PROLOGUE

Sunday, May 15, 7.11 a.m.

Their hands were cuffed and gags were winched behind their teeth. They were half lifted, half shoved into the back of an unmarked van. It felt like they'd stumbled into a *Law & Order* episode, but without a soundtrack to know when the scene was going to end.

She hadn't managed to scream. She'd been too shocked. In the distance, the constant thrum of traffic on I–40 sounded almost like water. Birds twittered mindlessly in the trees. She kept thinking someone must have seen, someone would call for help, someone would come.

No one came.

But these backwater Tennessee roads were empty even at the busiest times. Seven in the morning on a Sunday, there was no one on the road; it was too early even for the church crowd.

No one but the men in the van, with their hands slick

as machine-gun barrels and their orders to obey.

At least the men hadn't shoved their heads into burlap sacks. She'd seen a movie like that once, where a rich woman kidnapped for ransom was placed in a sack and had inhaled fibers and was asphyxiated, and then the criminals had to figure out how to dump the body and conceal the crime.

Maybe she, too, had been kidnapped for ransom.

But she knew, deep down, that she'd been taken for a different reason entirely.

It was because of Haven.

It was because they'd escaped.

She tried to listen, to keep track of where they were heading as the van picked up speed, bumping them down the road. The potholes threw them so high before slamming them down again that tears came to her eyes when her tailbone hit the van floor.

The ride smoothed out once they were on the highway. It was thunderously loud, like huddling under the bleachers while a homecoming crowd drummed their feet in unison. She felt like a slab of bacon stuck in somebody's hold. With no sunlight, she quickly lost track of time. Her throat was sore and it was difficult to swallow. The fibers from whatever they'd gagged her with tickled her nose and tonsils. It tasted like a sock.

Maybe they'd bought a pack especially for this purpose.

Her wrists hurt. She wondered whether handcuffs came in extra large, for heavier inmates, the way that condoms came in Magnums, which she had learned only last week, when April gave her a box as a joke. *For your very first boyfriend.*

Your boyfriend.

His chest was moving fast, as if he was having trouble breathing. His eyes were closed and he'd scooted back against the trunk. His head knocked against the doors every time they hit a bump.

She nudged his ankle with a foot to make him look at her. There was a small bit of blood at his temple where one of the men had hit him, and looking at it made her queasy. She counted the freckles on his nose. She loved the freckles on his nose.

She loved him, and hadn't known it until that instant, in the back of the van, with cuffs chafing the skin off her wrist and blood moving slowly toward his eyebrow.

She tried to tell him that it would be okay – wordlessly, with her eyes, with noises she made in the back of her throat. But he just shook his head, and she knew he hadn't understood, and wouldn't have believed her, anyway.

First published in Great Britain in 2017 by Hodder & Stoughton
An Hachette UK company

1

Copyright © Laura Schechter 2017

The right of Laura Schechter to be identified as the Author of the
Work has been asserted by her in accordance with the Copyright,
Designs and Patents Act 1988.

A CIP catalogue record for this title is available from the British Library

Hardback ISBN 978 1 473 61504 5
Trade Paperback ISBN 978 1 473 61505 2
eBook ISBN 978 1 473 61503 8

Printed and bound by Clays Ltd, St Ives plc

Hodder & Stoughton policy is to use papers that are natural,
renewable and recyclable products and made from wood grown in sustainable
forests. The logging and manufacturing processes are expected to conform
to the environmental regulations of the country of origin.

Hodder & Stoughton Ltd
Carmelite House
50 Victoria Embankment
London EC4Y 0DZ

www.hodder.co.uk

GEMMA

LAUREN OLIVER

RINGER

GEMMA

HODDER &
STOUGHTON

PART I

ONE

ONE

'PICK,' APRIL SAID, AND THEN leaned over to jab Gemma with a finger. 'Come on. It doesn't work if you don't pick.'

'Left,' Gemma said.

With a flourish, April revealed the bag of chips in her left hand: jalapeño-cheddar flavored. 'Sucker,' she said, sliding the chips across the table to Gemma. 'Maybe if you'd been paying attention . . .' She produced a second bag of chips, salt and vinegar, Gemma's favorite, and opened it with her teeth. She offered the bag to Gemma. 'Good thing I'm so nice.'

This was a tradition dating from midway through freshman year, when the school had for whatever reason begun stocking various one-off and weird chip flavors – probably, April theorized, because they got them on the cheap in discount variety packs. They'd made a game of picking blind – one good bag, one bad – even though they always split the salt and vinegar anyway.

But Gemma wasn't hungry. She hadn't been hungry in weeks, it seemed, not since spring break and Haven and Lyra and Caelum. Before, she'd always been hungry, even if she didn't like to eat in front of other people. Now everything tasted like dust, or the hard bitter grit of medicine accidentally crunched between the teeth. Every bite was borrowed – no, stolen – from the girl who should have come before.

She, Gemma, wasn't supposed to be here.

'Hey. Do I have to get you a shock collar or something?' April's voice was light, but she wasn't smiling.

Gemma reached over and took a chip, just to make April feel better. Across the cafeteria, the Bollard twins were huddled over the same phone, sharing a pair of headphones, obviously watching a video. Brandon Bollard was actually smiling, although he didn't seem to know how to do it correctly – he was kind of just baring his teeth.

'Did you know some twins can communicate telepathically?' Gemma asked suddenly.

April sighed so heavily her new bangs fluttered. 'That's not true.'

'It is,' Gemma said. 'They have their own languages and stuff.'

'Making up a language is different from communicating telepathically.'

'Well, it's both.' It was weird to see Brandon and Brant

together. Brandon was dressed all in black, with a fringe of black hair falling over his eyes and a sweatshirt that had two vampire fangs on it. Brant was wearing blue Chucks and low-rider jeans, and his hair was brown and curly and kept long, supposedly because Aubrey Connelly, his girlfriend and the most coldhearted of all the coldhearted pack wolves, loved to pull it when they were having sex in the back of her BMW.

It didn't make a difference: they had the same slouch, the same lips, the same wide-spaced brown eyes, the same way of slugging through the halls as if the destination would come to them and not the other way around.

'Did you know that sometimes twins, like, absorb each other in the womb?' Gemma went on. 'I watched this thing online about it. This woman thought she had a tumor and then they found teeth and hair and stuff inside. Can you imagine?'

April stared at her. 'Eating,' she said, except she had just taken a bite of her sandwich and it came out *eaffing*.

'Sorry,' Gemma said.

April swallowed and took a huge sip of coconut water, eyeing Gemma the whole time, as if she were a bacterial culture in danger of infecting everybody. 'You're not hungry?' she said.

Gemma moved her sandwich around on her tray a little. 'I had a big breakfast.' She wouldn't meet April's eyes. April always knew when she was lying.

April shoved her tray aside and leaned forward to cross her arms on the table. 'I'm worried about you, Gem.'

'I'm fine,' Gemma said automatically. She must have said it a thousand times in the past few weeks. She kept waiting for it to be true.

'You are *not* fine. Your brain is on autopilot. You're hardly eating anything. Suddenly you're *obsessed* with the Bollard twins—'

'I'm not obsessed with them,' Gemma said quickly, and forced herself to look away from Brandon, who was slouching toward the door, so pale he could have been the ghost of his twin brother.

'*Obsessed*,' April repeated. 'You talk about the Bollard twins more than you talk about *your own boyfriend*. Your new boyfriend,' she continued, before Gemma could open her mouth. 'Your new *awesome* boyfriend.'

'Keep your voice down,' Gemma said. At the next table, she caught a group of sophomore boys staring and made a face. She didn't care if they thought she was crazy. She didn't care about any of it.

April shoved her hands through her hair. April's hair was like some kind of energy conductor: when she was upset, her curls looked like they were going to reach out and electrocute you. 'Look,' she said, lowering her voice. 'I understand—'

'You don't,' Gemma said, before she could finish.

April stared at her. 'I saw it too,' she said. 'Pete saw it. We were there.'

It isn't the same, Gemma wanted to say. But what was the point? Just because they had seen the same things didn't mean they felt the same way.

'Haven isn't your problem anymore. It's not who you are. Lyra and Caelum are safe. There are people, major top-level people, investigating Dr Saperstein. Your part is done. You wanted to know the truth and now you do. But you can't let it destroy you.'

Gemma knew April was trying to help. But something black and ugly reached up out of her stomach and gripped her by the throat, a seething anger that had, in the past three weeks, startled her with its intensity.

'I mean, plenty of people have seriously screwy backstories.' That was April's big problem: she never knew when to stop talking. The anger made Gemma's head throb, so she heard the echo of the words as though through a cloth. 'You know Wynn Dobbs? The sophomore? I heard her dad actually tried to *kill* her mom with a shovel, just lost it one day and went after her, which is why she lives with her aunt . . .'

April couldn't understand what it meant for Gemma to be a replica, and she didn't *want* to understand. Gemma was well and truly a freak, and though she and April had joked for years that they were aliens in high school,

Gemma might as well have been from a different planet. In fact, she almost wished she were an alien – at least then she'd have somewhere to go back to, a true home, even if it was millions of light-years away.

Instead she'd been cloned, made, manufactured from the stem cells of her parents' first child, Emma. She was worse than an alien. She was a *trespasser.* It felt now as if she were living her whole life through one of those vignette filters, the kind that eats up the edges and the details. As if she'd hacked into someone else's social media accounts and was trying to catfish. Emma should have been sitting at this table, happily crunching through a bag of chips, stressing about her precalc exam. Not Gemma.

Gemma should never have been born at all.

'Gemma? Hello, Gemma?'

Somewhere in the deep echoes of the past, her lost twin, her lost replica, cried out soundlessly to be heard.

What was the point of trying to explain *that*?

Gemma forced herself to smile. 'I'm listening,' she said.

On days that April stayed after school for chorus, Gemma had always taken the bus, refusing her father's offer of a driver because it would only make her more of a target. But now Pete drove her home, at least on days when he wasn't working behind the register at the Quick-Mart.

It was Wednesday, May 11, nearly three weeks since she'd last seen Lyra. Pete had gotten rid of the eggplant-colored minivan they'd driven down to Florida. He said it was because of the mileage, but Gemma suspected it was because of the memories, too. Even when they were riding around in his brown Volvo station wagon – the Floating Turd, he called it, although it was definitely an improvement over his last ride – she imagined dark-suited men and women passing her on the streets, tailing her in featureless sedans.

Paranoia, obviously. Her dad had taken care of it, he'd promised her, just like he'd taken care of springing Lyra's dad from jail and setting him up with a job and a mobile home in some big Tennessee trailer park Gemma had never known he owned. April was right, at least about that part: Lyra and Caelum were safe, and staying with Lyra's father. Dr Saperstein had survived the explosion and subsequent fire at Haven, but he and his sick experiments would, her dad assured her, lose their funding after the disaster at Haven. She couldn't bring herself to ask what would happen to all the replicas who'd managed to survive, but she liked to believe they would be placed somewhere, quietly fed into the foster care system or at least moved into hospice care before the disease they were incubating chewed them up for good.

Pete always held her hand on the way to the parking

lot, and even though the drive was only fifteen minutes, it often took them nearly an hour because he was always pulling over to kiss her. Whenever Gemma's mom was home, she invited him in for sweet tea made by their housekeeper, Bernice, who came in the morning. The whole thing was so normal it hurt.

Except that it wasn't, because *she* wasn't, and they weren't, and the more she tried to pretend, the more obvious it was that something had cracked. Meeting Lyra and Caelum, knowing they were out there, knowing Haven and the people in charge of it were still out there somewhere – it had knocked her life off its axis. And Pete and April thought they could make things right just by *acting* as if they were all right. Gemma felt all the time as if they were circling a black hole, bound by the gravity of their denial. They would fall: they had to.

'What is it?' Pete brought a hand to her cheek. She loved the way he did this, touched her face or her lips with his thumb. They were parked at the very end of her driveway, the final quarter-mile stretch through graceful birches and plane trees whose branches interlocked their fingers overhead. 'What's wrong?'

She wondered how many times he'd had to ask in the past weeks. 'Nothing,' she said automatically. 'Why?'

'Your eyes were open,' he said. 'Like, staring. It was like kissing a Chucky doll.'

That made her laugh. That was the amazing thing

about Pete, his special talent: he could make anyone laugh. 'Thanks a lot.'

'Let's try again, okay?' He leaned into her. She closed her eyes. But she couldn't relax. Something was digging into her butt. She must be sitting on a pen. This time, she was the one to pull away.

'Sorry,' she said.

For a split second, Pete looked irritated. Or maybe she only imagined it. The next moment, he shrugged. 'That's all right. We should probably keep it clean for Ms. Leyla over here.' He reached out and flicked the hula girl on the dashboard, who promptly began to shimmy. Then he put the car in drive again. Gemma was relieved, and then guilty for feeling relieved. What kind of monster didn't want to make out with her adorable, floppy-haired, freckle-faced, absolutely-scrumptious-kisser boyfriend?

A monster who couldn't move on. A monster who felt like moving on was giving up, even though there was nothing, anymore, to fight for.

'Where'd you get this thing, anyway?' She leaned forward and gave the hula girl another flick. Her face was chipped away and the only thing left was a small, unsmiling mouth.

Pete shrugged. 'Came with the car. Your dad thinks she must have good engine juju.'

Gemma got a weird prickly feeling, like a spider was

walking on her spine. 'When did my dad see your hula girl?'

'When he dropped the car off.' He shoved the gearstick into park as they pulled up to the house, which never failed to emerge suddenly, enormous and unexpected, from behind the long column of trees. If a house could pounce, Gemma's would have.

Pete caught her staring at him. 'What? He didn't tell you? His friend was selling the car and he knew we were looking to cash in the Eggplant. He offered to make the trade. It was *nice*,' he said, frowning, and Gemma knew she must have been making a face.

'Sure,' she echoed. 'Nice.'

This time, he was definitely annoyed. He rolled his eyes and got out of the car without waiting for her to unbuckle her seat belt. Already the front door was open; Rufus bounded outside, as quickly as he could given his age, and began licking Pete's kneecaps. Gemma's mom, Kristina, appeared in the doorway, waving overhead with a big, beaming smile, as if she were heralding him from across a crowded dock and not from twenty feet away.

It was a stupid thing. Tiny. Minuscule. So what if her dad had a friend selling some shitty old turd-colored Volvo? Her dad had friends everywhere. Friends in the police department. Friends at the Formacine Plastics Facility, where Rick Harliss was now employed, a short ten-minute bus ride from the Winston-Able Mobile Home Community and Park, where he, Lyra, and Caelum were living.

Still, she didn't like it. She'd told her father weeks ago she would come home only if things changed. It would be her rules. Her life now. And yet weeks later she was as trapped as she'd ever been. They were trying to soothe her, appease her, distract her, make her forget. Even Pete wanted to forget.

It's too big for us, he'd said to her, shortly after they returned home. *It's too heavy for us to carry.*

Gemma knew exactly what he meant. She felt the weight too, the constant pull of something deep and black and huge. Except she wasn't carrying it, not even a little.

It was carrying her. What would happen, she wondered, when she fell?

TWO

'NO WAY WILL WE PUT troops on the ground.' Gemma's father talked through a mouth full of half-chewed tenderloin. Geoffrey Ives believed strongly in table manners – for other people. 'No way will the American public stand for it.' He leveled a fork at Ned Engleton, an old friend of his from high school, now a detective with the Chapel Hill Police Department. 'Patriotic outrage is all well and good, but once you start shipping out these poor kids from Omaha, Des Moines, wherever, it's a different story. I've seen robotics stocks go up tenfold the past month. Everyone's gambling on drones. . . .'

'May I be excused?' For the past few weeks, Gemma had seen her father for dinner more than she had in the previous ten years. Usually, Gemma and Kristina ate take-out sushi in front of the TV in their pajamas, or Gemma was left to scour the refrigerator for whatever Bernice had left her while Kristina floated between various benefits and social obligations.

But after Gemma had come back from Florida, and Lyra, Caelum, and Mr Harliss had been packed off (*protected*, Kristina said; *given new life*, her father said, although Gemma thought it was more like out of sight, out of mind), Gemma's parents had determined they needed more *together time*. As if everything Gemma had learned, everything she'd seen, was just a nutritional deficit and could be resolved by more home-cooked meals.

It turned out Geoffrey Ives's idea of family time was simply to bring his business home. In the past week alone they'd had dinner with a professor of robotics at MIT; a General Something-or-other who'd helped Ives land a lucrative consulting contract with a biotech firm that did work for the US government; and a state senator on recess whom Gemma had surprised later on that night in her kitchen, standing in his underwear in the blue light of the refrigerator, staggering drunk.

'You may not.' Geoff forked some more steak – home-cooked by Bernice, of course – and barely missed a beat. 'But I don't think air strikes are going to get the job done, not when these psychos are so scattered. Warfare keeps evolving, but have our methods evolved with it?'

Gemma felt a sudden hatred light like a flare inside her. She turned to Kristina, who had said next to nothing.

Normally she didn't pill-pop when they had company. But Gemma thought she was getting worse. Two, three, four glasses of wine, a Valium or two, and by bedtime she could hardly speak a word, and her smile was blissed out and dopey, like a baby's, and made Gemma sick to look at.

'I'm thinking of going to visit Lyra this weekend,' Gemma said loudly, and there was a terrible, electric pause, and then Kristina let her wineglass drop, and suddenly Geoff was on his feet and cursing and Gemma felt sorry and triumphant all at once.

'I spilled,' Kristina kept saying dumbly. Red wine pooled over her plate and made a handprint pattern on her shirt. 'I spilled.'

Geoff was shouting in staccato bursts. 'For God's sake, don't just sit there. The carpet. Gemma, get your mother something to clean up with.'

In the kitchen, Gemma wound a long ribbon of paper towel around her hand like a bandage. She was shaky. It felt as if someone was doing a detail number on her insides, vacu-sucking and carving and hacking her raw. Muffled by the door, Kristina's words took on the bleating, repetitive cadence of an injured sheep.

Before she could return to the dining room, the door opened and Geoff appeared. She was sure he was going to yell at her for mentioning Lyra's name in the presence of a guest – not that anyone could guess who she was.

But he just took a step forward and held out a hand for the paper towels.

Feeling bolder, she took a deep breath and repeated herself. 'I want to see Lyra this weekend,' she said. 'You promised I could.' For a second, their hands touched, and she was briefly shocked. They almost never touched. She didn't think her father had hugged her more than once or twice in her life. His fingers were cold.

'This weekend is your mother's birthday,' Geoff said. 'Did you forget about the party?'

'I'll go Sunday,' she said, unwilling to give up. She half suspected that he was filling her time with celebrations and dinners and obligations precisely so she *couldn't* see Lyra.

'Sunday we're going to church,' he said, and his voice was edged with impatience. 'I've told you we're going to do things differently from now on, and damn it, I meant it.'

'I'll go after church,' Gemma said. She should have dropped it. She knew her dad was getting angry; a small cosmos of broken blood vessels darkened in his cheeks. 'I'll get Pete to drive me. It'll only be a few hours—'

'I said no.' He slammed a fist on the counter so hard that the plastic kitchen timer – untouched by anyone but Bernice – jumped. 'Sunday is a day for family, and that's final.'

Gemma turned away from him, balling her fists tight-tight, as if she could squeeze out all her anger. 'Some family.'

'What did you say?' He got in front of her, blocking her way to the stairs, and for a moment she was gutted by a sudden fear. His eyes were hollowed out by shadow. He looked almost like a stranger. She could smell the whiskey he'd had at dinner, could smell the meat on his breath and the way he was sweating beneath his expensive cashmere sweater and she remembered, then, seeing her mother once sprawled at his feet after one of their arguments.

She tripped, he'd said. *She tripped.* Gemma had never known whether to believe it or not.

And in that second, weirdly, she felt time around her like a long tunnel, except the tunnel collapsed, and became not a road she was traveling but a single point, a compression of ideas and memories; and she saw her father with a dead baby, his first and only born, and knew that he'd done what he'd done not from grief but because it offended him, this natural order over which he had no control, the passing of things and the tragedy of a world that whip-snapped without asking his permission. He'd done it not for love but to restore order. Nothing would break unless he was the one to crush it. People didn't even have the right to die, not in Geoffrey Ives's house.

'Whether you like it or not, you follow my rules,'

he said, and she wanted to cry: this was her father, who should have been both a boundary and a promise, like the sun at the edge of every picture, the thing that gave it light. 'You're still my daughter.'

'I know,' she said, and turned away. But in her head she said *no*. In her head, and in the deepest part of who she was, she knew she wasn't. She was born of the sister, the self, who had come before her. She was the daughter of a silent memory, except the memory wasn't silent anymore. It had reached up out of the past and taken Gemma by the throat, and soon, she knew, it would begin to scream.

THREE

GEMMA COULDN'T REMEMBER THE LAST time her father had been home for one of Kristina's birthdays, or for one of hers. Last year, she had been patched through to the Philippines by his secretary so that he could wish her a happy fifteenth. She dimly recalled a party when she was five or six at a petting zoo, and crying when her mother wouldn't take her closer than ten feet from the animals, fearing Gemma would catch something.

The guests began to arrive midafternoon. For a short time, she forgot about Haven and poor Jake Witz, who had died trying to expose the truth about Haven and Spruce Island; she forgot about the feeling that she was sleepwalking through someone else's life. Her parents often hosted parties, mostly to support one of Kristina's dozens of causes – the Mid-Atlantic Breast Cancer Prevention Society, the North Carolina Nature Refuge, the

Equestrian Society, the Garden Club – or a political dinner for some local candidate Geoffrey was supporting.
Those parties were stiff-backed and yawningly boring,
and usually Gemma stayed out of the way or hung out in
the kitchen stealing leftover nubs of filet mignon from the
caterers and anxiously tracking how often Kristina came
into the kitchen to refill her glass in private.

But this was a real, true, honest-to-God party.

The theme was Hawaiian, a nod to the bar that Kristina had been working in after college, where she and
Geoffrey had met; Geoff liked to tell people that he'd
never seen a girl make a grass skirt look so classy. Fifty
or so of her parents' friends had been invited, including
April's moms, who both showed up wearing coconut
bras over their regular clothing. April's mother Diana
was a computer programmer and software engineer who
designed malware detection systems for big companies;
Gemma had hardly ever seen her in the daylight hours.
April's other mother, Angela Ruiz, was now a renowned
prosecutor for the state. Watching them swish around
with leis and fruity cocktails gave Gemma the same dizzying upside-down feeling of trying to do a cartwheel.
Meanwhile, April stomped around, looking absolutely
miserable, dressed pointedly in all black.

'What happened to aging gracefully?' she muttered,
gnawing a pink cocktail spear she'd been using to stake

olives from the bar. But Gemma thought it was funny, all her parents' friends in ugly Hawaiian shirts and plastic flower crowns, getting drunk on piña coladas and rum punch.

Kristina had suggested she invite Pete, and he came dressed up, as she'd known he would, in a loud-print Hawaiian shirt he proudly announced he'd purchased from the gas station during a week of random travel promotions. Gemma couldn't understand how he pulled it off, but he did. The shirt showed off his arms, which were long and tan and just muscle-y enough, and deepened his eyes to the rich brown of really good chocolate.

There were ribs smoking in a rented barbecue, honeyed ham with grilled pineapple, coconut shrimp circulated by waiters wearing grass skirts over their jeans. The grown-ups set up a game of bocce, but Gemma and April soon took over, making up their own rules so they wouldn't have to learn the real ones, and Pete refereed and narrated through a fake microphone, using made-up terminology like *the looping cruiser* and *the back-switch hibbleputz* that made Gemma laugh so hard she nearly peed.

Gemma had determined that at the party she would ask April whether she'd had any luck getting into Jake Witz's computer. April was sure Diana could get past Jake's security measures and had come up with a convenient excuse to get her mom on board: the computer, she claimed, had been left at the public library, and they needed to get into the system to find a registration and return it.

Gemma had bugged April for days after turning it over, until April threatened to karate-kick her spleen if she didn't stop. That was ten days ago. Gemma had figured she would slip it into conversation when April was relaxed, when they were having a good time, after she had proven she wasn't obsessing, like April said she was.

But somehow, she couldn't. For the first time in weeks she actually *felt* normal – she felt happy, and she wasn't faking it. Neither Pete nor April was staring her down like she was in danger of morphing into a feral animal. Geoff and Kristina were actually *dancing* – there, on the deck, in front of everyone – as the sun broke up into layers of color and the fireflies lifted out of the dark. Pete had his hands around her waist, humming into her neck to the cheesy eighties music her parents still adored. His breath was warm. The sky was big, the stars new and shimmering, and though the world was large, she was safe inside it.

Standing there, she even thought that maybe, just maybe, she could choose to forget after all. April was right – lots of people had fucked-up childhoods – and Pete was right, too, that what had happened at Haven was too big for them to make better. Lyra and Caelum had a place to live, and her father had promised he would figure out a way to get Caelum papers so he could be legal, so he could exist. It wasn't like they'd been trying to reach her. They hadn't called her, not even once, since they cleared off. Maybe they were doing just fine – maybe they, too, wanted to forget.

If they could, she could: forget where she'd been made, and how. Forget about Emma, her little lost shadow-self. Maybe there was nothing to being normal except the decision to do it. You had to simply step into the idea, like wriggling into a sweater.

She should have learned, by now, that nothing was ever so easy.

Pete had moved off to check out the party's main attraction: a full-on spit-roasted pig to be wheeled out and served before the hired Hawaiian dancers shimmied and hip-jiggled their way through dinner. But he came back and found her, his hair smelling sweetly of smoke, his hand warm when he interlaced their fingers. He was wearing half a dozen leis around his neck, on his wrists, even looped around his head.

'Come with me,' he said.

'Where are we going?' she asked.

He turned briefly to bring his mouth to her ear. 'Somewhere we can be *alone*,' he said, and his eyes were bright and alive with reflections. Her stomach dipped, not the way it usually did when they began to kiss and she felt herself seize up with panic, but like when riding a roller coaster: like good things were about to happen.

He pulled her up the stairs onto the deck and toward the sliding doors. Luckily, all her parents' friends had the sleepy-blissful look of tipsiness and were too wrapped up in their own little dramas to do more than wave. In the kitchen, Bernice was hustling the caterers around. When she spotted Gemma, she winked.

The hall felt even cooler after the dampness and warmth of outside, and when Pete stopped her and pushed her up against the wall to kiss her, she could smell charcoal in his hair and on his fingers. For once she didn't feel like a monster, didn't feel ugly or badly formed, and she stepped into him. He put his hands on her waist, slid them up her stomach, fumbled at her bra. . . .

Down the hall, a bathroom door opened, and Gemma heard the sharp rise of a woman's voice – Melanie Eckert, one of her mom's country club friends, sounding drunk. 'I *told* her too much filler would split her like a pumpkin. Have you seen her now?'

Gemma launched herself across the hall and yanked open the door to the basement, practically shoving Pete down the stairs before Melanie could see them. For a second they stood together on the landing, breathless and giggly, until Melanie's voice had faded.

'Is this where you murder me?' Pete whispered, bumping his lips against her neck in the dark.

She knew he was kidding, but a sudden vision of Jake Witz returned to her the way she'd last seen him, standing at the door, angling his body so she couldn't get inside, trying to warn her. Trying to save her. *Jake Witz is dead.* She was glad she hadn't seen the body but had read, anyway, that people sometimes choked on their tongues when they were hanging, or broke their nails off trying to loosen the noose.

She hit the lights, relieved by the bland normalcy of the carpeted stairs leading down to the basement.

'You wanted to be alone,' she said, taking his hand, eager to get back the good feeling she'd had only a minute ago.

The basement was a clutter of old furniture, dusty table tennis equipment, a pool table with stains all over its felt (Gemma's father kept a second, nicer pool table in the library upstairs), and old toys. Metal shelves, like the kind you might find in a library, were packed with massive jugs of bottled water, Costco-sized packages of toilet paper, cartons of canned soup, enough ketchup to fill a bathtub.

'Nothing says romance like industrial-sized rolls of toilet paper,' Pete said, and she laughed. 'Are you guys preparing for the apocalypse or something?'

'Prepared. Past tense. In case you haven't noticed, my

dad's kind of a freak.' She drew him between the shelves, moving deeper and deeper into the basement. It was like a spiny city built out of boxes of shredded wheat and stacks of Dove soap. And despite the musty smell of the basement and the bright overhead lights and the cheap gray wall-to-wall carpeting her parents would never have allowed anywhere else, Gemma felt in that moment, with Pete's hand in hers, that it was the most beautiful place she'd ever been.

They started kissing again: first they stood, and then, when Pete bumped her against one of the shelves and nearly toppled it, they lay down together. He got on top of her. Her whole body was breathless and hot, as if she were nothing but breath, nothing but the inhale-exhale of their rhythm together. He was struggling to get her shirt off and fumbling with her bra, and for once she wasn't worried about anything or even wondering how far things would go. Her nipples touched the air and he pulled away to look at her, to look at the long Y-shaped scar on her sternum that had earned her the name Frankenstein at school.

'Beautiful,' was all he said, touching her scar gently, with a thumb. She was liquid with happiness. She believed him. Weeks ago, someone had thrown a Frankenstein mask through the window. She knew now that it had been a warning from Lyra's father, Rick Harliss, but at the time she'd been convinced that it was from Chloe DeWitt and the pack wolves.

But maybe everyone was wearing a mask. Maybe no one was completely normal.

Maybe she *was* beautiful.

She wanted him. The want, the desire, was so huge she felt it incinerate her in a split second, burn her up to a single driving instinct: closer, more. She loosened his belt and undid his jeans without any trouble; it was as if she'd been practicing her whole life, as if she'd carried the knowledge of him in her fingers.

Suddenly, the basement door opened and footsteps came down the stairs.

'Glad you could come. Thought you might've gone back to town already . . .' Her father's voice. Of all the stupid luck. She'd never once *seen* her dad use the basement.

'Shit.' Pete pulled away, his face almost comical with panic. *'Shit.'*

She sat up. Her fingers turned clumsy again, stubborn with disappointment. She struggled to get her bra reclasped, and put her shirt on backward the first time. At least they were concealed behind several aisles of shelving, which, through a kaleidoscope of different supplies, gave them a patchwork view of the stairs.

Allen Fortner, a military guy her father knew from

West Point ages ago, passed momentarily into view, and suspicion scratched at the back of Gemma's mind. Fortner was FBI, and he and her father hadn't seen each other in years.

So what was he doing here, at Gemma's mom's party?

'. . . wasn't sure what side of the fence you were on,' Fortner was saying. 'Trainor never thought you could be bounced this way.'

'Trainor's an idiot,' Geoffrey said easily. They had moved out of sight, but Gemma could still hear them perfectly. 'Besides, it's not about loyalty. It's about future growth.'

Pete made a movement as if to stand, but she grabbed his arm to stop him.

'Aren't you worried about exposure?' Fortner asked.

'It's my wife's fiftieth birthday party,' he said. 'You're an old friend of the family. What's to expose?' Then: 'You didn't think we invited you for the pig roast, did you?'

In the long pause that followed these words, all of Gemma's earlier good feeling collapsed. She knew that this conversation, this man and her father standing between old furniture and rolls of extra toilet paper, was the true reason for everything: the skirts and the music and the honeyed ham and her mother's happiness.

A cover.

'All right,' Fortner said at last. 'Talk, then.'

Geoff's response was immediate: 'I know where they are,' he said. And then, when Fortner was silent, 'The subjects. The missing ones.'

Gemma's heart was a balloon: all at once, punctured, it collapsed.

'Christ. It's been three weeks.'

'Your guys lost track. I didn't.'

'We didn't lose track,' Fortner said, and he sounded irritated for the first time. 'We were dealing with containment issues. Civilians, data leaks—'

'Sure. Harliss. I know.'

Next to her, Pete shifted. His knee knocked a shelf containing dozens of bottles of water. They wobbled but didn't fall. Gemma held her breath.

Neither Fortner nor her father seemed to notice, because Fortner went on, 'You were the one to spring him.' He must have been pacing, because he passed into view again. Through the shelves packed with Christmas ornaments and old memorabilia, Gemma saw Fortner bring a hand to his jaw. It was like he was a robot with only a few preprogrammed modes. But when he spoke again, he just sounded tired. 'I should've known.'

'That's the problem with your end of the business, Allen. No local connections. A guy down at the precinct in Alachua County played basketball with me at West Point. It wasn't hard.'

'Why now? Why not before?'

Again, silence. Gemma felt a finger of sweat move down her back. She was in a crouch, and her thighs were beginning to shake.

'I made a promise to my daughter,' Geoff said, and Gemma heard the words as if they had glanced off the lip of a well high above her.

Allen Fortner obviously didn't buy it either. 'Come on,' he said. 'You can't be serious.'

'I promised her I wouldn't be the one to hand them over,' Geoff said. 'And I won't be. That's what your people are for. And I wanted to make sure the Philadelphia team was ready. I did some digging in DC, too, felt out the lobbies. Saperstein's done, even if he won't admit it. But that doesn't mean there won't be a place for the tech. I've spoken to Miller, and he thinks we're ready for a big policy push.'

Pete reached for Gemma's hand. She pulled away, balling her fists instead, squeezing until she felt pain. She couldn't touch him. Her whole life was a lie, and it had festered and turned poisonous.

She didn't want to infect him, too.

'What's the end goal?' Fortner said. 'Talk quickly, now. Your wife will be expecting a cake and her sing-along.'

That almost killed her, right there. She was still breathing, though. It was amazing the little deaths that she had lived through.

'We get the contract. Simple enough.' Through the

shelves, Gemma caught only quick glimpses of her father, still wearing his party outfit, his colorful Hawaiian shirt. All show. 'Triple the size and change the objective, at least in part. There will be a medical aspect, sure. That's where Miller and our friends in Congress come in. But there's a bigger endgame, too, to get costs down and make mass production viable. Saperstein bled money out of that place for a decade. His focus was too narrow and his production was too small.'

'We got functional variants. We got real-world observation.'

'You've got billions of dollars sunk into that shithole, a containment mission on your hands, and a PR shitstorm that will take a quarter of Washington. Come on, Allen. You know as well as I do that Saperstein's interest was ideological, not functional. He just wanted to prove he could make test subjects from scratch.'

From scratch. Gemma felt like she was going to throw up. *From scratch.* Like pancake batter, or Lego kingdoms.

After a pause, Fortner cleared his throat. 'Keep talking.'

'I'll give you the location. Everyone feels good. The mess is cleaned up, no one's in trouble, we move on.' Geoff leaned on the TV console that had once been upstairs. He looked almost bored. 'It's like making toy soldiers,' he added. 'Think of how many lives we'll save.'

Fortner was quiet again. Gemma's heart was emptying

and filling, turning over like a bucket. She felt as if she might drown.

'You said you promised your daughter,' he said finally, and just hearing the word made her body go tight. 'What made you change your mind?'

'I kept my promise. I won't be the one collecting. Besides – he threw up his hands, a gesture Gemma knew well, like, *what does it matter, Kristina, kale salad or arugula, it's all a bunch of rabbit food* – 'what would it have done before now? I knew Saperstein would hang himself by his own rope. The Haven team has proved its own incompetence. Billions of dollars down the drain, and enough cleanup to keep a thousand crisis managers employed for a decade.'

'Where?' Fortner asked finally. For a split second, Gemma still held out hope that her dad would lie.

'I put them up in a trailer on one of my investment lots. Winston-Able, right off Interstate 40. Lot sixteen, a double-wide. Not far from Knoxville. Didn't even remember I owned the damn thing until the federal government reminded me in April.' This made Fortner laugh. It sounded like a cat trying to bring up a hairball. 'Pulled some strings and got her dad working at Formacine Plastics out there. You know it?'

Fortner sighed. 'I'll talk to my guys about Philly. See what strings I can pull.'

'I'm sure you'll figure it out. Saperstein shot himself in the dick. He doesn't listen. This is a new age, Allen. We got the chance to change the world here. ISIS, the Taliban, Al Qaeda, you name it – they don't follow the old rules.'

'You're preaching to the choir.'

'They're gonna brainwash their army of human IEDs, no reason we can't *make* ours.'

'Like I said, preaching to the choir. But I'm going to have to go up the chain on this one.'

'I believe in you,' Geoff said, sounding faintly sarcastic.

Gemma had lost the thread of the conversation, but it no longer mattered. She understood everything that mattered: her father had betrayed Lyra and Caelum. He'd betrayed her, and his promise. She should have known he would.

Finally, Fortner and Geoff moved toward the stairs together. She could have cried from relief. Gemma's feet and legs had gone numb.

But at the last second, Fortner hesitated. When he turned back to Geoff, Gemma saw his face – cold and long and narrow, like an exclamation point – before he passed once again out of view.

'Your daughter,' he said, and Gemma's blood turned thick and heavy. 'She was made at Haven. One of the first.' It wasn't a question, but Gemma could hear a question layered beneath the words, like a knife angled up through a fist.

'She was born there, yes,' Geoff said, and Gemma heard the importance of the correction – *born*, not *made*. But did it matter? Made, spliced, implanted – she might as well have been a fast-growing variety of bean sprout.

Fortner coughed. 'You ever wonder what makes the difference?' When Geoff said nothing, he went on, 'You want to put the replicas to good use, and I'm with you. But what makes them any different from your girl?'

'What do you think makes them different?' Geoff's voice had turned cold. 'Someone wanted her.'

Someone. Gemma noticed that he did not say *I*.

FOUR

THE PARTY WAS STILL GOING. Of course it was. They'd been in the basement for probably an hour. And yet somehow Gemma had expected to resurface and find the whole party incinerated, like Pompeii, vaporized in just a few seconds of suffocating ash. She wouldn't have been surprised to walk through empty rooms filled with cast-off trash, to find everything grayed with decay, to see her parents' friends transformed by the alchemical power of disaster into skeletons.

Now she saw the party for what it was: packaging. Pretty lies packed, beveled, and neatly shaped together, like an intricate sand castle, teetering at the edge of a creeping tide. The leis, the guests, the vivid cocktails colored like drowning sunsets: all of it an excuse for her father to see Allen Fortner, to negotiate with him. Even the cake was bullshit. When was the last time her mom had eaten cake, let herself consume a single thing that wasn't low-calorie, high-protein, grass-fed, non-GMO?

They were only playing parts, and Gemma had been playing right along with them.

Again.

'Gemma. *Gemma.*'

She'd made it outside before Pete caught up with her. The air was alive with fireflies. Someone had lit the tiki torches; even burning could be made pretty, so long as it was contained. Gemma was struck instead by how insubstantial it all looked, the shadows and the light, the women in their bright dresses: like the scrim that dropped during a play so all the stagehands could get the furniture into position. She spotted her mother and father at the center of a group of dancers. It made her sick, that he could dance like that, arms up, not a care in the world, while in the background a faceless army prepared the audience for the next illusion.

'Talk to me,' Pete said, and put his hands on her face. 'Please.'

Before Gemma could answer, April shouted her name. She came ripping out of the crowd, and Gemma had the impression of a curtain swinging aside to release her.

'Where have you been? I got stuck talking to—' She caught sight of Gemma's face and broke off. 'What happened? What's wrong?'

'My dad lied to me.' She felt as if she had to say the words through a fist. 'He gave Lyra and Caelum up.'

'Gave them up?' April repeated the words very slowly, as if Gemma were the one in danger of misunderstanding. Gemma felt her anger, so poorly buried, give a sudden lash.

'That's what I said. He gave them up. He sold them out.' She felt like screaming. She felt like taking one of the stupid tiki torches and lighting the whole place on fire. 'Haven's a PR crisis. That's what he said. And they're the biggest leak.' The worst was that she couldn't even be angry at her dad, not really. He was a liar, and lying was what liars did.

She was the bigger idiot. She'd actually believed him.

April's eyes passed briefly to Pete – so briefly that Gemma almost missed it. *Almost.*

'I'm sorry,' April said, and reached out, as if she wanted to touch Gemma's shoulder, or maybe pat Gemma on the head.

Gemma took a step backward, out of reach. All at once it was as if she was the torch: she was burning with rage, combusting. 'You're *sorry*?' As if that was it, end of story, too bad. As if Gemma's favorite toy had just been stolen. 'You know what this means, don't you? You remember how they *cleaned up* Jake Witz?'

'Keep your voice down,' Pete said, although it hardly

mattered. Everyone was so drunk she could have been shouting.

Gemma spun around, stumbling a little on the grass, too furious to look at either of her friends. But April and Pete caught up to her almost immediately. Pete tried to take her elbow, but Gemma shook him off.

'Gemma, please,' Pete said again. 'Can you just . . . I mean, can we all stop and *think*?'

But she couldn't stop. There was no time. She closed her eyes and saw Jake Witz, the geometric perfection of his smile, the way he neatened his silverware, the intense stillness of his gaze, as if his eyes were a gravity trying to hold you in place. Already, her memories of him were fading. Too often, she saw him now as she did in her nightmares: half alive, half dead, lisping details about the constellations with a swollen tongue.

She kept stumbling on the grass, and nearly twisted her ankle when her wedge drove down into a soft bit of soil. She kicked off her shoes and didn't bother picking them up. She didn't have a plan, she didn't know what she would do now that Fortner had a head start, but she knew she had to keep moving, she had to go fast, she had to outrun Jake and her nightmare vision of his face and the sly orbit of Lyra's and Caelum's faces, moving eclipse-like to hang in his place. Pete and April could easily outpace her, but she was first to the narrow path that interlinked the front and back yards, and that was so hemmed in by growth they had no choice but to fall back. They were maybe a step behind her, but she heard them the way she heard the distant twitter of birds in the morning – all noise, all background.

'Christ, Gemma, will you *wait* for a second?'

'Can someone please just tell me *what the fuck happened*?'

She broke free of the tangle of azaleas. The cars in the driveway looked like a freeze-frame of a collision about to happen. But before she was halfway to the driveway, Pete had his hand on her arm.

'Jesus *spitballs*.' He was practically shouting. She'd never seen him mad before, not like this, and a small, distant flare of love went up through the smog of her own pain: you could count on Pete to make up a curse like *Jesus spitballs*. 'Will you talk to us for a minute? Will you actually *listen*?'

That word, *us*, extinguished the flare right away. April and Pete were on the same side, which meant Gemma was left out. Alone.

'What?' she said. 'You want me to listen? So go on. Spit it out,' she prompted, when he said nothing. A floodlight came on automatically, triggered by their movement. In its light, Pete looked hollow and exhausted, and for just a moment, she felt guilty. Then she remembered: it was two against one. All her life she'd felt as if she was trying to play a game from outside the stadium, trying to intuit the rules from brief and distant snapshots. But at least April had been with her, and Pete.

By learning the truth, she'd gone somewhere they couldn't follow. And that was just a fact.

April rocketed out of the growth looking as though she'd done personal battle with every inch of it. There were leaves in her hair, on her shirt, clinging to the wet of her shoes. 'I won't,' she panted, 'ask' – more panting – 'again.' But she did anyway. 'What. The. Hell. Happened?'

Pete still wouldn't meet Gemma's eyes, and for some reason that alone made her queasy: it meant for sure he had something to say that she wouldn't want to hear.

'Lyra and Caelum are in trouble,' she said, keeping her voice as measured as she could. 'I have to help. It's my fault, don't you get it? I walked them into this. I hand-fed them to my dad. If anything happens to them—' She broke off, suddenly overwhelmed.

In her dreams, Jake spoke to her even with the rope around his neck, puckering the skin around it. In her dreams, they were back on the marshes, and sometimes when he opened his mouth, he had beetles on his tongue.

Would he still be alive if she hadn't shown up to ask for his help?

'It isn't your fault,' April said. 'You couldn't have known.'

'Let's hope I get a big *E* for effort, then,' she said.

Pete looked at her then, and she wished he hadn't. His mouth was like a zipper stuck hard in a bad position. 'If the *military* is going after Lyra and Caelum, like you said, you can't stop it. You're in danger, too.'

'I don't have to stop it,' Gemma said. 'But I can warn them. I can give them a head start.'

'How?' Pete's tone sharpened. 'You don't even have a car.' *Bang, bang, bang.* Little shrapnel words.

'You can't even drive,' April added. This felt like a low blow. Her parents wouldn't let her learn to drive: another way they kept her bubbled off in glass, like one of those dumb ballerinas at the center of a snow globe.

'I'll take the bus,' she said, and turned around again, so Pete and April had to jog to keep up with her.

'You don't know where you're going,' Pete pointed out. 'It's almost eleven. It isn't safe for you to travel on your own. Besides, I doubt they have all-night service to Rococo.'

'Ronchowoa. So I'll hitchhike. Or I'll take a bike. I'll take a horse.' But Gemma's throat was all knotted up. She turned away, swiping her eyes with her wrist.

'Jesus, Gemma. Will you listen to yourself? You aren't thinking.' He wasn't shouting – not even close, not compared to what Gemma's dad could do – but still, Gemma pulled up as if she'd reached an unexpected cliff. 'If the military or the feds or whatever are trying to do a cover-up job – if they're willing to kill people to make sure the truth never leaks – you're a target. You were a target before, but you'll be a bigger target now. I won't—' His voice broke. 'I'm not going to risk you again, okay? Not for Lyra. Not for Caelum. Not for any fucking person on the planet. I won't do it.'

She started to cry, obviously. Trying not to cry was like trying to hold on to water by squeezing it. She cried until she gasped. 'Don't you see? I have to *do* something. I have to help them. They're my people. They're like me. . . .'

But by then she couldn't go on. Fear and guilt came down on her mind like a veil, rippling all her words into distant impressions. In the house, Rufus began to bark, as if he was determined that she not cry alone.

And, weirdly, just when it felt as if she could cry until she drowned, she felt a sudden pressure, an invisible presence. It was as if an unseen person had just stepped up to place a hand on Gemma's shoulder and whisper in her ear. *It's okay,* this other person said, and Gemma recognized in the silence the voice of Emma: the first, the original. *It's going to be okay.*

Pete came forward to put a hand on her back. 'It's okay,' he said, and Gemma startled, turning around to face him. Her impression of Emma's voice broke apart on the wind. 'I'll drive you.'

Behind him, April's face was narrow with worry, but she didn't argue. And Pete even managed to smile. He didn't look angry anymore.

'We're your people too, you know,' he said. 'We'll always be your people, if you let us.' He ran a thumb over her lips. His skin tasted like smoke.

FIVE

THE WINSTON-ABLE MOBILE HOME PARK was just under six hours away, forty minutes outside Knoxville. Pete and Gemma drove mostly in silence, with the radio off and the windows down, except when Pete asked whether it would be all right to stop and get coffee.

The drive, the tension, the wind blowing in the wake of passing semis and the windshield dazzling with headlights: it all felt like they'd tripped over a wrinkle in time and wound up back where they were three weeks ago. Gemma tried to sleep but couldn't. Whenever they passed a cop on the road, she got jumpy. Gemma had told her mom she was going to sleep at April's house, and Pete had told his parents he was sleeping in one of the Ives's guest rooms, and April had, after much protestation, gone home so that she could run interference if Gemma's mom called the house before Gemma got back. April's moms had left the party early, so there was no reason to think her cover story had been blown so quickly. Still, if worse came to worst, Gemma hoped her mom would assume she had merely lied in order to sleep over at Pete's house (which Kristina seemed to suspect Gemma was always angling to do – seemed to *hope* for it).

But she knew, too, that anything was possible. Her dad might have gotten suspicious. He might have radioed friends in the force, friends at the tolls, friends even now crawling dark highways, waiting to stop her and bring her home. A network of owed favors, backroom deals, contracts and alliances: the whole world was a spiderweb and all the threads were made of money.

Geoffrey was the spider. Which made people like her, and like Lyra and Caelum, the flies.

It was just before six o'clock when they spotted a sign for Ronchowoa, a dump of a place whose claim to fame was one of Tennessee's largest privately owned plastics manufacturers. By then, the darkness was letting up a bit, but the air was smudgy with chemical smoke and had its own gritty texture. Gemma remembered that her dad's brother, Uncle Ted, had helped restructure the Knox County debt, but she was still surprised to see a strip mall – containing a hair salon, a liquor store, a check-cashing place, and a local bank – sporting the name Ives.

It made sense. The Ives brothers loved nothing so much as ownership.

The trailer park was at the end of a long dirt road that badly needed paving. They went so slowly it felt as if they might simply be rolling in neutral. Gemma was itchy with anxiety, as if she were wearing a full-body wool sock. She saw no sign of Fortner or whoever he had sent to do his business. There were no other cars on the road, no strangers lurking around in the early morning shadows. Then again, she knew there wouldn't be. People like Fortner worked fast and clean.

Most of the time, at least.

What if they were too late?

She wished for the millionth time that Lyra had called her, and wondered for the millionth time why she hadn't. Gemma had told her to call first thing after their phone got set up, and had spent hours watching her cell phone, as if she could will it to ring through the pressure of her eyeballs.

Despite the grid of dusty, dirt-rutted streets, none of the trailers seemed to be in numerical order. Gemma's father had said that they were in number 16; she assumed that the unnumbered trailer between lots 15 and 17 must be the one they were looking for. But then she spotted the plastic children's toys scattered in the patchy yard. This wasn't it – couldn't be.

Still, they got out of the car, moving slowly, quietly, so

they wouldn't startle anyone. Gemma wasn't in the mood for a showdown about trespassing – and besides, it was possible that even now they were being watched. Spiders had eight eyes, enough to see in all directions. But human spiders had hundreds, maybe thousands, more.

She was almost relieved to hear a dog barking. Everything until then had been so still, so silent, she might otherwise have thought they were too late, that the whole damn place had been rounded up.

Gemma was turning to shush the dog when she saw movement from a dingy white trailer set behind a scrub of balding bushes across the street. A girl or a boy – she couldn't tell from a distance, not in the half-light – slipped outside and turned to lock the door.

As soon as the girl started down the stairs, Gemma knew her.

'Lyra,' she said. Her voice sounded hoarse. It was the first time she'd spoken in hours. 'That's Lyra.'

She and Pete jogged to catch up. Lyra was already moving away from them, head down, as if she was afraid of being followed. Did she know she was in danger? Where was Caelum? She must have heard them approach, because suddenly Lyra whirled around, hands on her backpack straps, elbows out like miniature wings.

'Lyra.' Gemma felt out of breath, though they'd gone barely one hundred feet. Lyra was more beautiful than she remembered. Funnily enough, she was wearing eye makeup. Not just a little, either. Shimmery, smoky, purple eye makeup, the kind April applied to Gemma when she was 'practicing her technique'. She'd dyed her hair, too, a platinum blond. She had gained badly needed weight.

'What are you doing here?' Typically, Lyra didn't smile or even seem that surprised to see them.

Despite having come to warn her, Gemma found at the last second she couldn't say the words – couldn't admit to Lyra that everything her father had promised was a lie.

Instead, it was Pete who spoke.

'You're in danger,' he said. 'The people who killed Jake Witz are tracking you and Caelum. They're probably on their way now.'

Lyra hardly even blinked. 'I know,' she said. 'They were here already.'

Gemma's heart fell through a hole. 'Is Caelum . . . ?'

'Gone.' She frowned a little, as if the word carried an unexpected taste.

The world tightened around them. Even the air seized up and grew too heavy to breathe. 'They – they got him?'

Lyra shook her head – a quick, spastic movement, like an animal trying to shake off a fly. 'He was already gone. I saw them come, and I hid until they left.'

'They'll be back,' Gemma said. She could barely understand what Lyra meant – Caelum gone, but not taken, and Lyra now alone. But she knew for sure they would come back. 'They'll be back any second. You have to come with us.'

'I can't,' Lyra said abruptly. And then, an afterthought: 'Thank you. I'll be careful.'

She turned and started walking again. For a second, Gemma was so stunned she could only stare after her. Then she registered the red backpack Lyra had on, bulging with belongings. Where was she going, at just after six in the morning? Where had Caelum gone?

'Wait,' she called out. Lyra turned around, still with that same blank expression, a little bit patient, a tiny bit irritated, too. Unexpectedly, Gemma was furious. That was the good thing about anger: it was always bigger than fear, always bigger than guilt or disappointment. You could count on anger. 'What do you mean, you *can't*?'

'And where's Caelum?' Pete was on Gemma's team again, bound to her by exhaustion and frustration. 'Where did he go?'

'Home,' Lyra said, as if that made any sense at all. 'I'm going after him.'

'I don't think you understand,' Gemma said. The long night was starting to catch up to her. Whenever she closed her eyes, she saw starburst colors, quick explosions in the dark. 'The people who came here won't just quit. They'll look until they find you, wherever you are.'

'They're looking for Caelum *and* me,' she said. 'They

won't expect us to split up. And they won't expect us to get far. They don't think we're smart enough.' Her expression changed, just for an instant, like a plate shifting deep undersea and causing ripples at the surface. 'Besides, what other choice do we have?'

'You could come with us,' Gemma said. But she knew that Lyra had made her decision. Gemma was fumbling for a way to convince her, hauling at a line stretched thin to a breaking point. 'We could drive you somewhere far away,' she said. 'Maine. The Oregon coast. Canada. Wherever.'

'Not without Caelum,' Lyra said simply.

'You'll never find him,' Gemma argued. 'Do you know how many people there are in this country? Millions and millions.' But there was no way to explain to Lyra how big the world was, and how far it went. Until a few weeks ago, her world was by the water, by a fence that ringed her off into a few square miles.

'You just said the people who came from Haven will find *us*.'

'That's different,' Gemma said. 'They're . . . bigger than we are. Do you understand that? They have cars. They have drones, and money, and friends everywhere.'

Lyra's face changed again. A new current swept away all the feeling, shutting her down to a perfect blank. 'You forget what they made us to be, though,' she said – softly, gently, as if Gemma were the one who needed to understand.

Gemma shook her head. Her heart was beating through her whole body. Every minute the sun leeched away more cover.

'Invisible,' Lyra said, so softly Gemma almost missed it.

Then she smiled. Gemma thought it was the first time she had ever seen Lyra smile, and the effect was dazzling, like watching the sun slide behind a prism and light it up in various colors. 'Thank you, though. I mean it.'

'Please,' Gemma said, as Lyra turned away. 'Take this, at least.' Gemma took her wallet from her back pocket. It was cheap, plastic, and covered in smiley faces, and April had bought it for her as a joke their sophomore year. There were probably sixty bucks inside, plus an Amex tied to her parents' account, a debit card, a non-driver state ID, a folded-up note April had given her on their first day back in school after break – *This note certifies I give zero fucks* – and, in the little coin pouch, a nest of unspooling thread she'd picked off Pete's pocket the first time she'd worn his sweatshirt to school. She could get new cards, and even an ID wasn't that difficult, especially since she didn't drive. She had only a few hundred dollars in her bank account, anyway. She mostly regretted that bit of thread. 'You'll need money. You know how to use an ATM card, right, to get money? The code's easy. Four-four-one-one. Can you remember that?'

'Thanks.' Lyra managed to smile again. Then she did something funny: she reached up and placed two hands on Gemma's shoulders. 'See you,' she said.

That was it. She turned and disappeared. At least, to Gemma it seemed like she disappeared, even though of course Lyra was actually visible for a while, moving between cars, heading in the direction of the highway, and finally passing into a thicket of disease-blighted trees. The sun had finally come up for good, and Gemma found her eyes watering in the sudden bright. She should run after Lyra. She should beg her, or scream at her, or force her to come with them.

But she knew it wouldn't do any good, and she didn't move, and couldn't breathe. She knew they would never see each other again. Lyra would be cleaned up, like Jake had been. Caelum too.

'Gemma?' Pete found her hand and held it tight-tight, as if she was in danger of falling off a ledge. 'You tried, okay? You did everything you could do.'

Gemma said nothing. It didn't matter if she'd tried. She'd failed. And that was the only thing that counted.

'You can't feel guilty about this, okay? You can't save her. You can't save any of them. I want you to say it.'

She was surprised when Pete pulled her into a hug. His shirt still smelled a little like the tiki smoke, his skin like the sweet punch they'd been drinking. She felt like crying again. But she kissed his collarbone through his shirt, and tilted her head to catch his Adam's apple, too.

'I tried,' she said. 'I can't save them.' As quickly as the urge to cry had come, it was gone. It wasn't that she believed it, exactly, but that it didn't matter anymore. What she had said to Lyra was true: the people working against them were too big. They were too strong.

Lyra and Caelum would die by their will, just as Gemma had lived.

The hand of misery that had been squeezing her for weeks unclenched. She felt light. Free. She saw now that her only mistake had been in thinking she had a choice.

There was evil everywhere in the world. Liars outnumbered truth tellers, probably by three to one. So what did it matter, one more or less? She might even be able to look at her father again. 'Let's go home,' she said.

For the first time since they'd left the party, Pete smiled. 'Now you're talking,' he said, and kissed her hand even as he interlaced their fingers. He seemed happy. He thought she was happy.

She didn't have the heart to tell him the truth. There was no need, anyway. Happiness never lasted, because happiness didn't pay dividends.

That was just the way the world worked.

SIX

THEY WERE ONLY A FEW miles out from the dump of run-down fast-food restaurants that counted for the center of Ronchowoa when they came across the accident: a big delivery truck and a sedan nosed together at a right angle so they blocked the road entirely. The truck driver was visible in his cab, hunched over the phone. The woman was pacing, and when she spotted Pete and Gemma she flagged them down, as if they might otherwise have any choice but to stop.

'Don't get out,' Gemma said, when Pete unbuckled his seat belt. 'There must be another way home.'

'She could be hurt,' he said.

Gemma was too tired to care, and too tired to feel guilty. 'She isn't hurt,' she said. 'She's walking. See?'

And she was — the woman was heading straight for them, gesturing for Pete to roll down the window. When he did, she leaned down to squint into the car. She had the washed-out coloring of an old T-shirt, but her eyes were dark and Gemma didn't especially like them. They were the kind of eyes that worked like specimen pins, as if they were trying to nail things down in their proper place.

'Sorry to bug you,' she said. 'Do y'all have a cell phone I could borrow? Mine's out of batteries. And this guy won't give me his info, won't speak a word to me.'

Gemma's phone was also dead, so Pete handed his over. Gemma did feel a little guilty then. The woman's hands shook badly when she tried to dial the police, and it took her several tries before she could get the number right. She moved away from the car, plugging one ear with a finger, while the truck driver climbed out of his cab and glared at her. Gemma didn't like the look of him. He looked big and ropy and mean.

The woman hadn't even hung up before the police were on the scene: two of them, a man and a woman, who arrived in an unmarked sedan.

Every minute it got hotter. Gemma and Pete sat and watched the woman and the truck driver argue and the cops look on impassively – they were too far to hear what was being said.

'Should I ask for my phone back?' Pete asked. Gemma shook her head and said nothing. She was too tired to think. When he keyed on the engine so they could use the AC, the female cop turned in their direction, as if seeing them for the first time.

'Great,' Pete said. Now it was the cop's turn to approach. 'Just great.'

'Step out of the car, please,' she said, in the flat drawl of someone extremely bored by her job. Gemma could see the sky mirrored in the woman's sunglasses, and she straightened up as fear twinged her spine.

'Hang on a second,' Pete said. 'We didn't do anything.'

'Please step out of the car.' She showed her badge – a flash of gold, and then it retreated.

'But we didn't do anything,' he insisted. 'We were just driving home and we came across the accident.'

'I understand. If you would both just step out of the car, we'll get you on your way in a minute.'

'Just do it,' Gemma whispered to him. Now the other cop was sauntering over, hands on his belt, working a piece of gum in his mouth.

They got out of the car. The backs of Gemma's thighs were slick with sweat from where they had stuck to the seat leather. It was bright and very quiet. A dozen cows stared dolefully at them from behind a rotting fence. From their perspective, Gemma and Pete were the ones fenced in.

'You see what happened?' the female cop asked.

Pete was getting agitated. 'No. I already told you. We had nothing to do with it.'

Now the male cop chimed in. 'You from around here, then?'

Pete hesitated. His eyes slid to Gemma's. Once again she felt a pinch of worry – could they be sure these were real cops? She'd only seen the woman's badge for a second. They weren't driving a squad car, and though they were in uniform, it wasn't like she could pick out a fake. Still, she knew they were safe so long as there were witnesses.

'We're from Chapel Hill,' Gemma said. Right away, she knew she'd made a tactical error.

The male cop's eyebrows blew up to his hairline. 'You're quite a little ways from home,' he said. 'Whatcha doing in Tennessee?'

'It isn't any of your business,' Pete said. Gemma nearly told him to calm down, but she didn't want to make things any worse.

The cop gnawed his gum some more. 'You two got some ID?'

Gemma's heart sank. She didn't have ID – she'd given Lyra her wallet. Pete seemed as if he might argue the point, but at a look from Gemma, he turned and moved back to the car, muttering. Gemma waited in the agonizing silence, half wondering why the truck driver and the woman he'd smashed were being so patient. If she'd been in an accident, if the cops were wasting their time on two nobodies instead of helping, she would have lost her shit. But they just stood there, dumb and practically silent, as if the cops' arrival had turned them into statues.

Pete was taking too long. He searched the front seat. He appeared to crouch, as if searching the floor. When he straightened up, his face was hollowed out with fear.

'I – I can't find my wallet,' he said.

Gemma felt the ground buck like an animal beneath her. 'What do you mean?'

'What do you *think* I mean?' He threw open the door to the backseat and disappeared again. 'I can't find it. It's gone.'

'That's – that's impossible.' But as Gemma closed her eyes, she remembered that they'd stopped for coffee a few hours before dawn. She saw Pete, juggling a Styrofoam cup and a water bottle, slide his wallet on top of the car so he could reach for his keys. What if he'd left it there? They'd been so tired.

It was possible.

Pete slammed the door shut. Then, suddenly, he aimed a kick at the rear tires. Gemma shouted. The cops started toward him and he backed off, holding up both hands. 'I'm all right,' he said. 'I'm all right.'

'Why don't you have a seat here on the curb?' The

male cop reached for his belt – Gemma saw a flash of metal handcuffs.

'What – are you going to arrest me now? We. Didn't. Do. Anything.'

'Settle down, son. No one's accusing you. No need to get so defensive.'

'I'm not defensive—'

'Early in the morning, wearing party clothes, maybe you been drinking some, decided on a little joyride—'

'Jesus Christ. This is *insane*. We weren't *joyriding*—'

'Pete.' Gemma's voice cracked. Everything was happening too fast. Gemma felt as if she were listening to a song at triple, quadruple speed. There was a high ringing in her ears, like the sound of electricity through a live wire. Danger. 'Please. We weren't joyriding. And we haven't been drinking. We have . . . we have friends nearby.'

'Friends?' Too late, Gemma knew she'd made another tactical error. 'These friends have names?'

Pete jumped in again. 'We don't have to tell you anything. You don't have any reason to hold us.' He was almost shouting. But for a second, the cops seemed to realize the truth of this, and froze where they were. 'Can I have my phone, please?'

These words he directed at the female driver, the one who'd originally flagged them down. Funnily enough, however, she didn't move. She didn't even blink. Again, Gemma had the impression of a statue.

No. Not a statue. An actor – a bit-part actor whose lines have come and gone, contentedly watching the rest of the play from the wings.

Too late, Gemma understood. Too late, Gemma knew there were no witnesses, and no one to hear them scream.

SEVEN

THE WORST THING ABOUT BEING kidnapped with your boyfriend, it turned out, was having to go to the bathroom. First Gemma thought she could hold it. Pete tried to get his hands free so he could at least pee in the corner, in a pile of rags or the empty water bottle that rattled across the floor whenever the van made a turn.

But he couldn't get his hands free.

She pretended to be asleep, choking on her own panic, on tears she couldn't even wipe away, while the van filled with a sharp metallic stink. Later it was her turn, and she felt a flood of shame that made her want to die, truly die, for the first time in her life.

Instead, she slept. Unbelievably, improbably, mercifully, she slept, with her head knocking against the filthy floor and the stink of ammonia everywhere.

Every hour or so, the van came to a stop: the drivers

were in no particular hurry. Every time, Gemma woke with a start, hoping they'd come to a checkpoint, or a roadblock – hoping, though she knew it was impossible, that someone had already realized she was missing, that police had been mobilized across fifty states – but no one came to let them out, and every time, after they lay there in the sweating quiet for agonizing minutes, the van simply started up again. Who knew whether the strangers who'd cuffed and gagged them were fake cops or the real thing, just paid off by somebody higher up? She understood that the truck had been brought, and the accident staged, specifically for the abduction. It was likely Fortner's friends had blocked off all the roads around Winston-Able with more fake accidents or fake checkpoints, scanning for a boy and girl traveling together, acting weirdly, no convincing story about who they were or where they'd come from.

By the time the van stopped for good, Gemma and Pete hadn't looked at each other in hours. Her jeans were wet. His, too. She was still wearing her party top, which had beaded sequins along the hem. He was in his Hawaiian shirt.

She nearly toppled over when she had to stand. The man who'd masqueraded as the truck driver took her arm, surprisingly gentle, as if they were on a date and she had caught a heel in the sidewalk. But the woman who'd posed as a cop stepped forward and seized Gemma roughly.

'I'll take this one,' she said simply.

It was dark except for a ring of headlights in the distance that might have been Jeeps, more vans, some kind of security cordon. There were streetlamps, but most of them were missing bulbs. People on foot patrolled with flashlights, and in the distance, Gemma made out a big, low, slope-roofed building, barely speckled with light.

Long runways of pavement, distant fists of furry trees, signs (A–32i, B–27a) blinking in the sudden clarity of the guards' flashlights. It was an old regional airport; she could even now make out a single hangar, illuminated by the temporary sweep of passing headlights.

Where were they? Not Tennessee. They must have been driving for twelve hours at least. She smelled running sap, tilled mud, even a very faint tang of fertilizer. Farmland.

Crickets cut the air into sound waves. Stars wheeled prettily above them. Ohio? Indiana?

Their abductors removed their gags at last; they were wet and heavy with saliva. Tears of relief burned Gemma's eyes, even though she still couldn't speak: her tongue felt swollen and painful, her lips were raw, and her throat dry. She wondered why they'd been gagged in the first place – whether it was just to keep them from talking to each other, or so they would be afraid.

Voices shouted in the dark. Someone called, 'Hot shit!' and there was even a smattering of applause, as if the people who'd seized Gemma and Pete had instead won several rounds in a bingo tournament.

'Where are you taking us?' Pete's voice was hoarse, too. She wanted to reach over and squeeze his hands. But she was filthy, ashamed, and besides, her hands, still cuffed behind her back, were numb.

'Nowhere.' The guy who'd been playing male cop sounded tired. Almost reproachful. Like, *hey, buddy, I've had a long day too. At least you didn't have to drive.*

'Don't answer it,' the woman said. Hearing Pete referred to like that, like an *it*, sparked a new terror.

'My name is Gemma Ives.' Gemma's words tasted a little like vomit. They were coming up quickly on the airport – too quickly. A few distant lights had swelled from fireflies to windows: in a few of them, she could make out concrete interiors, wires nested like intestines in the ceiling, banks of leather chairs still bolted to the floor. 'I'm the daughter of Geoffrey Ives. My dad was one of the original investors in Haven. This is my boyfriend, Pete. You've got it all wrong. We're not who you think we are.'

'I told you –' the woman sighed, speaking directly over Gemma's head, as if she were nothing but air – 'not to talk to it.'

'What does it matter, anyway? You want to know

where we're going, kid?' Her partner, or whatever he was, wouldn't look at Pete or Gemma, even when he was addressing them. 'Nowhere. We're already here.'

The old airport terminal rose steep-faced and ugly, like someone's blunt and splintered jaw. There was a faint hiss in the dark, and then the wheeze of rusted hinges: a door.

Gemma had known they were in trouble – big trouble. In the van she'd sat there grinding her teeth and trying to force her thoughts to settle, to pin them down whenever they flitted out of reach, like trying to catch horseflies by hand. They'd been followed. The military, or whoever was in charge, had figured out that they were trying to help Lyra and Caelum. Maybe they even knew that Caelum had managed to slip away, and somehow they blamed Gemma and Pete.

But now, for the first time, she understood. The people who'd abducted them didn't think Gemma and Pete had helped the replicas escape.

They thought Gemma and Pete *were* the replicas.

EIGHT

INSIDE: THE SMELL OF SHOE polish, sweat, gunmetal. Two soldiers wearing military fatigues straightened up at their post. They were in a tight corridor, carpeted and filthy. A narrow set of stairs, dirty with footprints, rose into the darkness. Gemma knew once she went up the stairs – wherever they led – things would be hopeless.

'You're making a big mistake.' Gemma's voice cracked. How many hours had it been since she'd had anything to drink? 'Call my dad. Call him.'

'We should have left the gags on,' the man holding Pete muttered. He nudged Pete toward the stairs. Unexpectedly, Pete broke loose, reeling like a drunk. His hands were still bound, but he cracked his head into the man's jaw; Gemma heard the impact of it, a hollow sound.

Suddenly, everyone was shouting. Gemma screamed as both soldiers launched for Pete at once.

'Don't hurt him! Please. *Please.*' She was too scared even to cry. For a second, she lost sight of him in the shuffle of human bodies. One of the soldiers accidentally caught her with an elbow and she bit down on her tongue.

'Easy, easy, easy.' The two soldiers hauled Pete to his feet, pinning him between them. Still, he struggled to break loose. Gemma had never seen him look the way he did then, and she thought randomly of a video April had once shown her during her vegetarian phase: how fighting dogs were burned with cigarettes, beaten with sticks, until they were so angry and desperate they would tear each other up, actually tear each other into pieces.

The dogs in the video knew they were going to die, and that was what made them fight. They had nothing to live for.

'Let go of me.' Pete's face was so twisted with raw anger, even Gemma was afraid of him. 'Get your fucking hands off me.'

'You better tell your boyfriend to calm down.' The man who'd been holding Pete was massaging his jawbone. He glared at Gemma. 'Or he's going to get his head blown off.'

'Please.' Gemma's voice cracked. 'Please, Pete.' At the sound of her voice, he finally went still.

'Good boy,' one of the soldiers said. 'We don't want to hurt you.'

Neither Gemma nor Pete bothered pointing out that that was very hard to believe.

'Take him up,' the man said, still rubbing his jaw and looking pissed about it.

This made Pete go wild again. 'Let me stay with her.' But the soldiers pivoted him, with difficulty, toward the stairs. 'Let me stay with her. Please.'

Gemma let herself cry then. She couldn't help it. She felt as if she were watching Pete through the wrong end of a telescope, getting smaller and smaller, though he was only a few feet away.

'It's okay, it's okay,' she kept repeating, even as his voice splintered into echoes and then grew fainter, even though it was obviously not okay, nothing was okay, nothing would be okay ever again.

'Please.' She tried one last time to make them listen. 'Please,' she said. 'I'm telling you the truth. Geoffrey Ives is my father. Ask Dr Saperstein, ask anybody—'

But she went silent as, down the hall, a door opened and spilled a gut of light.

'What's all the shouting for?' A woman's voice, low and surprisingly warm, floated out to them. For a moment, she was silhouetted in the light. As she came forward, Gemma experienced a shock of displacement: the woman looked like a soccer mom, like one of Kristina's lunch crew. She was even wearing yoga pants.

'Nothing.' The man finally quit massaging his jaw and straightened up. 'Is Saperstein back?'

The yogi shook her head. 'Tuesday,' she said.

Gemma's mouth tasted like plaster, like the soft crumble of a pill. Saperstein knew her father. She'd been counting on the fact that he, at least, would be able to help. She'd comforted herself with the idea that wherever she was being taken, Saperstein would be there.

What would happen to her, and to Pete, before Tuesday when he returned?

'He didn't go to Penn after all, did he?'

'No. Washington.' The yogi's eyes swept Gemma. 'Where'd you find her?'

'Where we were supposed to.' Gemma's captor was squeezing her arm so tightly, Gemma could feel her fingernails. 'She says it was all a big mistake. She says she doesn't belong here.'

'Is that right?' The yogi was still watching Gemma curiously – not meanly, not with disgust or contempt, but with true curiosity. 'Well, someone's been feeding her, at least.'

A fist of hatred tightened in Gemma's stomach. 'I'm not lying,' she said. 'I can prove it. Call Saperstein. Ask him yourself.'

Gemma couldn't tell whether the yogi woman was even listening. She only looked puzzled, as if Gemma were speaking in a different language. After a moment, she withdrew, and Gemma heard the murmur of distant voices: she was speaking to people out of sight. Gemma was dizzy with fear. What was she doing?

A minute later, several people wearing medical scrubs flowed down the hall and moved up the stairs without acknowledging either Gemma or the man and woman who'd brought them. They had the same look as all medical staff: harried, professional, too busy to be bothered. The colossal, patchwork strangeness of it all – the yoga pants and the doctors' scrubs and the soldiers with assault rifles and the reek of sweat – made a sudden rise of hysteria lift in Gemma's chest.

The woman in yoga pants returned, turning her face to the ceiling as if listening to the pattern of footsteps above them.

'Should I take her up?' Gemma's captor asked, and she shook her head.

'In a second. I'm going to bring them down first.'

'Bring *who* down?' Gemma blurted out.

The woman didn't answer right away. Just then, the sound of footsteps above them grew louder. The door at the top of the landing creaked open, and the doctors, or nurses, or whatever they were, returned.

They had brought along three Gemmas.

Three Gemmas crowded the stairwell. Three Gemmas

gazed down at her. Three Gemmas, scalps shaved clean, wearing filthy T-shirts and pants that bagged from the hollows of their hipbones, chittered like small mice, as if at a fun-house reflection.

Gemma lost her breath. A hole opened up beneath her feet. She dropped straight through the floor.

Dimly, she was aware that the woman in yoga pants had turned at last to address her. 'My proof,' she said simply.

NINE

FINALLY, GEMMA WAS ESCORTED UPSTAIRS. The airport terminal was crawling with military personnel, but also people in medical scrubs, rendered identical by their dirty hair and look of shared exhaustion. One woman dressed in a pantsuit, who resembled a fashion mannequin on Fifth Avenue, kept massaging her forehead with perfectly manicured fingers. Gemma didn't even want to know what government agency *she'd* crawled out of.

The airport was dizzying not so much because of its size, but because of its regularity, the identical halls stripped of furniture, counters, vendors, arrivals screens. There were very few working lights, and new ribs of plywood divided room from room. The ceiling panels were missing.

Gemma was led to a bathroom with no stalls at all, just toilets bolted to the floor at regular intervals. A nurse was summoned – she was wearing a shapeless medical smock over her street clothes, and had that blind-mole look of someone who'd just been asleep – to unbutton Gemma's reeking pants and underwear and haul them to her hips while Gemma peed, since her wrists were still bound.

The nurse's hands were cold. Gemma tried to blink away the sudden pressure of tears: the woman's fingers swept the place between Gemma's legs when she went to hitch up Gemma's underwear and then jeans.

'Sorry,' the nurse whispered. 'We'll find you something dry to put on in a bit.' But Gemma felt something come down around her, some inner space collapsing.

There was no air-conditioning. If it wasn't obvious enough from the smell of must and raw wood, from the filthy corners and cables of dust visible through open gaps in the walls, it was clear to her now: whatever this place was, it wasn't like Haven. There was no experimentation here, no medical treatments or analyses. This was a holding pen, pure and simple.

Outside the bathroom, the woman in the pantsuit was waiting, yawning behind a hand. She straightened up and frowned briefly at Gemma. 'Well?'

'Well what?' the nurse responded, keeping a hand on Gemma's elbow. Her touch was surprisingly gentle, as if she wanted to make up for what had happened in the bathroom.

'That's the last of them, isn't it?'

'How should I know?' The two women obviously despised each other. 'That's your business. What I'm supposed to do is keep them *alive*.' Gemma disliked the way she emphasized that. It suggested the other woman's business was something else entirely.

'No need to get defensive. I was just asking. They all look the same to me, even the ones that aren't doubled.'

'I bet.' The nurse's voice was hard with sarcasm. 'We still have bodies to match. Some of 'em no more than fingers − thanks to you.' She sniffed. 'But if you say so, you say so.'

They moved again down the hall, cavernous with shadow, and half-splintered spaces suggesting their original purpose: countertops, old glass display cases where she imagined sandwiches withering behind glass.

Something smelled: a trash smell, an inside-of-the-body smell. The scent of urine was strong. They stopped to draw water from a long industrial sink: plastic cups overflowed a massive trash can. The nurse had to hold the cup while Gemma suckled at it like a baby, but she was too thirsty to say no. Then, to her surprise, the woman turned Gemma and released her handcuffs. Gemma nearly fainted from the rush of pleasure, of relief, when she could move her shoulders freely.

But she understood, as the woman gestured her on,

why the restraints weren't necessary: patterns of footsteps sounded softly on the linoleum, overlapping, like the drum of distant rain. Soldiers with guns. Even when they hung back in the dark she could see the barrels winking like animal eyes.

'Be a good one, now, and you won't get in any trouble,' the nurse said. For the first time since being taken into the van, she felt a spark of hope. This woman wasn't evil. Maybe she could be made to understand. To believe.

'Please listen to me.' Gemma spoke in a whisper. Her throat was raw from crying. 'My name is Gemma Ives. I live in Chapel Hill, North Carolina. I have parents. They're looking for me.'

She couldn't tell whether the woman was even listening. This part of the airport was almost completely dark: a runner of cheap battery-pack lights lit a narrow aisle of floor, like those on an airplane designed to help you find your way to the emergency exit. Around them furniture was lumped and piled and stacked in the darkness. It looked like a whole warehouse had been emptied. The smell was terrible, too. It was so bad it had weight, and form, and even movement. They paused briefly in front of a set of plastic shelves piled with cheap T-shirts and plain cotton pants, laundered to the point of stiffness.

'Laundry day's Friday,' the nurse said. 'You'll get a replacement soon as you turn in this pair.'

'Please,' Gemma said. She found herself speaking in a whisper, as once again fear flooded into her, poured down her throat like the taste on the air, like the grit of human skin and nails. 'I don't belong here.'

Someone moaned. Then a cry in the dark, quickly stifled. But the sound seemed to find Gemma, to burrow deep in her chest, like a hook. And at the same time her eyes adjusted, she realized that what she'd mistaken for piles of furniture were really people, girls: hundreds of girls, dressed identically, some of them visibly wounded, others so thin they looked like a wreckage of bones; sleeping on the floor, on mattresses, on piles of fabric and tarps, on stacked blankets.

'Nobody belongs here, child,' the nurse said. She was holding her throat. Gemma saw a small gold cross nested between her fingers. 'Not even the devil himself.'

PART II

TEN

KRISTINA IVES SPENT THE FIRST day of her fifty-first year crying and picking the cuticles of her fingernails until they bled, and then shivering damply in bed, waiting for the Xanax to take effect, and the second day counting all the ugly things she could find on the way to Nashville, Tennessee.

A dead deer, mangled on the side of the highway. A house punched in by age and neglect, spilling its rot onto the porch, as if it had been gutted. Billboards advertising strip clubs, XXX stores, erectile dysfunction clinics.

Since having Gemma, she'd hardly ever traveled: she liked to be home with her things, in the beautiful house with the rugs that went *hush hush*, with Rufus and the cats and the pool in summertime where she could lie out with a book, her feet damp with dew and new grass, the hum of a lawn mower in the background like the pleasant buzz of one of her pills.

They had a house in Vail and Geoff hosted clients there several times a year, but she hadn't been, not since Gemma was a toddler. Though Geoff had urged her to learn to ski, she could never see the point in it, the suiting up and the rentals and the waiting in line to crank all the way to the summit only to plunge down the mountain again.

One time, only one time, he'd convinced her to put Gemma in ski school. She was maybe four years old, so young even she didn't remember the experience, and Kristina had stood with a crowd of other parents in the lodge while outside a group of fluorescent children made pie-wedges with their skis. No one else was worried – the other mothers and the scattered fathers drank spiked hot cocoa or went off on runs of their own – but Kristina had stayed at the windowpane, her breath misting the glass, watching the little gob of purple that was her only daughter, funny-faced and precocious with cheeks so fat Kristina had to stop herself from biting them.

She'd read once that during World War II many of the Jews had sewn their precious belongings, jewels and watches and things, into the lining of their coats before fleeing, and she'd immediately understood: Gemma was like that, like a secret, precious thing sewed not into the lining of her coat but into who she was deep down, at her core, as a person.

She saw it even before it happened. Saw Gemma's

puffy-coated arms begin flapping frantically, saw her teeter on her tiny skis. And she saw, at the same time, beneath Gemma's coat and beneath her skin, to the webbing of her narrow bones and all the fragile organs tucked among them, so easily punctured, ruptured, burst; and she was out the door and running, calling for Gemma to stop, be careful, stop, so that Gemma, looking up at her mother, lost her balance and fell.

So Kristina didn't go to Vail anymore. They had a place in the Outer Banks, but there, too, she rarely went. Gemma loved it, but Kristina could never keep down images of Gemma drowned in the waves, pummeled by sand, her lungs bloated with seawater. And she had another fear – that she would have to bring Gemma to an unfamiliar hospital, that blood would be drawn, or bones X-rayed, and somehow, the doctors would know. That evidence of Kristina and Geoff's crime might be encoded in every single one of Gemma's cells, embedded in the filaments of her DNA.

She'd been in the kitchen, rinsing out stray wineglasses that Geoff must have collected from the deck, when the call came in. Sunday: her favorite day. She never minded washing dishes, even though they had help to do that. She liked the sound of rushing water, the soap-steam clouds, the way the glasses chimed when she tapped them with her nails.

'Gemma?' she answered the phone automatically. No one else would be calling so early on a Sunday.

But it was April. And as soon as Kristina heard the sound of April's voice, she knew.

'Ms. Ives?' That was a tell, too – April never called her anything but Kristina, not since she was in third grade. 'I'm worried about Gemma.'

And then, in a rush, April had told her everything: that Gemma had not, in fact, slept over; that she had gone with Pete to see Lyra down in that tragic little shoe box her husband had shoved Rick Harliss into; that she should have been back already.

She wasn't back, though, and she wasn't picking up her phone, and Pete wasn't picking up, either.

By some miracle, Kristina had managed to locate a telephone number for Rick Harliss, scrawled on a notepad and wedged deep in the junk drawer, along with all the other miscellaneous things they couldn't stand to look at but knew might prove useful someday.

Rick's home number just rang and rang, and his cell phone went straight to voice mail.

She went right away to Geoff, as she always did, as she had been trained to do. He had the idea to check Gemma's debit card activity and see whether she had taken out any money. In the very early morning, Gemma had purchased tickets from Knoxville, Tennessee, to Nashville.

In the afternoon, she had taken out two hundred dollars from an ATM in Crossville, Tennessee. Around midnight, someone used her ATM card to check into a Four Crossings Motel in Nashville, and although by this morning that proved to be a false lead – the girl and boy in room 22 had obviously stolen Gemma's wallet, although they claimed simply to have found it.

Still, they must have stolen it *from* Gemma. Which meant she had gone to Nashville.

But why? For what reason? And why was her phone dead, and Pete's too?

Where, for that matter, was Rick Harliss?

You promise you know absolutely nothing about this? she had asked Geoff, after a terrible, sleepless night, half drowning in barbiturate dreams. *You swear you had nothing, nothing at all to do with it?*

Of course not. Geoffrey's answer was quick. *How could you even think that?*

And she believed Geoff because that was what she did, what she was compelled to do, the way the earth was compelled to go around the sun. They'd built the belief together, carefully, spinning turrets, ice-thin pillars, delicate vaulted ceilings alive with all the stories they'd made. Even a single crack would make the whole thing come down.

Now she counted: a truck overturned on the other side

of the highway. A highway memorial to someone who had died. A sign warning of a nearby maximum security prison. Ugly, ugly, ugly. Concrete sprawl and withered shrubbery baking in the heat. And Gemma, little Gemma, her small, glowing secret, somewhere out there. There weren't enough pills in the whole world to shave Kristina's fear into some manageable shape, a small white sphere she could swallow and let dissolve in her stomach.

A sign blinked, and disappeared behind them. Thirteen miles of highway left until they reached Nashville.

ELEVEN

'WHERE DID IT COME FROM?'

On Monday, those words had pulled Gemma from one nightmare into another: *mirrors,* she thought confusedly.

Three-dimensional, living mirrors: three Gemmas wore identical expressions of bland curiosity, three Gemmas had been split and fissured from a single central image. Unconsciously, she brought her hands to her face, her arms, her thighs, to make sure they were still intact. To make sure *she* was still intact.

'Which number are you?' asked one of the mirrors.

'You're not Cassiopeia,' said another.

The third one said, 'Cassiopeia is dead.'

'I'm Calliope,' said the first one. She added: 'Number seven.' In her eyes, Gemma was reduced to a narrow reflection. A reflection in a reflection in a reflection. Gemma thought of a double helix that mirrored even as it turned and turned. Symmetry, but a terrible kind. She sat up, half expecting the other Gemmas to move in response. But they didn't.

'You think it's dumb?' one of the girls said.

'Dumb how?' one of the others asked.

'Dumb like number eight,' the first one replied, and turned. 'Like Goosedown.'

Thud-thud-thud.

Only then did Gemma see another one, a fourth one, even skinnier than all the rest, crouched in the corner not far from them. Her legs were bare and covered with scabs. She was wearing a diaper. She was so thin her head appeared gigantic, her features too far apart, as if they were wrapped around a fishbowl.

Thud-thud-thud. As Gemma watched, she lifted her head and slammed it, once, twice, three times, against the wall; the sun caught a mesh of plaster fine as dust hanging in the air, sifting above her head, before slowly, it began to fall.

The sickest replicas were segregated from the rest of the population, concealed behind rudimentary curtains of burlap, kept mostly unconscious through regular dosages of morphine, at least according to what Gemma overheard. She might have been tempted to peek beyond the curtains and see for herself were it not for the smell.

Blood. Bodies in a constant state of hemorrhage, of organ failure, of beginning to turn.

Someone was always getting sick – in the toilet, in a trash can, on the floor when they couldn't make it to a trash can. Gemma knew that prions weren't contagious, at least that they couldn't be spread by breathing, but still she couldn't help but see prions turning invisibly on the air like sharp-pointed snowflakes, like dandelion fluff, like burrs that would stick in her lungs when she inhaled.

Diapered toddlers who had never learned to walk instead crawled among the wreckage of dirt, or simply sucked their fingers and cried.

Nurses still wandered the halls, like bewildered ghosts, as if questioning why on earth they couldn't just move on. They did the best they could to help, with limited supplies, dwindling medication, and power that failed regularly.

A single building, L-shaped, and boys and girls separated by security at the joint. Soldiers moved through crowds of standing cadavers – hollow-cheeked and fire-eyed, dizzy with disease and starvation – by parting them with their rifles. When one of the soldiers, a girl with tight cornrows, stopped to comfort a bawling replica, another soldier reprimanded her.

'You'll give them the wrong idea,' he said. He was tall, with pale eyelashes and a burst of acne across his forehead. 'It'll only be worse in the end.'

Gemma tried to find her way to Pete, to make sure he was okay, but was stopped by a redhead in full-on camouflage who looked like someone who might have been in her English class.

'Turn around,' he said. 'You speak English? Turn around.'

Another soldier, a girl with her nails painted different rainbow colors, was sitting in a single plastic chair still bolted down in a waiting area otherwise empty of furniture. 'They all speak English, dummy,' she said softly. She was playing a video game on her phone. Gemma could tell from the sound effects.

'Doesn't seem like it, half the time.' Gemma had turned away from him but not quickly enough to miss what he said next. 'Shit. I don't even like *twins*.'

She wanted to scream, but just like in her dream she couldn't. *Not me,* she wanted to say. *You've got the wrong girl.*

But how could she? Three other Gemmas tailed her. Three Gemmas who stood shoulder to shoulder, blink-blink-blink, breathing with *her* lungs, twitching with *her* hands, turning their heads on her own too-short neck.

No one would come to save her. Not a single person in the world knew where she was. Even when Pete's car was discovered – which she had no doubt it had been by now – there was nothing to suggest where they had gone, not a trace of evidence, no ransom notes, no trail of blood.

Her only hope was that somehow, her parents would catch up to Lyra and Caelum and realize what had happened. That her dad would charge in here in his Big Suit way, threatening to sue everyone from Saperstein to the president of the United States, and she and Pete would be saved. But she knew, too, that would mean that Lyra and Caelum would have to take their place. Maybe the whole thing had a sick poeticism. After all these years, she'd finally ended up back where she started. Where she *belonged*.

It was better not to think. She gave up on trying to speak to anyone and didn't bother trying to get anyone to speak to her. When Dr Saperstein came back, he would see her, know her, and realize his mistake – that is, if her dad didn't find a way to track her down first.

Until then, she simply had to survive.

TWELVE

THERE WAS NOTHING TO DO. No books, no magazines, no computers, no phones. Nothing but mattresses
jigsawed on the floor and hundreds of girls sticky with
injuries sitting or lying around.

Some of the replicas had made up their own games,
rolling pen caps or stacking coffee cups. She even saw a
girl, maybe three or four years old, playing with an old
syringe. When Gemma tried to take it from her, the girl
turned unexpectedly vicious, spitting in her face, going
for Gemma's eyes. Gemma stumbled backward, and
someone reached out to steady her. Again, Gemma had
the sense of falling into a mirror: one of the reflections,
one of her *clones*, had followed her.

'Don't worry about the Browns,' the girl said. Her
eyes were always moving – around and around, taking in
Gemma's hair, and stud earrings, and fingernails, which

were painted yellow and green, alternating – as if trying to generate some centrifugal force that would pull Gemma closer. 'They're all soft in the head.'

Gemma went from feeling angry to feeling sick. She turned around again and saw the girl had resumed her play, pulling up wool fibers from a patch of dirty carpet. Another girl, identical to the first, had scuttled closer to watch. Looking at them side by side made Gemma dizzy.

'You're not one of us,' the girl said. Her breath reeked, and Gemma felt sorry about being disgusted. 'You were made somewhere else. There were only five genotypes at Haven. Numbers six through ten. And number six is dead.'

'I know,' Gemma said automatically. 'I saw her.' It made a twisted kind of sense that this girl could see what the people in charge couldn't, or wouldn't. To them, the replicas weren't people. They were lab rats. Or they were things, manufactured shells, like so many plastic parts cut from the same mold. It must be hard to keep track.

The girl leaned closer, and Gemma had to stop herself from flinching. At the same time, she was seized by an impulse to dig her fingers into the girl's eyes, to pull them out, to tear off her skin. She wanted her face back.

'Number six was named. We called her Cassiopeia. Dr O'Donnell named me, too. My name is Calliope. Are you named?' Calliope's eyes were huge. Hopeful. April called it Gemma's *sad kitten face*.

Gemma nodded. 'Gemma,' she said.

Calliope smiled. Two of her teeth overlapped. She hadn't had braces, obviously, like Gemma had. 'Gemma,' she repeated. 'Where were you made?'

Gemma was exhausted again, though it couldn't be much past noon. She wondered whether the girl had ever met anyone new, at least anyone who would talk to her. 'I was made at Haven, like you, but then I went somewhere else.'

'Outside,' Calliope said, exhaling the word as if it were the final piece of a powerful magic spell.

After that, Calliope wouldn't leave Gemma alone. She followed Gemma when she walked the 282 paces she could walk, between the curtained-off wing where the sickest replicas lay mangled, tethered weakly to life by grim-faced nurses working a dozen machines; to the two bathrooms, men's and women's, in the no-man's-land between the gendered sides.

When Gemma sat, Calliope sat a few feet away, watching her. At one point Gemma lay down and pretended to sleep. Still, she felt Calliope watching, and she sat up, finally, relieved to realize that she was angry, that there was another feeling elbowing in besides fear.

'What?' Gemma said. Looking at Calliope still gave her a terrible sense of vertigo, like being spun around blindfolded and then discovering, with the blindfold off, that the world was still spinning. 'What do you want?'

She'd meant to scare her, or startle her away, but Calliope kept staring. Gemma couldn't shake the feeling that Calliope had crawled into Gemma's body, that she wasn't another person but a shadow, a squatter. That would explain the tight, airless feeling Gemma had, as if when she breathed it had to be for both of them.

'I'm looking at you,' she said, 'to see what the outside looks like. You have hair like the nurses. And you're fatter,' she added, but not meanly at all. Of course, Gemma realized, she didn't know that this was mean, like she didn't know it was rude to stare.

This made Gemma feel sorry for hating her face, for hating to see her, for wishing she would disappear.

Calliope tipped onto her knees and pulled herself closer, then rocked back on her heels again. She might have been Gemma's age, but she seemed younger. 'Do you know Dr O'Donnell?' she asked. 'She's the one who named me. Then she left. A lot of them leave but most of them not for good. She's outside, too,' Calliope clarified, as if Gemma might not have understood.

Gemma tried to swallow and couldn't. How to begin to explain? 'I don't know Dr O'Donnell,' she said at last.

'What about Pinocchio?' Calliope asked. 'Do you know Pinocchio?'

'*Pinocchio?*' Gemma thought Calliope must be joking.

But she was completely serious. Her eyes were moon-bright, huge in that thin face – familiar and also totally foreign. It occurred to Gemma that she'd never heard Lyra make a joke. She'd never even heard her be sarcastic.

'Pinocchio's made out of wood just like a doll,' Calliope said. She slid fluidly and without warning through different ideas, through fiction and reality, the past and present. 'Wayne calls me Pinocchio, and I don't say how Dr O'Donnell named me first. Names are like that. You have to be careful – once someone names you, you belong to them for life. Pinocchio wanted to go to the outside and be a real boy.' Once again, she leapt to a new stream of thought: she had no meaning, no system to unwind them, to decide what was important and what wasn't. 'He got ate by a whale but then he made a fire in the whale's stomach.' She laughed and Gemma flinched. It wasn't exactly a laugh, more like the sound of a hammer against metal. 'He made a fire just like the one at Haven. He lit it right in the whale's belly, right here.' She pointed to her own stomach. She seemed to find this hilarious. 'Wayne told me how he did it. And so the whale had to spit him up. I seen fire at Haven and I wasn't scared, not like some of thems.'

Untangling Calliope's speech took almost physical effort. She nearly explained that Pinocchio was only a story, but stopped herself.

'Outside is huge,' she said instead. 'Much bigger than you can imagine.'

Calliope hugged her knees, shrugging. 'I know. I seen it through the fence and on TV, too. Who cares, anyway? It dies, it dies, it dies.' She turned and pointed casually to three replicas. 'It dies.' She pointed to herself. Before Gemma could say anything, before she could deny it, Calliope was talking again.

'Haven is much bigger than where here is. Here is only the size of how A-Wing is at Haven. But there's more doors at Haven, and more nurses, too. I don't like the nurses, except for some of them are okay, because they feed us greens and blues for sleeping. One of the guards let me touch her gun.' She spoke quickly, hardly pausing for air, as if the words were a kind of sickness she had one chance to get out. 'At Haven we can't go in with the males because of their penises and how a normal baby gets made. So we have to stay away, except at Christmas for the Choosing.'

Something touched Gemma's spine and neck, and made the fine blond hair April had always called her *goose down* lift on her arms, just like that, like bird feathers ruffled by a bad wind.

'What do you mean, the Choosing?' she asked, but Calliope wasn't listening. She was pinballing between stories and ideas, feeding Gemma all the words she'd had to carry alone.

'Have you ever used a penis to make a baby?' she asked, and Gemma, stunned, couldn't answer. 'The doctors still don't know if they can, I mean if we can, the its. Pepper got a baby in her stomach, but then she cut her wrists so afterward they all got more careful.'

Gemma could hardly follow the story – Calliope combined pronouns or used them indiscriminately. She'd heard Lyra and Caelum refer to themselves as *it* at different times. All the replicas confused phrases like *want* and *ask, make* and *own.*

I owned it, one of the replicas insisted, when a nurse tried to take away a mold-fuzzed cup of old food remnants she'd been concealing beneath a panel of loose floor tile. *I owned it. It's me.* And some of the replicas couldn't speak at all – they could only growl and keen, like animals.

'So the doctors don't know.' Calliope was still talking, working a fingernail into a scab on her knee; when the blood flowed she didn't even wipe it, just watched it make a small path down her shin, as if it was someone else's blood entirely. 'Some of the its are too skinny for the monthly bleeding, but I have mine. Wayne said that means I'm a woman now.'

Nausea came like movement, like the rolling of a boat beneath her. 'Who's Wayne?'

'He's the one who told me about Pinocchio.' Her eyes weren't like eyes at all: they were more like fingers, grasping for something. 'I always wanted a baby,' she said in a whisper. 'Sometimes I used to go to Postnatal and hold them and say nice things to them, like I made them instead of the doctors.'

Blood was rushing so hard in Gemma's head she could hardly hear. Infants. Babies. She hadn't seen any since she'd been here. What had happened to all of them?

But she didn't have to ask. Calliope leaned forward, all big eyes, all hot little breath, all *need*. 'Postnatal burned fast,' she said. 'The roof caved in and all my babies got smashed.' Gemma turned away from her. But there was nowhere to go.

Nobody belongs here, child. Not even the devil himself.

Calliope pulled away again, smiling to show her teeth. 'I like Haven better for most things. But here's better because of the males and how you can talk to them if you want.' She said it so casually that Gemma nearly missed it.

'Wait. Wait a second.' She took a deep breath. 'What do you mean, you can talk to them?'

Calliope smiled with only the very corners of her mouth, as if it was something rare she had to hoard. 'You can come with me,' she said. 'You can see for yourself.'

Calliope came for her in the middle of the night. It could have been midnight, or 4 a.m.; there were no clocks in the holding center, and since arriving Gemma had truly been aware of the rubbery nature of time, when there were no watches, phones, or activities to pin it down to.

'Follow me,' she said, and took Gemma's wrist. Gemma had seen staff members guide the replicas this way, and imagined this was where she'd learned it.

They moved through the maze of sleeping replicas, most of them drugged up on sleeping aids distributed by the nurses before lights-out: pills for the replicas whose pain was greatest, and, when these ran out, simply plastic mouthwash cups full of NyQuil. Gemma had thrown hers out, as she assumed Calliope must have, too.

As they passed through the darkness, Gemma again had a strange doubling feeling, as if she and Calliope were two shadows, two watermarks identically imprinted. Or maybe she was the shadow, and Calliope the real thing.

Only one nurse, nodding to sleep in a swivel desk chair despite the lack of desk, jerked awake to ask where they were going. Calliope whispered, 'Bathroom,' and the nurse waved them on.

'Be quick,' she said.

No-man's-land: the makeshift kitchen, the bathrooms, a plastic card table covered with scattered magazines and phone chargers, what passed for a break room for the staff during the day. A light in the kitchen was on, and as always the coffee machine was burbling and letting off a burned-rubber stink. There was always coffee brewing, at every hour, although so far Gemma hadn't actually seen anyone drink from the machine.

Only a single soldier was on duty, the same red-haired guy with a pimply jawbone. He couldn't have been older than nineteen.

'That one never plays,' Calliope whispered to Gemma.

'Plays what?' Gemma whispered.

But Calliope just shook her head. 'He thinks it's bad luck.'

Gemma saw a quick look of pain tighten the soldier's features, as if seeing them together hurt. He turned away again as soon as they veered right, toward the bathrooms.

At the last second, instead of going into the girls' bathroom, they simply went left, into the boys'. Unbelievably simple. Gemma doubted the soldier had even noticed. He probably thought the replicas were all dumb, anyway. It was reasonable to expect they'd make mistakes.

The bathroom was only half-lit. Most of the bulbs had burned out in the ceiling, and a sink filled with paper towels had overflowed, leaving puddles of water on the floor. The tiles seemed to pick up her voice and hurl it in a thousand directions. But the boys' bathroom had stalls, at least, as well as two puddly urinals.

'What now?' Gemma asked.

'We wait,' Calliope said. 'Come.' She took Gemma's

hand and pulled her into one of the toilet stalls. She closed the door behind them and sat down on the toilet seat.

Less than a minute later the bathroom door opened again. Calliope held up a hand, gesturing for Gemma to be quiet. For a long second there was nothing but the *drip, drip, drip* of water from the faucet.

Then a boy: 'Hello.'

Calliope stood up then. 'In here,' she said, and opened the door.

He was younger – maybe twelve, thirteen. It was difficult to tell, since all the replicas, skinny as they were, with no concept of words they hadn't experienced directly, like *snow* and *cross-country*, seemed younger than their true age. But Calliope looked pleased anyway.

'A male,' she said, as if Gemma might not be able to tell. The boy had very dark skin and perfect features and the kind of lips Gemma's mom's friends paid money for. He would grow up to be beautiful. *If* he grew up.

'What crop are you?' Calliope asked.

'Fourteen,' he said. 'A White.'

This made her smile. 'Like me,' she said. 'The Whites are the most important.' She turned back to Gemma again. 'Well? What do you want him for?'

'I need you to give someone a message for me,' she said. He showed no signs of having understood. 'Another male. Like me, from the outside. His name is Pete. Can you ask him to come? Can you bring him?'

The boy looked at Calliope. She nodded, barely. 'What's for me?'

She tilted her head to look at him. Once again, Gemma had the uncanny doubling sensation of watching herself in a fun-house mirror, the kind that elongated and thinned.

'Observation,' she said, and held up one hand. 'Five seconds.'

He frowned. 'I want to stethoscope,' he said.

She shook her head. 'Observation.'

He looked away.

'Ten seconds,' he said finally. 'Five now, five when I bring him.'

Finally, Calliope shrugged. Before Gemma could stop her, she lifted her shirt, exposing her chest: ribs visible, small pale nipples identical in shape to Gemma's, breasts stiff and small and hard, like little knots. Gemma was so horrified, she froze, and by the time she thought to grab Calliope's arm, to haul her shirt down, Calliope was already finished.

'Five seconds,' she said. She didn't seem bothered at all, and the boy didn't seem all that interested. 'Now go.'

He turned and left the bathroom. As soon as he was gone, Gemma said, 'You shouldn't have done that.' She felt sick. They hadn't even cared that she was there, that she was watching. It hadn't *occurred* to them to care. She supposed *observation,* for them, happened in front of lots of people. She wondered if they even knew what privacy meant. 'You didn't have to.'

Calliope looked puzzled. 'It's only observation,' she said. She smiled and showed her crowded teeth. 'I've observed with twelve males so far. Only number forty-four is ahead of me. She's observed with fourteen. Plus, she lets anyone stethoscope with her, even the guards if they want.'

She spoke matter-of-factly. There was no playfulness to it. It wasn't pleasure, just something to do. It wasn't at all like the party games people had played in middle school, Seven Minutes in Heaven, the stoplight game, all of them excuses to squeeze a nipple in a dark room and knock braces for a bit. All night, Gemma imagined, the bathroom would fill and empty with replicas meeting to touch and bargain and barter and stare.

Gemma leaned up against the counter, not even caring it was wet. The half-light made strange looping shadows on the walls and ceiling. 'Stethoscope?'

'Like how the doctors and nurses do it,' Calliope said. She placed a hand on her own chest to demonstrate, inhaling deep. Then she shifted her hand again, and again. Stethoscope: they'd invented their own term for second base. She dropped her hand. 'Have you ever done stethoscope?' she asked.

'No,' Gemma lied. She thought of being with Pete in her parents' basement, next to the rows of canned goods and bottled water, and how he'd traced the long scar between her chest and navel. It could have been a memory from someone else's life.

She had the crazy idea that maybe Calliope and her other replicas would take not just her skin and hair and freckles, but her past, her life, her memory. The longer she stayed here, the less she would have that would belong to her and to her alone.

She was losing it. She opened her eyes and fumbled to turn on the faucet, drinking from a cupped palm. Behind her, Calliope's face was a narrow shadow of hers.

'Then there's the full examining,' Calliope was saying. Gemma didn't have to ask what that was. She could imagine well enough. 'But I never done that yet. I tried one time with a Green, but he got sick right in the middle. Then one of the guards came in and yelled.'

Gemma seized on this. 'Didn't you get in trouble?' she asked. She didn't want to talk about *examining* and *stethoscope* and *observation* anymore. She didn't want to think about these broken kids playing doctor.

Calliope looked puzzled. 'Lots of the guards play too,' she said.

Gemma understood, now, what Calliope had said to her outside the bathroom, and why the red-haired soldier had looked at them the way he did. He must know what went on at night, and what the other soldiers did with the replicas when they thought they could get away with it.

The door opened again. The boy, the White, had returned, alone.

Gemma's heart broke, actually broke – she felt it crumble in her chest, like a nub of chalk – but before she could ask what had happened to Pete, the door opened a second time and there he was.

Pete. He looked as if he'd been shocked into aging a hundred years. Feathery white eyelashes, hollows beneath his eyes, skin leached of color.

And yet, when he saw her, he smiled, and everything changed. Her whole world tilted, and slid her toward him, into his arms.

'Fancy meeting you here,' he said. His voice was the same – he might have been teasing her during a long car ride, and she tasted salt before she realized she was crying.

'Hey,' he said, pulling away to take her face in one hand. He wiped her tears with a thumb. 'Hey, now. It's all right.'

'Are you okay?' She couldn't stop crying. Both Calliope and the male replica were watching them, truly curious, and Gemma could almost see Calliope calculating, trying to understand the way she and Pete were holding each other, what it meant, and what kind of *examining* this was. 'Did they hurt you?'

'I'm okay, Gem. I promise. I *swear*.' He ducked a little to look in her eyes, keeping one hand beneath her chin. 'The food sucks and this whole place could really use some body spray, but I'm *fine*.'

It was unbelievable that he could make her laugh, but he did. And then she choked again, and he held her, and she heard his heartbeat through his chest, and tasted her own breath on his T-shirt, and she lost track then of exactly who was who and where she ended and he began. It was like losing yourself in the softening of a warm bed you've been looking forward to all day.

Then Gemma felt Calliope's fingers on her arm – cold fingers, needy.

Only when Pete sucked in a breath did she realize how strange it must be for him to see both of them together, and when he took a quick step backward, something dark and heavy opened in the bottom of her stomach.

'We have to go now,' Calliope said. 'We had our turn.' But Gemma couldn't shake the feeling that Calliope had merely wanted to interrupt. She didn't like how Calliope looked at Pete. Like someone starving who just wants to eat and eat and eat until she pukes.

'Christ.' Pete exhaled and put a hand through his hair, tufting it like a bird's. They hadn't shaved it. That was one good thing, at least, that they were giving him that. He managed another smile. 'Sorry,' he said to Gemma. He reached out and took her hand, but his palm was sweating now. 'It's just . . .' He shook his head.

'I know,' she said. 'You don't have to say it.' That cold, dark thing was still writhing at the bottom of her stomach, and Calliope breathed next to her, clinging to her like a film. She kept his hand in hers and pretended not to notice he was sweating. 'You'll meet me here again tomorrow night?'

'Every night,' he said. His eyes moved to Calliope and back again. Gemma pretended not to see that, either.

She took a step closer to him. 'They're not going to let us out, Pete,' she said, in a low voice, though there was no point in trying to keep it a secret. Calliope could hear everything. Maybe she could even hear inside of Gemma's head. 'We know too much.'

'We'll find a way,' he said, and his eyes softened.

Then Calliope took Gemma's hand, and Gemma wondered whether she had just learned that kind of touch from watching Pete. How many of the other things she did and said were just imitation?

Simulacrum. *A slight, unreal, or superficial likeness.* Calliope's fingers were long and very bony.

'We had our turn,' she repeated. 'More of them get to go.'

'I didn't get my second observation,' the boy said.

Calliope turned back to him. 'Next time you'll have stethoscope, then,' she said, as if it hardly concerned her.

'Tomorrow,' Gemma said to Pete, even as Calliope drew her toward the door.

'I promise.' But he was looking at Calliope, not at her, and she felt a sudden dread. Now it was Pete doubling, splitting in two, and becoming a twin version of himself who looked the same, who talked the same, but was, deep down, a stranger.

THIRTEEN

SHE WOKE TO THE DEEP navy light of a predawn sky.

Already, the holding center was full of voices and movement, the scuffle of rubber sneakers, the tooth-chatter of heavy equipment scraped along the ground.

She sat up, edging away from Calliope, who had insisted on sharing the twin mattress. When she stood she was dizzied by a sharp, sudden hunger. She'd received a minuscule ration of spongy baked pasta for dinner, spooned from a tinfoil-covered catering tray of the kind Gemma associated with school fund-raisers.

Gemma knew that meant there must be civilization nearby – a restaurant, a deli, something. She'd even found a receipt for a Joe's Donuts in Windsor Falls, Pennsylvania, coasting on a surf of overflowing trash outside the bathroom.

But Pennsylvania or Pakistan, what did it matter? No one knew where they were.

The sleeping replicas, motionless in the half dark, were so closely fitted together that they took on the quality of a single landscape: mounds of soft earth, ridged spines and shoulders.

A sudden light dazzled her and she turned to the window to see a van wheeling away, its headlights briefly revealing funnels of rain. More vans were arriving.

She saw soldiers jogging with rain slickers pulled down to protect their faces. Someone was using orange light sticks, like a real airport ramp handler, to indicate where the vans should park. And out of the airport came a constant flow of equipment: staff members passed in and out hauling plastic bins and waste containers, paperwork lashed into waterproof boxes, medical equipment, stacks of unused linens, snowy piles of plastic-wrapped Hanes T-shirts, hundreds of them, of the kind that were given to the replicas.

Gemma felt as if the rain had found its way inside. She was suddenly very awake and very cold.

They were closing up shop.

She picked her way between the replicas to the central corridor, full of a deep and driving panic, half expecting to find that she was alone, that the walls had been dismantled and the rug pulled up, that she had been left behind. Several nurses, bleary-eyed from lack of sleep, pushed past her wheeling IV carts. The atmosphere was tense, almost desperate.

'What's happening?' Gemma asked, without expecting anyone to answer, and no one did. 'What's going on?'

A patrolling soldier frowned briefly at Gemma before turning her attention back to several staff members trying to work a medical cart through a door down to the loading dock. 'Careful,' she said. 'Stairs are wet.' Gemma noticed her fingernails were painted pink.

She kept walking, feeling as if she were in the beginning of a nightmare. Even before anything bad has happened, you *know*, you're sure, that bad things will come. When guards in no-man's-land prevented her from going any farther, she went again to the window, mesmerized by the look of all the headlights through the rapidly ebbing dark. How quickly would it take them to clean the place out, to erase all the evidence that Haven had ever existed?

And what would they do with the replicas?

Why the sudden urgency? Why now?

But the last question, at least, was answered even as she stood at the window, squinting through a mist of condensation.

Because a new vehicle was arriving, not a van but a regular sedan, like the kind of shitty rental a budget travel agency might give you. From the driver's seat came a tall man with a dark beard and glasses. He stood for a second, squinting up at the airport, his glasses, in the glow of the exterior lamps, so bright it looked like they themselves were glowing.

He grimaced a little as the rain hit him. Then he ducked and began to jog through a slosh of puddles toward the door, and Gemma saw a flurry of movement, flapping raincoats and umbrellas, as he was enfolded by staff members and hustled inside.

Dr Saperstein was back.

A woman in a tailored pantsuit came for Gemma mid-afternoon. It was the same woman Gemma had pegged for a government slug when she had first arrived. As far as Gemma could tell, it was the same suit, too.

They went through a door marked with a sign that unnecessarily stated *Authorized Personnel Only,* guarded by two soldiers with long-range rifles. Down a set of stairs, the same ones they'd climbed Sunday night. Gemma knew they must be level with the tarmac, imagined phantom travelers hurrying with rolling suitcases and duffels toward waiting short-haul jets.

Through another door for Authorized Personnel, they reached what must once have been the airport's administrative hub, an inner funnel of connected rooms still showing the ghost-marks of old desks. The overhead lights were out, and a few standing lamps left whole areas oily with shadow. There were tubs of plastic containers full of shrink-wrapped sterilized needles and miniature urine collection vials. Two fridges were marked with handwritten signs: *Live specimens, do not open.*

Hidden generators bled thick cables across the floor, and Gemma thought of bits of dark hair clinging to the damp floor of a gym. Stacked messily on a folding table were cardboard boxes full of translucent medical gloves and antibacterial cloths, cotton swabs and rubber thermometer tips, laptops wired to a single power strip, and three-ring binders. Here, she knew, must be the remains of Haven's record keeping, the experiential evidence it had accumulated over decades and had not yet had a chance to move elsewhere or destroy.

Another woman, this one a stranger, leaned knuckles-down on a desk, in the posture of a gorilla, peering over the shoulder of a red-haired guy at a computer. She immediately straightened up.

'Ah, shit.' The woman had to step over the fluid ropes of electrical cable to get close. Her hair was cut short. She reminded Gemma of one of her favorite nannies, Laverne, a soft-spoken Haitian woman who'd come up from Louisiana and gave hugs that felt like being wrapped in a blanket. But the impression was over the moment she spoke. 'What a mess.'

'Hi yourself,' said Gemma's escort.

'Not what you thought?' The red-haired guy was still lit faintly by the computer screen, and the glare in his glasses had the weird effect of erasing his eyes beneath them. There was something wrong with the skin on the left side of his face, and his chin beneath his lips. It looked weirdly shiny, as if it were covered with a layer of Vaseline. He'd been badly burned, Gemma realized, and her stomach yanked: he'd been at Haven.

Laverne-not-Laverne took two sudden steps forward and snatched up Gemma's chin, as if it were a fish that might otherwise dart away. She angled her face left and right before Gemma managed to pull away.

'I don't know where she came from.' Her eyes on Gemma's face felt like mosquitoes, circling and circling without landing anywhere. 'She's not one of ours.'

'I *told* you,' Gemma said, though it was obvious the woman wasn't speaking to her. She let her hatred narrow like a knife inside her. 'You guys fucked up, big-time.'

Not-Laverne was still staring. 'Werner, pull up Sources, will you?' She pivoted, finally, and moved behind the computer again, leaning over to point. 'D–101,' she said. 'See here? Some of our first donor tissue. And these are the genotypes that took. Numbers six through ten.'

'Number six is Disposed,' the man, Werner, said.

The woman in the suit was sweating. 'You told us a boy and a girl. This one and her boyfriend fit the description.'

'They aren't ours.' Not-Laverne looked green. Werner was chewing on an unlit cigarette. Then: 'Dr Saperstein will nail you to the wall for this.'

Gemma was sick of being spoken about as if she wasn't in the room. 'My name is Gemma Ives. Ives,' she repeated, and saw Not-Laverne register the name, saw it pass through her like a current.

'Ives.' Werner nearly choked. He wet his lower lip with his tongue. 'Is that like . . . ?'

But he trailed off nervously as behind Gemma another door opened and then closed firmly with a click. The sudden silence filled the room by emptying it of pressure. She felt a pop in her ears, as if they'd just dropped altitude on a plane.

She turned, knowing already what she would see: Dr Saperstein, smiling, holding his glasses in one hand, shaking his head, like some kindly guidance counselor who'd discovered a mistake in her first-period schedule.

'The last time I saw you, you were six months old,' he said. He looked shorter and older than she'd been picturing him – of course, the photographs she had were outdated, and she'd been a baby when her father had severed his connection to Haven.

She felt a surge of hatred so strong it scared her: it was a hand from the dark side of the universe that reached up to turn her inside out. 'You've seen plenty of me,' she said, but heard her voice as if it was a stranger's. 'Four, by my count.'

'Looks can be deceiving, believe me. There is only one Gemma Ives.' He smiled again at this. Patient, indulgent, very slightly embarrassed. *Sorry about the confusion. These little mix-ups do happen.* 'Your parents, I'm sure, would agree.'

'Dr Saperstein—' The woman in the suit began to speak, but he cut her off.

'Later.' For a split second she saw, from beneath the surface of his expression, something sharp and mean solidify: it was like the sudden vision of a very sharp tooth. But almost instantly, it was gone. He smiled at Gemma again and opened a door that led to a small and very ordinary-looking office. 'Why don't you have a seat inside? I'm going to grab a soda. You want a soda? Or something to eat?'

Gemma shook her head, although she was desperately thirsty, and weak with hunger, too. But she didn't want to take anything Dr Saperstein offered.

'Go on. Make yourself comfortable. I'll be right with you.' When she didn't move, he hitched his smile a little wider – she could actually *see* the effort, watch individual muscles straining to achieve the right look. 'Go on. It's all right.'

'No,' she said. She wanted to scream. She wished she

could open her mouth and let her rage come up like a sickness. 'It's not. It's definitely not all right.'

'Well, that's what we're going to try and sort out.' He spread his hands. As if she were the one who'd screwed up and now refused to admit it. 'Look, I highly doubt you want to stay here. Right? So go on and have a seat, and I'll be with you as soon as I can scare up some caffeine.'

FOURTEEN

DR SAPERSTEIN RETURNED WITH TWO cans of warm Diet Coke, even though she'd said she didn't want one. She didn't want to sit and planned to say no, but at the last minute she was worried about her legs, which had begun to shake. So she sat, tucking her ankles together, pressing her hands between her thighs, hoping he wouldn't see how afraid she was.

He poured his soda into a plastic cup, took a sip, and made a face. 'Why does the diet stuff always taste like the back of a spoon?' He shook his head. 'The real stuff always goes first around here.'

Gemma felt more confused than ever. Dr Saperstein didn't look evil. She tried to paste what she knew about him onto his face, to make the images align. Emily Huang, those photographs of the two of them together. Jake Witz and his father. Those hundreds and hundreds of starved and broken people he treated like possessions, disposed of by burning them in the middle of the ocean after drilling their bones or opening their skulls for marrow and tissue and cell samples.

But she couldn't make it hang there. She couldn't make it fit.

He leaned forward. 'I can't tell you how sorry I am that you're here,' he said. Shockingly, she believed him. 'I've been in Washington, DC, crawling around on my knees trying to save this place. . . .'

'What – what *is* it?' She had to swallow hard against the feeling that she would begin to cry. 'What are you *doing* with all of them here?'

He shook his head. 'Nothing, now,' he said. 'I drove straight from DC this morning. Our funding's been cut.' This time, his smile never traveled up past his lips. 'Twenty years of research. Twenty years of effort, incremental gains, mistakes and corrections. All of it . . .' He gestured as if to scatter something into a passing wind.

'And what happens to them?' Gemma said, through a hard fist in her throat. She was still too afraid to ask what she really wanted to know: what would happen to her? And to Pete?

Dr Saperstein took off his glasses to rub his eyes. 'How much did your father tell you about Haven?'

'He didn't tell me anything,' Gemma said. Dr Saperstein

looked surprised. 'But I know that you've been using the replicas to grow prions.'

'To *study* prions,' he corrected her. 'You make them sound like petri dishes.'

'Isn't that what they are?' The pressure in Gemma's chest was so great she felt as though she was speaking around a concrete block. 'It was all for the military, wasn't it? It was all to make weapons.'

He raised his eyebrows. 'I won't ask you how you know that,' he said. She could tell she'd impressed him and, weirdly, felt happy about it. Then she hated herself. Why did she care about impressing him? 'Look, you obviously know quite a bit about Haven. But there's a lot you *don't* understand. The US military gave us one of our biggest contracts, yes. But it wasn't our only one.' Then: 'You know the word *prion* wasn't even coined until I was in college? It's been more than thirty years since then, but until I took over the Institute, we'd discovered almost nothing more about the way prions work, or how they progressed, or how fast.' The overhead light grayed the look of his skin. 'Prion disorders share traits with some of the most crippling brain diseases we know – diseases like Alzheimer's, which affects millions of people per year. Diseases we can't cure or even help.'

'I don't need a lecture,' Gemma said. 'I asked what happens to the replicas now.'

'There are protocols,' he said gently. 'I'm sure you understand that. Haven deals with – dealt with – deadly biomaterials. We're talking about a major health hazard.'

Deadly biomaterials. Otherwise known as: replicas. Gemma recognized the technique: every so often her father hid behind words too, not big words but acronyms, military slang, a patter she could never understand. But she knew what Saperstein was saying, and no amount of fancy vocabulary could make it any less horrible.

'You're going to kill them,' she said. Though it was what she'd been expecting, it was terrible to say the words out loud. The room seemed suddenly to be filling with fog. Or maybe it was her head that was filling up. She couldn't make his face come into focus. 'What about me? Are you going to kill me, too?'

'Kill you?' He actually laughed. 'Last time I checked, that was still illegal in this country. I'm going to make some calls, and sort out some details, and get you home to your father. Then I'm going to hope he doesn't kill *me*.'

He didn't sound like he was lying. 'What about Pete?' she asked. She thought, though she couldn't be sure, that for a split second he froze, and a sour panic rose in her throat. 'If you don't let him go, I'll tell everyone. My dad will track you down and murder you—'

'Gemma, *please*. Of course Pete will go home.' If he'd hesitated before, now he spoke easily. 'I know you think

Was it possible? In the letter Emily Huang had written to her friend, she'd made it sound as if it was all Dr Saperstein's idea. But what if she'd lied? What if she was ashamed of her own role?

What if she *had* killed herself after all? Out of guilt and shame and a sense of remorse?

'You covered it up,' Gemma said. 'You lied and you made everybody else lie, too.'

'What else was I supposed to do? We would have lost everything. Then there would have been no reason for any of it.' He leaned forward and his eyes screwed onto hers like metal caps. 'We're talking about research that directly impacts Alzheimer's research, research into what makes the brain deteriorate, how to stop it. We're talking about research that could have spared the lives of thousands of civilians stuck in hellish war zones, that might have been used in targeted attacks to prevent the horrific casualties of innocent people. We're talking about research critical to modern food supply. I regret some of the things we did – and some of the things done in our name. Of course I do. But we were fighting a countrywide campaign against reason – against *research*.'

'That still doesn't give you the right,' Gemma said.

He ducked his head and sat for a few seconds with his eyes closed, almost as if he were praying. When he raised his head again, he looked even older, as if several years had elapsed. 'Do you use shampoo?'

She was so startled by the question she couldn't even nod.

He went on anyway. 'Do you take cold medicine when you're sick, or Advil when you have a headache? How about vaccinations? Been vaccinated for mumps, rubella, tetanus? Vaccinations are diseases, you know. They're nothing more than weak concentrations of the exact disease they're designed to prevent.'

'What's your point?' She felt shaky, almost dizzy, as if she'd stood up too quickly, although she was still sitting across from him.

'How do you think those drugs came to market? How did the Advil get into your bathroom cabinet? How did the Sudafed land on your bedside table? How did we cure polio? Tuberculosis? Smallpox? How did we save hundreds of thousands of people, millions of people, from diseases big and small?' His smile was thinning. 'Hundreds of thousands of mice, rabbits, primates killed. Humans, too, of course – volunteers, desperate people, sick people. Some of them dead because of side effects, unpredictable responses, bad science, or just bad luck. I'm one of only thousands of scientists and researchers doing similar work, dangerous work, work that requires living people to die, so that in the future, people can keep living. A terrible paradox, but there you go. Did you know that a former staff member of mine is up and running in Allentown, Pennsylvania? All our funding will go to her. And the cycle continues.'

The name registered dimly in Gemma's memory, but she didn't know why.

Saperstein wasn't done. 'And those are just the medical casualties. Noble, really, by comparison to what we do every day, in thousands of places across the globe, all for cheaper products and more of them, new clothes every season, new cell phones, faster cars.'

'That's different,' Gemma said. But she couldn't think how.

'Is it?' He shook his head. 'I don't think so. Everything we have, everything we know, everything we own, has been paid for in someone's blood. Once you understand that, you understand we're just talking about ratios. Percentages. Math.'

He was confusing her, like her father always did, twisting things around somehow.

'How many people have to benefit from a cure before you risk the life of a single test patient? Ten? One hundred? How many people might live easier lives because of a new technology before you can justify disrupting the livelihoods of those who benefit from the old one? What does help have to look like? Do you have to help them a little, or a lot? Help them now, or in the future? Tell me. If you have the formula figured out, tell me.'

Of course she couldn't. There was no answer; she didn't know.

'What about all those children who work backbreaking hours for pennies at factories across the globe to make the T-shirts you and your friends wear, who die early of tumors caused by fumes, smog, chemicals? How about boys sold into slavery on fishing boats to haul smelt and plankton so that we can eat fresh shrimp all year round, how about girls half your age helping to make your shoes, your lip gloss, your phone covers, your accessories? What about children blown up mining minerals we use for the memory chips in your cell phone, and children eviscerated by drone strikes in countries we spent decades squeezing for their oil, whole countries decimated, populations starving to death slowly? What about them? Who's crying for them?'

Gemma *was* crying. She couldn't help it.

'We never cloned people at Haven. That's what you have to understand. That's impossible and always will be. We cloned genetic composition, fetal cells, *structure.*' Gemma could tell by how easily and quickly the words came how often he had repeated them to himself. She could tell he really believed them. 'You can't make people with science. We're all born a collection of cells and senses and chemical patterns. We have to *become* human.'

Gemma thought of Calliope, and the bulwark of her ribs beneath her skin, the way her hand, slick with sweat, had held to Gemma so tightly. A terrible sadness touched her.

'The replicas can't feel loss, or love, or empathy. When they die, no one grieves for them, and they grieve for no one else. Any one of them would kill you, or me, if it suited them, if they needed to. Any one would lie or cheat or rob you, and never feel bad about it. They wouldn't even know the difference. To them there is surviving and not surviving, and that's it.'

Was any of it true? Did it even matter? 'You make them sound like robots,' she said.

'Not robots,' he said. And for a brief second, a look of terror moved like a hard storm across his face. 'Animals.'

FIFTEEN

THERE WERE DIFFERENT SOLDIERS ON duty outside the bathrooms that night, a young man and woman, maybe early twenties. The card table was gone: it must have been packed up and shipped off. Gemma had lost count of how many vans had left throughout the day. Though the airport was still crowded with clutter, medical equipment, and mattresses, curtained-off alcoves and makeshift break stations, it felt incalculably emptier. It felt like being sunk at the center of an old ship while it was hollowed out by bottom-feeding fish.

The rain, still drumming the windows, filled the terminal with hollow echoes.

As soon as the female soldier saw them approaching, she stood up abruptly and vanished, as though by pre-arranged signal. The guy was older, maybe twenty-four or twenty-five, with a blunt jaw and a prominent forehead that made his eyes appear to be hiding out in his face.

'That's Wayne,' Calliope said. She had taken Gemma's hand again, and Gemma was both glad of and frightened by her grip. 'Wayne was the one who told me about Pinocchio and how he got spitted up by the whale.' A strange expression pulled briefly at Calliope's face: if Gemma hadn't known better, she would have called it joy.

They had to wait for Wayne – an ugly name, she'd always thought, made even uglier now by him – to acknowledge them. Calliope didn't tense up or even seem uncomfortable when he stared baldly at her breasts and legs, at the space *between* her legs. She was used to it, Gemma knew, and that was the most terrible thing of all: her body had never belonged to her, not for a second.

Animals, Dr Saperstein had said. But animals had the urge to protect themselves, to protect one another. The replicas were like human photo negatives: like they weren't alive at all, only giving the impression of it, but always just a little bit off. Even tonight, moving through the darkened puzzle of bodies, Gemma had the strangest feeling that none of the replicas were sleeping at all – that this, too, was illusion, bodies laid down to rest while their spirits roamed elsewhere, hungry and awake.

'All right,' Wayne said finally. 'But quick. Fifteen

minutes.' As soon as they started toward the bathroom together, he called them back. 'See me after,' he said to Calliope.

Gemma was surprised and relieved to find Pete already waiting for her, leaning heavily on the counter, head bowed. For a second, she hung back. His face was so serious, so sad, it made her ache.

But when he caught sight of her, his face rearranged into the one she knew so well, and it was like two plates slid together deep inside her and sealed off a rift. Her anger went, and so did her fear. If she could just stay with him, everything would be fine.

She was grateful that Calliope let her go, and even hung back when Pete hugged her, and kissed her gently, lips, nose, forehead, and lips again. It was funny: as soon as Pete had become her boyfriend, she had started being more careful about her looks, not less. She put on lip gloss and mascara; she always made sure her hair was blown straight; she agonized about what she wore. She told herself she wanted him to be proud of her, but it wasn't that, not exactly. Really, she wanted to make sure he wasn't *embarrassed*.

But here, in this place, even though she hadn't showered — a ritual that, like laundry day, occurred once a week, in which replicas were shuffled in and out by the dozen to hose off in a dim concrete room with open holes for drainage – even though the toothbrush she'd been given had disappeared earlier that morning, even though she was braless, her breasts sticky-heavy beneath her shirt, she realized it didn't matter at all. She loved him and felt, in that moment, truly loved: the feeling of being saved, of coming home after a long night at a terrible party, and getting to wipe your makeup off and take off uncomfortable tights and slip into a pair of worn pajamas.

'Another day in paradise, huh?' Pete said, touching her face.

She could feel Calliope watching them, and was struck by Calliope's stillness, her complete absorption. She was reminded, then, of the way her cats, Bean and Ender, sat in the window seat to watch the geese that landed on her lawn on their way south. It was as if Calliope's whole body was funneled into her eyes, and the desire to consume.

She was going crazy. She was going to lose her mind in this place.

'You okay?' he asked. She tried to smile but saw her reflection thrown back at her, ghastly.

'I'm okay,' she said. 'I saw Dr Saperstein today.' She lowered her voice, hooked her fingers into the neck of her T-shirt. Hers, familiar, real. 'It's all over. They're shutting down.'

'Yeah, I kind of got the idea. I'm surprised they haven't

shipped out the toilets yet.' Then, unexpectedly: 'Three replicas died today. I saw them packed up. They were loaded onto a gurney like – like meat or something. All bundled in plastic.' His voice was too tight, like fabric stretched thin by too much use. 'There are children tied down in place. One of the nurses said that otherwise they'll try and chew their own fingers, or scratch themselves until they bleed. And the *nurses* . . .' Finally, the fabric snapped. His voice cracked. 'Nurses, doctors, soldiers . . . everyday people, good people. It's like they've all gone blind. It's like this *place* has blinded them. How can they stand it?'

'Pete.' She couldn't make it better. She couldn't explain. There *was* no explanation. They had to get out of here before they were poisoned. She took his hands. They were very cold. 'Pete, listen to me. Dr Saperstein is making arrangements with my dad,' Gemma said quietly. 'He's going to let us go.'

His eyes were like windows, suddenly shuttered. She was aware of a strange tension, not just here but every-where, as if an enormous underground rift was slowly widening, as if they might all drop.

'We don't have a choice,' she added. She seemed to smell smoke. Memories that weren't even hers flowed to her, of Haven on fire, of the island burning and bod-ies bleeding out into the marsh. Maybe Calliope wasn't feeding off her. Maybe she was feeding from Calliope, collapsing into her. 'But the important thing is that we're getting out of here. They're letting us go.'

He looked away. A muscle pulsed in and out in his jaw. 'When?' he said finally.

'Tomorrow.' Still he wouldn't look at her. She followed his gaze and saw that he was staring at Calliope in the mirror. But she wasn't looking back at him. She was standing, motionless, staring up at the ceiling with the strangest smile on her face, as if she was listening to a favorite song played far away. 'I don't know when. I think Dr Saperstein's scared. He'll have to . . .' *Negotiate,* she nearly said, but stopped. The word wouldn't make it out beyond a sudden tightness, a feeling of burning.

'I won't go,' Pete said. 'I can't.' And she heard the crack of the fault line beneath their feet. She saw that they were already falling.

'You can't save them,' she said, but she felt a rising panic as the dark rose up to reach them. She heard her own voice faintly and heard, too, the echo of Dr Saperstein. 'It's already done.'

'I can't just walk out of here.' He turned back to her but now she hardly recognized him. His eyes didn't seem brown so much as gray. Smoke-gray. 'I can't just *forget.*'

'I'm not asking you to forget,' she said. She realized she was going to cry and had to swallow fast. 'But there's no other choice.'

'There is,' he said sharply. 'There always is. There has to be.'

'Would you rather stay here?' She was cold and hot all at once. She was losing him. 'What about your parents? What about how worried they must be?'

Pete stepped away from her. 'So that's it, we leave, and your dad's the big hero.' He looked so different when he frowned, older and harder, somehow. She'd nearly always seen him smiling, had even begun to believe it was his natural state, like having blond hair or freckles like a scattering of brown sugar. 'And then what? We go back to school? We hold hands after chem and I drive you home and feel you up in your driveway and that's *it*, that's all we have, that's all—'

He broke off, as if the words had driven the air from his lungs on the way out. 'Sorry,' he said, in a different tone of voice, and, turning back, tried to put his hands on her shoulders. 'I'm sorry. I didn't mean that.'

'Don't,' she said. If he touched her, her skin would burn away, she would disappear into smoke. All along she'd been wrong. All along he *had* been ashamed of her – ashamed and disappointed, and trying to hide it only because she was the best he could do right now.

'Gemma, please. That came out all wrong.' He looked truly upset but she didn't care, didn't feel sorry for him at all. 'You know I didn't mean . . .' When again she stepped away from him, he let his hand hover there for a second. 'What I meant was I can't go back. I can't just rewind. Do you understand?' His voice was climbing registers, clawing up toward a point of panic. She saw him bloated by misery, choking on its fumes. 'I can't unsee what I've seen, I can't unknow what I know. I *can't*.'

'Keep your voice down,' she said. Something really was burning. She wasn't imagining it. She could smell smoke now, for sure. Confusedly she thought Calliope must be smoking. But that was crazy – Calliope was still smiling her secret smile, still absorbed in her own invisible kingdom – and besides, the smell was too strong for that.

Pete hadn't heard or didn't care. He was talking louder than ever, as if he weren't so much speaking the words as letting them rattle through him. 'I can't walk out of here and know that these people – people, Gemma, not experiments, not test subjects, human beings – are going to die. I—'

But then he broke off again, and she knew that he, too, had felt the change: the approach of danger that, like a storm, sent invisible messages ahead.

Just as suddenly as clouds might vault from the horizon, Gemma found the source of tension, grabbed it, and tracked it to its source. Calliope was laughing.

Gemma remembered going with her parents to their

house in the Outer Banks one summer and hearing coy-
otes shrieking in the night. They laughed when they
killed, her father told her later, but she would have known
anyway. It was cruelty set to music: it wasn't even the
pleasure of the *kill*. It was the pleasure of pain, the pleasure
of watching small things die slowly.

And now, here, in this bathroom in an old airport that
might as well have been hell on earth, Calliope laughed
just like that.

'You're wrong,' Calliope said, and her words still carried the echo of something old and predatory and hungry.
'You mixed it all up. You got it backward.' She was still
standing there with her head tilted, still staring vaguely
at the ceiling. But by then, of course, Gemma knew. She
wasn't staring. She was *listening*. And by then Gemma was
listening, too: the shouts, the sharp punctuated cries, and
footsteps vibrated the floor.

The stinging in Gemma's throat had been real. Smoke
was texturing the air, giving it the appearance of a solid,
and somewhere solid matter burned, and transformed to
smoke.

'What are you talking about?' Pete asked, and Gemma
could hear that he, too, was afraid.

'You said we would die. You said you don't want to
leave us.' She shook her head. She was smiling in a way
that Gemma had never seen before. It was as if her smile

was actually consuming her face backward, trying to reveal her skull. 'But you said it backward. The us won't die.' She bit her lip, and Gemma tripped over the image of her own habit, her own nervous way of correcting herself. '*We* won't die.'

In Gemma's head, she saw smoke trails plumed over Haven, saw men with rifles, working in the rubble; she saw fireworks leave tentacle trails of smoke across a bloody dawn sky. *Crack. Crack. Crack.* But these weren't fireworks. They were bullets that cracked sound in two when they leapt, explosively, from their long slick barrels. They were bullets that made a lot of noise and then killed silently.

People were screaming.

'What's happening?' Gemma asked. Her voice sounded like it was coming to her from the other side of a tunnel.

Calliope finally looked at Gemma. She was radiant. And in that split second, Gemma saw that both Pete and Dr Saperstein were wrong. Calliope wasn't an animal, and she wasn't a human, either. She was something darker and older and far more dangerous, she was something *deeper* – a compression of matter and space, a possibility collapsed into the narrowest, narrowest place. Being, urge, energy – emotionless, unthinking, unfeeling – funneled so deep, for so long, that it became an explosion. She was a black hole that could take a planet apart forever, in endless slow motion.

'It's starting,' she said, and reached up to touch Gemma's face. Her fingers smelled like metal.

Her fingers smelled like blood.

SIXTEEN

THEN A BULLET BLASTED THROUGH the bathroom door, ricocheted off the counter, and blew the pinkie finger off Gemma's left hand.

It was the craziest thing. One second she had five fingers, and the next, her pinkie was missing and blood had patterned the linoleum. And yet at first she knew it had happened only because of how Pete began to shout. For a long, watery second she floated somewhere outside her body, and observed the blood and the missing finger and the raw exposed muscle of her hand with a kind of detached curiosity.

And then the pain came, like a gigantic rubber band that snapped her back into the bathroom, into her body. It was pain like nothing she'd ever known, like the kind of high vibration that could shatter glass, like a full-body flu that burned even in your bones. She couldn't even scream. She couldn't try and stop the bleeding, couldn't move, could only stand there, staring like an idiot, as the blood kept pooling at her feet.

Somehow she ended up on the floor. She wasn't sure whether time had leapt forward or she'd simply, for a half second, lost consciousness. She no longer had the strength to stand up.

All this happened in three seconds, maybe quicker. When she did finally speak, she could only say, 'My finger,' over and over. By then Pete had found a roll of toilet paper – from God knows where, the girls' room never had any – and he was frantically unwinding it, half the roll at one go, and packing it against the wound. The pressure triggered a new surge of pain and brought her stomach into her mouth.

He wrapped a fist around her hand to stanch the bleeding. It hurt so much she wanted to pull away, to yell at him to stop, but the pain had her in a chokehold now, and she couldn't.

'It's okay, Gem, you're going to be okay,' Pete kept saying. He looked as if he was going to cry. 'Deep breaths, you're going to be fine, I know it hurts, but you're going to be okay. . . .'

Another bullet blasted through the door, this time punching out one of the overhead lights. Calliope ducked and scuttled beneath the sinks as a spray of plastic and glass sifted down on them like a snow. Still keeping her injured hand wound tightly in his fist, Pete put an arm around Gemma, herding them inside one of the bathroom stalls. She leaned against the hollow of his chest, and he whispered *it's okay, it's okay, it's okay,* so many times the word and his heartbeat became confused in her head, until she heard in its rhythm that same exact message.

The initial shock had passed and already her body was working to absorb the pain, accept its reality, to find equilibrium inside it: a process she knew intimately after so many hospital visits, so many surgeries and scars. She missed her mom with a sudden sharpness even worse than the physical pain – how she sat next to Gemma's hospital bed, whispering *it's gonna be okay, I'm here,* just like Pete was doing now; how she'd climb into bed next to Gemma, making a seashell-curve of her body, and the two of them would fall asleep. She missed her mom and wished, more than anything, that she could say she was sorry. She'd been so angry with Kristina that they had barely spoken in weeks, and Gemma could see the way it was killing her mom, coiling her down around an internal misery like a winch.

And now it was too late. They would die here. She closed her eyes and tried to hang on to an impression of her mom's voice, soothing her to sleep.

'Hush, hush.' It was Calliope's voice she heard instead.

During a break in the rhythm of gunshots, Calliope came toward her. She moved quickly, propelling herself with her palms and sliding belly-down on the floor with the sinuous grace of an eel. Gemma, still half-blind from pain and shock, was repulsed. The gunshots started again, and Gemma found herself briefly fantasizing about a bullet cleaving Calliope's head in two, or just evaporating her, as her finger had been evaporated.

Calliope crowded into the stall with them and began touching Gemma, stroking her arms, her wrist, her thighs. 'Hush, hush, there's no reason to cry,' she said. 'It's a finger, just a little finger.'

'We need to get out of here,' Pete said. He hadn't let go of her injured hand, not for a single second, but already the toilet paper was nearly useless, soggy with blood. 'She needs a doctor.'

Calliope looked briefly annoyed. 'She doesn't need a *doctor,*' she said. 'I'll take care of Gemma, don't worry. Just as soon as it's over.'

'This isn't one of your fucking games.' Pete's voice edged toward a shout. 'She's hurt, can't you see that? She needs *help.*' Gemma wanted to tell him to be quiet – they would be heard, they would be found, they would be killed – but she couldn't. She didn't even know who to be afraid of. She was as terrified of Calliope, of her strange little smiles and the light touch of her fingers, as she was of the guards who were shooting, still shooting. She heard screaming and pictured hundreds of replicas simply mowed down where they were sleeping, a surf of blood rising, coming to drown them all.

'It's not a game,' Calliope said, and she drew away from Gemma, looking hurt. 'It was never a game. But you can't leave now, anyway, not until it's sure.'

'Not until *what's* sure?' Gemma said. Her voice sounded as if it had been punched through with holes. Calliope chewed the inside of her cheek and didn't answer. She was angry, Gemma knew, because Pete had yelled at her. 'Please, Calliope.'

'It's like Pinocchio, like I told you,' Calliope said, sounding almost bored. 'He got swallowed up, so he started a fire to get out.' She held up her left hand, turning it, admiring it from several different angles. Then she began to touch her pinkie finger, bend it and flex it, as if to see whether it, too, would evaporate now that Gemma's was gone. And yet each time she moved or stroked her finger, Gemma felt a phantom stirring in her own hand, and a new wave of triggered pain.

'You started a fire?' Gemma said, trying to hang on to the thread, to stay focused, to make sense of the nightmare. They'd been so close to being released.

'*I* didn't,' Calliope said, still sulking. 'Some of the other thems did.'

Gemma remembered feeling, earlier tonight, as she and Calliope wove through a slum of bodies and filthy mattresses, that the replicas weren't sleeping, only pretending to. She felt suddenly dizzy. How many replicas were there in the airport? Five hundred? Six? More?

And maybe three dozen, four dozen guards, a handful of doctors and nurses.

'Wayne thought he taught me something about fire because of his friend Pinocchio,' Calliope said, with new scorn in her voice that made her seem older. 'But I knew about fire forever. When I was little, there was a kitchen fire, and we didn't use the Stew Pot for days.'

'This . . . this was your idea?' Gemma asked. She remembered what Dr Saperstein had said. *The replicas can't feel loss, or love, or empathy. To them there is surviving and not surviving, and that's it.*

Calliope ignored that question. 'The people always think we don't remember,' she said. 'They think we don't pay attention, that we don't listen, that we're all soft in the head. But I've been listening. I know plenty. I know how to use a gun.'

Immediately, as if in direct response to that statement, another quick-fire burst of rifle fire just outside the bathroom sent terrible echoes through Gemma's head and the back of her teeth. She heard a man's voice shout – a plea, a call for help, she wasn't sure – and then another gunshot.

But the voice was enough. She had recognized it, and her stomach pooled all the way down in her feet, a terrible, sick helplessness, like having to sprint for the bathroom.

It was Wayne's voice, Wayne on the ground, Wayne crying for help. And though Gemma couldn't feel sorry for him, she knew what that must mean: the replicas had taken control.

They were taking revenge.

'It's always fire, isn't it?' Calliope said then. 'In all the stories, there's always a fire. Does it hurt to burn, do you think?' And she turned back to Gemma, eyes bright and big and curious, and not unhappy at all.

SEVENTEEN

THEY HAD TO MOVE. THE smoke had sniffed out the corners and ceiling, and it rolled down now in heavy waves, turning the air gritty. Gemma didn't know where she'd read that during fires most people don't die from the fire itself, but from inhaling too much smoke. Even now her lungs felt heavy, wet, like a towel soaked through with rain.

'It's okay now,' Calliope said, and the words were so absurd that they came to Gemma like sounds in a language she didn't know. *It's okay now.* The pain in her hand was a rhythmic throbbing, and she thought it must be her pulse, beating out her blood. When they stood up she saw a butterfly pattern of blood, absurdly red, soaking the toilet paper, and so much of it: it was insane that it should all have come from her, that she would have so much to begin with.

She was freezing. She remembered, then, a bath when she was little, maybe eight or nine, and hearing her parents begin to argue. She'd stayed there, motionless, until the water was freezing: she didn't know why, in retrospect, she hadn't just drained the tub. But it hadn't occurred to her. If she didn't move, she'd thought, she wouldn't exist, and if she didn't exist, she could stop hearing them.

'You're okay, Gemma.' Pete kept his arm around her, even when he bent to cough. His eyes were tearing up. 'It's going to be okay. I promise.' He was using the same sounds as Calliope, and none of them made sense, and she couldn't stop laughing, laughing and shivering. 'She needs a doctor,' he said – shouted it, actually, his throat raw from smoke, as if he expected someone to hear.

Calliope was at the bathroom door. She touched the handle lightly with a finger, to feel if it was hot. 'There are no doctors,' she said.

Only then did Gemma realize that there were no more shots, no more sounds of gunfire. Just the noise of fire getting fat on drywall and ceiling panels and support beams, gobbling up filthy rugs and mattresses, swelling itself with sound. They never told you that about fire, how loud it was, as if everything it touched started to scream.

Outside the bathroom, Gemma was relieved to find no fire. She could hear it close, though: the *pop* and *boom* of things changing form suddenly, exploded from solid to gas, a noise that sounded just like terror. But the smoke was even worse, so bad she could hardly see, and a single breath made her choke.

'Get down,' Pete said. He had to repeat it before she understood. In a crouch, he took off his shirt and wound it tight against her fist, since the toilet paper had begun to come apart. They went, crawling, Calliope in the lead. Gemma wanted to leave Calliope – she wanted Calliope to vanish, to disappear into the smoke like a mirage – but she was also terrified of losing her. She would never be able to find the exit. She couldn't think at all, didn't know which way the stairs were, thought that everything had burned already, the doors and windows and the way out, that they might be crawling their way to an exit that no longer existed.

In the stories, there is always a fire.

The floor was slicked with blood, and there were bodies everywhere. Gemma wondered whether one of them was Wayne's. She had the urge to shout for everyone to wake up, to run, to get out, although she knew they were all dead, replicas and soldiers, humans born by chance and by design, all of them sleeping together under a veil of smoke. She was glad that the darkness softened dead bodies into shapes: already, they were losing reality.

But she had to crawl around a dead replica who'd lost

half her head to a bullet. She still had a gun in her hand, and Gemma noticed her fingers, long and pale and lovely, and imagined that they still stirred, like underwater plant life moved by a current of water.

The stairwell was impassible. Even the door marked *Authorized Personnel* was warm, and Gemma could hear the fire beyond it humming, shredding the physical world into vibration. Calliope tested the door handle, then quickly pulled her fingers away and sucked them into her mouth.

Trapped. They'd waited too long to get out.

They headed back across the scrum of debris, of broken bodies and cotton drift. Everything was dark with ash, everything looked like the grit of burning, and even as they made it to the windows, the fire finally punched its way up to the second floor, collapsing a portion of the wall near the stairwell and tonguing its way over the blood-sticky floor.

A sudden sweep of fresh air made Gemma want to cry. Several windows were missing where people had crashed through them. Gemma, Pete, and Calliope leaned out into the night air, still fizzing with rain, and in the distance Gemma saw dark figures escaping into the trees, pouring through the open gate, shaking the fence to dismantle it: replicas, hundreds of them, making a run for it. Two vans were on fire and half a dozen bodies – soldiers and replicas, it looked like – were scattered across the parking lot, like dolls abandoned by a careless child. Most of the usual Jeeps and trucks were missing. Probably the soldiers had gone, carrying their wounded, or maybe seeking reinforcements, and whisked Saperstein and the other staff to safety.

'We're going to have to jump,' Pete shouted. 'It's the only way.'

Gemma nodded to show she understood. The drop was twenty feet, and almost directly beneath them two replicas lay, half-naked and entangled, their eyes unblinking, exposed to the wind and rain. She didn't know whether they'd landed wrong or been shot, but it didn't matter. She would have jumped if the distance was twice as great, would have catapulted into the air without looking back – anything to get out, to get away, as far from the choke-hold of the smoke and the fire feeding off bits of skin and scalp and hair as possible.

She jumped.

She was screaming through the air, and her lungs were bursting with the joy of oxygen, and then she landed hard in a barren patch of dirt, next to a scrub of bushes. Her right ankle rolled and she knew right away she'd twisted it, but the pain was nothing compared to the red-funnel fire that burst in her vision when she drove her injured hand down into the ground for balance. It was like the missing finger had instead folded up inside her and shot all the way to her throat; she nearly gagged.

Pete landed with a grunt and scrabbled quickly away from the bodies. Now that Gemma was closer she saw they'd been shot, probably from the air: there was a pattern of blood spatter on the exterior wall. It was Calliope, funnily, who hesitated, teetering on the windowsill, looking now not like the monster Gemma had seen in the bathroom but like a sister Gemma might have dreamed. Smoke undulated and roiled behind her.

'Jump,' Gemma found herself shouting, though minutes earlier she'd been hoping Calliope might simply disappear. 'Jump!' Her throat was raw from smoke, and when she tried to draw air again, she began to cough.

Calliope jumped, and for a second Gemma saw her framed in the air like a bird, arms flung wide and mouth open, suspended in the glitter of the fine rain.

Then she landed, gracelessly, but on her feet. Gemma felt the impact herself, whether from the vibration of the ground or because of the doubling effect, she didn't know. When she stood up and tested her weight, her ankle held, barely.

'What happened?' Pete had already moved to take hold of her injured hand again, but she drew away. It was too painful, too awful, and numbly she half believed she could make everything that had happened untrue again.

'I landed wrong,' she said. 'It's nothing.'

'Keep pressure on your hand,' was all he said. He'd always looked thin but now, in the slick light of the remaining streetlamps, covered in blood that wasn't his, he looked truly sick.

They moved across the parking lot, leaving the ruins of the airport behind. Gemma kept expecting to hear a ricochet of shooting, to be stopped, to have her legs eviscerated by bullets. But other than the sound of the fire and a few distant shouts, it was quiet. Why was it so quiet? The fire must be visible for miles. Shouldn't there be sirens already? Ambulances? Shouldn't someone have noticed and responded? It was as if . . .

As if they were miles away from anyone.

It felt to her that they were in the open forever, inching across that bleak expanse of gray pavement, with the painted silhouettes of old parking spaces still faintly visible and bodies flung at intervals facedown on the concrete. But finally they were at the woods, which would hold them and hide them: and at the far end of the woods would be roads, and gas stations, and telephone wires, and help.

Then an explosion made waves of sound that made the ground shudder and vibrated in Gemma's teeth as she turned around. A portion of the roof had collapsed, and flames shot suddenly to the sky, illuminating a low-hanging covering of red-tinged cloud, before retreating again. Gemma and Pete stood stunned, watching the last of what had once been science's greatest experiment consuming itself.

Only then did Gemma see Calliope a short distance away, standing next to a sedan leaning on a flat tire, windshield shattered. It had obviously been heading for the gate. Gemma couldn't see Calliope's face, but she was strangely immobile, as if something inside the car fascinated her. And for whatever reason Gemma found herself backtracking, limping on her injured ankle. Forever afterward she couldn't have said why she was compelled to the window of that sedan, only that she was.

When she was still twenty feet away from the car, Calliope leaned in through the open window. Gemma couldn't see what she was doing, but she thought she heard a shout. This, too, she couldn't absolutely swear to afterward.

By the time Calliope withdrew, Gemma had come up beside her. It was brighter now: the burning airport had created an artificial dawn. When Calliope turned, Gemma nearly screamed: her hands, her wrists, her shirt, all of it was soaked in blood.

'I tried to help him,' Calliope said quickly. 'It was too late.'

For a moment, Gemma couldn't make sense of what

she was seeing: a confusion of glass and blood and steel, the horrible staring face, and the metal finger jointed to its forehead. It looked like one of the cubist paintings her father collected, a nonsense-jumble of shapes.

Then, in an instant, she understood: the blood leaking from his mouth, the air bag pinning him to his seat, a steel rod that must have rocketed from the building just before the roof collapsed, whipped through the windshield, and punctured Dr Saperstein between the eyes. His glasses were gone. In death he looked suprised, and vaguely puzzled, as if he'd come across an unexpected turn in a familiar road.

'Poor Dr Saperstein,' Calliope whispered, and almost sounded as if she meant it. What had she been doing when she leaned into the car? Why was she so covered in blood?

Gemma turned to look at her. Calliope's face rapidly shuttered into an expression of disgust. Like a mirror, it rearranged itself to reflect back what it saw. It was very fast and extremely convincing, but Gemma had caught her too early, had seen the truth nesting like an insect beneath her skin.

Of course, that was the problem with simulations. They were never exactly like the real thing.

EIGHTEEN

GEMMA COULDN'T HAVE SAID HOW far they walked that night looking for a road — miles, maybe, or maybe no distance at all, turning circles in the pitch-dark. They had no water, no flashlight, no matches, no way of getting food and shelter. They had managed to stop her bleeding, and Pete had bundled her hand tightly by rebandaging her fist as best he could with his T-shirt, already soaked with her blood. Still, she could easily get an infection, if they didn't die of hunger or thirst first, or get eaten by wild hogs or wolves or bears or whatever might be prowling in the woods.

Finally, they were forced to stop. Gemma's ankle was so swollen she could hardly put weight on it.

They slept sitting up between the thick roots of an oak tree. It was still raining. The ground was wet and cold. Gemma leaned against Pete to keep him warm. He had no shirt. She expected to have nightmares, but instead sleep came to her like the numbing cold of anesthesia: she dropped.

It seemed to her that only a few minutes passed before she woke again, and her dreams – liquid nightmares of dark-beaked birds, sticky with blood – scattered sleekly into memory. Sometime in the night, Pete had moved: he was now curled on the ground like a sleeping animal, his hair lifted by a light breeze.

Calliope was gone.

Gemma's hand was full of a throbbing pain, as if pressure was building up beneath her skin. It took a moment to remember what had happened – her finger, gone. The bullet that had shaved off her finger, the smoke-filled bathroom, the escape. Dr Saperstein, dead. The replicas, escaped.

And yet the birds were twittering in the trees and shafts of sunlight pinwheeled between branches budding with the pale-green leaves of late spring, and the world was intact.

She let herself cry a little, turning her face into the crook of her arm to muffle the sound. She was cold, and exhausted, and her throat, raw and swollen from all the smoke she'd inhaled, hurt when she swallowed. She was hungry. They'd crawled through a slick of blood and jumped from a second-story window to escape a torpedo of flame, and she cried because she would have killed for some cornflakes, for french toast with butter.

But she was quickly cried out. She kept hearing her father's voice: *No one ever solved a single problem by shedding tears about it.* It was yet another of his master-of-the-universe pronouncements, like, *the world is full of sheep and lions, and I know which I'd rather be,* but in this case it was probably true. They were out of that awful place, at least, and she knew there must be *something* nearby – why build an airport in the middle of nowhere? Besides, there had been sandwiches brought in, and coffee. They just had to pick a direction and stick with it.

Pete turned over, muttering in his sleep. His lips were purple. His skin looked so pale, so fragile, like tissue paper, and she was suddenly terrified for him.

'Pete.' She leaned over and touched his face. 'Pete, wake up.' She was reassured when he opened his eyes almost immediately.

'Is it time to go to school?' His voice cracked but he managed to smile. Gemma found herself laughing. If she *was* going to die, she was glad that Pete was with her. He sat up slowly. 'How's your hand?'

'It's fine,' she said, and pulled away when he tried to take it into his lap. She was too afraid to see how bad it was. 'Calliope's gone.'

'What do you mean, she's gone?' Pete's tone sharpened.

He leaned against the oak tree to climb to his feet, holding his ribs as though they hurt. She saw there were cuts on the palms of his hands, where he must have crawled over broken glass. 'Where did she go?'

'I don't know. I woke up and she was gone.' Every time she thought of Calliope standing by the car window, staring down at broken Dr Saperstein, of the look on her face before Calliope managed to recalibrate her expression to something more appropriate – not joy, exactly, but *excitement,* and total absorption, like proof of the entire universe was contained there in that car – she felt a strong pull of hopelessness and nausea. Calliope and the other replicas had planned all of it.

Gemma could understand escape. She could even understand revenge. But that – the massacre at the airport, and whatever Calliope had done to Dr Saperstein – was something different. That was *pleasure.*

Pete was quiet for a minute. His eyes were almost gold in the early morning sun, and she found herself wishing she could curl up inside them, float away on all that color.

'We can't wait for her,' he said finally, and Gemma was surprised by the intensity of her relief. 'We need to get help. Christ.' His voice cracked. This time, when he smiled, he couldn't quite get it right. 'A fucking cell phone, right? My kingdom for a cell phone.'

'There must be a town *somewhere,*' Gemma said, partly

to reassure herself. 'This is America, not Siberia.' That was another thing her father had liked to say. *In America, you can count on only two things. Taxes, and finding a McDonald's.*

'Right,' Pete said. 'Sure.' But his face was like a dying bulb, full of flicker and uncertainty. She hated to see Pete scared even more than she hated being scared herself. She wished she could stuff Pete's fear and pain down inside of her, pack it down her stomach like newspaper, just so he could be okay.

But she hadn't quite forgotten what he'd said to her in the bathroom, how he'd looked at her as if she were at the very distant end of a telescope and he was surprised to find, after all that, how dim and small her light was.

Pete hacked his way into the undergrowth to find her a walking stick; her ankle was still the size of a grapefruit. At a certain point she realized she could no longer hear him moving around in the trees. Suddenly terrified that he had left her, she was about to cry out for him when she heard a shout. In answer, Calliope's voice lifted over the trees.

'It's just me,' Calliope said. 'It's all right.'

They came out of the woods together, Calliope and Pete, like some warped vision of her own life. When Calliope saw Gemma she actually laughed, and ran to her, taking up both of her hands and sending another shock of pain, like a hot white light, through Gemma's whole body.

'Outside is so big,' Calliope said. 'I walked for ages before I found a wall.'

She was wearing a long cotton dress and slip-on shoes – she'd found new clothes. And she didn't look tired. She didn't even look scared. She looked like the sun had invaded her, glowing beneath her skin. Gemma couldn't shake the feeling that Calliope was somehow feeding off Gemma, siphoning her strength and energy. Taking over.

Gemma jerked away.

'Poor Gemma,' Calliope said, but the words didn't quite sound sincere. 'You're sick.'

'I'm not sick,' Gemma said, even though she felt terrible – dizzy and light-headed, as if the smoke she'd inhaled hadn't fully left her. 'I'm hurt. I'll be fine.'

'You'll be fine,' Pete echoed, which actually made Gemma feel worse. Like he needed to say it to make it true.

'It's hungry,' Calliope said soothingly. But she couldn't conceal her happiness: Gemma had noticed she messed up her pronouns when she was excited. 'I found a wooden house. There's clothing there, and beds. Food to eat. There's a water pump. We can live there, the three of us,' she said. 'We can make a new Haven, but this time we're the gods. I can nurse you,' she added, because she must have seen Gemma's face. 'I know how.'

Gemma wanted to recoil when Calliope touched her face. But she didn't. A house meant people, which meant phones, which meant safety. 'Can you find your way back?'

Maybe she'd hurt Calliope's feelings. Calliope took a step backward.

'I think so,' Calliope said, angling her hand to examine her nails, as if she'd lost interest in the conversation.

'Please, Calliope, we need you.' Pete's voice was gentle and made Gemma ache: it was the voice he'd used when he lifted her shirt in the basement and, without blinking, said *beautiful*. She wondered now if that had been put on too, to appease her, as he was trying to appease Calliope.

Was there anything in the world that wasn't just pretend?

Pretend or not, it worked. Calliope smiled again. 'I made a path back,' she said, addressing Pete directly. 'You can follow me.'

Gemma went slowly, leaning heavily on her walking stick with every other step. Almost immediately she fell behind, though Pete stopped and waited for her whenever he saw that she was struggling,

Calliope often darted ahead, vanishing among the trees, so they had to call her back. She touched every-thing: tree bark, slender branches pale and new, even the pulp of rotten leaves, bending down to run her fingers in the dirt. Gemma couldn't imagine what she was thinking, free at last in a world she didn't know at all, and wondered at how unafraid she seemed.

Gemma had been enclosed too, in a way, bound by her father's rules and her mother's concern, and yet she understood now why people released from prison sometimes wished to go back. She longed for walls, for narrow hallways, for doors that locked. She longed for her old life back, for its sharp angles and clarity: who was wrong, who was right.

In this new world, things doubled and mutated. People had faces beneath their faces. Dr Saperstein was a monster *and* he wasn't. She was afraid he'd been right about the replicas raised at Haven. Calliope was made of the same material as Gemma was, and she was also a monster. Whenever Gemma caught her eye, Calliope smiled, but always a fraction of a second too late. She remembered what Saperstein had said: *To them there is surviving and not surviving, and that's it.*

Calliope had said she had made a path, left markers so she would be able to find her way back, but if she had, Gemma couldn't see them. It all looked the same to her, and as the sun rose and the insects rose with it, hovering in swarms, buzzing around Gemma's wounded hand, she began to think Calliope was either lost or deliberately leading them through the same narrow tunnel of trees. Gemma was so exhausted her vision was blinking out, periodically going to black. She didn't know why April was always going on and on about saving the trees – there sure as shit seemed to be plenty of trees already, doing fine.

Just when she was about to call for another rest, Pete shouted. And limping toward them, she saw a low post-and-beam fence, rudimentary and half-rotten, and beyond it: fields. Pastures and farmland. Cows blinking sleepily in the sun.

Farmland meant farms meant *people*. And people meant they were saved.

'See?' Calliope said. 'I told you I could find my way back.'

Despite everything, Gemma could have kissed her. She laughed, and a group of birds startled, as if they, too, were shocked by the sound. 'You're brilliant,' she said, and couldn't help it: she put her arms around Calliope, as she would have with April. Calliope tensed, and in her arms she felt so small, trembling slightly, a fine wire coiled and coiled almost to breaking, and Gemma felt terrible and guilty. Calliope just stood there, arms pinned to her sides, and Gemma realized she had likely never been hugged, not once in her life.

It wasn't her fault she had been made this way, forced

to observe and imitate, strange and kind and cruel by turns. Maybe she could be taught. She could learn.

Maybe Gemma could teach her.

As she pulled away, Calliope smiled – a real smile this time, that lit her face all the way to her eyes. And looking at her, Gemma's vision doubled again, but this time she saw not herself but the face of that lost sister, the original daughter, *Emma*. An echo seemed to reach her from a lost world, and she knew then that Calliope was her chance to sew the past and the present together. She could love Calliope, and by loving Calliope she could make up for what her father had done, for the fact that she was alive in Emma's place.

Calliope seemed to know exactly what she was thinking. She put her hand on Gemma's heart. She pressed, and Gemma realized she was reading her pulse, trying to get the measure of her heartbeat: the only way she knew to care for someone else.

'You can be mine,' Calliope said. 'You can be my replica.'

NINETEEN

IT WAS LIKE WALKING INTO a portrait: the red barn, its weathered doors partially open; a tidy white house with faded curtains sitting in a dip of land, an old stone well and a bucket lying next to it on the grass, all bound together in the middle of so many rolling fields Gemma thought of a ship moored to an ocean of green.

Gemma couldn't shake the idea that no one had been home in a hundred years. There were no cars in the driveway. She saw no wires, no satellite braced to the roof, nothing but old-fashioned rakes and shovels, neatly cleaned, as if polished by invisible hands after the original owners had departed. The cows in the pasture stared at them with deep and mournful eyes, and they, too, could have been ancient, could have been standing there for ten decades. Gemma's relief gave way again to anxiety. It was wrong. It was like a photo with a too-obvious filter:

somehow, beneath the brightness, you could see a truth that wasn't nearly so pretty.

Pete veered toward the barn doors, maybe thinking he might find someone at work. But Calliope grabbed his wrist and shook her head.

'Don't,' she whispered. For the first time, she looked really afraid. 'The barn is where the animals go to die.' It was funny, what she knew and didn't know.

'The barn is where the animals go to *sleep*,' Pete corrected her. But he let Calliope pull him toward the house.

Only when they came around the house and saw a buggy did Gemma understand.

'Amish,' Pete said.

'There won't be a telephone,' Gemma said, fighting down a fear that she couldn't exactly justify. Where was the family who lived here? They hadn't driven off, obviously. They weren't out catching a movie. The fields glimmered in the sun and yet there was no one turning them, raking, planting – Gemma didn't know exactly what, but she knew on farms there was always work to be done.

Calliope was already at the front door. She turned back to gesture them inside. 'Come, Gemma-Pete,' she said, as if their names were a single thing. 'Come see.' In her dress, she looked as if she truly belonged. It was as if she learned by absorption, and had, like a chameleon, changed her skin to match her new surroundings.

'Well, whoever lives here will have to come back eventually,' Pete said. 'We can rest. Have something to eat. Wait it out.' He managed a small smile. 'At least we know they aren't on a road trip.'

He was right. Besides, Gemma knew she couldn't have gone much farther on foot anyway. Her ankle was so swollen it no longer even looked like an ankle. It wasn't even a cankle – more like a purplish skin-bandage rolled and strapped around where her ankle should be.

The house was unlocked. Inside, it was very neat and full of sunlight. There was a gas stove and, Gemma saw, a small refrigerator cabled neatly to a battery. But no microwave, no digital clocks, no phones or iPads left casually on the counter, no mail, even. The lights were wall-mounted gas lanterns. Again she was struck by the weighty stillness, as if time had turned heavy and dropped like a hand over the whole place.

There was a plate on the table, toast half-eaten, along with a mug of unfinished coffee. This bothered her for some reason – why leave the house so neat but not clear your breakfast?

Calliope caught her staring. 'There was a male,' she said. 'He ran off when he saw me.'

'Why?' Gemma asked, and Calliope shrugged. It seemed weird to her that a boy in his own house would run at the sight of a girl on his land, but then again, she didn't know much about Amish culture. Maybe he'd run for help, and even now there were people on the way who could take them to a town, or point them in the right direction, at least. 'He didn't say anything? He didn't speak to you at all?'

'He just ran,' Calliope said.

They drank water from a sink that worked with a hand pump and came out cold and tasting deliciously of deep earth. Instantly, Gemma felt better. They ate bread and fried eggs with yolks the orange of a setting sun, and Gemma nearly cried: she'd never been hungry before, truly hungry, in a way that torqued your insides. She couldn't even feel bad about the food they were stealing. They would pay it all back, anyway, she would make sure they did, once she got home.

In a cellar, Pete found an old-fashioned icebox, and in a closet, coarse linen hand towels that he used to make a pack for her ankle.

'We need to wrap your hand again,' he said, and Gemma didn't want to but knew he was right.

He crouched in front of her and began to unwind the T-shirt they'd used to stop the bleeding. When it came away, Gemma was shocked by the sight of her missing finger: she couldn't understand, for a moment, where it had gone, still felt it buzzing and tingling.

She bit her lip as tears broke up her vision. Pete said

nothing. He didn't look disgusted. He didn't try and make her feel better. He just dampened a clean towel and slowly wiped the blood off the back of her hand, off her fingers. She bit the insides of her cheeks when he touched the wound itself, so hard her mouth flooded with a metal taste. Pain came down on her like a shutter, and then it passed.

'We have to keep it clean,' he said, rebandaging it, and she knew that was his way of saying *I'm sorry.*

How could they ever survive what they had seen together? They would be like tumors to each other: a nest of dark things, terrible memories, questions they wanted to forget.

They could never go back to how things had been. If they wanted to go forward, she feared, they would have to cut those tumors out. They would leave all their pain in the past. They would bury it so deep that even their heartbreaks couldn't hurt them.

Still, no one came. It hadn't been long, but Gemma grew anxious and increasingly restless. She desperately wanted to move on, to reach an end point, to hear her mom's voice, to see gas stations and telephone poles and parking lots and all the ugliness of life that now seemed beautiful: maps, grids, roads, wires. She craved fluorescent lights and boring TV and normalcy. But she also knew it would be risky to leave. They might be ten miles from another settlement, maybe more.

Pete was right: it was better to wait.

He left Calliope and Gemma alone when he went to clean off in the old-fashioned tub, which also functioned with a pump and drew no hot water. She wondered if he felt the same way she did, like they'd been slicked all over with death, like it would never wash off.

In the kitchen she watched the sun turn dust motes in the air, wishing she could shake the feeling of terrible intrusion – a sense that had less to do with being in a strange house and, like Goldilocks, eating and drinking and consuming, and more to do with a feeling that they'd stumbled on a sleepy mystery best not to awaken. She was almost afraid to breathe too hard.

Calliope, on the other hand, moved from room to room, opening drawers, touching everything, marveling at soup spoons and wooden tongs, can openers and mason jars, salad bowls and flower vases, needlepoint pillows and woven place mats. She disappeared and reappeared wearing a second dress on top of the first one, a knit sweater that hit her at mid-thigh, and a wide-brimmed hat. Gemma wanted to say something, to tell her not to, but the words kept swelling in her throat like a sponge. She kept having the crazy thought that Calliope wasn't wearing different clothes, but different skins; that the clothes were like the discarded shells of long-dead cicadas.

Calliope wasn't sick: it was an obvious realization but one that came late. Calliope was thin, way too thin, and her head was shaven, and she had crooked teeth. But she wasn't like Lyra. Lyra was sick in a way that showed itself even when she was desperately trying to hide it. Gemma knew that the replicas had been given different variants of prion disease, some of them much faster-working than others. There would have been control groups, too.

The idea of Lyra being selected and Calliope being spared made her sick, even though she couldn't say why she cared so much. When it came down to it, she hardly knew Lyra. When it came down to it, she was here because of Lyra. And Lyra had thanked her only once, and probably wouldn't care whether Gemma lived or died.

'You shouldn't touch everything,' Gemma said at last, when Calliope crouched, letting her dress pool on the floor, to examine a fat-bristled broom next to the stove.

Calliope threaded a finger through its bristles, then tugged, so some of them came away in her hand. She let them scatter. 'Why not?'

Exhaustion now felt to Gemma like a weight, like pressure bearing down on her from outside. 'Because these things don't belong to you,' she said. 'This isn't your house.'

A shadow moved across Calliope's face. 'Why not?'

Gemma stared at her. She realized she had no idea how to begin answering. *We can live here,* Calliope had said. Did she not understand what belonging meant?

'Because . . . people live here. They're coming back. They use those spoons and cups and hats and . . . and everything.'

Calliope removed the hat and turned it over in her hands. 'But we used them too,' she said after a moment. 'So doesn't that mean we own them now?'

'No.' Gemma reminded herself that Calliope didn't understand, and that it wasn't her fault. 'It's not about who uses what. They just – the house is theirs. They own it.'

Calliope frowned. 'Why?'

'Just because,' Gemma said. 'Because the house is theirs, it was always theirs. They probably built it—'

'So if you build something, it automatically belongs to you?' Calliope's voice had turned sharp, and Gemma realized she'd said the wrong thing.

'No,' Gemma said carefully. 'Not always.' Calliope looked down. Her knuckles were very white on the brim of the hat. 'You don't belong to Haven, Calliope. You never belonged to them.'

Calliope said nothing for a while. 'It's just I've never seen so many things before,' she said, so quietly the words touched Gemma like a wind. She immediately felt terrible. 'I always wanted, for my own. All of us wanted things. Only people could own anything.'

'I'm sorry,' Gemma said. She really was. How would she ever be able to fix Calliope? How could she even start? 'It isn't the owning that makes a person, you know. It has nothing to do with that.'

'Then what?' Calliope said. 'What is it?'

Gemma couldn't answer that either. Calliope looked down at the hat, turning it again in her hands.

'At Haven the nurses left things without meaning to. Clips to put in your hair, except we didn't have hair, we weren't allowed. Number forty liked pens. She liked to suck on them. Her tongue was always black with ink. Maybe that's why she was an idiot. I found a whole package of gum, once, and Cassiopeia got a bracelet and I wanted it bad, but she hid it so them wouldn't take it.' Calliope shook her head. 'But I got even better than she did, in the end. It was because of watching. Most of the other thems never paid attention. But I always paid attention. I saw how the people talked and how they did things.'

Wind briefly stirred the curtains, and made phantom shapes: faces appeared in the cloth, rippled, and were gone.

'The nurses hid in the bathrooms to use their cell phones.' She said *cell phones* the way someone else might say *church*: as if the words carried special power. 'They weren't supposed to, but they did anyway. I found a cell phone of my own one day. It was just sitting there. I kept it hid. I was very, very careful. When they turned up Ursa Major with Nurse Maxine's wallet, all of us got searched. Ursa Major got hit so bad her face swole up and she had to go to the Box.'

A terrible taste soured Gemma's mouth.

'The first day I was so happy. I hid far on the other side of the island and missed Stew Pot and all my testing, and I got in trouble from nurses afterward. But it was worth it. Sometimes the cell phone did nothing, and other times it lit and played music. Once I saw lots of numbers and I pressed all the buttons and I must have pressed at the right time and somebody spoke to me. "Hello," she said. "Hello." I was too scared to talk back. I liked to listen, though.' Calliope scowled. 'And then the phone made music too loud and the nurses took it away from me. Nurse Maxine said she would cut my fingers off if she ever caught me stealing again. I was happy when Haven burned,' she added abruptly, and her voice sharpened. 'I was happy when the roof exploded. I hoped she was inside, I hoped all her skin was burning, her and all the other nurses.'

Gemma took a deep breath, fighting the hard tug of nausea. 'But think of how many people died,' she said.

'And – and all those babies, the infants in Postnatal, the ones you liked to visit? Remember, you told me that?' Calliope's face didn't change. 'They're dead.'

Calliope shrugged. 'Things die,' she said. 'At Haven, things died all the time. The Pinks and the Yellows, mostly all of them died. Browns too. They got sick early and started walking into things. Forgetting where their cots were and being stupid clumsy.'

'So that's it?' Gemma's voice was inching into a scream, and Calliope looked up, frowning, as if the tone bothered her. But Gemma couldn't stop it. She couldn't calm down. 'You don't feel *bad*? You don't feel sorry?'

It was like watching a shutter latched tight against a storm: all the expression went out of Calliope's eyes. For a long time, she stood there, staring at Gemma in silence, still holding the hat she'd found in one of the closets, her long white fingers knuckle-tight on its brim.

'If it isn't the *owning* that makes humans,' Calliope said finally, and her voice was all knit together, interlaced with tension, 'and it isn't the *making*, either, then maybe it's the *un*making?'

Before Gemma could stop her, Calliope had ripped the ribbon from the crown of the hat. She tossed it on the ground and began to stomp it with a heel. Her face flattened, like a reptile's, into an expression of cold anger.

'Stop it.' Gemma struggled to get to her feet. Calliope

swept a hand over the kitchen shelves, crashing mugs, bowls, and plates to the ground. 'Calliope, *stop.*'

She didn't stop. She turned and darted into the living room. With two hands, she yanked the mirror from the wall and threw it. Gemma had to duck out of the way, folding her ankle again and barely catching herself on the counter. When the mirror hit the wall, the glass slid out of the frame and shattered.

A curse, was the first thing Gemma thought. A curse of bad luck.

'There,' Calliope said. Glass crunched beneath her shoes. 'Now it's ugly. Now it's ruined. Now no one can have it.'

'You shouldn't have done that,' Gemma said, tasting blood and tears in her mouth – she'd bit down on her tongue. Calliope lunged for her and Gemma screamed. But Calliope just gripped her by the wrist, squeezing so tight Gemma could feel the individual impressions of Calliope's nails.

'What if they never come back?' Calliope asked, so quietly Gemma nearly missed it. Terror swept down her spine, like the touch of an alien hand.

'What?' she whispered.

Calliope was careful not to look at her. 'You said the people who live here will come back,' Calliope said. 'But what if they don't? What if they stay away forever?'

Dimly, over the thunder of her heartbeat, Gemma heard Pete creaking down the hall. Calliope released her quickly – but not quickly enough.

'What the *hell*?' Pete had changed into a pair of loose drawstring pants and a clean shirt, and there was color in his face again, although his eyes were still too bright, as if he had a fever. Gemma was shocked by how intensely relieved she was to see him.

For a second Calliope just stood there, breathing hard. Then she shoved past Gemma and hurtled out the door, letting it slam behind her.

TWENTY

'SOMETHING'S WRONG,' GEMMA SAID. SHE thought of the way Calliope had flown at her, her sharp-fisted hands, the sour heat of her breath.

What if they never come back?

'That's an understatement,' Pete said. He smiled, but only halfway, as if he couldn't quite remember how to do it.

'*No.*' He didn't see. He hadn't seen how Calliope looked, and hadn't heard what she'd said. 'I mean, whoever lives here should have come back by now. They should have come home. Why haven't they?'

'Hey.' Pete had to step very carefully: he wasn't wearing shoes, and the floor was still littered with glass. 'Deep breath, okay? You're just scared.'

'What if – what if Calliope did something to them—' She choked on the words, on the very idea of it, and Pete put his arms around her, as if he knew it was the only way to keep her on her feet.

'Come on,' he said. 'It's all right. Home stretch. You're exhausted.'

'You're not listening to me.' Gemma pulled away and saw reality for a moment like a fabric sail, blowing away from its mast, straining in invisible currents. 'She asked me what would happen if they never came back.'

'She's never been outside, Gemma,' Pete said. 'She has no idea what to think.'

Gemma shook her head. Her mouth tasted like vomit. She was dizzy with confusion and fear. 'Where are they then? You said yourself – it's not like they went on a road trip.'

Pete's hair was wet: when he pushed a hand through it, water sprayed through his fingers. 'Maybe they walked into town.'

'What town?' Gemma no longer cared that she was shouting. 'I haven't seen a town, have you, Pete? In fact, I think the whole reason we're here is that there is no fucking town.'

He threw up his hands and let them fall hard, a clapping sound that made Gemma flinch. 'So maybe they went to a picnic. Or a ukulele bonfire. Or to make soap out of lye or something. How should I know?' Pete was doing his best to be nice, but she could tell he was losing patience.

His irritation kept showing, like the nub of something sharp rubbing up beneath a sweater, distorting the fabric. 'I mean, shit. She doesn't even know what a barn is. What could she possibly have done?'

'She knows what a barn is,' Gemma said: a stupid response, but she was on the verge of tears again. 'She called it by name. She's smarter than you know.'

Pete frowned. She was worried he would tell her she was being crazy again, and that she would start to cry, but he just shook his head.

'Look. I can't imagine what it's like for you—' He broke off, shaking his head. 'I mean, being with her. Seeing your *face* . . .' He smiled but only barely. 'It's weird even for me. When you're standing next to each other . . .' He reached out and knuckled the counter, like there was an insect there he needed to crush. 'I'd be freaking out too.'

Gemma felt a chill go through her. She was a cold mist, barely hanging together. 'You think I'm freaking out,' she said.

He looked at her. Pale eyelashes. Freckles, lips, the coral inside of his nose. She'd studied his face so often – thinking it beautiful, thinking it hers. But the face was just collision, random physical accumulation that meant nothing.

'Anyone would freak out.' He tried to take her hand but she balled her fist, and weirdly enough her other hand, the injured one, pulsed with sudden pain, as if she'd balled that instead. 'She's not you. She's nothing like you. You shouldn't be afraid.'

'I don't think she's like me,' Gemma said. 'I don't think she's anything like me.'

But she realized, even as she said it, that this wasn't exactly true. Wasn't that the whole point? She could have been Calliope, and Calliope could have been her. People became different bodies by chance or accident or God, depending on what you believed; but if you had the same body, the same voice, the same hair and fingers and eyes and nails, then how did you know the difference? She would have to separate from Calliope, cleave her like some horrible head in a fairy tale, and even then she would have that doubleness inside her.

'Go rinse off,' Pete said, in a voice she hated: it was a tone her father used, hooking onto an *I know best* kind of thing. 'It will make you feel better. I promise. By the time you get out, what do you want to bet we'll be hitching a ride back to the twenty-first century in a buggy?'

Gemma couldn't smile, even though she knew he was only trying to help. She wouldn't let him help her to the washroom, either, even though she was hobbling on her swollen ankle and had to lean on the furniture for support.

The bathtub was old and spotted with rust. Pete had left blood behind, too, a faint ring of it where the water had turned color, and more funneling toward the drain. She pumped for water and was shocked by how cold it was. But at the same time she liked it, and liked the smell, too, like spring soil, and dirt newly turned over.

She stripped out of the clothes she'd been issued at the holding center and maneuvered into the tub, trying not to put weight on her ankle and careful, too, not to use her left hand. The shock of cold water even at her ankles made her gasp, and instinctively she went for a knob that wasn't there. Then she wanted to cry again, not for the lack but for all the things she had always used, for how lucky she was and for her life, pure and simple, for the ability to stand naked and hurt ankle deep in cold water. She was alive: she'd made it out. Goose pimples raised the hair on her thighs and forearms. The water took blood from her skin and swirled it into pink. She was ugly and damaged, and for an instant, she didn't care: she was alive. Her ribs held her, her heart held her, the world held her. It bound her like a promise.

Pete was right: she did feel better, infinitely better, once she'd watched a film of soot and dirt and blood wash away, as if it was carrying the memory of what had happened. Still, she was uneasy. She hadn't heard anyone come back. The house was still silent, still wound up, like a coiled spring.

There were towels pegged to the wall, and she took

one. In an adjacent room she found a closet full of dresses like the one Calliope had chosen, and she rooted around in a drawer until she found pants, a white shirt, and a dark vest, all of them obviously meant for a guy. But a pair of sandals wedged beneath the simple bed fit her pretty well, and she almost laughed when, feeling something crunch in the pocket of the vest, she fished out a half-empty pack of Marlboro Lights and a Bic lighter decorated with a peeling Steelers logo.

So. There were rule breakers here, too.

Pete wasn't in the kitchen, although he'd swept up the glass. Calliope wasn't back, either. In an instant, all her good feeling was swept away; she stood drowning in the air, in the emptiness. She was alone.

She was suddenly terrified. She launched herself to the door, ignoring the pain in her ankle, crying out: there was something behind her, something too terrible to look at; the weight of her fear had transformed into a monster.

She was outside, and the light was blinding. The cows moving across the pasture calmed her only slightly. She was alone and lost. She was shouting Pete's name without even meaning to, and when she saw movement inside the barn, the shift of color and shadow, she went toward it with her arms outstretched.

'Don't. *Don't.*' His voice stopped her. She'd never heard anyone sound like that, and in that moment, though she was still standing in the sun, the shadow of the monster behind her reached out and swallowed them. 'Don't come in here. Don't.'

For a moment he was still invisible. He was corners of himself, an arm and a leg, trying to move out of sticky darkness. And she was drawn toward him, to reach him, to pull him away, and so even as he plunged outside, like someone diving in reverse, she saw behind him the shoes attached to the ankles, and an arm – a small arm, a young arm – held motionless in a slant of light. Even if she hadn't, she would have known by Pete's face: it was as if all the skin had come off, as if the fear had come down and planed away everything else.

The barn is where the animals go to die.

He grabbed her, and this time Gemma felt that he was the one in danger of falling. 'We can't stay here,' he said. 'We've got to get out of here. We have to get out now.' There was blood on his shoes.

She couldn't move. Her thoughts had frozen: they were rattling together like cubes in a tray. 'What happened?' she asked, even though she knew. But she couldn't quite make sense of it – that pale child's arm reaching into a triangle of sun, and a man's feet fanned apart. *Bodies.*

'Jesus.' Pete was crying. He turned away from her and bent to put his hands on his knees, trying to breathe, retching a little. 'Jesus Christ.' He just kept saying it, over and over, *Jesus, Jesus,* and Gemma felt the clean brightness of the sky above them, felt all the emptiness of that endless hurtle into space.

'She killed them,' she said. The words didn't sound real. Pete just nodded. He was still doubled over. She wanted to put a hand on his back, but she couldn't make her arm obey the command.

The barn is where the animals go to die.

Where was she now? Where had she gone? Gemma was freezing, gripped by fear. In the distance, the woods rippled as a breeze passed through the trees. Was someone shouting? She couldn't think. She thought she heard voices crying out.

'We can't stay here,' she said, as Pete had. But neither of them moved. It was like a nightmare. Too bright, too warm, too empty.

Voices. She definitely heard voices now, not the phantoms but real people. In the distance a long trail of orange dust unfurled, and then she saw horse carts, three of them, and a cluster of people. They were coming fast, and for a moment she felt nothing but relief. They were saved.

Pete had her shoulders. He shook her, and her teeth jumped together. 'You need to run. Don't you understand? We can't be here. They can't find you here.'

'What are you talking about?' Her thoughts were still frozen into uselessness. The wagons were closer now. The ground shivered under the vibration of so many hooves. She could make out the men inside them, all men, all dressed in black, all shouting. There was a boy, too, maybe thirteen or fourteen. He was standing, balancing like a sailor on a rolling sea deck, scouting for sure. He was pointing.

'Listen to me, Gemma.' Pete was shouting, but she couldn't hear him properly.

'Run, Gemma. Listen to me. You gotta move.'

She'd already lifted a hand to wave back, to hail the people in the wagon, because they were waving too, because the boy in front, the one who reminded her of a sailor, was pointing at her.

Pointing, shouting. *Angry.*

And suddenly she remembered what Calliope had said: *There was a male. He ran off when he saw me.*

The cooled coffee with milk congealing into a pale skin on its surface. Half-eaten toast.

You can be my replica.

The men were pouring down off the wagons now, shouting, as the boy still stood with a finger raised, trembling and white-faced with fury, and finally Gemma heard him over the rattling of her heart, over the fear that had her in its grip.

'That's her,' he was saying. He had the beginnings of a beard, dark and patchy, and a long, narrow face, but it was his eyes that struck her. They were large and terrible, like holes that had been gouged into his face. 'That's her. That one. That's *her*.'

Pete shoved her. The shock of pain when she stepped on her ankle jolted her into her body, into understanding: Calliope had killed people and Calliope had disappeared and Gemma, her replica, would be her substitute. *'Run.'*

They were swarming toward her, jackets flapping in the wind like capes, so she was reminded of insects, of biblical locusts coming down to bring punishment.

Finally, Gemma ran.

TWENTY-ONE

SHE LOST SIGHT OF PETE almost immediately.

Pain darkened her vision every time she put weight on her left ankle, and her ankle kept folding, rolling her down to her hands and knees. She lost one sandal. She fell, got up, fell, got up. She could hear the men shouting behind her, tunneling toward her like a wave, but she was too afraid to look and see how close they were.

She was choking on her own spit, blind with pain and panic. Down, up again. In the fields the cows watched her lazily, flicking their tails. The woods were impossibly far. She kept running anyway, up and down the swells of land, falling and climbing again to her feet, swallowing her snot.

Then she had crossed the expanse of green and hit the fence, running into it with hardly a break in her step, simply plunging over it, toppling, rolling on her shoulder and then hauling herself again to her feet, sheltered in the sudden shadows, ping-ponging from tree to tree, using her good hand. She tripped and slid down a steep embankment, through a mulch of rotting tree bark: at the bottom of the slope, an enormous felled tree wheeled its roots to the sky. An overhanging lip of earth made a kind of tunnel, and she saw at once this was her only chance: to hide, to wait, to hope that the men missed her. She scuttled backward into the soft rot of this long, damp space. The air smelled like moisture, pulped leaves, and decay.

She waited, shivering, her arms around her knees, listening to the distant shouting of her pursuers. At one point they seemed to be almost directly on top of her, and fear turned her stomach to liquid. But then they passed on.

She lost track of time. Her terror turned every second into a swampy hour, a long agony of waiting. Finally, she realized the woods were quiet. She couldn't hear anyone shouting.

She hadn't heard anyone shout in a long time.

Carefully, she shimmied out of her hiding place, still pausing every few breaths to listen for footsteps or the sound of voices. Nothing. Now that her panic had eased up, the pain in her ankle had redoubled. It took her twenty minutes to work her way up the slope she'd tumbled down in seconds.

At the top of the embankment she stood, trying to catch her breath, waving away a cloud of gnats that rose in a swarm. Afternoon sunlight made elegant angles through the trees. That meant hours had passed. She hoped the men who were after her had given up.

She wondered what had happened to Calliope – whether she, too, had made her escape through the woods.

She thought she remembered which direction she'd come from. She would have to go the opposite way, or risk ending up right where she started. If this was farmland, she comforted herself with the idea that she would have to reach another farm eventually – preferably one wired for the twenty-first century, where no one believed that she was a murderer. Even better, she might find a road full of traffic, full of normal people, soccer moms and dentists and teenage drivers with both hands on the wheel.

She swore then that if she ever made it home she would never complain, ever, about being bored. She wanted to be bored every day of her natural life. She wanted to die of boredom, literally.

So she went on, hobbling, limping, leaning heavily on a stick she fished out from the underbrush. She had to stop and rewrap her ankle twice, clumsily because she had only one hand, because she was shaking so hard, and the skin was so enormously puffy it frightened her. Miles of land, tight-knit woods of oak and maple and birch, dappled sun and the sky held at bay by the canopy of branches, the occasional flash of a deer bounding off in the distance, broken stone foundations that might have existed since the days of Paul Revere. She kept telling herself there had to be a road soon, soon, soon.

The afternoon lengthened. The shadows turned the color of a bruise. More than once, she imagined she heard the noise of traffic – there, over that ridge, just behind that stand of trees, she could swear she heard a horn blowing. She was desperately thirsty, and her head hurt. She'd been crying for an hour without realizing it, and squinting hard to try to make treetops into rooftops or telephone poles. In the thickening shadows, she could almost believe it. She'd lost her second sandal too, without realizing it.

And now it was getting dark.

She began to shout for help, no longer caring who found her, wishing, now, she'd never run in the first place. She shouted until her voice broke and she couldn't bear it anymore. No one came, anyway.

And then she saw, in the distance, deliverance: a stone house, a roof overgrown with green moss, but a *house*. No – more than one house. Three houses lumped next to one another, like faerie houses dropped by some miracle in the middle of the woods.

If she'd been less desperate, she would have noticed the

shattered windows, the doors angled off their hinges, the wood rot, and seen it for a settlement no one had entered in years, possibly decades.

If she'd been less tired, she would have noticed the low circle of stones indicating an old sunken well, with only a flimsy covering of ancient wood to keep animals from falling in.

But she was desperate, and tired, and the woods were dark.

She tripped on the edge of the sunken well and saw, briefly, the small covering of ancient wood, like a trapdoor set in the ground. Then she crashed through it and tumbled down into the long, sleek mouth of a thirty-foot hole.

PART III

TWENTY-TWO

AT ALMOST THE SAME TIME Gemma fell, Kristina and Geoffrey Ives arrived at a Bruinsville, Pennsylvania, police station, not ten miles from the old stone well in the middle of the Sequoia Falls Nature Preserve where their daughter now lay unconscious.

They had arrived in Lancaster County the night before, after one of Geoff's many military contacts, Captain Agrawal, had signaled that Saperstein might have mistaken Gemma and Pete for the replicas they were pursuing, only to discover a calamity: an explosion at the private facility where Saperstein had been licking his wounds and trying, without success, to rally new financial support. Kristina refused to consider the possibility that Gemma might be among the dead bodies excavated from the wreckage. She wouldn't even think it.

They were ushered by Captain Agrawal down a narrow

hallway to the locked and windowless evidence room in the back. Kristina had to reach out a hand to steady herself against the file cabinets.

How had she ended up in a police station with her daughter missing and children turned to ashes? There seemed to be a gigantic hole in her life that she couldn't bridge. She couldn't remember her way across it.

A sudden swoon of terror darkened her vision, made her dizzy on her feet: she imagined they were bringing her inside to show her Gemma's body, still and cold and lifeless, her lips dark as a bruise.

Years ago, she and Geoff had refused to accept the death of their only child. They had transgressed the natural order: they had taken their child back, after death had already claimed her.

She couldn't shake the idea that death had come, now, to settle the score.

When the door opened and instead she saw Pete Rogers, bloodless and exhausted-looking and definitely alive, she almost cried out. He was sitting at a table wedged between the metal shelving, which had been cleared of everything but a few cardboard boxes – or maybe that was all the evidence of crime in this part of Lancaster County. He was gripping a Styrofoam cup of what smelled like hot chocolate, and he had a blanket draped around his shoulders. The room was cold and extremely bleak, with a cement floor and exposed wire-encased lightbulbs.

'It's the only room that locks besides the drunk tank,' Agrawal said, as if he knew what Kristina was thinking. 'I wanted to be sure he had privacy.'

'Pete.' Kristina's relief lasted only a second – fear grew almost immediately again inside her, a hard, cold metal thing that stuck in her throat. The night before, she'd gone instinctively for the Klonopin in her purse, only to find that suddenly her throat wouldn't work to swallow. She literally could not get the pill down.

She hadn't been this sober in years. She hadn't been this afraid, either.

'Pete.' She went to him and knelt, taking his hands, which were cold, noting the bruised color of his eyelids and the capillaries broken across his cheeks and forehead. 'Pete.'

He showed no sign of having heard her.

'He's in shock,' Geoff said, as though it weren't obvious.

'One of the troopers picked him up right on the shoulder of the turnpike a quarter of an hour ago, near the intersection of Route 72,' Agrawal said. 'My guy nearly plowed him.'

'He needs a hospital,' Kristina said. She had a memory of seeing Pete, April, and Gemma laughing together at her birthday party, playing bocce barefoot on the lawn. Pete's pants were rolled to the knees and Gemma had several paper cocktail umbrellas tucked behind her ear. She was laughing. Could that really have been only four days ago?

'We've got a team from Lancaster General on their way now,' Agrawal said. 'I wanted to bring you in first. In case . . .' Kristina didn't miss the look Captain Agrawal gave her husband.

'Gemma's still out there.' Pete's voice was so raw it hurt just to hear. It was as if he was speaking through a mouth full of thorns. He started to stand up, lost his balance, and sat down again. 'I lost her. We have to find her.'

'Shhh.' She put a hand on his forehead, which was clammy with sweat. She smoothed back his hair. She had met his mother once – a cheerful, round-faced woman who'd arrived with paint still smudged on one cheek. She was a kindergarten teacher, she'd explained, and Kristina had immediately envied her warm, chaotic friendliness. 'It's okay. Just tell me what happened.'

He was grabbing the table as though he still worried he might fall down, even though he was sitting. 'It was Calliope,' he said, his voice cracking over every syllable. 'She must have had the whole thing planned from the start. Gemma tried to warn me and I didn't listen. I didn't believe her.' He was shaking. Kristina reached out and put a hand on his back, trying to rub some warmth into him. 'There was so much blood. . . .'

Immediately, it was as if the cold had flowed into her body as well. 'What – what do you mean?' Memories swept suddenly through her head, brightly awful, like dead leaves: Gemma's veins threaded with tubes and needles, like some kind of alien plant; Gemma's mouth leaking blood the first time she'd lost a tooth; the thick Y-shaped scar across her chest, so similar to the incision that morticians made after death.

'There were three of them,' Pete said. 'One of them was just a kid.'

'What are you talking about?' Kristina's voice sounded loud in the little room. 'What's he talking about?'

'He means those homicides off Hemlock,' Agrawal said quietly, avoiding Kristina's eyes. She knew that something terrible had happened to one of the Amish families in the area, but she had deliberately tried not to listen. She had enough tragedy of her own. She couldn't handle anyone else's. 'He was on the scene.' But Kristina had the feeling that there was more, that there was something he wasn't telling her.

'I told Gemma to run,' Pete said. He wouldn't look at her. He was staring at his fists, balled now in his lap. 'They were coming after her. There was no other choice.'

The cold made Kristina's fingers and lungs tingle. '*Who* was coming after her?'

Pete shook his head. It was as if he'd forgotten anyone

else was in the room. 'They thought she was Calliope,' he said. 'That was the whole point. That was what Calliope wanted.'

Kristina imagined herself freezing, like a pane of glass webbed with frost, filling with tiny cracks. 'Who's Calliope?'

Pete met her eyes, finally. 'Calliope's one of Gemma's replicas,' he said.

'One of . . . ?' Kristina tried to take a step backward and knocked one of the shelving units behind her. There was nowhere to go, no space at all. She couldn't breathe.

'All right, that's enough.' Geoff came forward and tried to put a hand on Kristina's shoulder, but she jerked away. 'The kid is in shock, Kristina. He needs to go the hospital, like you said.'

'Numbers six through ten,' Pete said, as if he hadn't heard. Now that he was looking at Kristina, she wished that he would look away. 'Five in all. But Calliope wanted to be human.'

'He's confused.' Geoff's voice seemed to reach her from a distance, as if she really were hearing him through a thick layer of ice. The air had frozen in her lungs. She couldn't speak. She had the sense that she and Pete were alone at the bottom of a lake, that everyone else, the whole world, was held at bay by thousands of tons of water.

'That's why Calliope did it,' Pete said, in a whisper. 'She wanted to switch places.'

TWENTY-THREE

GEMMA BLINKED INTO CONSCIOUSNESS AGAIN, tossed up by a hand of pain. Something screamed. Or rather, she screamed and it screamed, and it was impossible to tell who started first. Leathery wings swept her face and the tangle of her hair, and her voice reached registers she didn't even know she could hit: a high-C, horror-movie scream that echoed back to her as the bat winged up toward the moon, probably just as scared as she was, knocking against the sides of the well in its effort to get out.

It was silhouetted briefly, a black blur against the sky knotty with clouds and a moon just easing out of the darkness, and then it was gone, and with her terror ebbing, the pain came grinding back instead, and the memory of what had happened: the long, limping escape through the woods, the sudden realization that she was lost. The house in the glen – now, in memory, so obviously abandoned, maybe for a century – and the soft splinter of wood breaking apart beneath her.

The well.

She was at the bottom of a well, alone, in the middle of the woods.

She was shivering. The well smelled, strangely, like the inside of a dirty produce drawer, like the chill of old vegetal rot. The mud was puddled with old water and debris, with a tangle of tree branches and miscellaneous trash. She was lying in the rot of the old well, and when she shifted, she heard the crunch of small animal bones beneath her. High above her, a portion of the well cover was still intact. It blotted out a sweep of sky and reminded her of a half-closed eyelid.

'Hello?' she whispered. Of course no one answered. She cleared her throat and said, louder, 'Hello?' Her voice rolled off the stones and then dropped.

Panic came up from her stomach, sharp-clawed and frantic, like some kind of rodent. She could barely sit up. Her back hurt; everything hurt. Nothing seemed broken, at least.

'Hello!' she tried again. 'Help me!' There must be someone out there, someone who would hear. The well tunneled her voice into echoes, so even when her voice began to crack she was momentarily surrounded by the cascading responses of her own words, *help me*. 'Help me! Hello! Help!'

She shouted, over and over, into the thin night air, but her voice, still raw from overuse, gave out quickly. It dropped into hoarse croaks and then into whispers. Finally, she couldn't even do that, and when she opened her mouth, nothing came out but a soft whistling, like a leak from a faulty kettle.

Still no help arrived. No one came. No one answered.

There was no one around to answer, no one for miles and miles. Only the bats, blind and hungry, clicking their way through the dark.

TWENTY-FOUR

IN THE CURDLED LIGHT OF a new dawn, while a hundred police officers from all over the state began to gather in the parking lot outside the Bruinsville police station to smoke cigarettes and drink coffee and blink the sleep out of their eyes, while four bloodhounds lashed to the wrist of their handler sniffed experimentally at shoes and car tires and the crusted remnants of someone's dropped bacon, egg, and cheese, Gemma woke up to the pressure of a light rain that had started hours earlier and to a voice calling softly to her.

She blinked. Rain blurred her vision, and she swiped it from her eyes, disappointed when she realized that the voice, and her name, must have been part of a dream. There was no one above her, no one looking down on her at all: just the sky, a small and narrow mouth, graying above her. Staring up at the knit of clouds, she thought of the surface of a distant mirror.

A shadow moved: she saw her own reflection peering down at her as she peered up at it.

She blinked again through the long tunnel of rain.

Calliope.

'Hello, Gemma,' Calliope said. Then Gemma knew that hers was the voice she had heard calling softly to her in her sleep.

It took Gemma a long time to sit up. An eternity to claw, inch by inch, to her feet. 'Calliope.' Her mouth was dry. She opened it to the rain. 'Please. Help me.'

Calliope's face was a small, shifting pattern of shadows. 'Don't be afraid,' she said in a sweet voice, like the subtle pressure of a razor on Gemma's skin. 'Be a brave girl, now.'

Calliope disappeared again. When Gemma opened her mouth, when she screamed, she felt as if more fear flooded in, instead of being expelled.

'*Please.*'

Calliope reappeared almost immediately, and Gemma felt a small flicker of hope. Calliope had murdered all those people. Calliope was sick. She was evil. But she was still *someone*. She was a chance. Gemma couldn't stand to be alone. She couldn't bear it.

'Please, Calliope.' She licked her lips. 'I – I want to help you. If you get me out of here, you can come and live with me. We can be like – like sisters.'

'Sisters?' Calliope repeated the word in a puzzled tone of voice.

'Like friends,' Gemma said desperately, realizing Calliope likely didn't know what sisters were. 'Like best friends, who share everything.'

For a long time, Calliope looked at her. She seemed to be considering it. Gemma allowed herself to hope.

Then Calliope said, 'I'm tired of sharing.'

This time, when she vanished from the lip of the well, Gemma heard almost immediately the scrape of something heavy on the ground. And then a portion of the sky above turned black. Gemma thought, confusedly, of an eclipse.

'Goodbye, Gemma.' Calliope was invisible, hidden somewhere behind the curtain of black that began to inch slowly across the opening of the well.

A door, or some kind of table: Calliope must have found it in one of the old cabins.

She was using it to cover the well.

She was using it to seal Gemma inside.

Terror turned Gemma inside out. 'No!' She pounded the walls with her fists, as inch by inch the daylight narrowed to a finger, to a line, to a single point above her. 'No! Please! *No!*'

The covering slid into place. Now she could see nothing but a faint gray web of sky, where gaps in the planks revealed razor-thin slices of daylight. Calliope's voice, when she spoke, was so faint Gemma couldn't be sure, afterward, that she hadn't imagined it.

'Goodbye.'

Gemma screamed for hours. She screamed, again and again, calling for Calliope, calling for someone to help. But no one answered – only the rain, scissoring through the rot of old plywood, a quiet shushing.

She slept again. She woke up crying, from a dream of rescuers, of friendly voices drawing closer. Wishful thinking, like people who saw mirages of floating water in the desert.

But then, once again, she heard them.

She sat up as quietly as she could, as if by making too much noise she would frighten off the distant voices. And for a second, she thought she had: she couldn't hear them anymore, and she strained so hard to listen that she felt the effort traveling all the way through her jaw.

Then they came again, nearer this time. She could make out only a few phrases, which carried through the woods and, like water going off a cliff, tumbled down into the well: 'clear,' 'no sign,' 'radio.' Cops. So someone had been sent to find her. In all likelihood, that meant Pete had escaped and found help.

She was saved.

'Down here,' she yelled, and was horrified when

instead what came out was a fragmented whisper, like the rough sound of dry leaves skittering in the wind. She could barely hear it over the drumming of her heart. She cleared her throat and tried again. 'Help me. Please. I'm down here!'

A whisper. A croak. A fish opening and closing its mouth soundlessly beneath the water.

She'd screamed for hours.

She'd screamed herself hoarse.

Already, the cops were drifting away – their words lost shape and edge, and their voices became tones, low notes of regret and disappointment. She grabbed a piece of wood from the splintered pile next to her and tried to beat it against the stone, but it crumbled moistly in her hand.

Help me.

Please.

Please.

She crawled, digging a hand into the loam of rot at the bottom of the well, until she found a rock. Loosing it from the mud, she drove it hard against the side of the well, again and again, rhythmically, and the sound traveled as a shock from her wrist to her elbow and up to her teeth.

But it was too late.

She was alone again.

TWENTY-FIVE

SHE WATCHED THE RAIN BEAD along the fine prism of a spider's web. The spider, black-bodied with furred white-and-black legs, had been at it for hours, leaping and soaring beneath the splintered remains of two shattered boards, trying to restore what had been lost when Gemma had fallen. It was amazing how pretty the web looked in the rain, in the trickle of light that reached her down here.

She lay there, cheek pressed to the mud, breathing in the smell of rotted wood and leaf rot, surprised that she wasn't afraid, wasn't in pain, wasn't feeling much of anything. She was content simply to watch the spider. She wondered how many times over the spider had seen its own web destroyed, and how many times it had simply begun to reweave. Ten? Twenty? One hundred?

She wondered if Pete was okay, and if he'd made it back to civilization, whatever that meant. She wondered if he'd managed to convince anyone of the truth, or whether he'd been shunted off into some psychiatric hospital.

She had no idea what time it was, only that it had been hours since the voices had gone, and so far they hadn't come back.

In Chapel Hill, her classmates would be drinking bad coffee in the cafeteria, finishing last-minute homework assignments, sweating through pop quizzes, ducking outside to smoke weed behind the music building.

She had to get up. Her stomach hurt. She had to use the bathroom. There was a bad smell permeating the air; she realized that it was coming from the filthy cloth still tightly wrapped around her hand.

She had to get out of the well. Not tomorrow. Not when − or if − someone found her. Now. Today.

She kicked through the rubble at the bottom of the well. Wood splinters. A soda can − that got her interest, that was good, it meant there were other people who came this way, hikers or picnickers, and she couldn't be that far from help. She found a textbook, too, from someone's history class − the pages warped, the type blurry and mostly indecipherable. That almost, almost made Gemma smile. She and April had hurled their biology textbooks onto the train tracks once, just to watch them get mowed over, even though both of their parents docked them allowance for the cost of a replacement.

There was no ladder. No booster rocket. No flare gun, or charged cell phone. Big surprise.

The well walls were moss-slicked but studded with rocks that made decent handholds. She wished now more than ever she'd been allowed to participate in gym – her mom had always insisted she be excused, claiming a weak heartbeat, concerned that Gemma might flatline in the middle of a game of dodgeball – and that she'd learned rock climbing during the aerial unit last fall. She couldn't climb one-handed, anyway, but when she tried to use her left hand, thinking that with four good fingers, she'd be okay, the pain was so bad she nearly peed herself and stumbled backward, gasping.

So. She couldn't climb.

She thought of piling all the rotted wood together, stacking it carefully in a cross-hatch pattern, hoping that by some miracle of geometry she would be able to climb the pile like a footstool and reach the top of the well. But the wood was soft and rotten and there wasn't much of it to begin with: it boosted her barely a foot. Her voice was still shot, still coming out in a bare croak, like the throaty wail of a dying frog.

Stretching onto her tiptoes, she managed to get a hand around a root exploding through the rot between stones. Maybe she could climb it, brace her feet against the wall and get some leverage – it would take her only a quarter of the way toward the top, but a quarter of the way was better than nothing.

But here again, she failed. She could barely support her weight with one arm, and her feet slipped as the wood rot crumbled beneath her. She slammed into the wall with a shoulder and dropped on her knees – remembering, at least, to shield her left hand, so she didn't accidentally put pressure on it.

She sat there, panting, her nose leaking snot into the mud. She was too scared even to cry. She might actually die here. Here, at the bottom of some shitty hundred-year-old well, in a state she didn't even *like*. She would die a virgin, alone, unloved.

Funnily enough, it wasn't Pete she thought of then, or April, or even her mom. It was Lyra, the way she looked when Gemma had last seen her: still fragile but also full of life, something hatching. When Gemma closed her eyes, she could hear Lyra's voice, whispering to her across a distance.

Gemma, her voice said. *Gemma.*

Gemma's heart nearly cracked. She opened her eyes again.

But still she could hear Lyra's voice, louder now.

'Gemma, Gemma.' And Caelum's, too, a lower, deeper echo of hers: 'Gemma, Gemma.'

She climbed to her feet. She couldn't quite believe it. They were so distant, she almost feared she really had snapped, and that what she heard was just the transformation of her memory into sound. But no – there was an unfamiliar voice, too, a man's voice. And how could she remember something she'd never heard?

That meant they were here. Close.

Instantly, she was seized by terror: they wouldn't hear her. They would leave, like the police had left, and no one would ever think to look for her here again.

The rock was still where she'd dropped it, exhausted, after an hour of banging fruitlessly, hoping someone would come. She picked it up again and slammed it hard against the slick wall, and the noise it made was of an old stone mouth, clicking its tongue in disapproval.

Not loud enough. Was it her imagination, or were the voices receding already?

She banged the stone again and again. Now she *was* crying, from terror and frustration. How could they not hear? How could they not *see*? Of course, she hadn't seen it either: the well was separated from the houses by a hundred yards, and tucked behind a stand of trees.

She thought of throwing something into the air, in case they happened to be looking in her direction. But it was no use. She could barely lob the rock ten feet in the air, much less hope to break through the wood that Calliope had used to conceal the opening.

The well smelled like her own sweat, like a hard panic. She wasn't imagining it. Lyra's voice was receding.

They, too, were going away.

She was shaking and burning hot, too. She shook off the wool vest she'd taken from the farmhouse — a sudden vision of the boy, red-faced, enraged, pointing at her, as the wagon crested the swell of the hill, overwhelmed her — and as she did, the cigarettes and the peeling lighter thudded out of one pocket.

Gemma's breath seized in her throat.

Could she . . . ?

It had been raining on and off all night. The wood was damp, although not as damp as it could have been — Calliope had done her this favor by covering the well.

She bent down. The lighter was cool in her hand. She thumbed a flame to life and was shocked by how vivid it was, how bright against the darkness.

Could she . . . ?

It was risky. It was dangerous. She remembered how quickly the airport bathroom had filled with smoke, how quickly she'd felt she couldn't breathe. She had no idea how far Lyra and Caelum had traveled already, and whether they'd even *see* the smoke.

On the other hand, she didn't know how much longer she'd survive.

And what had Calliope said?

In all the stories, there's always a fire.

TWENTY-SIX

AND THEN, WHILE SHE WAS still hesitating, still trying to decide, three gunshots cracked out in the silence.

That settled it. Three gunshots meant a gun and someone to fire it: someone was still near, and she would take her chances that it was someone who would help, and not Calliope or some psycho Amish guy with a rifle from the 1800s. Maybe Lyra and Caelum had even gotten hold of a gun. Maybe they were trying to signal to her.

She hoped and prayed that they weren't on the wrong side of the bullet.

Either way, she would have to take her chance.

Gemma had never built a fire before – three of the four fireplaces at home were electric and functioned at the push of a button – but she'd watched her mom do it a few times, amused that Kristina had once been a tomboy and had spent her summers camping and hiking and hitchhiking between different beach towns, and amused, too, that Kristina always got so offended when Gemma said she couldn't imagine it.

Quickly, quickly, before they went away.

She tore handfuls of paper from the old textbook, saying a silent apology to the Book Gods for ruining the binding – and was pleased to find many of the pages at the center very dry. They lit up easily, flaming quickly into little bright universes that soon shriveled and burned up to nothing.

The wood was harder. She discarded all the wettest pieces and wound up with a small pile that she layered on top of a pyramid of crumpled pieces of paper. It would have to do.

She was shocked by how much smoke there was right away: smoke curled off the wood as if being planed by an invisible machine. The chemical smell of ink made her cough. She crouched as low as she could, suddenly very afraid. What if the wood *did* burn, so well, so quickly she couldn't control it?

Smoke climbed up the well, rolling from one side to another, like someone rappelling down a cave but in reverse. Gemma tilted her head and gasped with relief: the smoke had sniffed its way to the open air, had begun to trickle through the narrow gaps in the wood and lift toward the trees.

Someone would have to see.

Please, God. Let someone see.

The wood was still smoldering, releasing long tendrils of blue smoke that reminded Gemma of dark hair, that felt like hair in her mouth and in her throat. Her eyes and head hurt. Already, the air was very bad.

Should she put out the fire? Her head hurt so badly, she had trouble thinking through the pain. One more minute. She would wait one more minute.

The wood burst into flame, at last.

Gemma began to cough.

Her head now hurt so badly she couldn't think of anything at all.

She was very tired and thought, maybe, she should just lie down for a while, down in the mud, where it wasn't so hot. . . .

TWENTY-SEVEN

GEMMA DREAMED SHE WAS RIDING on the back of a giant bat, cupped in the soft leather of its wings. She dreamed that a veil had been placed over her face, to keep her from looking down and getting afraid, to keep her from crying out and startling out of the sky. But she couldn't breathe. The cloth was wet from her breathing, and it flowed into her open mouth. It tasted like smoke.

Briefly she woke up to the sound of voices and lights — hands everywhere, leathery hands, unfamiliar, and faces she didn't know — but she hovered there, on the edge of consciousness, for only a few seconds before the bat enfolded her in its wings and once again swept her up, this time loosing itself from the trees and hurtling across the clean, cool night air.

She could breathe again. The veil had come loose. Her sister had unhooked it, because she didn't like how it looked.

That's better, her sister, Emma, said. Except that Emma had Lyra's face, and Gemma knew, in her dream, that all along Lyra-who-was-Emma had simply disguised herself to give Gemma time to adjust to having a sister.

The bat had turned to a trundling donkey, and Gemma rocked back and forth, back and forth, while Lyra, who was her sister Emma, walked beside her. The sky above them was the color of milk. Was she dreaming or not? She was bound up in white sheets, as if prepared for burial, but she didn't feel afraid, not with her sister Lyra standing next to her and whispering to her, over and over, *Shhh. It's okay. You're okay now.*

TWENTY-EIGHT

'IS IT TRUE? DID YOU really lose a *finger*?' April didn't wait for Gemma to answer. 'That's so *awesome*. You got your finger blown off. Is it your middle finger?'

'Pinkie,' Gemma said.

'Oh, well, thank *God*,' April said. 'How else would you flick off Chloe DeWitt and the pack wolves? Seriously, that is the most badass thing I've ever heard. You're going to be Instagram famous, like, immediately.'

'Sure,' Gemma said. 'Maybe I'll even become a hand model.'

'Uh-huh.' April fed a Twizzler into her mouth, then offered one to Gemma. 'Maybe I'll get my finger blown off too. You know, so we can be twins.'

Gemma rolled her eyes. 'You're certifiably insane. You know that? You should be locked up.' But the knot in her chest had loosened. April had that effect: like a warm bath after you'd almost frozen to death.

Since Gemma had woken up – nearly eighteen hours since she'd first been admitted, time enough for April and her mothers to catch a flight to Philadelphia and then make the drive to Lancaster General – April had barely paused for breath.

She told Gemma how her mom Diana had helped her crack into Jake's computer after April admitted the story they'd cooked up about finding it in the library was in fact a fabrication.

'I should have known,' Diana said. 'When's the last time you two were at the library?'

'It took her, like, two seconds,' April said, deliberately ignoring the question. 'Meanwhile she can't use Snapchat to save her life.'

April had been hoping that there might be information on Jake's computer that would help them locate Gemma. Instead, she had found passwords to HavenFiles.com, lists of bloggers and journalists who'd expressed interest in what was really happening at Haven, hundreds of names and connections, data that Jake, out of precaution, out of fear, had kept secret.

But April, God love her, had never kept a secret in her whole life: she had flooded HavenFiles.com with new uploads, had emailed every single whistle-blower she could find online, had started a Truth Apocalypse, as she put it. Her mom Angela had even contacted the *New York Times*.

'Some detective talked to me,' she said. 'He wanted to know all about the Haven Files. All about Jake Witz, too.'

'Is April bugging you, Gem?' Diana asked, ruffling her daughter's hair.

'Yeah,' Gemma said. 'For about the past ten years.'

She was kidding, of course, though in truth, she didn't want to think about Jake Witz, or detectives, or the replicas escaped from the airport, and what would happen when the truth about them began to break. That would come later. For now, though, she liked to hear April's voice, and see Angela and Diana bickering over whose turn it was to run down to the canteen for coffee, and sit in the sun with her mother, clear-eyed, sitting next to her.

'Har-dee-har.' April made a face through a mouthful of Twizzler. 'All I'm saying is, when the shitstorm hits the—' But she didn't finish, because just then the door opened behind her, and Lyra and Caelum edged shyly into the room.

Gemma's heart leapt. They were both wearing hospital gowns, and Lyra was painfully pale, and still far, far too thin. But she was smiling, and alive.

'Looks like you have some more visitors,' Kristina said, reaching out a hand and smoothing Gemma's hair back.

'You're awake,' Gemma blurted. She had been asking since she had woken up that morning.

April treated Lyra and Caelum's arrival like she treated everything: as if it was exactly what she had expected all along. 'You're *heroes*,' April said, and then held out her bag of Twizzlers. 'Twizzler?'

Lyra shook her head. Caelum, however, took one, and Gemma couldn't help but smile.

'Come on.' Angela put a hand on April's shoulder. 'Let's leave them alone for a bit, okay?'

Gemma's mom stood up. 'I could use a cup of coffee, actually.'

April made a face. *Leaving Gemma alone* was not a concept April had ever been particularly good at. It was one of the things Gemma loved most about her.

'Yeah, sure,' she grumbled. 'But we'll come back, right? You can't get rid of me that easily.' She pointed a Twizzler at Gemma.

'I wouldn't dream of it,' Gemma said. Lyra and Caelum exchanged a look. She thought she saw a smile pass between them.

Kristina bent down to kiss Gemma's forehead. 'I'll be right back,' she said, and Gemma nodded to show it was okay for her to go.

'How are you?' Gemma asked, as soon as everyone else had left. She was worried about how pale Lyra looked. 'How are you feeling?'

But Lyra answered immediately.

'We're fine,' she said. Caelum took Lyra's hand, and Gemma felt a surge of love for them both. She struggled to find the words to express how she felt – how grateful she was.

'April was right,' she said at last. 'You're both heroes. I can't believe you found me.'

Slowly, Lyra smiled. It was the funniest thing. Her smile was like something that snuck up on her, like the kind of sun that begins by planting an elbow through the clouds and then begins to push, and push, until the whole sky is exposed.

'That's what friends do,' Lyra said. 'They find each other.'

Gemma knew, then, that Lyra understood. That the terrible things that had happened to her hadn't, after all, been more important than the love she had found.

'Exactly,' she said.

Suddenly, unexpectedly, Lyra came forward and put her arms around Gemma's shoulders, and squeezed. They had never hugged before. Gemma blinked away tears. She could feel Lyra's ribs through her back. She thought of a bird; she thought of the dream of being carried to safety on a pair of wings.

'Thank you,' Lyra said, twice. Then she pulled away, almost as if she was embarrassed. Without another word, she turned for the door.

Caelum lifted a hand, and quirked his mouth into a smile, and waved. Then they were gone.

Not a minute after they left, Kristina was back and fussing over Gemma. 'She's going to be okay, isn't she?' Gemma asked, after Lyra had slipped out, promising to lie down. She was consumed by a strange anxiety, a premonition that she wouldn't see Lyra again – or that she wouldn't see her for a long time.

Kristina sighed. She looked down at her hands. 'Lyra's very sick, Gemma.'

'I know that,' Gemma said. 'That isn't what I meant.' But she wasn't sure what she *did* mean. She was scared all over again, scared and full of love: she knew she couldn't save Lyra, and that was the scariest thing of all.

'I wish I had the answers,' Kristina said. That was one of the things Gemma loved about her mom: she wasn't a liar.

Kristina moved to the window and drew the curtains to let in the sun. Gemma blinked. Outside her window, a spider was weaving in one corner, putting the finishing touches on a web that looked like a blown-up snowflake.

'Your father called,' she said at last, almost casually. 'He wants to talk to you.'

'I don't want to see him,' Gemma said. 'I don't want to see him ever again.'

'Well.' Kristina turned away from the window again. She had no makeup on. Gemma couldn't remember the last time she'd seen her mom with no makeup. She looked gorgeous, Gemma thought. 'You can't avoid him forever.'

'Why not?' Gemma asked.

Kristina bit her lip. For a second, Gemma was sure – sure – she had been about to smile. But she sighed instead, and came toward the bed.

'Listen, Gem.' This time, when she brushed the hair out of Gemma's eyes, Gemma nearly cried. She'd missed her mom so badly. She'd been so afraid they'd never see each other again. 'I think . . . I want you to know – and I know this will be hard for you – that I don't think I'm going to go home. To your father, I mean. I think I'd like to get my own place. A place for just you and me.' Her throat was moving up and down, up and down, as if it was doing double duty just to get the words out. 'What do you say? I know things will be different. . . .'

But she didn't finish. Because Gemma started to laugh, and cry, both, imagining a little house where she and her mother would live together, she and her mother and their animals, all covered in pet hair, and nothing white at all.

TWENTY-NINE

DEEP DOWN, GEMMA HAD KNOWN that when Lyra hugged her – their first hug ever – she had meant it as a goodbye. She was right. By the next morning, Lyra and Caelum had vanished.

According to the nursing staff, they must have slipped out around dawn, unseen even by the stubbornest bloggers and tragedy tourists, through a little-used stairwell right by the ladies' room that led down into the parking lot.

They had practice, Gemma knew, in turning invisible.

She couldn't say she blamed Lyra and Caelum. They'd spent so much of their lives in closed rooms, surrounded by charts and IVs and sharp-edged equipment made for cutting. Gemma didn't blame them for not wanting to waste another minute.

'They'll be back,' Gemma said to her mother. 'They'll find us again, when they're ready. That's what friends do.'

She was sure, absolutely sure, that it was true. They just needed to find their own way back.

She was both desperate to see Pete and dreading it, but she couldn't delay it any longer; he was asking for her. Pete had gone into shock soon after being picked up by the police, and for nearly twenty-four hours he'd been in critical condition, floating in and out of consciousness, while they tried to regulate his organ functions and his temperature. His parents had flown up from Chapel Hill, and they told Gemma only after she'd been admitted did he stabilize. Even though he was unconscious, by then, kept under by a course of anesthesia, it was like he knew.

He'd been moved only that morning from the ICU to a recovery floor. Still, the room they had him in was dark, all the blinds sewn up against the light – 'so he doesn't get overwhelmed,' his mom said, and gave Gemma a hug, before slipping outside with her husband to give Gemma and Pete privacy.

He was propped up on several pillows, but his eyes were closed. She inched toward the bed, scared of waking him, and scared, too, that he wouldn't wake up. He was so pale, even in the dark she could see veins in his forearms and his chest. He was hooked up to an IV, and an EKG, and the sound brought Gemma back to her childhood, and terrified her: what if Pete was sicker than anyone thought?

But he opened his eyes when she kneed the bed accidentally, and smiled.

'Gemma,' he said. His voice sounded raw. Just hearing him say her name like that, like it was the name he'd been waiting to say his whole life, made her lose it.

'Oh my God.' She started to cry. She couldn't help it. She loved him so badly; she wanted him to know that. It didn't even matter whether he felt the same way. 'You look terrible.'

'Thanks,' he said. He cracked the smallest, faintest smile. 'I forgot my mascara at home.'

It was the second time in a day she'd laughed and cried at the same time. She managed to adjust the hospital bed, so she could climb in next to him, and he laid his head against her chest.

'I thought I would never see you again,' he whispered.

'Shhh.' She put her hands through his hair. 'I'm right here.'

'I was so scared.' His voice broke. In the dark, their bodies lost form: they could have been a single person, a single body entangled together in the sheets. 'What's going to happen, Gemma? What's going to happen to us?'

Gemma leaned back and closed her eyes. She imagined, somewhere in the woods of eastern Pennsylvania, a spider weaving a web in a well. After rain or wind came to destroy it, it wove. It wove with thread so fine it was almost invisible, and she wondered if the spider was ever afraid, that its life was bound up in something that could be blown away with a breath. It wove anyway, either way.

Spiders were funny that way. They leapt first, and the web followed. It was a kind of biological faith, that demanded belief and then turned it real.

'It's going to be okay,' Gemma said. 'Trust me.' She didn't know if it would. But she didn't know it wouldn't be either, and that, she thought, was what being human meant. You built your life into meaning, you transformed it into liquid faith, again and again, like a web; you did it blind, by instinct, because to not do it would be to stop living. And the darkness sieved through. It flowed and gathered and dropped, but it wasn't strong enough, wasn't real enough, to touch what you had made.

That was the true gift: to have a story that was still unfolding, like a thread unspooling, and as it did, this single thread separated light from dark, meaning from senselessness, hope from fear.

'It's going to be okay,' she repeated. She put a hand on Pete's chest, above his heart, and he put his hand on top of hers, so the rhythm of his heart passed through her palm and back to his. She heard, for a split second, the sound of his life and hers, drawn together along the string of an ancient instrument, and that string hummed with the sound of a thousand thousand other lives, and when she closed her eyes, she saw a spider buried deep underground, spinning music, pure music, for the world.

PROLOGUE

Monday, May 16, 3.19 a.m.

They looked nervous.

'Jumpy, you know,' he would say, and each time he saw them clearly in his mind: both of them skinny, with complexions the color and texture of wet clay, and eyes like someone had knuckled holes in their faces when they were still wet. 'Like they were on the run.'

Of course, plenty of the people who walked into the Four Crossings Motel looked nervous: it was that kind of place. And even if Guy's mom, Cherree, was always telling him to turn away anyone with track marks or the jumpy look of a major addict, he knew they'd only bought the place because she'd wanted to cash in on the pill poppers and dopeheads, a whole new generation of druggies – suburban moms, and men still wearing their ties from the office, and thirtysomething dental hygienists – who needed a place to crash while they got high.

And then there were the usual cheaters and hookers and lowlifes who came in and out regularly. Guy even knew some of their names. He'd gotten a hand job from one of the working girls, Shawn, who wasn't a girl at all, more like forty-seven. Up close, she'd smelled like barbecue potato chips.

He knew what people looked like when they were sleepless, desperate, guilty, and plain high out of their minds.

Gemma Ives. The girl's ID was all messed up, warped like it had gone through the washing machine, and the picture was scratched. He could tell she'd lost weight, though, since the picture was taken – if it even was her in the picture. The guy didn't have a license at all. He just wrote his name down in the register. It was all about covering your ass, Guy knew, if somebody flatlined in one of the rooms. They just needed to show due diligence. But their debit card matched the ID, and it worked, so he figured fuck it.

'One room, one night,' was all the girl had said. She kept looking over her shoulder, and every time the insects pinged against the glass, she jumped.

As if she were being watched.

As if she were being *followed.*

Two hundred and forty miles away, a different girl and a boy, both dressed in stolen clothing, both with a stack of stolen cash rubber-banded in their jeans, and their hair cropped so short it might recently have been shaved, slept together in the very last seat of a northbound Greyhound bus. Who knows what they were dreaming about? A sign announced they were coming up on Philadelphia, but they didn't stir, and the bus didn't stop, and they sailed on.

LAUREN OLIVER is the cofounder of the media and content development company Glasstown Entertainment, where she serves as the president of production. She is also the *New York Times* bestselling author of the YA novels *Replica*, *Vanishing Girls*, *Panic*, and the Delirium trilogy: *Delirium*, *Pandemonium*, and *Requiem*, which have been translated into more than thirty languages. The film rights to both *Replica* and Lauren's bestselling first novel, *Before I Fall*, were acquired by AwesomenessTV; *Before I Fall* has been made into a major motion picture.

Her novels for middle grade readers include *The Spindlers*, *Liesl & Po*, and the Curiosity House series, cowritten with H. C. Chester. She has written one novel for adults, *Rooms*.

A graduate of the University of Chicago and NYU's MFA program, Lauren Oliver divides her time between New York, Connecticut, and a variety of airport lounges. You can visit her online at www.laurenoliverbooks.com.

FOLLOW LAUREN OLIVER ON

LYRA

LAUREN OLIVER

RINGER
LYRA

HODDER &
STOUGHTON

PART I

ONE

LYRA HAD STARTED COLLECTING THINGS. When she saw something she liked, she pocketed it, and usually by the end of the day she was weighty with the sloughed-off skin of someone else's life: losing lottery tickets, Snapple bottle caps, ATM receipts, pens, chewed-up foil that came off the cheap bottles of wine sold down at Two Brothers Beer & Liquor.

In the privacy of her small room in the double-wide trailer gifted to them by Gemma's father, which to Lyra, formerly known as 24, felt very luxurious, she shook out her new belongings on the comforter and tried to listen, tried to hear them speak to her of this new world and her place in it. Her old belongings had spoken: the bed at Haven had whispered, and the Invacare Snake Tubing asked questions, the snobby syringes had insulted her with their sharp little bite, and the long-nosed, greedy biopsy needles used for marrow extraction had always wanted gossip, more and more of it.

But these new objects told her nothing, spoke of nothing. Or maybe it was just that the outside world was so noisy she couldn't hear.

She was no longer a human model. She was a she, not an *it*. But it was now, here, with a room of her own and photographs from her earliest childhood Scotch-taped to the walls, that she didn't know who or what she was.

Here she could wake when she wanted and eat what she liked, although since she'd never prepared her own food, she and Caelum, who had been 72 until she named him, mostly subsisted on cans of soda and granola bars Rick bought from the grocery store. They did not know how to fry an egg. Rick taught her to use a can opener, but the microwave bothered her; its humming energy reminded her of Mr I.

Caelum spent hours sitting cross-legged on the couch, watching whatever channel happened to be on when he first pressed the power button: news channels, movie channels, and his favorite, the Home Shopping Network. Lyra had learned to read. Caelum learned how to watch. He learned the world through the things it bought and sold.

He did not want to learn how to read.

There were sixty-two trailers in the Winston-Able

Mobile Home Park, and the whole thing could have been slotted down comfortably in two of Haven's wings. But to Lyra it seemed infinitely bigger, because it was unknown, because of all the things she'd never seen before: wind chimes and old Halloween decorations and cars on cinder blocks and pink plastic flamingos; lawn chairs and bar-becues.

Caelum stayed inside and watched the world through the pinhole of the TV screen, and Lyra walked for hours a day and put things in her pockets and sorted through them like an archeologist trying to decode hieroglyphs. They were both trying to learn in their own way, she thought, but she didn't like it even so. Sameness was the only way she had ever understood who she was. What she was. Now, everything had changed. He was inside, and she was outside, and that made them different – at least, during the day.

Night came again and again like a tide foaming over the trailers and the cars and the scrubby trees, and turning it all to the same smudge of darkness, rubbing shapes into shadows. The night broke Lyra and Caelum's separate-ness. It collapsed the space between them; they fell into its depth and landed, blind, together.

Rick worked the graveyard shift, and when he didn't, he went to bed early, still sweating a faint chemical smell. Every night, Lyra and Caelum walked down to the unoccupied trailers on lots 57 and 58. He found a garden hose, and in the sticky air they'd let it flow, drink from it, throw water between their hands at each other just for the fun of it, because fun was new.

They kissed. They kissed for hours, until Lyra's lips were sore and tender to touch, still heavy with the pressure of his mouth. With her tongue she found the ridges of his teeth, and the soft rhythms of his tongue in response. She touched the vault of his mouth and the strange slick texture of the inner side of his cheeks. She let him do the same, let him learn her through his tongue. Sometimes it was kissing, and sometimes it was something like learning, like collecting seashells, the way Cassiopeia had, turning them over and over to memorize the miracle of ridges and whorls built by thousands of years of soft water.

They played a game where their eyes stayed closed and they had to see with their mouths instead. Lyra knew bodies for what they did and what they failed to do, and her only feelings had been in sickness or in pain. She learned the soft wonder of the human body on the planes of his chest, and on the angles of his shoulders, and in the soft fuzz of hair, like the gentlest kiss, below his belly button. She learned it on his scalloped ears, and on his kneecaps, and on his long and gentle fingers.

She learned his body, and she learned that her body

was a strange and watery thing that pooled and flowed and turned all at once to a current; the pressure of his tongue, on her neck, on her nipples, on her thighs, turned her into a million other things. She became air and the electric possibility of lightning. She became a furred animal, howling in summer. She became his mouth, and she existed in his mouth. She poured her whole body into the radius of the circles he made with his tongue. And at the same time her body became huge, like a long shout of joy hanging in the quiet.

They had a game to kiss each other on every scar, slowly, starting from the neck. They had a game to find the darkest place they could and touch each other until they couldn't keep track of whose body was where. *Your knee or mine?* he would say. *Your hand or mine?* They had a game to act like the night when it came, and erase all the space between them, to lose their bodies entirely, until they didn't know who was holding and who was being held. She didn't have a name for some of the things they did, only a melody, a rhythm that hummed in her skin after they were done.

She wanted things she hardly understood: to be closer, closer, closer than bodies could ever be. She wanted to take her body off and for him to shed his, too, and to stand like two shadows overlapping with not a shiver of space between them.

And she wanted to keep her body, so he would keep kissing it.

She learned how to tell time, and every morning, she counted the hours until dark, when Caelum was no longer Caelum, and she was no longer Lyra, and both of them became each other.

She was terrified that one day it wouldn't work, that the distance would put up a hand, and hold them apart.

TWO

AND THEN, ON THURSDAY, IT happened.

At Haven, Lyra had been bored so often that, para-doxically, she had almost never been bored at all. Little things consumed her attention: the petty squabbles she imagined between her belongings; the replicas who went to the Box or were disciplined by the nurses; her small missions, planned and executed with all the precision of a military invasion, to steal words from medicine bottle labels or even the nurses' cigarette packs.

But now that there was so much to see, so much to do, she was often bored. On Thursday, a bright day of puffed-up clouds, the world beyond her windows looked dizzy in its own light. But when Lyra suggested to Caelum that they take a walk, he looked at her with eyes burned like wounds in his face.

'No,' he said. And then, looking back at the TV, 'This isn't my place.'

Caelum had wanted to escape. He'd been Code Black. And now when Lyra thought of Haven and what had happened to it, her memories were intertwined with him, with the moment she'd slipped through the fence past the drums of old construction litter and biohazard signs and where he'd first touched her wrist. If she had known about the world, about space and time, she would have known that matter bends the universe around it. But even without knowing that, she saw how Caelum had bent her universe, and made everything change.

He had wanted to be free, and to see how real people lived. But now they were free and he wouldn't go outside except at night, when there was nothing at all to see. He learned the world only from what he saw on TV.

'It will never be your place if you don't try,' Lyra said.

'It will never be my place even if I do,' he said.

She went alone. Going anywhere by herself thrilled and terrified her, no matter how often she did it. At Haven she had almost never been alone. There were nurses to accompany them everywhere, and researchers to watch behind glass. There were the silhouettes of the medical machines themselves, and the doctors to operate them. And of course, there were thousands of replicas, all of them dressed identically except for their bracelet tags. They ate and bathed and showered together. They moved together as a single mass, like a swarm of gnats, or a thundercloud.

'Hey. You. I'm talking to you.'

Lyra turned around, still unused to people who addressed her directly, who looked in her eyes instead of at her forehead or shoulder blades. Something strange had happened to her in the outside world: she had begun to forget how to stay invisible.

The girl outside lot 47 was chewing gum and smoking a cigarette from something that resembled a pen. After a closer look Lyra recognized it as the kind of e-cigarette some of the nurses had smoked. 'You're new here,' she said, exhaling a cloud of vapor.

It didn't sound like a question, so Lyra didn't answer. She put a hand in her pocket, feeling her newest acquisition: a cold metal bolt she'd found half-embedded in the dirt.

The girl stood up. She was skinny, though not as thin as Lyra, and wearing low-waisted shorts and a shirt that showed off her stomach. She had a birthmark that made a portion of her face darker than the rest. Lyra had once seen something similar, on one of the infants in the Yellow crop before they died in the Postnatal wing.

'My friend Yara thinks you're a bitch,' the girl said calmly, exhaling again. 'Cuz you never talk or say hi to anyone. But I don't think you're a bitch. I think you're just scared. That's it, isn't it? You're scared because you came from somewhere else and never expected to end up here, and now you're wondering if you'll ever get out.'

Once again, Lyra said nothing. She didn't know what a bitch was, although she thought, years ago, she might have heard the word – something to do with Nurse Em, one of the other staff members complaining about her.

'So?' The girl's eyes were a dark, rich color that reminded Lyra of the mud along the banks in the marshes, teeming with invisible life. 'Who's right? Me or Yara?'

'Neither,' Lyra said. She was startled by the way her voice rolled across the short distance between them. Even though it had been weeks since she'd left Haven, she wasn't in the habit of speaking. When Caelum came out with her at night, or when he snuck into her room and slid into bed beside her, they rarely spoke out loud. They breathed and touched, communicating through language of the body: pressure and touch, tension and release. 'I never thought I'd end up here. I didn't know there was a here to end up. But I'm not worried about getting out. This *is* out.' She stopped herself from saying anything she shouldn't.

To Lyra's surprise, the girl smiled. 'I knew you weren't as dumb as you looked. Half the people round here could double for shitbricks, so you never know. I'm Raina. What's your name?'

Lyra almost said *twenty-four*. Rick always called her Brandy-Nicole. But she had lost so many things in her life; she wasn't ready to lose her name, too, and the memory of the woman who'd given it to her.

'Lyra,' she said.

Raina smiled. 'You drop out of school or something?'

Lyra didn't know how to answer.

'School's dumb anyways,' Raina said. 'I finished last year and look at me now, on the nine-to-five shift at Fantasia.' She tilted her head and Lyra thought of the funny, knob-kneed birds that used to scuttle through the gardens at Haven, looking for crabs as small as the fingernails of the infants in Postnatal. The only part of her that wasn't skinny was her stomach, which had the faintest swell, as if there were a tiny fist inside of it. 'You want a Coke?'

Lyra almost said no.

But instead, almost accidentally, she said yes.

Lyra was with Raina, and then she was home, and she couldn't remember anything that had happened in between. She'd obviously fallen down. Her palms stung and there were flecks of gravel in her skin. Her knee was bleeding.

It was happening more frequently now, these jump cuts in her mind. She knew that what they'd done to her at Haven, what they'd grown in her, was to blame, and remembered that Gemma had said prions made holes grow in the brain, slowly at first, then faster and faster.

That was exactly what it felt like: like holes, and hours of her life simply dropped through them.

Rick's car, tawny with dust, was parked in front of lot 16, and the lightning bugs were up, as well as swarms of no-see-ums that rose in dark clouds. She heard raised voices as she came up the porch steps, but it wasn't until she was standing inside, under the bright overhead lights on a secondhand *Welcome Home* mat, that she saw Caelum and Rick had been fighting. Their last words slotted belatedly up to her consciousness.

It's enough now. You can't stay here if you don't find a way to help.

Both of them turned to look at her. Caelum she couldn't read. But Rick's eyes were raw, and his expression she knew from the youngest researchers at Haven whenever they accidentally messed up an IV and blood began to spurt or the replicas cried out: guilt.

'What's going on?' she asked.

'Nothing,' Rick said quickly. Patches of scalp showed through his hair, shiny and bright red. 'Nothing. Just having a family talk, that's all.'

'You're not family,' Caelum said. 'You said so yourself.'

Rick stared at him for a long minute. Then he shook himself, like a dog, and moved for the door.

'I'm working a double,' he said. 'I just came back for a bite. I'll be home later tonight.' He stopped in front of her and reached out two fingers to touch her shoulders. This was a gesture they'd agreed on, an expression of affection she could tolerate. 'Will you be all right?'

'Yes,' Lyra said. She knew he wanted more from her but wasn't sure what or how to give it to him. Sometimes Lyra tried to see herself in his nose and jaw and smile, tried to climb down a rope of feelings to get to one that made sense, but he still looked like a stranger, and felt like one, too. He had given her photographs from when she was a baby, but they felt like images from someone else's life.

'Okay. Good. Okay.' He dropped his hand. The noise was loud in the quiet. Then he was gone, leaving Caelum and Lyra alone.

The room smelled faintly sour, as it always did. Another thing Lyra had not gotten used to was the dirt in the corners and the insects that tracked behind the faucet, plates and pans half-crusted in the sink when Rick went to work, fruit flies that lifted in clouds from the garbage, and the giant water bugs that came up from the drains in the shower.

Caelum stared at Lyra for a second, then turned back to the TV, although he didn't sit down.

'What happened?' she said. It wasn't the first time that Caelum and Rick had fought. Several times she had been startled into awareness by the sound of raised voices, or come out of her bedroom to find them standing too close together. 'What did he say to you?'

'Nothing.' Caelum turned up the volume. Words flashed on the screen, but they were gone too fast for Lyra to read them. 'What happened to your knee?'

So he'd noticed. Lyra bent down and thumbed the blood off. She'd heard at Haven that blood was only red after it oxidized. Strange the way everything changed on contact with the world.

'Nothing,' she said, since that was the answer he'd given her.

'You were gone for a long time,' he said. It wasn't exactly a question, but Lyra nodded. 'Where were you?'

'I made a friend,' Lyra said, and nearly regretted it when Caelum looked up, his face seizing around a quick spasm of pain. 'She invited me to a party on Saturday. You're invited too.'

'A party,' he said. He said the word as if it were in a different language, the way the birthers had said *water* or *help* or *doctor,* if they spoke English at all. 'Why?'

'There's no reason,' she said. She didn't have an answer. But this made her defensive, not embarrassed. 'It's what people do.'

'People,' he repeated. Now he made the word sound like a medicine that turned bitter as it dissolved. '*Your* people.'

'Don't,' she said. They had gone through this before, when Gemma had first told her that she had a father, that she wasn't really a replica. *I thought we were the same. But we're not. We're different,* Caelum had said, but she hadn't believed him then.

But now a new voice began to whisper. *Maybe he was right.*

'I can't stay here much longer,' he said. '*He* doesn't want me here.' Caelum refused to use Rick's name. 'And you don't, either.'

'Of course I do,' Lyra said.

Caelum just shook his head. 'You have a new life here,' he said.

All the anger she'd been keeping down broke free. It was like a rope whipping up words in her chest. 'Why did you leave Haven?' she burst out. 'Why did you run away? What do you *want*?'

'I got what I wanted,' he said, and with a quick step came closer to her. In an instant everything stilled and went white, and she thought he was going to say *you*, and wings of feeling lifted in her chest. But instead he said, 'I wanted to do something on my own. For myself. I wanted to choose.'

'So you chose. Congratulations.' In words, now, she heard the echo of Raina's voice, the edge of her sarcasm. 'Are you happy now?'

'Happy.' He shook his head. 'You even talk like one of them now.'

'So what?' She hated him then. More than she'd hated any of the doctors or the nurses or the sanitation teams who'd bundled up the dead replicas in paper sheaths, making jokes the whole time: *How many clones does it take to screw in a lightbulb?* 'So I talk like them. So maybe I have a friend. What's wrong with that?'

'It's a lie, that's what's wrong with it,' he said. 'You're sick.'

'You don't seem sick,' Lyra said automatically, and only registered a split second later that he hadn't, in fact, said *we're sick*. And with a kind of yawning horror she realized that what she had said was true. Caelum had been so skinny when they met that his collarbones stood out like wings. But he had put on weight. He didn't get nauseous, not that she could see, and he never got confused, like she did.

There was a long, terrible moment of silence.

'You're not sick,' she said at last. She could barely get the words out. Then: 'What cluster were you in?'

He looked away. She closed her eyes, tried to picture him as she'd first seen him, his wild eyes and dirt-encrusted fingernails, the wristband looped around his dark skin . . .

He said it at the same time she remembered. 'White.'

It was stupid she'd never wondered, stupid she'd never asked. It was all her fault.

White was *control*.

And control meant that he was fine.

'Lyra . . .' He tried to reach for her and she backed away from him, nearly toppling the table in the front hall, bumping against the door. 'I'm going to find a way to fix it. I promise. I'm going to find a way to help.'

When he tried to touch her again she lurched past him, knocking a coat from the rack pegged to the wall. She felt like she would cry. She hardly ever cried.

Maybe this too was something that had *oxidized*: her feelings had changed color, and flowed more quickly now. She imagined that inside of her, the prions pooled like dark shadows, waiting to swallow her up.

'You can't help me,' she said. 'No one can.'

THREE

FOR TWO DAYS, SHE HARDLY saw Caelum at all, and she felt nothing but terrible relief, like after you finally drop a glass that has been slipping for some time from your fingers.

Caelum was her tether to Haven, but he was also her anchor. Around him she felt stuck in her old life, stuck in her old name. 24. The escaped replica, the human model, the monster.

Rick told her that he'd put Caelum to work. There was little he could do, because in order to become someone in the outside world, you *already* had to be someone, which required pieces of paper and numbers from the government and identification that neither Lyra nor Caelum had. But Rick had met a guy who owned a tow company and impound lot and needed help on the grave-yard shift, from midnight to 8 a.m. He was prepared to pay cash, and he would ask no questions.

Money, Lyra was learning, was a source of near-constant worry in the outside world, as it had been in Haven. At Haven the staff had talked constantly about budget cuts and even the possibility of having funding cut off completely. But it surprised her to find out that money everywhere was so difficult to get and hang on to. Gemma's father had offered them a large sum of money, but Rick had refused it, and when Lyra asked him why, his face darkened.

'Blood money,' he said. 'It's bad enough I have to lean on him for a roof. I won't take a dollar I don't have to.'

She had a hard time thinking of Rick Harliss as poor, since he had a car and his own TV and his own narrow house, a bathroom only the three of them shared, multiple sets of clothes – all things that to her seemed rich.

But they *were* poor, at least that was what Rick said. And while Lyra was his daughter and it was his duty to protect her, Caelum was freeloading – *stealing time from the clock,* Rick said – and would have to figure out how to make his own way in the world.

Lyra should have heard the threat in those words: that Caelum would have to leave, sooner or later.

On Friday and Saturday morning, after his first two shifts, Caelum left piles of dollar bills on the small kitchen table, secured beneath a can of Hormel chili, and Rick took the money wordlessly and bought more Hormel chili from the store, more toilet paper and toothpaste, more pairs of socks and books for Lyra to read, all of them with creased pastel covers and heroes who always arrived at the right moment.

For two days, Lyra was happy – despite the holes dropping hours of her life, despite the fact that she and Caelum had had their first fight ever, despite the way she had to pick through the boredom of the day on her own, collecting ever more pieces of trash, arranging them and rearranging them as if they would someday yield a sentence. She visited with Raina, and was absorbed in an endless funnel of people, ideas, and places she'd never heard of – Los Angeles, the neo-Nazis in lot 14, veganism, YouTube, Planned Parenthood, the Bill of Rights.

She was angry at Caelum for lying to her, even though she realized he'd never said he was sick and she had never asked. Still, she was angry. He resented her for becoming something he could never be, but there was no greater abandonment than this: she would die, and he would live.

Even so, she never thought she might lose him for good. He had been absorbed into her life, into the constellation of her reality now growing to include the small trailer on lot 16; moths beating against the screens and spiders drowning in the sink, Raina and her parties, clothing purchased from the Salvation Army by the pound. Her whole life she'd experienced as a series of circles, days that repeated themselves, procedures that happened again and again weekly or monthly or yearly, birthdays that passed without celebration to mark them. Even the fence at Haven had been a rough circle, and Spruce Island had been bounded by water on all sides.

Things didn't change. They just returned to what they were before. And she and Caelum would return, again and again, to each other.

She should have learned, by now, that nothing was ever so easy.

On Saturday, she didn't see Caelum at all. In the morning, she found his mattress – concealed behind an ugly fuchsia curtain Rick had strung up from a shower rod – empty and the bed neatly made. But he'd come home at some point: she saw that he'd left money for Rick. Next to the bed was a shoe box he used for his belongings, and when she opened it, she felt like someone had just tapped the center of her rib cage. He, too, had obviously been collecting things when he went out: old coins, a bus schedule, an empty cigarette pack, a brochure, a receipt carefully unfolded and weighted beneath a tin labeled *Altoids*. She felt a sudden, hard aching for him. At Haven, she had once had an Altoids tin, had kept it stashed carefully in her pillowcase.

He wasn't home by the time she left to meet Raina, and she couldn't leave a note for him. She didn't know how to write and he wouldn't be able to read it. She wasn't sure what she would say, anyway.

She and Raina walked together to Ronchowoa, a town lobbed down in the middle of nowhere as if it was made by God's spit. (That's how Raina put it.) Lyra still didn't like being out on the road, and got jumpy whenever she saw a sedan with dark-tinted windows. But it was hard to be nervous when Raina was around. She never stopped talking, for one thing. Just listening to her took up all of Lyra's attention.

'The Vasquez brothers will be there for sure, they think they're hot shit because their dad has four car dealerships in Knox County. Watch out for Sammy Vasquez, he'll have his hands down your pants before he even knows your name. . . .' She laughed. She had a laugh like a solid punch. 'I don't know. Maybe you should let him. I hear you got caught tonguing your own cousin.'

Caelum and Lyra had said they were cousins when they first arrived, because Rick had said it and then they'd repeated it, if anyone asked. 'He's not exactly my cousin.'

'Yeah, I got some *cousins* like that.' Raina smirked. 'What is he, anyway? Chinese or Korean or something? He's all mixed-up-looking. Cute, though.'

'I don't know,' Lyra said. Many of the replicas had been

grown from stem cell tissue purchased on the sly from clinics and hospitals, and no one knew exactly where the genotypes had come from.

'It's all right. My first was a Haitian. My mom nearly flipped her shit. You know, you could be pretty if you weren't so *basic*.' This was another thing Raina did: slid sideways into new thoughts without any warning. 'You ever think of cleaning up a bit?'

They went to the big Target, whose bright-white look and antiseptic smell reminded Lyra painfully of Haven. In the cosmetics aisle Raina opened tubes of lipstick and little plastic-shrouded tubs of eye shadow, experimenting with color on Lyra's cheeks and on the back of her hand, keeping up her nonstop stream of conversation.

'You got big eyes, that's good, and your lips are decent too. . . .'

She'd almost finished with Lyra's eyes when a woman in a red polo shirt came to yell at them. 'What do you think you're doing? Those aren't for sampling.'

'Well, how was I supposed to know?' Raina made her face go blank and dumb, and Lyra had a sudden memory of some of the Yellow crop back at Haven, a bad crop full of replicas who *failed to thrive*. After the Yellow crop, God mandated that all the newest replicas needed at least two hours of human contact a day.

'Don't give me that duff. I've seen you in here before.'

The woman had a name tag, S-A-M. 'I've half a mind to call the cops on you myself.'

'Don't,' Raina said. 'We'll pay for everything. We always meant to, anyway.'

The woman shook her head again. But she said, 'All right. Follow me.'

They were halfway to the checkout lanes when Raina gripped Lyra's elbow and steered her instead toward the exits. They were almost at the door before S-A-M realized they were no longer following and shouted.

'Run,' Raina said, and keeping her grip on Lyra's arm, she and Lyra hurtled toward the exit. An alarm screamed. Memories lit up flash-like in Lyra's head: Code Black, the sweaty heat, a spring storm that knocked out the power and forced the generators on. They were in the parking lot. They were laughing, and the sky was spinning overhead, and Lyra was dizzy with a sudden happiness that punched her breath out of her chest. She had never laughed like that – she was surprised by how it came, in waves that rocked her whole body and made her feel fizzy and bright and airless.

Raina's trailer was the same size as Rick's but even more cluttered, and Lyra felt a pang to see so many possessions worn and used and taken for granted – family photos hung crookedly in plastic frames, throw pillows shaggy with dog hair, mugs holding a crown of pens. By comparison, Rick's trailer was as cold and impersonal as the hallways of Haven.

On a side table sheeted with mail, she noticed the same glossy brochure she had seen in Caelum's shoe box of belongings. This time she focused on the letters until they ran into meaning: *Nashville Elvis Festival.*

Raina caught her looking. 'Don't tell me you're an Elvis freak too?'

Lyra didn't answer: silence, as always, was like a corner for retreating.

'My mom goes every year. Can you believe she met her boyfriend there? Look. He even made it into the brochure.' Raina shook out the folds of the brochure so it opened suddenly into a fan of narrow pages, and Lyra lost her breath.

Replicas. Dozens of them, all men, identically dressed in white, but not in hospital gear: in suits with beautiful detailing.

They looked well-fed. They looked well, period.

'That's Mike,' Raina said, and plugged a finger on one of the replicas in the third row. 'He won two years ago. My mom saw him perform "Hound Dog" and walked right up to him and asked him out.' She rolled her eyes. 'It's been true love ever since.'

'I don't understand.' Lyra's voice sounded distant to her. 'Where is this place?'

Raina shot her a puzzled look. 'You've never been to Nashville?' When Lyra shook her head, Raina frowned. 'Where did you come from, again?'

'Florida,' Lyra said, although she had never known where she was from until Gemma had told her. She knew only Haven, and Spruce Island, and Barrel Key. She hadn't understood the world was so big it had to be endlessly divided: into countries, states, towns, neighborhoods. Was it possible the world was so big it included places, like this Nashville, where replicas were made and lived happily, in the open? 'We – we had replicas there too.'

Raina squinted, like she was trying to see Lyra from a distance. 'Impersonators, you mean?'

Lyra shook her head; she didn't know. Her body had turned to vapor. She was suddenly overwhelmed by a sense of all the things in the world she didn't understand coming toward her, a hard high wave she couldn't duck or ride. But she clung to the idea of a place where replicas could smile and be photographed in the open: it was a reedy, ropy line of hope.

'I think the whole thing's stupid,' Raina said. 'A bunch of grown men dressing up like some dead rock star from a thousand years ago. I mean, his music isn't even that good.'

'What do you mean, dressing up?' Lyra asked.

'Well, you know, dyeing their hair, growing sideburns, shopping for costumes and stuff. I mean, it's just make-believe. But Mike acts like he really *is* Elvis.' Then, seeing Lyra's face: 'Don't tell me you don't know who Elvis is.'

Lyra, miserably confused, said, 'He's like the God in Nashville?'

She was reassured when Raina laughed and agreed. 'Oh, for sure,' she said. 'He is definitely the God in Nashville.'

In the bathroom, Raina finished Lyra's makeup, and then dressed her, too.

'You look nervous,' she said, when she stepped back to evaluate her work. 'Are you nervous?'

Lyra shook her head. In her mind she had already passed through the party and returned home; Caelum would for sure have come home by now. She didn't know whether he'd collected the brochure by chance. She didn't know whether he'd even looked through it – surely he would have told her. And that meant that *she* could tell *him*. She would give him this enormous gift, and he would understand that she had forgiven him and that they were still, after all, the same.

'You ever been to a party before?'

There had been a Christmas party at Haven every year, but only for the nurses and researchers and staff. For weeks, administrative staff bolted garlands of sweet-smelling greenery to the walls and lumped colored tinsel across the security desks and strung big red ribbons in the entry hall. The night of the party only a skeleton staff remained, and they were blurry-eyed and rowdy, wearing crooked fur-trimmed red hats and strange bulky sweaters over their uniforms.

Then, the Choosing: a handful of male doctors who came staggering into the dorms sweating the smell of alcohol swabs.

'Not exactly,' Lyra said.

'Didn't think so,' Raina said. 'You'll love it. Trust me.'

Raina put cream in Lyra's hair – which was longer than she'd ever had it, feathery and thin, the color of new wood – and set a timer for fifteen minutes. By then the sting of chemicals made Lyra's eyes water. Lyra bent over to rinse out the dye and afterward Raina finger-combed it and set it with gel.

'Don't look,' she said, when Lyra started to turn. 'Not yet.'

She sprayed Lyra down with something called Vixen. She reached into Lyra's shirt, and hoisted her breasts in their borrowed bra, and laughed when Lyra didn't even flinch. Then she spun Lyra around to face the mirror.

The girl looking back at her was a stranger, with white-blond hair and smoky eyes and a tank top that barely cleared the bottom of her breasts. Tight stomach, hips suctioned into their jeans.

'How do you like that, Pinocchio?' Raina slung an arm around her shoulders. 'I knew I'd turn you into a real girl.'

FOUR

IT WAS NEARLY EIGHT O'CLOCK when they set out, and the sun was low. Lyra had always liked this time of day, when the light turned everything softer and edged it in gold. Even the Winston-Able Mobile Home Park looked beautiful at this time, all the slinky cats sunning their final hour and patchy gravel roads deep with shadows and everyone coming back from work but not drunk or angry yet. She felt new, walking with Raina, her friend, side by side, smelling like a stranger, in borrowed clothes. She *felt* like a stranger, as if she'd put on not just someone else's clothes but a whole identity.

All her life she'd been smoothed and blunted down to an object, had her body handled, touched, manipulated without her permission, until even she had come to see it as a kind of external thing, a stone or a piece of wood. For the first time she felt her breasts and legs and hips as *hers*,

truly hers, a delicious inner secret like all of her belongings, tucked away for safekeeping in her room.

They stopped by lot 16 to see whether Caelum had
come home yet, even though Raina made fun of her
for having a kissing cousin. ('That's some real hick shit,'
she said. 'Too hick even for us out here.') But he hadn't
returned. His bed was still neatly made. Lyra didn't know
whether to be relieved or disappointed and was a bit of
both.

Eagle Tire was a big factory on the other side of the
weigh station. To get there, Lyra and Raina shimmied
beneath a fence and skirted between enormous trucks,
then had to pick their way over a trash-strewn lot.

Inside, and despite all the blown-out windows, it was
hot. It smelled like smoke and urine, and the walls were
soot-blackened from a decade's worth of fire pits, since
transients and homeless people squatted there when it
started to get cold. Almost immediately, Lyra regretted
coming. All the kids knew one another, and half of them
snickered when they saw Lyra, as if they could also see
24, sticking out at awkward angles, underneath. Some of
them were from Winston-Able, and a few girls asked her
where her *cousin* was, lingering on the word and making
it sound like something bad Lyra had done.

'Ignore them,' Raina said, as if it were that easy. Lyra
didn't see how she could ignore them when *they* were

everywhere. There were more people massed into the empty rooms of Eagle Tire, more people crunching over broken glass and shouting through the cavernous halls, than she had ever seen outside the Stew Pot at Haven.

At Haven there had been rules, the explicit ones – rise at bell, listen to the nurses and doctors, stay out of all the doors marked with a circle and a red bar, don't bother the guards – and hundreds of secret rules, too, that grew invisibly and were absorbed like mold spores through the skin. She'd thought it was because Haven was an institute, but out here there were just as many rules, as many codes and ways of behaving. And Raina's explanations only made Lyra more confused.

'There are those bitches from East Wyatt; just because they got rezoned into PCT now they think they're hot shit,' she said. 'Oh. And check it out. Those are the McNab sisters; don't talk to them, whole family's cursed, their grandfather killed himself and that's what got it started. You know, because of it being a sin and everything.' In the dark, Raina looked much paler, like one of the silvery fish that finned through the shallows near the beach at Haven. 'Now every generation, someone dies in a freak accident. They lost their mom to a fluke at Formacine Plastics last year.'

What was rezoning? Or a bitch, for that matter? What

did it mean to be cursed? She knew what sins were –
Nurse Don't-Even-Think-About-It had often quoted
from the Bible – but not why it would be a sin to commit
suicide. At Haven, it was only a sin because the replicas
were expensive to make.

But regular people came cheap. Didn't they?

Before she could ask, Raina seized her arm. 'Don't
look now,' she said. 'Remember those Vasquez boys I was
telling you about?' She got no further. Two boys shouldered through the crowd, one tall and skinny with the
crowded eyes of a fish, the other shorter, more muscular,
his arms dark with tattoos.

'Oh no,' one of the Vasquez brothers said to Raina.
'Who let the dogs out?'

She crossed her arms. 'Same person who let you out of
your cage, I guess.'

Lyra found herself standing next to the other brother,
the shorter one with the tattoos. 'Cool hair,' he said. He lit
a cigarette that didn't smell like a cigarette. It was stron-
ger and reminded her not unpleasantly of the smell of the
marshes when the tide was low. 'You know what they say
about girls with short hair?'

'No,' she said.

'Freaks in bed.' He exhaled. It was so dark she could
hardly see his face, just the wet glistening of his lips. 'Is
it true?'

'Go suck on a tailpipe, Leo,' Raina said, and put a hand on Lyra's arm to steer her away. 'I *told* you they were retrogrades,' she said. 'Their mom's a boozehound. Must have dropped them one too many times on their heads, that's what I think.'

The next room they came to must have been an office once: it was smaller and reeked of cigarette smoke. Someone's belongings were piled on a mattress in the corner. All the walls were covered with writing, but she couldn't make out what the words meant. Tendrils of wire punched through the walls and ceiling. Someone had brought speakers and people were dancing. A boy offered her a drink in a can and she took it, thinking it was soda. Then she took a sip and immediately spat it out, wetting Raina's shoes.

'Oh, for fuck's sake,' Raina said, and for a quick second, a new face dropped into place over her old one and she looked annoyed – annoyed, and embarrassed.

All at once, Lyra knew she shouldn't have come. Raina didn't want her there. Lyra could see it. She recognized the look on Raina's face; it was the way the nurses looked when they discovered that one of the replicas had wet the bed or gnawed the edge off a pillow or been eating paint chips from the windowsill, like 108 had done when she was hungry.

'I'm sorry,' Lyra whispered.

Raina's expression softened. 'That's okay. I hate Bud Light, too.'

But it was too late. Lyra, ashamed, knew how Raina really felt. She was Raina's project, and she was failing, and they both knew it.

She shoved her way back through the room, which had only gotten more crowded. The echo of so many voices had invaded her memory, so all the shouting seemed to be coming from some old association; she was worried she might throw up, or drop into a hole and lose minutes, hours. Someone grabbed her and she nearly screamed, but it was just a girl with hair sculpted high and breath that smelled like hand sanitizer, saying, 'Watch where you're going, bitch.'

Lyra pulled away. Somehow she made it outside. She crunched over the vacant lot, watching for needles, as Raina had instructed her to do. She passed between cargo trucks at the weigh station next to the fizz and hiss of highway traffic and ducked beneath the loose fence. Her eyes burned. She rubbed them with a fist, smearing her makeup.

She'd been stupid to believe, even for a second, that she might someday belong in this world, among these people. She belonged only to Haven, now as ever. Caelum was right all along.

She was cutting between the straggly overgrowth that

had reclaimed the abandoned trailers at lots 19 and 20 when she heard the murmur of voices. Edging past the water hookup across a splinter of exposed concrete, she saw through a web of blistered tree branches an unfamiliar sedan parked directly in front of lot 16, not ten feet away. A man and a woman stood together on the porch. The woman was trying to see in past the slat of drawn blinds that covered the window.

Lyra froze. Although they were dressed in normal clothing, she had no trouble at all recognizing them. She had spent her lifetime around Suits. She read power from minor details, from small differences in the way people stood and spoke and acted. And on the strangers, power was like an oil slick. It darkened everything around them. She could see it, dark and wet, everywhere they put their hands. She felt suffocated by it. Her breath was suddenly liquid and heavy.

'Think someone tipped them off?' the man said. He spoke quietly, but it was late and for once, no one was shouting or playing music. The sound wouldn't have carried far, but it carried to her.

'Nah. Doubt it. They're probably out with Harliss.'

'At midnight?' The man shook his head and reached in his pocket for a cigarette pack, then shook one out into his mouth. 'Nice family gathering. What do you want to do?'

'What can we do?' The woman took a seat on the porch, resting her elbows on her knees. Next door, their neighbor had rigged a floodlight to deter thieves – he imagined anyone under the age of forty was a would-be thief – and the artificial brightness hacked her face into exaggerated areas of hollow and highlight. It was a good thing, though. She would be blind, or almost – and hidden in the shadows, Lyra would be practically invisible.

She thought about trying to backtrack, but she was worried her legs would betray her, too scared they would hear her cracking through the undergrowth. Instead, she lowered herself carefully to the ground, hardly daring to breathe. Though she didn't know where the strangers had come from, she knew plainly enough that they were here to take her away. Caelum was still missing. Where was he? And where was Rick? She hoped he was still at work, and safe; it didn't look like the strangers intended to leave anytime soon. If they would wait, so would she. She could only hope that Caelum didn't come home in the meantime.

'What a mess,' the man said. When he exhaled, he tipped his head to the sky, exposing a dark ribbon of throat. Lyra fantasized about putting a bullet right through his skin, sending it back through the architecture of his spinal cord. Why wouldn't he just let them be? 'Sometimes I envy the paper pushers.'

'You'd lose your mind.'

'One more all-nighter and I might lose my mind anyway.' Then: 'It doesn't make any sense to me. If CASECS wants to go public next month, why wipe out the old specimens?'

'The DOD's got Saperstein's ass to the wall. It isn't CASECS that wants to clear the slate. They've got nothing to do with it.' She put her hands through her hair and looked up. 'Besides, they were smart about it. They did the lobbying first. They got the Alzheimer's lobby, the cancer lobby, the MS lobby – everyone's lining up. They're going to go at it from the direction of public interest.'

Hearing God's name was like a wind. It made Lyra shiver.

The man came down off the porch. For minutes, he and the woman said nothing. He smoked. She picked at something on her pants.

Then she looked up. 'You know Saperstein's supposed to be ribbon-cutting in Philadelphia on Tuesday.'

The man coughed a laugh. 'Bad timing.'

'Sure is. Danner told me that UPenn might disinvite him. The students are rioting. They want the name Haven stripped off the goddamn water fountains.'

'They don't know the half of it.'

'Sure. That's the whole problem.'

The man shook his head. 'Count no man lucky till he's dead, right?'

They were quiet for a bit, and Lyra was terrified they would hear her heartbeat, which was knocking hollowly in her throat. Then the man spoke up again. 'You ever think it's wrong? Making them in the first place?'

Though her face was still a cutaway of shadow and light, the woman's posture changed, as if she were hoping the idea would simply slide right off her. 'No worse than anything else,' she said. 'No worse than the air strikes last year – how many civilians killed? No worse than shooting soldiers up with LSD to watch what happens. No worse than thousands of kids slaving to make those sneakers you like. The world runs on misery. Just as long as it's not ours, right?'

'Just as long as it's not ours,' he echoed. Then: 'Those shoes aren't stupid, by the way. They're classics.'

Lyra didn't know how the woman would have responded, because a car was approaching. Tires crunched on the gravel, and a sweep of headlights appeared. The man put out a second cigarette and stood up, dusting himself off, neatening his cuffs as if he were there for an interview.

Lyra recognized Rick's car from the sound the engine made, a growl-spit that Rick was always complaining about. She hoped he would see the strangers and know what she knew, and turn around. Regular people knew so much and yet so little; they had never been taught to scent danger the way she had, to smell the metallic sharpening of tension on the air, the same odor as an approaching scalpel.

He didn't turn around. He cut the engine and climbed out of the car. 'What do you want?' was the first thing he said, and Lyra's stomach tightened. You did not speak to Power like that. Power spoke to you.

The man responded, with exacting politeness, 'Mr Harliss?' But Lyra wasn't deceived. At Haven, Dr Good Morning always spoke gently, and asked questions in just that kind of voice. But he liked to find all the replicas' weak spots – their poorly healed scars, their new abrasions – and plumb them with his fingers, as if manually drawing out the pain.

Then he would take notes on the way they screamed. Private research, he called it. To see whether their brains experienced sensation the same way.

Rick said nothing. He concentrated on feeding a cigarette from his pack to his mouth. Now it was the woman who tried. 'Are you Rick Harliss?'

'Depends on who's asking.'

'We're detectives with the county PD. We're investigating a pattern of B and Es and we have reason to believe your daughter – she pretended to consult a piece of paper, or maybe she really did – 'Brandy-Nicole, may have been a witness on the latest scene. We need to speak with her.'

There was a long, heavy silence. 'Bullshit,' Rick said finally.

This was obviously not the answer they had expected. 'Excuse me?' the man said.

'You heard me. Bullshit.' Rick got a cigarette lit, came a little closer, and blew a long plume of smoke directly in the man's face. Lyra couldn't have come up with the words herself, but in that moment a strong web of feeling knitted together in her chest, and she came as close to loving him as she ever would. 'Who sent you?'

There was another short silence. When the man spoke again, his voice was harder, and Lyra felt the impact of the words like little metal hammer blows to the base of her spine.

'You violated parole. You were caught with an illegal handgun. You assaulted a police officer. You jumped bail.'

'I didn't jump bail,' Harliss said. 'They let me go.'

'Our records say you jumped bail. That makes you a fug-i-tive.' He drew out the syllables, stretching them taffy-like between his teeth and his tongue.

Rick froze with his cigarette halfway to his mouth. Then, to her surprise, he started to laugh. But the noise was awful, and reminded Lyra of the way Nurse Don't-Even-Think-About-It used to cough up phlegm when her allergies were bad.

'Shit. He turned on me, didn't he? Fucking Ives. Piece of shit. Well. It's my fault for trusting him.'

'We need the kids, Mr Harliss. Where are they?'

'Fucked if I know.' He took another long drag and spoke with smoke ribboning out from the corners of his mouth. 'You don't believe me?'

'We don't want any trouble.'

'Neither do I. But it sure as shit seems to find me.' He shook his head. The light was a lurid yellow, and in its glow he looked exhausted, washed out, like an old photograph. 'I don't know where they are, I'm telling you. The boy took off sometime last night. Stole a thousand dollars out of a lockbox from the impound lot and made off with it. As far as I know, he hopped a plane to Mexico.'

'With no ID?'

'You can buy IDs, same as you can buy anything else. Ain't nothing and no one in this world isn't for sale. But you know all about that, don't you?' He smiled narrowly, through another mouthful of smoke.

'Careful,' the woman said. But Lyra could no longer follow their conversation, or the shifting currents of insult and threat that eddied around their spoken words. Caelum was gone. Caelum had stolen money and run off. She knew both that it was impossible – he would never leave her – and that it was true. It explained why he had consented to the job in the first place, and the bed he hadn't disturbed last night, and why he still wasn't home.

He had done what he did at Haven: he'd split.

'And the girl?' the woman said. But at that moment, Tank, the fluffy white dog Angie Finch kept in lot 34, started to yap, and Angie Finch's voice, thick with sleep, hushed him sharply. Something thinned on the air; Lyra had the impression of a drawstring cinched suddenly tight, squeezing out the possibility of escape.

'Look, why don't you come with us, get in the car, come on and talk about it,' the man said – in that fake lullaby voice, the kind Dr Good Morning used when he was knuckling new bruises until the pain sharpened to a kind of obliteration.

'I ain't going nowhere with you,' Rick said. His voice had changed too, and Lyra heard the warning in it. He took a last drag of his cigarette, fanning his fingers, making a show of it. 'Not unless you make me. And I can kick up a pretty big scene.'

He flicked the butt. Lyra watched it flash the distance between them, spinning through the web of old shrubbery – by bad luck it landed on her foot, a half inch from the sandal strap that would have protected her.

She swallowed a short cry, shuffling backward and disturbing a rustle of old leaves. Both strangers whipped around – and for a second, before she retreated farther into the shadows, she could swear that Rick's eyes landed on her. Or maybe he only sensed her presence.

She sat there, sweating in the darkness, stomach cramping from an agony of fear.

The woman took a step in her direction. 'You hear that? Something moved back there.'

'I wouldn't, if I were you.' Rick's voice was louder now, and froze the woman before she could come any closer. Lyra could see, now, the woman's heavy jaw and penciled-in eyebrows, her hair showing its real color at the roots. 'Not if you like your fingers. Had a lot of problems with coons these last few weeks. Had to shoot one myself. Rabid.'

Now she was sure he'd seen her. It was a lie. They'd had no trouble with raccoons, other than catching one rooting around in the garbage can one time they forgot to put the lid on overnight. Caelum had chased it off by shouting.

Angie Finch's dog was barking again. Angie's voice was muffled by the trailer walls. 'Shut up, you filthy animal!'

'Look,' Rick said. 'I don't know where they went. Like I told you, they could be halfway to Mexico. If you want to find them, you're wasting your time talking to me.'

The woman seized on this. 'You think they're together?'

Rick scowled. 'I'm done talking,' he said, as if they'd

caught him out in some kind of lie. She understood it was all an act. A show, so they would leave, so Lyra would have a chance to escape.

The strangers exchanged a look. The man cleared his throat. 'You know what I think?' He didn't wait for Rick to answer. 'I think you're hiding something.'

Rick said nothing. Lyra searched his face for the resemblance or the history he'd promised her was there, the story where she was a baby, loved, swaddled, wanted. But she couldn't find it.

Still, for the first time ever, she had the urge to call him *father*. She wanted to tell him to run.

'We can help you,' the woman said. 'Get those charges in Florida dropped once and for all. Clear your record, even.'

Rick appeared to be thinking about it. He gnawed the inside of his cheek.

'She isn't your baby girl anymore,' the woman said softly. 'It was a terrible thing that happened to her. Terrible. But all those kids raised out there on that island . . . they're all screwed up in the head. They're made all wrong. They're dangerous. You understand that, don't you? They're putting good people in danger.'

'She would never hurt anybody,' Rick said – but weakly, as if he wasn't totally convinced.

And he was wrong, anyway. Several times in the past

few weeks, Rick had walked her out behind lot 40, where someone had pinned paper targets to a rotting fence, and shown her how to shoot his gun. She had seen the guards aiming at waterbirds for target practice back at Haven, and had even heard some of the other replicas boast about trying it out for themselves – some of the male guards would let them do that, hold and fire guns, for exchanges Lyra understood only distantly. Haven was, in a way, like a large-scale replica of the minds it had grown: things needed to be neatly locked away, certain areas inaccessible, the whole place kept clean and bright and orderly so it could function at all.

Rick told her she was a good shot. She liked to imagine Dr Good Morning's smile wrapped around the aluminum of a beer can. She tried to picture God pinned to her targets, but whenever she did, her hand faltered. He was cruel and he had filled her with disease. He had done terrible things.

But he was still her God.

'She doesn't have to want to. She's sick. She's got a bad sickness inside her. If word gets out . . .' The woman shook her head. 'Can you imagine the panic? Can you imagine the protests, the violence?'

Rick stood there some more, acting out his uncertainty. Finally, he said, 'All right. All right. I'll come with you. But you gotta help me out, okay? I'm talking clean slate.'

'That's a promise,' the woman said, and the lie was like a long metal tongue, something smooth and slick and easy. When, Lyra wondered, did people learn to lie, so often and so well?

She wanted to scream, *Don't go.* But it was too late. He was getting into their car already.

The woman got behind the wheel, and the man took the passenger seat. Just a few seconds, and they might as well never have been there at all. Headlights dazzled Lyra as the car reversed. She was seized by the sudden memory of lying flat on an observation table, disembodied voices and hands touching her. She could see her father's face, framed briefly in the car window, and the sweep his eyes made as they looked for her again in the darkness.

A sudden panic overwhelmed her: wrong, wrong, wrong. It was like the alarm that had gone off during the Code Black, except this time the sound was inside her, in her chest, shaking her lungs. She had barely thought about Jake Witz and how she and Caelum had found him hanging from a door with a belt around his throat, but now she did; she saw Rick's face in place of Jake's, his skin a mottled purple and his eyes enormous with fluid. She had seen many corpses in her life, had watched countless replicas bundled and packaged onto the freight barge for disposal, but Jake's was different. Rick would die too, she knew that. That was what Power was – to decide who lived and who didn't.

Dad. The word rose in her chest, and pushed the breath from her lungs with its weight. *Dad.* She thought of running after the car, rocketing out from the shadows, and offering herself in his place.

But she stayed where she was. The taillights dimmed and then disappeared, and the growl of the engine quieted to a purr, and finally became the soft tutting of the crickets, singing endlessly from ten thousand hidden places.

Inside the trailer, everything looked the same way it always did. The warped mirror and the framed needlepoint *Home Is Where the Heart Is* were in place. The TV was still on. An open can of soda had left rings on the old wood coffee table, and next to the sofa the makeshift curtains were still drawn around Caelum's mattress.

He might have been sleeping. He might have been only moments from strolling through the door, wearing a salvaged T-shirt and jeans that hung below his hipbones, showing off the muscles, like wings, above his waistband.

She had traced those muscles with her fingers. She had licked them to know the taste.

She wanted to scream, to break something. Now she understood the replicas who spent hours knocking their heads against the walls, or who picked all the skin off their arms.

Rick was gone. He was as good as dead, and it was her fault.

Caelum had left her.

Was she still the same person without him? Who *was* she? Brandy-Nicole? Lyra? 24? Someone or something else entirely? She touched her face, her breasts, her thighs. She didn't seem to have cracked anywhere. Nothing had broken off. And yet she felt that something *had* broken, that there was a big gaping hole somewhere inside her, and air blowing through it.

She knelt on his sheets and put her face to his pillow. It smelled like him. She took the shoe box and carefully laid out the belongings he'd collected, placing them side by side on the mattress, as if they were runes and by some magic she might call him back. The brochure from the Nashville Elvis Festival. Bus schedule. A receipt. The plastic wrapper that had enclosed a utility knife. Several miniature Snickers, uneaten. Old batteries.

And then she blinked and the objects blinked too and became something else, something meaningful: not trash but a sentence written earnestly and urgently, just for her.

She smoothed out the receipt and read the list of things he had purchased from Able Hardware: one utility knife, one pocketknife, one flashlight and four packs of AA batteries, a butane lighter, a can opener. The bus schedule was from something called the Knoxville Transit Center. Her heart jumped. Someone had circled all the buses running between Knoxville and Nashville for Caelum.

Caelum had left her. That was true. Probably, like he'd

said, he thought she didn't want him around. He thought she'd be better off without him. But he'd also left her clues, just in case, and they all pointed to Nashville, where another God named Elvis had made hundreds of replicas.

Caelum had gone home, and she was going home with him.

FIVE

IT DIDN'T TAKE HER LONG to pack. There wasn't much she owned, and almost all of it had been owned by others first and would, she assumed, be owned by new people later: a bright-pink sweatshirt, a pair of sneakers and one pair of flip-flops, three T-shirts. Even the backpack Rick had purchased for her, red nylon and blotchy with old stains, was doodled over with someone else's notes and pictures, like a skin covered with faded tattoos. But she was careful to pack all the belongings she'd found, all the things she'd salvaged from the dirt: pens, metal soda tabs, loose coins.

She debated whether to bring Rick's gun with her, in case the man and woman – Suits, even if they had been dressed casually – caught up. But after weighing it in her hand, the metal oily like a slick of pollution, she put it back. She was afraid not that she wouldn't be able to use it, but that she would. That she wouldn't be able to stop.

Maybe, she thought, the strangers who'd taken Rick away were right. Maybe all the replicas were broken. Maybe they didn't have souls, like the nurses had always said. Maybe they were like the shells that Cassiopeia had sometimes collected, abandoned by whatever had once lived inside of them, full of nothing but a hollow rushing.

But if Caelum was broken, then she was broken in the same way. And she didn't know much, but she knew that had to count for something.

She was eager to set out as soon as possible, but her body was heavy with exhaustion and waves of dizziness kept tumbling her. She meant to close her eyes just for a minute, to catch her breath, to get her strength back, but woke up hours later in a panic, just as the sun was poking through the sagging blinds. Dawn already.

She shouldered her backpack and slipped outside, fiddling with the door handle, which was loose, to lock it. It gave her a brief pain to think of what would happen to the trailer with no one there to care for it: soon, she knew, it would be reclaimed by squatters, and the other residents of Winston-Able would strip it of its good furniture and sheets and dishware. Or they would gray the walls with cigarette smoke and carpet the floor with a surface of broken bottles, like in lot 48, where people went to get drunk and worse.

But she let this worry slip away from her, like a kind of smoke. She had learned long ago to let things go, to let them pass, to allow all her worry and hurt and need to simply drift, cloudlike, until it had left her behind.

Tank was barking, as usual, as if he knew where she was heading and wanted to be sure she didn't get there. She turned in the direction of the highway. She would cross through the truck weigh station again and have to pass Eagle Tire. She hoped she wouldn't see Raina but had no idea how long parties lasted. One time she had woken up at dawn after the Haven Christmas party to the sound of laughter and the crack of gunfire: a few doctors and some of the guards were taking turns hurling bottles and trying to shoot them in midair.

She heard a familiar voice call her name, but knew she must be imagining it: sometimes, in her dreams, she heard Dr O'Donnell call her voice in just that way. Only the second time did she notice a sharpness to the voice that didn't sound like dream or memory — and didn't sound like Dr O'Donnell, either.

She turned and saw Gemma and Pete. Gemma, flushed and pretty, was wearing clothes that struck her as exotic and reminded her of some of the birds that landed, occasionally, on Spruce Island: elaborately colored, sleek, showy.

'What are you doing here?' Lyra asked them. She

thought Gemma's house was far away, but she couldn't be sure. The journey from Florida to North Carolina, the meeting between Rick Harliss and Gemma's parents – seeing parents up close, even – was a hole all of its own. She felt if she got too close to the edge, she might fall into a place that had no bottom.

'You're in danger,' Pete said. 'The people who killed Jake Witz are tracking you and Caelum. They're probably on their way now.'

'I know,' Lyra said. She thought of Rick, and the way his eyes had swept the dark for her, trying to latch on. She thought of his pink scalp and his blunt fingers and his slow, shy smile, all of it soon to be reduced to nothing but skin cells and decomposition. A long rope of hatred coiled around her throat. 'They were here already.'

Gemma was sweating. 'Is Caelum . . . ?'

'Gone.' Lyra hated to hear the word out loud. It was like something rattling inside an empty tin can.

Gemma closed her eyes and opened them slowly, as if she was trying to pry herself out of a dream. 'They – they got him?'

'He was already gone.' She thought of telling Gemma and Pete where he had gone – that there might be others like them, free, and living happily in Nashville – but she was afraid that they would discourage her and that saying the words out loud would burst them like small bubbles, and make her see how silly she was to hope.

'I saw them come, and I hid until they left.'

'They'll be back. They'll be back any second. You have to come with us.'

'I can't,' Lyra said. 'Thank you. I'll be careful.' She knew they were trying to help. Rick had taught her to say thank you, like he'd taught her to say please, to look people directly in the eyes and say hello, too.

She turned and started off again, but before she had gone four feet, Gemma called her back.

'Wait.' Gemma's face looked unexpectedly altered, her eyes startlingly bright, as if they'd grown. 'What do you mean, you *can't*?'

'And where's Caelum?' Pete's whole face was pinched with exhaustion, as if someone had sewn his skin on too tight. 'Where did he go?'

'Home,' Lyra said, and ignored the way Gemma and Pete looked at each other. She knew they couldn't understand. The world had grown too big. She had to shrink it back to manageable size, back to the slender weight of the secrets that she and Caelum could carry together. 'I'm going after him.'

'I don't think you understand.' Gemma was trying to be nice. Lyra knew that. But her voice was razor sharp, as if at any second it would fall off an edge into hard anger. 'The people who came here won't just quit. They'll look until they find you, wherever you are.'

'They're looking for *Caelum* and me,' she said. 'They

won't expect us to split up. And they won't expect us to get far. They don't think we're smart enough.' She thought of the way the nurses and doctors had always spoken over their heads, had avoided their eyes, had joked and laughed about things in the outside world – never understanding that Lyra had been listening, learning, *absorbing*. And it struck her as funny, now: they hadn't thought to watch what they said because they believed they had complete power over her. But as a result, their power had become hers. She'd eaten just enough to survive. 'Besides, what other choice do we have?'

Lyra could tell that Gemma knew, immediately, that there were no other choices. Still, she said, 'You could come with us. We could drive you somewhere far away. Maine. The Oregon coast. Canada. Wherever.' Places that made Lyra feel uncertain again. Places she'd never heard of.

'Not without Caelum,' she said. Caelum was a person, but he was a place, too. He was her place.

'You'll never find him,' Gemma said. 'Do you know how many people there are in this country? Millions and millions.'

Lyra knew her numbers up to the hundreds, because there had been nearly twenty-four hundred replicas at Haven. But she didn't know what *millions* was. 'You just said the people who came from Haven will find *us*.'

'That's different. They're bigger than we are. Do you

understand that? They have cars. They have drones, and money, and friends everywhere.'

Lyra was surprised to realize she felt sorry for Gemma. Gemma was so desperate to help. She didn't understand that Lyra and Caelum were beyond reach. They belonged to a different world.

'You forget what they made us to be, though.' Lyra spoke gently. And then: 'Invisible.'

She managed to smile. Smiling had always felt strange, but now it was getting easier. 'Thank you, though. I mean it.'

'Please. Take this, at least.' Gemma dug in her pocket and found a small wallet that was covered in a repeating yellow graphic of smiling faces. Lyra was momentarily breathless when Gemma handed it to her. It was the most beautiful thing she'd ever seen or held, its plastic slick and new-feeling, bulky with whatever it contained. She wanted to smell it, to nibble on its edges. 'You'll need money. You know how to use an ATM card, right, to get money? The code's easy. Four-four-one-one. Can you remember that?'

She nodded. She had had to remember numbers for Cog Testing – words, too – and parrot them back for the proctors. She knew now that they had been testing the progression of prion disease, but at the time she had thought they only wanted to prove how smart the replicas had grown. She only wanted to do well.

'Thanks,' she said. She couldn't bring herself to decline it. Already, the plastic wallet had warmed in her hand, pulsing there as if it belonged. She took a step forward, overwhelmed by feeling, and, before she could decide against it, brought her hands to Gemma's shoulders the way Rick had for her. Gemma's face reminded her so much of Cassiopeia in that moment that she felt an unexpected doubling of her life before and after. She was two Lyras and she was no one: she was a hole falling through the past. 'See you,' she said, stepping quickly away, because for a split second a terrible urge possessed her to hang on, to stay with her hands on Gemma's shoulders and never let go – an urge she thought she'd been rid of long ago.

She turned away. She knew she'd never see them again. Let go. It was surprisingly difficult to walk, to *keep* walking, as if the air was throwing up extra resistance. But there was no other choice. Let go. It was the rule that bound everything, as true in the outside world as it had been in Haven.

Let go, let go, let go. She thought of wind through the trees, and laundered white sheets, and the warm fog of anesthetic. Let go. She thought of clouds and shadows and waves; she thought of the ocean, bearing away a boat filled with the small bundled bodies of the dead.

SIX

LYRA KNEW FROM THE BUS schedule that Caelum was heading to Knoxville, and from there to Nashville. She knew that Knoxville was a large city less than an hour away by car, because that was where Raina's mom worked at a twenty-four-hour restaurant called Big Tony's.

But she didn't know how to get there. The first person she saw, a guy unloading cartons from a grocery truck, pointed her in the right direction and even offered her a ride. But she didn't like the way he looked at her. 'Can't walk all the way to Knoxville,' he'd called out, when she kept going.

The next person she asked, a woman counting change behind the gas station counter, told her she couldn't get to Knoxville without a car. But a third person had overheard the exchange and told Lyra, outside, that she thought there was a local bus station that had buses to Knoxville.

She was black, with very red lipstick, and so tall the light haloed behind her, as if she were cracking the sky with her head. She smelled like Dr O'Donnell had, like lemon soap, very clean. Lyra thanked her and kept going.

It was a seven-mile walk along a bleak industrial road that kept edging close to the interstate and then away again. Stanton Falls was bigger than Ronchowoa but she didn't know by how much. She knew she was in town when she began to pass occasional strip malls of mostly shuttered stores. She saw a boat shop, too – funnily enough, since she had no idea where the nearest water was – with little motorboats displayed in the brown grass and covered with tarps. She couldn't have said what drew her across the yard and to the display, only perhaps that it reminded her of where she'd first met Caelum, in an overgrown section of Spruce Island, littered with old waste.

One of the tarps had been loosened and retied. She saw that right away. She tugged it free and knew that someone had slept there. On one of the benches the treads of a dirty sneaker had left marks. There was a crumpled Snickers wrapper, too, wedged between two seat cushions. Probably Caelum had arrived too early, before the bus was running, and had lain down to sleep for a bit.

She was catching up.

But in Knoxville, she lost hope again. Knoxville was by far the biggest place she'd ever been, full of so many people she couldn't understand how there was enough air to allow them to breathe, and the clamor of noise made the back of her teeth ache. Faces, faces everywhere – all of them looked the same to her.

The Knoxville Transit Center was huge, all glass and concrete and escalators rolling up and down, the loudness and the lights, and the *womp, womp, womp* of her own heart, like a fist punching her in the chest.

A man shoved her. A woman yelled at her for standing motionless in front of the revolving doors, unsure of how they worked. There were people in lines as if waiting to get medication, and big machines grinding out slips of paper, and numbers on big boards that blinked and changed, dozens of TVs, words everywhere, signs everywhere, the smell of sweat and perfume and bathrooms.

She found a bus after standing in the wrong line twice, and was handed a ticket and told by the girl who sold it to her that next time she could do it through the automated system and also that she had cool hair. 'I went short for a while too,' she said, 'until my mom said she would boot me from the house.' This gave Lyra a boost, however, as it always did when she went out into the world, into people, and *passed*.

Because at heart and despite what Raina or Rick thought, she knew the truth now: she wasn't one of them and would never be.

She had to wait because the bus wasn't ready to

board. She counted how many people wore red hats, and how many people wore black ones. She tried to close her ears to the unfamiliar voices, dozens of conversations that together sounded like the grinding work of one large machine, all stutters and beeps and sharp, hysterical alarms. Whenever an individual voice reached her, she was reminded of how the researchers had spoken, moving in packs down the halls as if they were cabled together invisibly, using English but somehow an English she didn't understand. A man sitting next to her on the bench picked dirt from his fingernails with a pen cap, and spoke in words that made her head ache for their foreignness. *Can't fault Walsh on that snap . . . you watch and see, Seattle'll blow holes in their defensive line. . . .*

Holes. She closed her eyes; she breathed carefully through her nose. She'd believed for a long time that the outside world might be as big as ten times Haven, and after escaping she knew it had to be at least ten times that. But a bigger vision was impossible. What she knew of Tennessee was Ronchowoa, and the walk to the Target and back, and the Winston-Able Mobile Home Park, and its grid of sixty-two lots.

In the end, she only knew the bus had arrived when a loudspeaker voice announced that it was getting ready to leave, and she had to run to the far end of the terminal, barely gasping through the doors before they shut behind her with a hiss that sounded ominous.

She lurched into a seat just as it began to move. The blur of landscape still made her dizzy. She leaned back, clutching the schedule she'd been given in one hand. It was already wet, damp with sweat. Three and a half hours to Nashville, with one stop at Crossville to pick up new passengers.

She got sick in the tiny, filthy bathroom once, twice, a third time, until nothing came up but bile. She couldn't rinse her mouth out. There was no water to drink. So she wiped her mouth with a sleeve, toweled off her face with a hem. An old woman seated near the bathroom shook her head and frowned, as if Lyra had gotten sick deliberately, when Lyra made her way carefully back to her seat. But she felt better. She was even a little bit hungry.

In Crossville, there was a layover of twenty minutes, and the passengers disembarked to use the bathrooms and buy food from the station. Lyra was feeling a little braver, so she showed the bank card Gemma had given her to a woman across the aisle.

'I need money,' she said, since Gemma had said that was what the card did.

The woman gave her a strange look. 'Well, there's an ATM right over by the bathrooms,' she said.

Lyra shook her head to show she didn't know what that meant.

The woman squinted, moved her gum around in her mouth. 'It's your card, isn't it? You've got a code?'

'Four-four-one-one,' Lyra recited, and the woman put up her hands to cover her ears, laughing.

'Whoa, whoa, whoa. You're not supposed to say it out loud.' She put her hands down again, and her son thought it was a game, placed his hands to his ears and down again, said, 'Whoa, whoa, whoa,' and cackled.

'Please,' Lyra said, getting desperate now. The bus would leave in twenty minutes. She was hungry – she had not had anything to eat in twenty-four hours – and the station smelled like frying meat fat, like the Stew Pot in Haven but better. 'I need money.'

The woman let out a *shush* of air, like the sound when SqueezeMe had finished hugging. 'Come on. I'll help you.' She took Lyra's arm, exactly where SqueezeMe would have in order to read her blood pressure. Her hair was gray and brown, both. Otherwise, she looked a little like Dr O'Donnell.

When they left Crossville, the bus was more crowded than ever, and Lyra's heart stopped when she saw that among the passengers was a replica like the kind she had seen in the Nashville Elvis Festival brochure: a slick of black hair and dark sunglasses, plus the same beautiful white jumpsuit with beading that caught the sun. She was desperate to ask him questions, but felt too shy; he was traveling with a large group and spent the whole time chattering with the other travelers, or crooning along to songs the bus driver piped from the speakers. At one point he stood, staggering a little to keep his balance, and danced along to the music, pivoting his hips and holding a soda bottle like a microphone. Everyone laughed and even applauded, and Lyra felt a vague sense of foreboding. It wasn't real. It couldn't be.

She was even more discouraged when the bus driver announced their arrival in Nashville. She had been hoping that Nashville would look like Haven: an orderly series of buildings contained by a fence. Instead, it turned out to be a city: stack-block buildings, signs puncturing the sky, roads like the serpentine trails left on the surface of the marshes by passing water snakes, the slow crawl of traffic. More people. Perhaps the world didn't end at all. Perhaps it went on and on forever. It occurred to her that if she didn't find Caelum, she wasn't even sure how she'd get back to Winston-Able, couldn't remember what bus line she had taken to Knoxville.

But maybe it didn't matter. Now that she knew the people from Haven were looking for her at Winston-Able, now that they had taken Rick away, she couldn't return anyway.

She followed the line of passengers off the bus, trying to work up the courage to speak to the man in the clean white suit. He moved quickly with a surge of other travelers toward the station doors, and she knew that as soon as he hit the street, she risked losing him. She was sure that she would find Caelum wherever the replicas were heading, and so she took a deep breath and jogged to catch up, with her backpack slamming against her lower spine and echoing the rhythm of her heart. She had to say *please* several times before he turned around. The people with him – regular people, none of them replicas, but none of them dressed as nurses or doctors, either – turned with him. Under the weight of their stares, Lyra felt suddenly shy.

'What's the matter, little lady?' he said. He had a deep voice that rumbled in his chest. 'You want an autograph or something?'

She knew what an autograph was – it was when a doctor put down his signature on a piece of paper. The nurses were always asking the doctors to autograph one thing or another: disposal orders, cognitive evaluations, the reports generated by the Extraordinary Kissable Graph. This gave her confidence.

'No autograph,' she said. 'I'm looking for all the others.'

'You're here for the festival, huh? You an Elvis fan?'

Raina had said that Elvis was the name of their God. 'I need to speak to him,' she said, which made the others laugh.

'Isn't she sweet,' one of them said.

But another one frowned. 'I hope she ain't on her own. She's too young for it.'

The replica with the dark hair inched his sunglasses down his nose. 'You want to talk to Elvis, do you?' he asked, and she nodded. 'Come on. Let me show you something. Come on,' he said, and gestured for her to follow him out the revolving door, into the bright afternoon sunshine, and the wet-tongue heat. In the distance, she could hear the faint roar of a crowd, like the break of ocean waves, and a cascade of music.

'You want to talk to Elvis, little lady, you just close your eyes and listen,' the male said. 'You hear that? That's Elvis talking, right there. You just gotta follow the music.'

SEVEN

LYRA DID AS SHE WAS told. She set off toward the music, and when she got lost, she simply closed her eyes and listened for the drumbeat rhythm of applause, and the crackle of distant speakers, and turned right or left. She wondered whether Caelum had been here, had waited at the crosswalk for the light to turn green as she was waiting, had thought of her or worried about her or wondered whether she would follow.

The streets grew more crowded and funneled a mass of people down toward the music. Colored flyers fluttered from the lampposts. People drank in the streets and leaned over the balconies of their high-rises to wave. Lyra was overwhelmed by the crush of people, by the blur of strange faces and a celebratory atmosphere she couldn't understand. Was this another party? She had yet to see any more replicas. The music picked up the tempo of her heart and knocked it hard and fast against her ribs.

Then she turned a corner and saw them: hundreds of identical men milling around a stage elevated in the center of the plaza, all with the same oil-black hair and sideburns and sunglasses, many of them dressed the same, too, in heeled boots and spangly white uniforms. She cried out without meaning to, filled with a sudden, cataclysmic joy.

Replicas. Hundreds of them. Alive, healthy, drinking from red plastic cups, posing for photographs with eager tourists.

But then she got closer, and her heart dropped. She saw at once she'd been mistaken. The men weren't identical at all. Some were fat, some were dark, others were pale. There were even women among them, with sideburns pasted to their skin that in places had begun to unpeel. They weren't replicas at all – they were simply regular people, costumed to look the same, for reasons she couldn't understand.

The disappointment was so heavy she could hardly breathe. All of a sudden she felt trapped – squeezed to death in the vast open space by the pressure of all the strangers around her, by the chaos of so many unfamiliar things. Speakers blew feedback into periodic screeches. Laughter sounded like explosions. The air stank of fried food and sweat. Caelum must have come here, and seen what she had seen. But where would he have gone afterward? He could have wandered in any direction. He could have left Nashville entirely.

She would never find him now.

She was suddenly dizzy. Turning to move out of the crowd, she stumbled.

'Whoa. Take it easy, there, lady. Are you okay?' A woman squinted at her and her dark wig – that's what it was, a wig – shifted forward an inch on her forehead. 'You need some water or something?'

Lyra wrenched away from her. She was hot. She couldn't think. She hadn't been afraid at all, not when she believed that in Nashville she would find more replicas. But now she was panicked, and her mouth flooded with the taste of sick. *Do you have any idea how many people there are in this country?* Gemma had asked.

You'll never find him, she had said.

She hardly knew where she was going. She just knew she had to get out, away from the noise, away from the music and the crowds. She was desperately thirsty, and whatever energy had carried her this far had abandoned her all at once.

She crossed a scrubby parking lot to a 7–Eleven, stepping onto the curb to avoid two boys smoking outside their car – when, just like that, in the space between one second and the next, she saw him.

Or not him, exactly, but a picture of him, taped to the window of the 7–Eleven.

The picture wasn't very good, and most of his features were obscured. But it was definitely him. She recognized the hooded sweatshirt he was wearing, which they'd found together at the clothes-by-the-pound thrift store Rick had taken them to when they'd first arrived at Winston-Able Mobile Home Park.

There were words on the page, but she had to blink several times to make them come into focus.

Smile! You're on candid camera.
Thieves will be photographed, shamed,
and prosecuted. Just like this one!

She didn't know what *prosecuted* meant. But she knew what a thief was. Had Caelum stolen something? Was he in trouble?

Suddenly, on the other side of the window, a man's face appeared: an ancient face, tufted with hair in strange places, and eyebrows that ran to meet each other above the nose. She took a quick step backward before remembering there was glass that separated them.

'In or out?' he said. His breath misted the window, and his voice was faintly muffled. 'Or you just going to stand there gaping?'

'I . . .' Before Lyra could think of an answer, he'd turned, shaking his head, and stumped back toward the cash register. She followed him. Inside, the air smelled like a shoe box. Several customers stood at the counter, waiting to have items scanned. She detached Caelum's photograph from the window where it had been hung. The old man scowled when she approached him with it.

'Hello,' Lyra said.

A guy so skinny his head looked inflated blinked at her. 'There's a line,' he said.

Lyra ignored him and spoke directly to the man behind the counter. 'I know him,' she said, and placed the picture of Caelum down on the counter.

The man just kept running items past the scanner. 'That boy is a thief, young lady,' he said. 'Tried to lift a package of jerky and a Coca-Cola, right from under my nose. I been in this business a long time. I know a bad seed when I see one.' He glared at Lyra as if to say that he was looking at one right that very second.

'Sorry,' she said – a default word of hers, a word that had always helped at Haven with the nurses and doctors. *Sorry I made too much noise. Sorry I'm in the way. Sorry I breathe, that I'm here, sorry I have eyes, sorry I exist.* 'I'm looking for him. That's what I mean. I need to find him.'

'You should stay far away from him, is what I think,'

the old man said. He'd finished ringing up the skinny guy and gestured the next customer forward.

'Please,' Lyra said. Her palms were sweating. The overhead lights were very bright. Remembering the lie Rick had coached her on, she added, 'He's my cousin.'

The old man shook his head again. But this time, his voice was a little softer. 'I'm not in the business of giving handouts, young lady,' he said. 'It's a store. Not a church. Besides, if I'd let him get away with it, who's to say someone else couldn't just waltz on in here and strip the place?'

'Do you know where he went?' she asked. Fortunately, her voice didn't shake. She had gotten very good at that, at hiding, at burying things deep inside of her.

The old man blinked at her as if she'd just appeared. 'Where do you think he went?' he said, scowling again. 'The cops took him down to the station. And if I were you, young lady, I wouldn't hurry to bail him out.'

EIGHT

IT WAS EASY ENOUGH, IT turned out, to find a police station, even if you had no idea where you were going. All you had to do, Lyra discovered, was start walking – and eventually, when it started to get dark, the police would find *you*.

She walked down a long street empty of cars. Lyra couldn't exactly be considered lost, since she did not know where she was going: still, she very definitely did not know where she was.

At some point, it had begun to rain. She crossed an empty playground darkened by shattered floodlights. Next to the swings, several guys paused to watch her, the happy rhythm of their conversation abruptly silenced. A woman with a big metal cart piled with plastic bags wheeled slowly down the sidewalk, her feet swollen with rags instead of shoes. Lyra saw a rat picking at trash bags piled on the street, and the gutters were knotty with empty bottles and old sandwich wrappers and cigarette packs.

She had been walking for at least an hour, wondering whether she would recognize a police station if she saw it, and if so, whether she would have the courage to go inside it, when a dark sedan pulled up beside her.

'Are you all right?' A man leaned over to squint through the passenger-side window. His skin was very dark, and his hair was threaded with gray. He was wearing a dark suit.

Lyra's immediate thought was to run. She knew sedans, knew the look of the Suits who drove them, knew that they carried smiles along with their guns. But she was trapped: he could easily follow her if she took off running down the block, and there was nowhere to hide, and no possibility of cutting across a nearby park that was hemmed in by a tall chain-link fence.

'This isn't a good place for you to be walking this late,' the man said. Lyra backed up, shivering, until the fence punched her between the shoulder blades. She wondered if she should scream. But who would help?

'Hey.' The man's voice got softer. 'It's all right. I only want to make sure you're safe out here.' Then: 'It's okay. You're not in any trouble.'

Lyra was confused by the tone of his voice – none of the Suits had ever spoken to her like that, or looked at her the way he was, as if his eyes were something warm he wanted to give her. And he hadn't come at her with a gun or tried to force her into the car.

Maybe, then, he wasn't a Suit.

Still, Lyra was frozen. The man didn't move, or get out of the car. He just sat there, looking at her, his face touched with light from a streetlamp on the corner.

'Do you speak English?' he asked. And then: *'¿Habla español?'* Then: 'My name is Detective Reinhardt. I work with the Nashville Police Department.'

Finally, Lyra eased her weight off the fence. She was positive, now, that he hadn't been sent to find her. And she had to be brave, if she was going to find Caelum, which meant she had to believe him.

She hesitated. 'I was looking for a police station,' she said finally.

He stared at her a second longer. 'Get in,' he said, and opened the door.

His car was very clean, which relaxed her. A picture of three girls was mounted to the dashboard, and when they passed beneath a streetlamp, she saw two of them were identical and felt a kind of ecstatic relief: twins, she knew, not replicas, but still it seemed like a sign. The other girl looked older, and she had the policeman's long nose and the same enormous eyes. She wore a bright-red headband and had her arms looped around the twins. Her eyes were closed and she was laughing.

He saw her looking. 'The twins are my nieces, my sister's kids. Jamie and Madison. And that's my daughter, Alyssia,' he said, thumbing the girl in the middle of the photograph. 'An old photo. She's in college now.'

'She's pretty,' Lyra said.

He smiled. 'Don't I know it,' he said. He had a little bit of an accent, like Nurse Curly, who'd come from a place named Georgia. 'What's your name?' he asked.

'Gemma Ives,' she lied quickly. Before leaving Haven she hadn't been a good liar, but this was a skill, she'd rapidly learned, that most humans had perfected; it was necessary to lie, living in the human world.

'Nice to meet you, Gemma Ives,' he said. His eyes were big enough to root her in place: as if he wasn't just seeing her, but absorbing everything about her, her past and even her future. 'You can call me Kevin.'

'Detective Kevin Reinhardt,' she recited, and he laughed.

'Just Kevin is fine, like I said.'

Lyra was glad that his suit was rumpled, and smelled like soft old wool. Not sharp, like the suits the military men and women wore when they came. 'Why don't you wear a uniform?' she blurted out.

He smiled. 'I'm a detective,' he said. 'We travel under the radar.'

Lyra nodded, though she didn't know what a detective did, exactly. But she was glad he wasn't in uniform.

Uniforms made her think of Haven and its guards, of the soldiers who'd pursued them out on the marshes. *You know how expensive these things are to make?*

'Now,' Detective Kevin Reinhardt said, 'why don't you tell me what you need a police station for?'

She wasn't used to being spoken to in that tone, as if she might have something valuable to say. She told him her cousin had been picked up for stealing.

'You know what precinct got him?' he asked.

She shook her head, and repeated what the man at the 7–Eleven had said: 'He tried to lift a package of beef jerky and a can of Coca-Cola. They took him down to the station.'

They were stopped at a red light. The policeman turned to look at her again. She felt the way his eyes moved from her hair, still shorter than most of the boys' she had seen since leaving Haven, to her bare arms, to the flimsy backpack with someone else's name written on it in marker.

'You know if you're in trouble, you can tell me,' he said, still in that same low and gentle voice, as if he was singing instead of speaking. He wasn't like other police officers she had seen on TV, or even the few she'd encountered since leaving Haven. His face looked as if it had been dimpled permanently into an expression of understanding. 'If someone's hurting you, you can just let me know right now, right here, and I'll help you out, and make sure you're safe and no one hurts you again. That's my job.'

The darkened city outside their windows was a wash of blue tones and hazy cones of color from the streetlamps; then she realized, to her shock, that her eyes were leaking. That's what they'd called it at Haven. Never crying. *Tear duct inflammation, leaking eyes, overactive lachrymal production. Crying* meant feelings, and the replicas didn't feel, or at least the humans pretended they didn't. Probably that made it easier for them not to feel, either. That way they could do their jobs, draw their paychecks, and sleep soundly.

For a second she fantasized about telling Detective Kevin Reinhardt everything: about all the pills and medications and lies, the harvesting procedures and the testing and the MRIs, the small prions, deformed like bits of melted plastic, whirring through her blood and bone marrow. In the end, what came out was half-truth.

'I'm sick,' she said. 'I'm dying. My cousin takes care of me. He's the only person in the world who does.'

'What about your parents?' the policeman asked. 'Where are they?'

She thought of Rick and the dry skin around his mouth, the way he squinted through his cigarette smoke when they were target shooting. The smell of hot dogs and frozen soup. She thought of Dr O'Donnell, her blond hair like a vaporous haze barely clinging to her head. She thought of Cassiopeia bleeding out in the marshes, of the Yellow crop bundled up for disposal, of Jake Witz hanging by his own belt.

'My parents are dead,' she answered. 'Everyone's dead. We came all the way from Florida on our own.'

'Florida,' he repeated. 'Must have been a long trip.'

'It was.' Suddenly, she couldn't stop talking. Words skittered off her tongue like insects trying to beat a path home before they were trampled. 'We lived on a small island and saw all the same people every day. There was water everywhere, in all directions. And alligators that lived in the marshes. There was a fence—' She sucked in a quick breath. She'd nearly revealed too much. 'There was a fence to keep them out.' She looked down at her hands, surprised at how badly she actually *missed* Haven. 'There were birds there. Lots of birds. More birds than people.'

'It sounds like a beautiful place,' Detective Kevin Reinhardt said, and turned off the car engine. They had arrived somewhere she assumed was a police station: a one-story brick building, and big windows through which more police in uniform were visible. 'How old are you?'

This lie came easily, too. 'Twenty-one,' she said, because she had learned from Raina that this was a magic age, even if she didn't quite understand why. Raina had complained about not being twenty-one yet, about all the bars and concerts and parties that were twenty-one and over, about getting kicked out of someplace for not being twenty-one, so Lyra figured that once you turned twenty-one you got special rights to exist.

'My niece had brain cancer,' he said finally. 'Jamie, the one in the picture. Took her when she was fourteen years old. Cancer's what you're sick with, isn't it? But there are clinics. Treatments. You should be under the care of a doctor.'

'I am,' Lyra said. 'That's where I'm heading. To UPenn in Philadelphia. To see my doctor.' As soon as she said it, she knew it was exactly what they had to do.

Lyra and Caelum had been wrong about Nashville. There was no God here. Which meant they had only one option left: they had to find their original God.

They would ask him to help. They would *demand* it.

Detective Reinhardt's relief was obvious. She could almost smell it coming off him, like a particular odor of sweat. 'My daughter almost went to UPenn. Opted for Columbia instead. Philadelphia's a great city. I know a guy at UPenn Hospital.' He looked at her sideways. 'Who's your doctor up there?'

This time, Lyra couldn't think fast enough to lie. She said, 'Dr Saperstein,' hoping he wouldn't recognize the name. Luckily, he didn't appear to.

He just gave her a quick pat on the knee. 'I'll take care

of your cousin, don't you worry. No one's going to jail for wanting a soda, all right? You just leave it to me.'

They got out of the car. A rush of black overtook Lyra when she stood up. The rain had turned to a heavy, hot vapor that hung in the air. Who knew what would happen to her once she followed Detective Kevin Reinhardt inside? He seemed okay, but the doctors and nurses at Haven had seemed okay, and all the time they'd been filling her up with disease, tending not her but the disease inside that would eventually sweep away her memories and her words, seize her arms and legs, numb her throat until she couldn't swallow.

Still, she followed Detective Reinhardt inside, shy in the sudden brightness. Police officers wove between a jigsaw puzzle of wooden desks. The room stank of old coffee and new ink. A phone seemed to ring every five seconds.

'Don't be shy, now.' Detective Reinhardt put a hand on her shoulder when she hesitated in the doorway. 'You go on and get comfortable and I'll be back in a hurry. Now, what did you say your cousin's name was again?'

Lyra froze. She pictured her mind as a series of computer monitors, all of them darkened at once by a power surge. There was no way Caelum would have given his real name. But she couldn't think of the name he would have invented.

But she was lucky. Finally, she was lucky. Because even as she hesitated, she heard someone shout.

Turning, she saw Caelum rising from a plastic chair to greet her, trying as hard as he could not to smile, not to *grin*, and failing totally, so they stood together twenty-five feet apart in a police station in Nashville, Tennessee, at 9 p.m. on a Sunday, and laughed.

NINE

DETECTIVE KEVIN REINHARDT KEPT HIS word and made sure that no charges were filed against Caelum. By the time he announced that Caelum was free to go, it was nearly midnight, and Lyra had fallen asleep in one of the plastic chairs in the waiting room with her head on Caelum's shoulder, directly beneath a large framed poster of the singer named Elvis she had originally mistaken for another Dr Saperstein.

Detective Reinhardt volunteered to drive them back to the Greyhound bus station, although he warned them it was likely the buses to Philadelphia wouldn't run until morning and that the neighborhood was a bad place to go wandering. Lyra told him they planned to wait inside the station, that they didn't mind spending the night on the floor.

'You got somewhere to stay once you get up to Philly?'

he asked them, once they arrived at the station. 'You got friends up there? People you know?'

'Oh, sure,' Lyra said. 'Lots of people. It'll be just like home to us.'

It wasn't exactly a lie. Lyra had told Caelum that they would find God there, at a place called UPenn.

It was a slim hope – Dr Saperstein might simply put them in a cage, as he had done back in Haven – but their only one. He had filled Lyra with sickness. He might, she thought, be able to remove it.

'You need help or run into trouble, you just give me a call,' he said, and gave her a small white card with his name printed on it, and more numbers she now knew must connect to his telephone. 'I want you to study that number. Memorize it, okay? Promise me.'

Lyra nodded, overwhelmed. Other than Gemma, Detective Reinhardt was the first person to give her a number, his number, to call. She felt, holding the card, as if she were holding something fragile, something sacred and beautiful.

She blinked to clear her eyes of tears and watched the numbers sharpen and flow into a pattern, make a sentence in her mind. 'I promise,' she said.

Climbing out of the car, however, she felt a strong pull of dread. She thought again of Jake Witz; of finding him swinging from a doorjamb, his face swollen and discolored, and the cleanup crew who'd come afterward to make sure that no one would ask questions. He, too, had offered help. Rick had helped, and she was sure that by now the people who'd taken him in their car had murdered him.

She hoped this man, Detective Kevin Reinhardt, wouldn't end up hanging from a rope.

It was by then after midnight, and no buses would run for hours. Several people lumped on the benches to sleep might have been distant rock formations. It was quiet and still, except for an old man pacing and muttering darkly to himself.

She wanted to ask Caelum why he had gone off without her, but she was worried about what his answer would be. Besides, she felt sick again. A seesaw was starting in the bottom of her stomach, back and forth, back and forth, slowly tossing acid up in the back of her throat.

They went in search of ginger ale: the vending machine at the station was out of everything but Coke. At Haven, she had had ginger ale regularly, because along with the antinausea drugs that got delivered orally or piped in through an IV, the nurses distributed warm ginger ale in small paper cups. The taste of ginger ale reminded her in equal measure of Dr O'Donnell and of the Box, and so she loved and hated it, also in equal measure.

Nothing was open this late. They kept walking. Lyra's

legs felt strange and sticky, as if they were made of metal that had rusted. She was exhausted. Her relief at being reunited with Caelum only made her aware of how lost she would have been without him; it wasn't, therefore, exactly relief. Though Detective Reinhardt had said it was a bad place to walk, she felt that with Caelum next to her, nothing bad could ever happen again. But several blocks from the bus station, Lyra became aware of a change in the shadows around them, a subtle rearrangement of the nighttime noise of that foreign city.

They were being followed. They'd been herded, actually. Unconsciously trying to outpace the voices even before they knew what the voices meant, they had wound up on a narrow one-way street that contained nothing but a shuttered auto-parts supply store and a vacant warehouse.

Before Lyra had a chance to warn Caelum, they were surrounded. Five men, not much older than Caelum was, and one girl who hung back, keeping her eyes on her phone. The light from the screen made strange shadows on her face.

The five boys tossed Lyra's backpack and took the wallet Gemma had given Lyra, which held Gemma's bank cards and all of her money. But what really made Lyra angry was the way they scattered her stuff: the bottle caps and old plastic bags filled with clinging browning plant matter and coins and a rusted pin shaped like an apple, all the things she'd collected and cared for at Winston-Able.

'You a trash lady or something?' one of them said, and hurled away a pen, her favorite pen, its end deformed by chewing.

They made fun of Caelum for the knife he carried – 'You need more than a pair of tweezers, you swag around here like we're supposed to know you' – and insisted he hand over his money (stolen, Lyra knew, from the cash box at work) and even his belt, which one of the boys wanted. Caelum did what they said without a word. Still, Lyra could feel anger like heat ticking off him, subtle waves of it that made her light-headed.

When one of the guys moved to touch Lyra's cheek, Caelum began to growl. At first the boys thought this was funny, and they laughed.

'Look at this guy. He's like a cat or something.' A second guy stepped forward and tried to push Caelum.

Quickly, even as a passing car threw light briefly onto the brick wall behind them and then darkness crowded in after it, Caelum changed. He was a person and then he was something less, something animal and old. He lunged, snapping his teeth.

The guy wrenched his wrist away, finally. 'Freaks,' he said. Though Caelum and Lyra were drastically outnumbered, the power had shifted. 'Freaks,' he said again, and when he met Lyra's eyes, he looked afraid. 'Come on. Let's get the fuck out of here.'

After they were gone, Lyra bent to retrieve her scattered belongings. But she couldn't distinguish her things, her special things, from the trash in the gutter, little knobby strangers that meant nothing to her – snub-nosed cigarette butts, tongues of gum stuck to their wrappers.

'Are you all right?' Caelum asked her. It was practically the first thing he had said to her directly since they'd laughed together like idiots in the police station.

She didn't answer him. She was nauseous, and tired, and they had nowhere to sleep, and no money to buy a bus ticket, either. She hated the group of boys who'd followed them and laughingly upended her backpack to shake her things into the gutter. She hated the girl who stood there with her eyes stuck to her phone screen, the girl who couldn't even be bothered to look. How could they be people the same way that Detective Reinhardt and Gemma and her friend April were people? The difference between people and replicas was one of ownership. Real people owned, and they took, and replicas *were* owned. A difference of action and object.

'Lyra,' Caelum said, when she didn't answer. How to sort out her things from the flow of human waste? Where did all these things come from, and who was discarding them so easily? It seemed to Lyra that the whole human world was built on waste, and trash, and things manufactured just so that they could be tossed out afterward. She couldn't save it all. She could never rescue everything. 'Lyra, please. Talk to me.'

'You left without me.' It wasn't what she had been planning to say, but once the words were out of her mouth, she knew that she was still furious at him. 'You were just going to leave me behind. You didn't even say goodbye.'

'I thought I was doing you a favor,' Caelum said. 'You seemed happy.'

'I was happy because we were together,' she said. 'I thought we would always be together, at least until . . .' She found she couldn't think about her sickness. She couldn't say the words out loud. At Haven, death had never seemed particularly scary. It was a bald, natural fact, like the transformation of food through the digestive tract. Replicas were born, they got sick, they died, their bodies were bundled and burned. Someday she would be ash, sifting through the ocean waves, to be consumed by half-blind deepwater fish.

'I'm sorry.' He knelt so she had no choice but to look at him. 'I didn't want to leave you. I didn't,' he said, reaching out to touch her face, so she couldn't turn away. He placed a hand on the back of her neck, and her body responded, as it always did, as if she were something hollow – a husk, a leaf – and he the wind lifting it. 'I thought it would be best. I thought I was protecting you.'

Another passing car threw up a quick wedge of light. Caelum looked so beautiful it was almost painful. She was relieved when the darkness chased the car away again.

She stood up. 'What are we going to do now?' They had nothing of any value, and Lyra knew by now that everything in the real world cost money. You needed money to eat, and money to sleep, and money even to use the bathroom in public places, which were *for patrons only*. Caelum was quiet. 'We'll find a way,' he said.

'What if Dr Saperstein won't help us?'

Caelum's smile was as thin as a razor. 'We'll make him.'

They backtracked to the station, thirsty now, and moneyless, and ticketless. They hunched down in a dark alcove near the men's bathroom, with its smell of armpits and old urine, and waited for morning to come.

Lyra balled her pink sweatshirt up beneath her head for a pillow. She closed her eyes and felt the nausea rise and fall like a swell of water, and she was scared. She pictured her own body like a night sky, a web of black tissue, and small disease cells burning like stars inside it; she closed her eyes and saw instead of darkness a blinding light, the compression of all that light, all that energy, into a single blazing explosion.

She woke up swallowing a scream that came up in the

toilet with splatter. In her vomit: small comet trails of blood.

Whether she made it to Philadelphia or not, she was running out of time.

PART II

TEN

BARELY SIX HOURS AFTER HE let the skinny girl, Gemma Ives, and her cousin off at the Greyhound station – regretting, on the one hand, not keeping them for more questioning, and on the other hand himself exhausted, eager to believe that they were indeed heading to see someone who could help her, that they were not just two more junkies busing toward their next high – the police commissioner in Nashville, Sarah Rhys, called Detective Kevin Reinhardt's supervisor, Captain Basher, to say that Mr and Mrs Ives would be coming by the station.

The day before, Gemma Ives's debit card had been used to purchase a one-way ticket to Nashville from the Knoxville Transit Center, and hours later she'd withdrawn two hundred dollars from an ATM at a rest stop in Crossville, suggesting she had, indeed, boarded a bus. It had been less than the requisite forty-eight hours since Mr Ives's daughter had gone missing. Nonetheless, Rhys was issuing an Amber Alert: the girl wasn't yet eighteen years old.

She was thought, perhaps, to be traveling with a boy.

Detective Reinhardt knocked his chair over in his hurry. He didn't even double-check the girl's likeness: her parents had sent the Crossville PD a series of photographic attachments, and Crossville had forwarded them on. Buses started running at 6 a.m. But she might still be there, he might have time to catch her, she needed sleep, there was still time. . . .

'Where you going with your pants on fire?' Officer Cader was checking her teeth in her computer monitor, working a fingernail between her incisors.

Christ. He should have been a dentist.

He should have been a bus driver.

He should have been something, *anything* else.

He was already through the revolving doors, into air swollen and thick with the promise of more rain, and sprinting to the car, thinking there was still time to catch her.

He plunged through the revolving doors at 6.17 a.m. exactly – record time – into the echo chamber of cell phone conversations and squeaky-soled sneakers, into a colorful foam of faces and rolling luggage. Any other person would have been overwhelmed, but Detective Reinhardt had been a cop for a long time, and his dad had been a cop, and his uncle was a cop, and so was his cousin

Rebecca. So he looked not where all the color and sound was but where it wasn't: the negative spaces, the empty corners and hallways and alcoves that regular people were trained to ignore.

His eyes leapt over the crowd. He let himself drift. He released the station so that it floated away from him, like a boat unmoored from the shore. The girl, the funny soft-spoken kid with the eyes made slightly bulbous from being too thin and the bright-red backpack, was the only thing he could have clipped onto.

Nothing. Nothing. Nothing.

'Now boarding, Gate 3, 405 north to Boston.'

And then: a glimpse of red, a flash of platinum-blond hair, a girl who moved like she was drifting.

Almost at once, the crowd re-formed and he lost sight of her. It didn't matter. He was shoving his way through the funnel of people churning toward the gates, swirling around the big departures board.

Someone stepped in front of him, and Reinhardt nearly went down over the wheels of a hideous green faux-alligator suitcase. The man looked outraged, as if it were an actual alligator and Reinhardt had just trampled its tail.

Only then did the loudspeaker voice touch his consciousness.

'Now boarding, Gate 3, 405 north, destination Boston, with stops in Washington, Philadelphia, and New York . . .'

ELEVEN

'NOW BOARDING, GATE 3, 405 *north, destination Boston, with stops in Washington, Philadelphia, and New York . . .*'

Lyra came awake to a booming electronic voice. A cop was frowning down at her.

'Can't sleep here,' he said. He had to speak loudly above the echo of so many voices. Spokes of sun, a blur of people holding briefcases, women in sneakers that went *squeak-squeak* and reminded her of the nurses, children shouting.

She got to her feet, leaning hard against the wall for support. Caelum was gone. Standing, she was even taller than the police officer. Sweat dampened her underarms, and she could smell herself.

The cop squinted at her. 'You all right?'

'Fine,' she said quickly. Her voice sounded like it had been chewed up. 'Just waiting for my bus.'

He nodded as if he didn't quite believe it but moved off anyway. She stood there breathing hard – even the effort of standing had made her dizzy – and tried to think. She couldn't remember why she was there, only that Caelum had been with her and now he was missing. The pattern of travelers was dizzying. Strangers threshed the lights into shadow patterns. A gigantic clock on the wall with tapered iron hands pointed to 6.09. She was going to be sick again.

She closed her eyes and leaned her forehead against the wall, grateful for the coolness of the stone. *Think.* But she couldn't think. She couldn't remember a thing. Images came to her in flashes: Detective Reinhardt's big cow eyes, throwing up in the toilet, the veins of blood.

When she opened her eyes again, she thought for a moment, through the thick haze of sun, she even saw him moving through the shifting crowd of travelers. But then the pattern changed shape and instead she spotted Caelum, dodging the crowd without appearing to notice anyone else.

'Here,' he said, when he reached her. He was holding a paper bag. From it, he produced a can of ginger ale. Cold.

'I thought you'd gone,' she blurted out. She lowered her mouth to the soda can, sucking along its rim, comforted by the taste of metal. This was a Haven taste, of tongue depressors and tubes behind the throat, even of

Thermoscan, though that had been made of plastic.

He just shook his head. He looked happier than she'd seen him in a month. 'I bought us tickets, too. The bus is boarding.' She remembered now, dimly: those boys moving out of the dark, an impression of wet mouths and the harsh birdlike cries of their laughter. She remembered kneeling in the gutter, trying to sort out her things from the collection of trash.

'How?' she asked.

He shrugged. 'I told you I was going to get our money back,' he said. 'And I did. Some of it, anyway.'

She still didn't understand. She could hardly remember what they looked like: to her they now seemed a blur, their faces eaten up by shadows, and all their mouths identical and grinning. 'You found those boys from last night?' she asked, but knew immediately, from his face, that wasn't what he meant.

He took her free hand, pressing something into her palm. She opened her hand and found a battered leather wallet. She saw a flash of wadded bills before he took it back again.

'They're all the same, Lyra,' he said. 'That's what you have to understand. Even the ones who say they'll help are the same.'

Her head was pulsing, like the rubber pump of a stethoscope when it was squeezed.

'You stole it,' she said.

'They took from us,' he said. 'So I took back from them.'

It was wrong to steal. Lyra knew that. Once Calliope, one of Cassiopeia's genotypes, had stolen a cell phone from the nurses' break room. Even though they'd found it tucked inside Calliope's pillowcase, Nurse Swineherd had insisted that *all* of her genotypes be punished. Privately, Lyra believed that that was when number 8 had gone so soft in the head, that maybe she'd been knocked too many times. Although the truth was that she had always been smaller than the others, and much dumber, too, so maybe she'd simply been born that way.

Caelum was right: why should they have to give so much, and never take anything in return?

If everyone believed they were monsters, shouldn't they at least be allowed to have teeth?

She could feel Caelum watching her, felt a question hanging between them like a very fine curtain of fabric. 6.20 now.

'Last call, Gate 3, 405 north, destination Boston, with stops in Washington, Philadelphia, and on to New York . . .'

She looked up. The curtain parted. 'We better hurry,' she said, 'if we want to catch the bus.'

They slipped easily through gaps in the kaleidoscope of people, like rats, like shadows. All the people Lyra passed did look the same. Their skin and hair and jaws began to blur into a smear of indistinguishable color, into people who were simply not like them.

But then, for half a second, her eyes snagged again on a vision of Detective Reinhardt pushing frantically through the crowd. This time, she was sure she hadn't imagined him.

She nearly lifted a hand to wave.

But then Caelum took her hand in his, and together they sprinted the rest of the way to the bus, slipping inside just as the doors were closing.

TWELVE

LYRA AND CAELUM ARRIVED IN Philadelphia just
after 11 p.m., and still a crush of people poured with
them into the station. Every time she thought she must
have seen all the people there were in the world, all the
buildings and cars, they kept coming: it was a little like
watching distant waves in the Gulf of Mexico, as she had
sometimes done at Haven, to see the way each wave in
fact hauled dozens, hundreds, thousands more on its back.

Lyra knew that Dr Saperstein was going to speak on
Tuesday at a place called UPenn – that was what the people who had taken Rick Harliss away had said. She had
been keeping careful track of the days, as Rick had taught
her to, and knew that they were a day early. Still, she was
nervous.

Remembering how helpful Detective Reinhardt
had been, Lyra suggested that they ask a police officer

for directions. Caelum was less certain – the day before, he'd been shunted between holding cells, and desks, and grim-looking officers for hours, waiting to be booked – but after two hours of wandering, he finally agreed.

They circled back to the bus station, where there were plenty of cops. But the first one just shook his head.

'If you're here for the protests,' he said, 'you'd be better off just turning right around. This country's got bigger things to worry about, and we've had guys down there clearing the roads for two days. Besides,' he added, narrowing his eyes, 'it's almost midnight. Don't you have somewhere to be?'

The second one, a woman with her hair in tight braids, like Dr Fine-Yes had worn back at Haven, just stared at Lyra for a long time, up and down, as if her eyes were a broom and Lyra a bunch of dust.

'How old are you, honey?' she asked, and Lyra grabbed Caelum's hand and hurried away without answering.

By then, Lyra was too tired to continue: exhaustion kept rolling up and crashing over her, hauling her down into brief, blinking moments of darkness, so she would come alert and realize she didn't remember crossing a park, or she didn't know how they'd ended up inside a neon-bright restaurant that sold hamburgers flattened like palms.

They found a Motel 6. They had no ID since Lyra's

wallet had been stolen, but the desk clerk just shrugged and handed over a key anyway.

'No smoking in the rooms,' he called out after them. 'I'm serious.'

In the room was a carpet the color of vomit, and ancient wallpaper that still exhaled the smell of old cigarettes and booze, two twin beds and an old, blocky TV, a bathroom where mold inched between tiles and decals on the tub floor peeled like brittle leaves. It was the prettiest room Lyra had ever seen, except for the one in the little white house where they'd first been taken by Gemma – she couldn't believe how big it was, how spacious, that it was all theirs for the night. How many rooms, she thought, must there be in the world: how many rooms like this one, folded across the vast space of the world, pretty and quiet and safe, with doors that locked? It was a beautiful idea.

She showered first, taking her time, letting herself imagine that her body didn't belong to her at all, that it was just an object, a broken-down chair or a table full of surface cracks, and that she herself was somewhere different, that she would not be affected if her body gave out entirely or was discarded. Afterward she stood in the cloudy bathroom, listening to the muffled noise of the TV from the bedroom, feeling suddenly nervous. She had been with Caelum countless times in vacant trailers and behind the supply shed, and played a game of kissing each other's scars, and the thin, fragile skin on the inside of the elbows and the back of the knees. But that was in the dark, at Winston-Able, in a room musty with spiderwebs and the smell of bike tires. That was washing up accidentally somewhere, and clinging to each other because there was nowhere else to go.

This was different.

She knotted a towel around her chest. Before Caelum could even turn to look at her, she'd slipped into the bed closest to the bathroom, shivering when the cold sheets touched her bare skin. She pulled the covers to her chin.

'Are you finished?' he asked, and she saw his eyes move down to her shape beneath the blanket, and this made her shiver, too.

The drumming of the shower in the bathroom, the murmur of TV voices – soon she was asleep, falling off the edge of sound into quiet.

She woke to movement, the rustle of sheets and the sudden touch of cold air. She'd fallen asleep in her towel, and she was cold. The lights were off, and the TV was off, and it was quiet except for the faint hum of an air conditioner. For one disoriented second, she didn't know where Caelum was: she had a vague sense of his outline standing beside her, watching her sleep.

'What are you—?' she started to say, but then Caelum

was sliding in next to her in bed, naturally, as if there was no other place to be. He looped a heavy arm across her waist. He wasn't wearing a shirt, only a thin pair of boxer shorts. She could feel his chest rising and falling, his breath on her cheek, his anklebones when he moved, and immediately she wasn't cold anymore. She was burning hot.

'Lyra?' he whispered, but before she could say *what*, he put his mouth against her neck. Then she realized that it hadn't been a question after all. He found a gap in the towel and slid his hand to her stomach. He touched the architecture of her hips. He moved a hand, carefully, gently, between her thighs. 'Lyra, Lyra, Lyra,' he said again, singsonging it, as if he were learning how to speak through saying her name.

She wasn't a human. She wasn't a replica. She was a star trail, burning through the darkness, lighting up the room in invisible spectrums of color.

'Caelum,' she said, turning over to him, and opening her mouth to his, letting him pour this new language inside of her, letting it transform them together into music.

THIRTEEN

IN THE MORNING THEY SHOWERED together, soapy, touching each other with slick-fish fingers, filled with the joy of the new. They packed their few belongings, and Lyra took a pen from the nightstand. She left behind the Bible she found there; she associated it too much with Nurse Don't-Even-Think-About-It, with quick and blinding sideswipes to the head.

They had better luck than the day before. The desk clerk didn't even blink when they asked for directions to UPenn. She just slid a paper map across the desk and charted the best route with a little ink line.

'It's a hike, though,' she said. 'You might want to Uber.'

Lyra just thanked her and said a quick goodbye.

It *was* a hike: an hour of slogging next to a sluggish gray river and a grid of barely flowing traffic. Lyra marveled at the look of the houses on the river, enormous and colorful, in a style she had never seen before. Caelum puzzled over the map, charting their progress carefully, inching a finger along the ink pathway when Lyra read out the names of the streets they were passing.

Finally, when his finger was almost directly above the little star indicating they had arrived, Lyra saw something that took her breath away. A group of boys and girls came toward her, singing. There were so many of them that Lyra and Caelum had to step off the sidewalk to avoid being bumped.

'Caelum,' she said, and pointed.

Several of them wore T-shirts marked with a logo she recognized. An electric thrill traveled her whole body. *The University of Pennsylvania.* Lyra knew it. Caelum knew it. Everyone at Haven knew it.

It was a place both Dr Haven and Dr Saperstein had come from. The bust in the entryway of admin wore a blanket bearing the same logo for a cape. On certain days, certain *game* days, God went into his office and didn't come out. Sometimes the staff members drank beer on those days, carted from the mainland in coolers on the boats, and sat for longer than usual in front of the TVs, watching sporting events whose rules Lyra didn't understand.

'UPenn,' she said out loud, and began to laugh as the group of strangers raised their fists and shouted, 'Go

Quakers.' Finally, she understood: UPenn meant the University of Pennsylvania, where both of the Gods of Haven had started.

Where the second God, Dr Saperstein, was soon due to return – and where she and Caelum would be waiting for him.

She'd assumed that UPenn was a single place, almost like Haven, that had produced both Richard Haven and Dr Saperstein. But once again the outside world smashed itself into a thousand different visions, into dozens of buildings, hundreds of people, noise and color and rhythms she didn't understand.

Kids sat cross-legged with homemade signs in front of the looming stone buildings, chanting. Others, ignoring them, lay out on blankets in the grass or played a game that involved a flat plastic disk and lots of running.

'I don't understand where they all come from,' Caelum said, and she knew exactly what he meant: how could all these people have been made if not on purpose?

'Come on,' she said, and took his hand. Caelum was agitated by the crowds. She remembered, suddenly, seeing an eclipse when she was younger, how the nurses had let them file out into the garden to look. Caelum became like that when he was nervous, like something dark that swallowed the light around him.

Lyra was anxious too. The swell of voices from

every direction made her head hurt. The blur of colors reminded her of the starbursts that crowded her vision when, stretched out on the examination table, she looked too long at the ceiling lights. If Dr Saperstein was here, did that mean that other people from Haven were here, too? Guards with guns? People like the ones who had killed Jake Witz, and had come most recently for Rick Harliss?

To her surprise, the first person they approached didn't hesitate when they asked whether she knew where to find Dr Saperstein.

'He's not coming,' the girl said. She was wearing lots of rings, and violet eye shadow that made Lyra think of Raina, and of the strange party where people stood in the half-dark together and also somehow alone, like the individual patches of land submerged in the marshes that only from a distance looked like solid ground. 'I mean, they haven't officially announced it yet, but he won't.'

Lyra's palms began to sweat. 'What do you mean?' she said, and repeated as faithfully as possible what she had overheard. 'He was supposed to be here Tuesday, for the ribbon-cutting.'

'Yeah, but that's probably not happening either. Have you been to the protests? There's, like, two thousand people outside.'

'Where?' Caelum asked.

'Over by the Haven Center. Or *whatever* they're calling

it now.' The girl rolled her eyes. When she saw that Lyra and Caelum had no idea what she was talking about, she sighed. 'Next to the medical school and PCAM. You know where PCAM is, right? The Perelman Center for Advanced Medicine? It's right next to the Haven Center. You can't miss it, it's right on Civic Center. You students here, or incoming?'

Lyra said nothing.

'Well, you'll get a real view of Penn, anyway. Protesters and crusty alums and all. Whose side are you on?' She smiled in a way that might not have been friendly.

'No one's side,' Lyra said, though she had no idea what the girl meant.

At the same time, Caelum said, 'Our own side,' and squeezed Lyra's hand even tighter.

They found PCAM and the medical school – an enormous modern complex, all steel and glass, which reminded Lyra of the real Haven – and next to it, the brand-new Richard C. Haven Center for Regenerative Research.

'He was here,' Lyra whispered excitedly. 'The first God was *here.*'

It seemed impossible that God, the first God, could have existed here, so many hundreds of miles away from Spruce Island. That here, too, in this busy city, he'd put a thumb in the soft clay of reality, he'd existed, people knew his name.

If there were a single place in the world where she

would find help, it had to be here, where the Gods of Haven would be once again reunited.

Despite the crowd gathered in front of it, the building itself had the whistling, empty look of an abandoned shell. The revolving glass doors were roped off behind a thick red ribbon, and Lyra's heart picked up – this, then, must be the ribbon Dr Saperstein was expected to cut. But the podium positioned directly in front of the doors stayed empty, the microphone crooked uselessly toward the open air, like a finger beckoning to no one. Police sawhorses kept the crowd a safe distance from the building.

Hundreds of people eddied around the steps, blocking the entrance. Lyra kept hold of Caelum's hand – she wasn't sure she would have been able to loose herself, he was squeezing so tight – as they edged along the periphery of the crowd, puzzling over what it meant. From the fact that the girl with the violet eye shadow had asked them whether they were students, she now knew this must be a school. Maybe this was simply how schools looked, how teaching took place.

Many of the students carried signs that said *Not Our Penn, Take Haven to Hell, Penn Students for Awareness.* Others waved school flags, or carried signs that said *Penn Pride* or *Penn Students for Science.*

Between the two groups there was obvious tension. A makeshift line divided them, like the finger of an invisible current had divided the crowd in two, and as they watched, two boys began pushing each other and one of them ended up on the ground, his glasses shattered.

Finally, she worked up the courage to ask a girl what all the shouting was about.

The girl, red-faced and sweaty, wearing mismatching shoes and thick glasses, was resting on a stone wall with a cardboard sign tucked between her legs. Because of the way it was angled, Lyra couldn't read what it said.

'You go here?' She squinted at Lyra and Caelum in turn, and when they shook their heads, seemed to relax. 'Oh. I was gonna say. What *planet* are you from?' She bent down to retrieve her sign, propping it on the wall next to her. This one said *Not Our Penn*.

Lyra tried a different tack. 'Do you know where to find Dr Saperstein?' she asked. The sun was too bright. In its glow she felt as if all her holes were visible, all the defects in her brain obvious.

'Oh, the ceremony's off for sure. They're just too spinecheese to tell us. You heard about what happened in Florida, right? I mean, you're not *actually* from Mars?'

'Don't be a dick, Jo.' This came from a boy sitting next to her.

'Florida.' Lyra swallowed. 'You mean what happened at the Haven Institute?'

The girl, Jo, nodded. 'Richard Haven was a professor here, like, a million years ago. He's been dead for, like, a whole decade.' She paused to let this settle in. 'Anyway, he went off and made fuck-you money doing biotech and who knows what, and he bought his name onto this building.'

'It wasn't biotech,' the boy said. 'It was pharmaceutical stuff.'

'No one knows what it was, and that's the point. No oversight. Typical one percent stuff, too big to fail. And Saperstein's just as bad.' That she addressed to the boy, and he raised both hands. 'Anyway –' she turned back to Lyra and Caelum, exhaling heavily, so her bangs moved across her sticky forehead – 'the Florida meltdown is, like, the worst environmental catastrophe *ever*.'

'Since the BP spill, at least,' the boy chimed in.

'Since the BP spill, for *sure*.' Jo glared at him. 'There are clouds of pollution, like seriously chemical clouds, practically *poisoning* everyone within eighty miles—'

'Not eighty miles,' the boy put in mildly. 'You're exaggerating.'

The girl didn't seem to hear him. She was getting worked up now. Her glasses kept slipping. Every few seconds, she thumbed them higher on her nose. 'They're saying there might be generational damage, plus it turns out Saperstein was *completely* skirting federal regulations, they're saying he was *cloning* people. . . .'

'*One* person is saying that,' the boy interrupted her

again, and nudged her. 'Didn't your mom ever tell you not to believe everything you read on the internet?'

Finally, she turned on him. 'Whose side are you on, anyway?' He shrugged and went quiet, picking at a pimple on his chin. 'The point is –' she said, rolling her eyes – 'I'm premed, and I don't want this guy's name on our buildings. How about Marie Curie? How about a *woman*? Richard Haven doesn't represent me. Not my Penn.' She pointed to her sign.

'But where is Dr Saperstein?' Lyra felt increasingly panicked. In the distance, she spotted a man uniformed in dark blue, wearing mirrored sunglasses: a guard, sent to collect her. Then he was gone, dissipated in the sweeping motions of the crowd, and afterward she wasn't sure whether she'd imagined him.

Jo blinked at her. 'I told you. He's not coming. He'll be lucky if he doesn't end up in jail.'

'Thank you.' Lyra remembered, just barely, to say it. Thinking of Rick, and the way he'd tried to teach her about manners, and how to talk to people, brought on an unexpected spasm of pain.

They turned away from the girl and her sign. Then Caelum pivoted suddenly.

'He *was* making clones,' Caelum said.

Both the girl and the boy stared.

'I'm one of them,' he said. 'I'm number 72.'

'Ha-ha,' the girl said flatly. An ant was tracking across her sign. She frowned, took it up between two fingers, and squeezed.

In the short time they'd been speaking to Jo, the crowd had grown even denser. Now the protest spilled up the steps, toppling the sawhorses, and as she watched, several students charged the podium and brought it crashing down. Lyra saw a blur of police uniforms among the crowd and felt suddenly as if she were going to faint. Reality slipped slowly toward darkness.

'We have to get out of here.' Caelum sensed the change at the same time: the current had tipped over to one of fury. The crowd seemed to pour into a single roiling mass, like a tight-knit cloud condensing on the horizon.

'He still might come.'

'You heard them. He's not coming. He's not—' But Caelum was whipped away from her when people surged suddenly between them, a wall of people pulsing together like an enormous organ, walls of breath and hair and sweaty skin.

Someone grabbed Lyra's wrist, hard. She turned and a scream throttled her, lodging somewhere in her throat.

Though she had seen him only from a distance, in the harsh glare of the floodlight, she recognized him: he was the same man who had come for Rick, but dressed up now like some kind of local security guard. But she would have sworn it was him. She recognized the flatness of his eyes, like the dead stare of a fish.

Are you okay? his mouth was saying. But she couldn't hear the words. Instead, she heard him laughing. She heard the guards on the marshes weeks and weeks ago, laughing as they toed their way through the blood of dying replicas.

You know how expensive these things are to make?

She wrenched away from him. She spun around – she had a brief impression of open mouths and shouting, a boy with blazing eyes shouting at her. A backpack caught her in the chest and she was knocked off balance. She was on the ground. Someone stepped on her fingers. Sneakers and legs, so many bodies – she was momentarily over-whelmed, she couldn't breathe.

Even as a girl reached to help her, the crowd moved. Suddenly everyone was shouting and she couldn't get up. Someone kneed her in the ribs. Through a rift in the crowd, she spotted Caelum, flying at the guy with the backpack. A girl screamed. Caelum was a sudden frenzy of motion; there were three guys fighting him now, and blood on his teeth. As she watched, trying to find the breath to shout, one of the boys caught him on the cheek and then another one on the back of the head, and then a third kneed him in the stomach. Then he was on his knees, spitting up blood, but she couldn't get to him – still they were separated by a hard blade of moving bodies.

Someone hooked Lyra by the elbows and got her to her feet. Air touched her lungs like a burn. She gasped and tears came to her eyes.

'Are you okay?' the guy shouted. He was wearing glasses with only a single lens. She recognized him as the boy who'd gone down before, shoved by someone. He kept a hand on her arm, even as Caelum finally pushed his way toward her. 'Animals,' the boy kept saying. 'You're all *animals*.'

Now Lyra could see the guards carving the crowd up, dispersing it. But the man with the dead fish eyes was gone.

Caelum's face was swollen where he'd been hit. Lyra could tell how much pain he must be in. His cheek was cut. One of the guys who'd hit him must have been wearing a ring.

'Goddamn. *Tell* me you aren't prospectives.' The boy in glasses looked furious. 'Come with me. Let's get out of here before these psychopaths start a riot.'

FOURTEEN

HIS NAME WAS SEBASTIAN, AND with his help they elbowed their way free of the crowd. From a distance, it resembled an organic mass, a seething, hungry creature.

Lyra was still having trouble breathing. She kept scanning the street for the man with the fish eyes, or the woman who traveled with him. She felt the weight of invisible observers watching their progress, the way she had always felt the Glass Eyes at Haven.

'Animals,' Sebastian said again, when they were several blocks away, and the noise of the chanting had faded. Lyra was surprised that it was still early afternoon, still sunny; that the cars still churned by slowly, that nothing else had stopped.

Caelum hadn't spoken at all. His left eye was swollen shut. When he leaned over and spat up a gob of blood, the boy shook his head.

'You should really get some ice on that. And clean the cut, too, so it doesn't get infected. I'm in med school,' he added, in response to a look from Lyra. 'If you want, my apartment's right around the corner.'

Lyra hadn't exactly recognized it as an invitation until he started walking again and Caelum, to her surprise, followed.

Sebastian lived in a small, bright apartment on the third floor above a sandwich shop. The whole place smelled like the inside of a book. Books sagged the built-in shelves lining the wall. The sun caught thick swaths of dust in the air and striped the room vividly in golden light. She couldn't see anything in the haze of sun.

'My roommate's a lit PhD student,' Sebastian said, when he caught Lyra pacing the shelves, running her fingers over the spines. 'Can you believe he still reads *paper* books? It's so nineteenth century.'

The sun made black spots in Lyra's vision. The room began to turn, slowly, and to stay standing she had to grip the table. Side effects. No. *Symptoms.*

'Do you have a bathroom?' she asked him. Sebastian had so many things it made her dizzy: paper clips and mugs, framed photographs and bundles of wire, coins and little porcelain trays to hold them. She could hear all of it screaming, crying out in neglect; she wanted to open her mouth and swallow the whole room. She wished she could stuff all of his belongings down inside her, like some kind of magical potion that would turn her human, totally human, at last.

Like some kind of magical potion that could make her well.

'Are you all right?' He squinted at her, and for the first time she noticed how nice his clothing was compared to theirs, how well it fit him, how healthy he looked.

'Bathroom,' she managed to say again, even as she felt bile biting off the edge of the word, making acid in her throat.

In the bathroom, she turned on the faucets and opened her mouth and let the black come up, waves of sickness that brought with them a sharp antiseptic burn in her throat and Haven's smell. They had failed to find Dr Saperstein, like they had failed to save Rick Harliss, or Jake Witz, or Cassiopeia in the marshes. Everywhere they went, they had left nothing but death behind them.

And she had nothing but death to look forward to.

She sat back on her heels, waiting for the rise and fall of the room to go still. Her face was wet. She was crying. A green toothbrush with its bristles splayed, tweezers, a scattering of clipped hair, an empty tissue box gathering dust, a straw basket piled with magazines and paperback books. She wanted things. She wanted a phone, an apartment full of books, tall glasses and ice cube trays and mugs for tea hanging from nails beneath the kitchen cabinets. She wanted a space she could fill and fill with her belongings, until no one could touch her, no one could even reach her past all of her beautiful things.

She took a paperback from the basket and opened to inhale its pages. She tore off a piece of paper, and then another, and fed the pieces one by one into her mouth until she felt well enough to stand.

She hadn't brought her backpack to the bathroom and that was a mistake. But she tucked the paperback into her waistband and found her T-shirt concealed it perfectly. She washed her mouth out. She felt better, with those pieces of paper pulsing their small words out from somewhere deep in her chest.

Hers.

Caelum and Sebastian had moved into the kitchen.

'I should have known the whole demonstration would be a disaster,' Sebastian was saying. Without his glasses, he was beautiful – not as beautiful as Caelum, but still beautiful. He had dark skin, high cheekbones, and eyes the same color as the afternoon sunlight on the wood floor. 'But people never listen to reason. They don't care about facts. They read one think piece in the *Times* and they get hysterical about everything. I swear, you can't even fart on this campus without someone screaming environmental policy at you nowadays. You want some water or something? Beer? I have wine but it's old.'

'Water's fine,' Lyra and Caelum said, at the same time.

'I'm not a conservative,' Sebastian said. He poured water from the tap into tall glasses, and Lyra marveled at how comfortable he was touching everything, as if the whole space was just an extension of his body. 'I understand we shouldn't have theaters named after Ponzi scheme billionaires, or slave owners — and in our country, that excludes more people than you'd think. But Richard Haven?'

He shook his head. 'His work on stem cell regeneration was pioneering. Do you know he built a lab in his room when he was in elementary school? He isolated his first nucleus when he was *nine*, using a kitchen spatula, basically. I'm exaggerating, but you get the point. He was a genius. You think Steve Jobs made people feel warm and fuzzy? Benjamin Franklin was a total prick, and so was Edison. He *bought* the idea for the lightbulb, by the way. He was basically just the licensor.'

He paused to take a breath and Lyra too felt breathless: so many words, ideas, names she'd never heard.

And she realized, then, that that was what being raised at Haven truly meant, and why she would never be entirely human. It wasn't that they'd inserted needles to draw bone marrow or fed her a diet of pills, that they'd called her 'it', that she had never been held or cuddled, that her head had been shaved to keep out lice, and small fatal disease cells had been introduced into her muscle tissue just to watch what would happen. She'd been completely torn away from the human timeline, from a vast history of events, achievements, and names spanning more years than she could think of.

She had no context. She was a word on a blank page. There was no way to read meaning into it. No wonder she felt so alone.

'Actually, that was one of the reasons I was hoping that Dr Saperstein would show up today – other than taking a stand, I mean. I'm interested in medical tech, and I'm curious about the IP aspect. They're saying Cat O'Donnell might be up for a Nobel Prize. But she wouldn't have a career if it weren't for Haven. The whole idea of individual-specific stem cell regeneration . . . It seems obvious now, but that was a revolutionary idea.'

The name O'Donnell touched Lyra like the electric zap of the Extraordinary Kissable Graph: one of the machines she'd loved the best at Haven, which read her heartbeats and then drew them, vividly, in climbing green lines and vivid peaks that recalled the mountains she'd seen only on TV.

'You . . . you know Dr O'Donnell?' she asked.

'I mean, not personally.' Sebastian gave her a look she didn't know how to decipher. 'I just know her because of what she's doing at CASECS. I heard she used to work with Dr Saperstein at Haven,' he added, almost as an after-thought. 'That's why he's suing her. I guess he thinks she stole some of his research. Meanwhile O'Donnell won't say a word about it. Still, pictures never lie.'

He pulled out his cell phone and made adjustments to it, tapping and swiping the screen. Then he spun it across the table to her and she lost her breath.

There, in miniature, was Dr O'Donnell, stepping off one of the trash ferries that used to travel back and forth to Haven. She was wearing regular clothing, and her head was angled toward Dr Saperstein, who was next to her, but Lyra would have known her just from the geometry of her ear where it joined her jaw, by the color of her hair, by the way her mouth flattened when she thought.

Dr O'Donnell had given them names from the stars, and so she had given them a whole universe.

And in a single instant, Lyra realized how wrong she had been, how stupid.

Dr Saperstein wasn't God.

Dr O'Donnell was.

FIFTEEN

LYRA DIDN'T LIKE TO STEAL from Sebastian. He was nice. He had helped them. He had resurrected Dr O'Donnell, and shown them where CASECS was, only a short distance away in a place called Allentown.

But she was beginning to understand that those things didn't matter. Whether he was nice or not, he had a phone that she wanted, and so she took it when he wasn't paying attention.

Richard Haven had a whole building. He had his name above beautiful glass doors. And he was not nice.

Being nice didn't matter. Only taking did, the way animals took.

They wouldn't get far, Lyra knew, before Sebastian realized that Lyra had stolen his phone.

But they didn't need to get far. They didn't need distance to disappear.

Being invisible had benefits: it was easy to shoplift, as long as you picked a crowded store (Caelum's mistake in the 7–Eleven had been to steal when there was no one around to deflect the clerk's attention; when he had, for a brief, flaring moment, become visible); to edge a little too close, or lean a little too hard, and come away with a phone or a wallet; to pass into a restaurant and then stand up and leave again before anyone could ask that you pay.

Lyra was now throwing up almost everything she ate, but that was all right, that didn't stop her.

They'd agreed their best chance of getting into CASECS to see Dr O'Donnell was at night. They were thinking, of course, of Haven's security and of Caelum's escape, which could never have been accomplished during the day. By evening Caelum had two cell phones and a new wallet of his own, plus more than fifty dollars he'd skimmed from the tables of restaurants and cafés, and Lyra had a leather billfold and several credit cards, plus a necklace she'd found coiled at the bottom of a woman's purse when she'd dropped her hand casually down inside it.

Everything she added to her backpack made her feel better, less nauseous, less dizzy. She didn't understand gravity, but she knew intuitively every bit of weight, no matter how small, slowed her, made her mind turn less quickly, made her feel less as if she might drop down into a place where no one could find her.

It wasn't yet dark when they hired a car to take them to Allentown: their first time in a taxi. Though they didn't have an address for CASECS, the driver managed to locate it easily enough on his phone, and told them the route would take roughly an hour and a half in traffic.

Maybe she should have felt bad. Maybe she should have felt sorry for all the things they'd stolen. She wondered whether Sebastian was angry, whether the woman with the bright-pink lips from whom she'd taken the necklace would be sad.

But she didn't feel bad. They were going to see Dr O'Donnell, and Dr O'Donnell would make it all better. She was happier than she'd ever been, sitting in a sticky backseat that smelled like bubble gum, her backpack heavy on her lap, Caelum's hand occasionally brushing her thigh, her hand, her shoulder, like a bird exploring the territory. She felt human. Didn't humans, after all, take what they needed? Wasn't that what humans like Dr Saperstein, like Richard Haven, had always done?

They reached Allentown just as dusk lowered like an eyelid. From one minute to the next, streetlamps blinked on, and buildings lost form and instead became beaded strings of lit windows. They wheeled off the highway into long bleak alleys of car lots, parking garages, blocky office buildings, industrial complexes with names like Allegra Solutions and Enterprise Data. Lyra lowered the window and smelled gasoline and tree sap, frying oil and a faint chemical tang.

The taxi driver slowed, leaning over his steering wheel to squint hard at every street sign. Finally, they turned down a street identical to all the other streets except in name. On the corner, a Kmart showed off a cheerful block facade that reminded Lyra of Haven. A good sign. They kept going, past a fenced-in parking lot and a flotilla of bright-yellow school buses, all sickly in the fading light and pointed in the same direction, like fish suspended in the deep.

Several blocks later, the street dead-ended in a scrub of thinned-out, trash-filled woods. But as they approached, a narrow drive appeared behind a low stone wall, moving out of the shadow of the trees like some kind of optical illusion.

CASECS was marked by a single sign planted low in the grass. The *No Trespassing* sign next to it was leaning at an angle, and half-swallowed by a hedge that had begun to lose its shape. There were no patrolling soldiers, no guard towers, no obvious security measures: just a long, narrow sweep of driveway that pointed to a simple guard hut. The institute itself was concealed by the curvature of the drive, but the distant lights winking through the overhanging trees suggested a building much smaller than she'd been expecting.

Her heart began gasping, and she imagined the organ like the bird she and the other replicas had once found near A-Wing, sucking in frantic breaths.

'Here,' Lyra said.

The driver met her eyes in the rearview mirror. 'Here? You sure?' When Lyra nodded, he said, 'You want me to wait?'

'No,' Lyra said. Suddenly her happiness broke apart. It lifted into her chest and throat, and beat frantic wings against her rib cage. What if Sebastian had lied? What if he was wrong? What if Dr O'Donnell didn't remember her?

The driver turned around in his seat to peer at Caelum and Lyra, as if he'd just noticed them. 'You sure you gonna be okay getting back?'

'We're not going back,' she said, and he just shook his head and accepted the money they gave him. Too much, probably – Lyra was too nervous to count and let Caelum do the paying.

They waited until the cab light became distant and then blinked out. From where they stood, Lyra could see one of Allentown's major arteries. But this road, sloughed off by the main thoroughfare, was totally without movement, except for the occasional approach of a car toward the Kmart. Haven's security had depended on its remoteness. But CASECS was hiding in plain sight. No one would ever believe anything of importance would happen here, down the street from the school bus depot.

They went parallel to the driveway, on the shadowed side of the stone wall that continued along its length, concealed by a vein of trees that ran parallel to the pavement. They moved in silence, stopping every few feet to wait, and listen, and watch for security. But there was no movement, no distant voices or footsteps. Lyra should have been reassured, but instead, she only grew more anxious: she didn't understand what kind of place this could possibly be.

They stopped a short distance from the guard hut, edging closer to the stone wall in a crouch, hoping to be mistaken for rocks. Now they had a clear view of the CASECS complex. It was a fraction of the size of Haven: three stories high, blocky white and bleakly rectangular. Security was tighter than it first appeared. A fence ringed at the top with barbed wire marked the periphery and made climbing impossible. Lyra noted, too, the presence of Glass Eyes everywhere, and small glowing pinpricks, like the burning embers of cigarette butts.

That left only one option: they would simply have to walk in, and hope they wouldn't be shot.

They crouched, and they waited, learning the rhythm of the traffic in and out – almost all of it, at this hour, *out*. A sweep of headlights, the occasional patter of conversation as the guard – a woman with a sweep of blond hair and a booming laugh – leaned down to greet the driver. The mechanical gate clanked and shuddered open, then closed again. They counted seconds: twelve, thirteen, fourteen. The gate was open for anywhere from ten to twenty seconds. More than enough time to run, if they were quick, if Lyra didn't stumble.

Still, they would be heading for the guard directly, and Lyra was sure that she had a gun. She thought she could even see it: a dark bulge on the woman's hip.

For the first time the whole thing struck her as funny, that they were risking their lives to get back into a facility like Haven after risking their lives to escape in the first place.

'Let me go alone,' Lyra said to Caelum. Suddenly it seemed important to her, critical, even. She would die anyway, whether pulled apart by the ricochet of bullets or by falling into holes that got ever deeper and harder to escape. Caelum was White. He could go anywhere – he could continue stealing wallets and cell phones, he could drift and disappear and reappear again. There would be other girls who loved him, and saw him as beautiful: human girls, who never knew where he came from and didn't care. They would do what Lyra had done with him in the hotel room. They could turn themselves into living strands of music that played together.

'Don't be stupid,' Caelum said. 'We're together.' He stood up. When she hesitated, he reached back and took her hand again. 'Come on.'

They moved a little closer, until they were only a few feet from the perimeter fence and another, larger sign that announced CASECS to visitors. The headlights of a departing car made Lyra throw a hand up, momentarily dazzled. The gates clanked open again and then closed. The car swam past them, so close that Lyra could make out the silhouette of a man behind the wheel, turning to fiddle with the radio.

'Next one,' she said. She was suddenly having trouble breathing, and after only a few seconds her feet and legs felt numb and bloated, as if they'd been submerged in freezing water. What if she ran into the driveway and then froze, couldn't remember where she was or where she was going? She hoped Caelum would hold her hand the whole way, but she didn't want to ask.

'No,' Caelum said. 'We wait for a car going in. The headlights will give us time. The guard will go blind for two, three seconds.'

He was right. They waited. She squeezed her toes. She named all the bones she could think of – ankle, clavicle, tibia. She would have looked for the stars, too, but they were invisible behind the light-smear from the city.

Lyra lost track of time. Minutes went by, or hours. The

parking lot continued to empty. All the traffic flowed the wrong way. But at last a car approached from the direction of the Kmart, its headlights skimming the stone wall and then latching on to the guard hut, the fence, the harried-looking trees.

'Now,' Caelum said, as the gate began to grind open and the rhythm of conversation reached them – *how ya doing, another late one, huh?* Suddenly Lyra found that she could not remember how to stand. She tried to shout the urge to her legs, but they didn't hear her. She was stuck where she was, and as Caelum tried to get her to her feet, she simply landed knees down in the grass instead, barely missing the stone wall with her chin. It was as if her ankles had been bound together by invisible cording. *Stand, run, walk,* she thought, but her body remained blankly unresponsive, filled with a useless static.

It was too late now: the car was passing inside the complex, tires fizzing on the pavement. Lyra's heart was so swollen with fear she could feel it in her head, in her mouth, in the bottom of her stomach.

'What happened?' Caelum's face was unexpectedly illuminated: fluid cheekbones, dark eyes. He was so perfect, so alive, and she was so broken. White cluster. Control. His blood, she imagined, was a deep and royal blue, hers dark and sludgy. 'What's wrong?'

Then she realized why she could see him so clearly,

why every eyelash was drawn so vividly: yet another car was coming. This time she didn't even have to tell her body to move. She didn't have to think at all. She was on her feet. Caelum cursed, but he was right behind her. She made it over the fence but tripped getting over the curb.

The guard had once again moved into the light to greet the driver, and she was so close Lyra could see the blunt bob of her hair cut to her chin, see her uniform straining over her breasts and revealing a narrow slice of her bra. Lyra couldn't believe the guard didn't see them, that she didn't begin to shoot, but Caelum was right: with the headlights in her eyes, she *couldn't* see.

They came at an angle, scuttling low around the back of the car – a sleek and silver thing, like an elegant fish – until they were pressed up against the passenger side. Lyra thought even if the guard couldn't see them, she would surely hear the way Lyra's breath tore at her throat. A second woman's voice, high and laughing, touched off a nerve inside of Lyra's whole body, like the memory of something bad that had once happened to her. The smell of exhaust made her dizzy.

'You have a good night.' The guard was retreating to her hut. The gate churned open and the car eased off its brakes.

Lyra tried to keep pace, flowing through the gate at the same time the car did – but even as she stood up, the darkness stood too, the sense of vertigo and falling. She was pulled up and down at the same time. She was trying to leap over holes burning open at her feet. Her mouth tasted like gravel, like chemicals, like metal. Someone was shouting. She was at Haven and coughing blood.

'Get up, Lyra. Get *up*.'

Her ideas rotated. They pivoted and suddenly the true picture emerged: she was on the ground. She'd tripped. She wasn't at Haven. She was here, at CASECS, in Allentown, Pennsylvania, and the person shouting wasn't a doctor but a guard, *the* guard, who must have heard her fall.

The silver car had stopped. A woman leaned out the window to shout. *What happened, what's the problem, I can't understand you.*

'Not you, not you,' the guard said. But the woman in the silver car was still confused, and the car exhaust kept stinging Lyra's eyes. 'Those two, behind you, two kids, out of the way.'

Caelum grabbed Lyra by the elbow. The guard was running, and Lyra, still on her knees, saw the shiny polish of her boots, the walkie-talkie strapped to her belt, the gun holster. 'Hey, you. Hey, stop.'

Lyra made it to her feet, finally, just in time. But Caelum's hand was torn free – she lost him, they started off in different directions. Now she heard the crackle of radio interference and the guard shouting again and at the same time Lyra hurtled to the left, the car decided to turn too: she was blinded by a funnel of white light, she saw the grille leap toward her shins and she couldn't turn, she had no time.

The car hit her or she hit it. She cracked against the hood, rolled off an elbow, and went down.

A woman screamed. Caelum shouted to her but she couldn't call to him. She was on her back now, breathless beneath a starless sky. She couldn't move at all, couldn't feel her arms or legs. Maybe her spine had snapped, maybe her head had rolled off her body.

A car door opened and slammed closed. Footsteps, muted voices, an explosion of radio static and distant voices communicating in a slang patter. The headlights made a halo of her vision. Someone came toward her – Caelum? the guard? – but in the high beams faces became formless shadows.

'Look at her. She's just a girl.' It was the driver, her voice like a hand that tugged at an ancient memory. Haven and clean sheets and pages that turned with the soft *hush-hush* of wind through the grass. Then: 'Oh my God. My *God*.'

The guard was talking into her radio, so many words that they themselves became static bursts. 'That's right, just two kids, some kind of prank, the girl's down, the boy beat it when I tried to grab him, looks like he headed into the parking lot—'

'I know her. Do you understand? I *know* her.'

Fingers cool on Lyra's cheeks. The woman slid like an eclipse across the blinding bright lights. Her hair was dirty-blond and gray and loose, and tickled Lyra's face where it touched her.

'She belongs to Haven. I'm sure of it, I'm absolutely positive. . . .'

Lyra fell. She sank toward a warm and forgiving darkness. The pavement softened beneath her back, the night dissolved into a memory of other nights and other places.

'Can you hear me, hon? Can you hear my voice? Open your eyes if you can hear me.'

She thought she opened her eyes. It didn't matter anyway. In the dark behind her eyelids she saw a face, so familiar, so often recalled: the freckles and the wide, flat mouth, the smile that said *welcome, I love you, you're home.*

'She must have hit her head bad. . . .'

'Her name . . . I wish I could remember. . . . She was one of the earliest ones. . . .'

'What?'

Dim voices, trailing across her mind like distant comets. One a flinty blue. One the soft white dazzle of a shooting star.

'We named them. Some of the replicas. It was a game we played. They only had numbers before. It wasn't Cassiopeia . . . what was her name?'

Lyra, Lyra thought. She opened her mouth. Her words evaporated into bubbles of air.

'Jesus. Looks like she's trying to talk.'

The woman leaned closer. Her hair tickled Lyra's cheekbone. 'What's that, honey?' she whispered.

'Lyra,' Lyra managed to say, and the woman cried out softly, as if the word was a bird, some soft thing that had landed in her palm.

'Lyra,' she said. 'Of course. Can you open your eyes, Lyra?'

Lyra did, surprised by how much effort it took. The pavement hardened beneath her again. There was pain in her ankle, a sharp pain behind her eyes. Her mouth tasted like blood.

'Do you remember me, Lyra? My name is Dr O'Donnell. I knew you at Haven. Remember?'

She reached up to touch Lyra's face. Her fingers smelled like lemon balm.

SIXTEEN

LYRA WOKE UP AND FOR a confused moment thought she was back at the Winston-Able Mobile Home Park: in the distance she heard the thud of music and people laughing, the scattered catcall of loud and joyful conversation. But it was too clean, and it didn't smell right. When she moved, she thumped her head on the arm of a sofa.

'Sorry for all the noise.' When she heard Dr O'Donnell's voice, Lyra remembered: the car, the driver, the cones of light, and Dr O'Donnell's hair tickling her face. She turned and a flock of birds took off in her head, briefly darkening her vision. She must have cried out without meaning to, because Dr O'Donnell reached out and touched her cheek.

'Poor thing,' she said. 'We wrapped your ankle up nice and tight. It doesn't look broken to me, thankfully.'

Lyra noticed then that her ankle had been wrapped

tightly in tape, and various cuts and bruises had been treated with CoolTouch: it had left a shiny film on her elbow and shins.

'Is this CASECS?' she asked. The room looked nothing like a hospital. There was a desk cluttered with belongings in one corner, and shelves filled with books. A miniature fridge hummed in the corner, and a stuffed bear wearing a *Number One Boss* shirt gathered dust on top of it. Lyra was lying on a scratchy dark-wool sofa. There were framed posters on the walls, giant posters of people she didn't recognize. There was a clock on the wall, and a paper calendar with cats. There were no keypads on the door and the only lock was the handle variety.

'This is part of it,' Dr O'Donnell said. She wasn't even wearing a lab coat – just jeans and boots and a light sweater. Maybe that was why Lyra felt so shy around her – that and the gray in her hair, the lines around her eyes, the sharp angle of her nose, all features Lyra hadn't remembered. She had changed or she was different from the start, and either way, Lyra was nervous. 'We're a small operation. We keep a staff of just under a hundred and fifty. That includes the cleaning crew.' She smiled.

Then Lyra remembered Caelum, the way he'd veered off in the darkness when the headlights swept him, and the guard radioing for backup. 'Where's Caelum?' she asked, sitting up and blinking at another rush of birds in her head.

'Caelum. Is that what you call him?'

'That's his name,' Lyra said, and felt anxious for reasons she couldn't exactly say. The laughter, the distant drumming of music, a faint smell of alcohol – maybe it all stirred memories of Haven Christmas parties, when the researchers would remove their shoes to slide down the halls in their socks, and the air was edged with a taut, superficial tension, like the lip of water in a glass about to overflow.

'Don't be afraid,' Dr O'Donnell said, and that, at least, reassured her: Dr O'Donnell still had that skill. She could look at something, or someone, and understand. 'He looked hungry. Sonja – she's my research assistant – went for pizza. Caelum's probably halfway through it by now.' Her smile made new wrinkles appear and others collapse. 'Are you hungry?'

Lyra shook her head. She was dizzy, and nauseous, and thirsty. But not hungry. *I'm sick,* she wanted to say. *Help me.* But she was too shy. She wished Dr O'Donnell had been wearing a lab coat. Wished she'd looked more like a doctor, and that the room looked more like a hospital. Here she felt her sickness was a stain, that it would be terribly out of place.

Dr O'Donnell got a bottle of water from the miniature fridge, which was also stocked with Diet Cokes.

'Drink this, at least,' she said, once again as if she'd read Lyra's mind. She took a seat, and Lyra was aware of how closely Dr O'Donnell watched her drink, no doubt taking note of the way Lyra's hand shook. But Dr O'Donnell didn't comment on it, and she didn't offer to help, either. 'I still can't believe it's you. Number twenty-four, wasn't it?'

Lyra nodded. It was strange to hear the words out loud, even after only a few weeks, strange to think of herself again that way, *one of a series,* something that could be stacked or arranged.

Dr O'Donnell was watching her. 'A Green. Is that right?'

Lyra nodded again, this time because her throat seized.

'And Caelum,' Dr O'Donnell said, 'is he a Green, too?'

'Caelum is a control,' Lyra said, surprised the words brought a bad taste to her mouth. She was expecting Dr O'Donnell to look sorry for her and was glad she didn't. But she was also confused. Did Dr O'Donnell know what that meant? Did she know that meant Lyra was dying, and Caelum had to watch?

Dr O'Donnell was good, but she had known about the sickness. She had known about the variants and the prions and the holes opening up in Lyra's brain, and she had lied, like all the others, and claimed that Haven existed for the replicas' protection.

But maybe Dr Saperstein had forced her to lie.

In the silence, she heard a new swell of music. Someone

shouted, 'turn it up, turn it up', and there was laughter.

'Is there always music here?' she asked.

Dr O'Donnell laughed. 'Sometimes. Not usually so late, though. Some of the staff members are celebrating tonight.' She seemed to hesitate. 'We had some good news today.'

Lyra waited for her to go on, but she didn't. It was, she realized, the longest conversation she'd ever had with Dr O'Donnell. 'What kind of good news?'

Dr O'Donnell looked surprised. She didn't know that Lyra had learned how to ask, how to say please and thank you, how to put on mascara and speak to males. *Boys.* 'We'll be able to continue our work here,' she said carefully. 'We had – well, call it a contest. CASECS was up for an important award. And we won.'

'Award.' Lyra held the word on her tongue, and found it tasted like coins. 'You mean like money?'

Again, Dr O'Donnell looked startled. But almost immediately, she was serene again, and Lyra thought of a stone disappearing beneath the surface of a still pond. 'Yes, like money.' She pronounced the word as if it were unfamiliar to her. 'But more than that. Support. People who believe we're doing the right thing.'

Lyra wanted to ask her about a cure, and about whether Dr O'Donnell knew how to cure the twisted shapes deforming her brain. But before she could, Dr O'Donnell leaned forward and took her hands, and Lyra was startled by their dryness, by the coolness of her touch, both familiar and totally foreign. For some reason she thought of Rick and felt a strong impulse to run, to backpedal into the darkness, to rewind the miles they had covered and return to Winston-Able.

But almost immediately, the impulse passed, and she couldn't have said where it had come from. Rick was gone. The past was gone. Dead. You had to sever the lines and let it float off on the ocean, or you would simply sink with it.

'Tell me what happened to you, Lyra,' Dr O'Donnell said softly. 'Tell me everything that happened. It's important.'

'Haven burned down,' she said simply. 'Everything burned.'

She waited for Dr O'Donnell to express surprise, but she didn't.

'I heard,' she said finally, when Lyra said nothing more. 'It was in the news. And besides, Dr Saperstein – well, we stayed in touch, in a manner of speaking.' But a shadow had crossed her face and Lyra knew enough, now, to read Dr O'Donnell's unhappiness. They had always been fighting, Dr O'Donnell and Dr Saperstein. Most of what they'd said was above her head, full of scientific words that had washed over her like breaking water. But there had been one memorable fight about the rats, and whether or not the replicas should be allowed to have some toys and games.

Still – if Dr O'Donnell had left Haven because she wanted to help, why hadn't she come back when she heard about the fire?

Lyra was having trouble pinning her ideas of Dr O'Donnell down onto the face in front of her. That was always the problem with faces, with bodies: they told you nothing. Like the genotypes who looked the same but acted completely different. Cassiopeia was proud and strange and angry, but she collected seashells, she scooped insects from the path so they wouldn't be stepped on.

Then there was Calliope, who would catch spiders just to pull their legs off, one by one. Who'd once stepped on a baby bird, just to hear it crunch beneath her shoe.

'Caelum escaped with me,' Lyra said. 'We ran and hid. We didn't want to go back to Haven. They were making us sick.'

She waited for Dr O'Donnell to apologize or say that Dr Saperstein had forced the doctors to obey. But she just said, 'That was weeks ago. Where have you been all this time?' She seemed truly curious. 'Who fed you? Who gave you clothes? Who brought you here, to see me?'

It annoyed Lyra that Dr O'Donnell assumed someone else had brought them. She didn't want to tell Dr

O'Donnell about Gemma, or about Rick – they were hers, she decided suddenly, like bed number 24 had been hers, like *The Little Prince* had been hers after Dr O'Donnell gave her a copy.

'No one,' she said. Her voice sounded loud. 'We came ourselves. We took the bus and a taxi. We slept where we could. And we took what we needed.'

'You mean you stole it?'

'We took it.' Lyra was more than annoyed now. She was angry. 'Everybody else has things. Why shouldn't we?' Dr O'Donnell's cell phone was sitting there, on the counter, next to a coffee mug ringed with lipstick, and this infuriated Lyra more: it was evidence. Proof. 'People take things all the time. They took what they wanted from us at Haven, didn't they? Didn't you?' She didn't mean to say it, but the words came out and she wasn't sorry. She was happy when Dr O'Donnell released her hands, happy to think she had caused Dr O'Donnell pain.

But when Dr O'Donnell spoke, she didn't sound upset. She actually smiled. 'You're tired,' she said. 'You're sick. And, of course, you're right. You're *right*.' And Lyra couldn't understand it, but Dr O'Donnell began to laugh.

SEVENTEEN

AFTER A DINNER OF SALTY soup and crackers that dissolved in the broth, Lyra worked up the courage to tell Dr O'Donnell what she had come for: she wanted to live.

Dr O'Donnell listened in silence, resting one hand lightly on Lyra's knee. Lyra should have felt happy, because Dr O'Donnell was obviously so happy to see her.

But a shadow had attached itself to her thinking; everything dimmed beneath it. Why hadn't Dr O'Donnell come to help? Why did she allow the doctors to make all the replicas sick? What was CASECS, that there were no hospital beds but only sofas and armchairs and corkboards, where the doctors wore jeans and sneakers and music played at midnight?

She was reassured, however, when after a long pause, Dr O'Donnell stood up. 'Wait here,' she said, and slipped out the door. When she reappeared, she was holding a small, unmarked bottle of fluid, along with one of the long-snouted syringes Lyra had despised back at Haven, for their cruel curiosity. Now she was relieved to see it.

'What is it?' Lyra asked. Dr O'Donnell found a pair of medical gloves at the bottom of a desk drawer and cinched them carefully on her fingers.

'A new medicine,' Dr O'Donnell said. She drew the liquid carefully into the syringe, keeping her back to Lyra. 'Very rare. Very expensive.'

'Will it cure me?' Lyra asked. Hope buoyed her, swelled her with air, and made her feel as if she might lift off toward the ceiling. 'Will it make all the prions go away?'

'With any luck,' Dr O'Donnell said. Then: 'Hold out your arm for me.'

Dr O'Donnell offered Caelum a couch in the office next to hers, which belonged to a beautiful woman named Anju Patel. But in the end, since Caelum insisted on sleeping next to Lyra, Dr O'Donnell and Anju maneuvered a second couch into Dr O'Donnell's office instead.

'Sorry if there are any crumbs in the cushions,' Anju said. She had appeared suddenly, practically careening through the door, wearing sweatpants and an inside-out T-shirt, as if she'd dressed in a hurry. Lyra had overheard

Anju tell Dr O'Donnell she'd been in bed when someone had rung her up to share the news of Lyra and Caelum's arrival.

The medicine had filled Lyra with a kind of happy warmth: already, she could picture the prions breaking apart, like mist by the sun.

'Cupcakes are my coffee. I need at least one a day just to keep moving.' Anju turned to Dr O'Donnell. 'Sorry, I don't – I mean, do they understand me?'

'We understand you,' Caelum said. 'You like to eat cupcakes?'

For some reason his voice made Anju startle. Then she began to laugh.

'Oh God,' she said. She had tears in her eyes, soon, from laughing, though Lyra didn't know what was funny. 'Yeah, I do. I really do.'

After Dr O'Donnell had cleaned and bandaged the cut on Caelum's cheek and set him up with an ice pack to help reduce the swelling around his eye, she left in search of Advil and something to help Caelum sleep. Anju Patel stayed, staring. Her eyes, dark as the nicotine candies Rick had sucked sometimes, were enormous, and Lyra had a sudden fear she would be spiraled down inside them, like water down a drain.

'Are you a doctor too?' Lyra asked, both because she was curious and because she was slowly learning to dislike silence. At Haven, silence, her silence, had not been a choice but simply a condition.

Anju Patel laughed again. 'God, no,' she said. 'I can't even get my blood drawn. I'm a baby for things like that.' Lyra didn't know what she meant, or why anyone would be unable to have blood drawn – for a second she thought Anju meant there was something physically wrong with her, that she couldn't. 'I'm in sales. Licensing, really.'

'What's licensing?' Caelum asked. Lyra, too, had never heard the word.

Anju Patel's face changed. 'Do you like to ask questions?' she asked, instead of answering. 'Are you very curious?'

Caelum shrugged. Again the shadow swept across Lyra's mind, like a dark-winged bird brushing her with its feather.

'When we don't know something,' Lyra said, 'we ask to know it.'

Anju nodded thoughtfully, as if there were something surprising about that. Maybe Anju was just very stupid. She took a long time to answer.

'Licensing is about rights,' she said finally, very slowly. 'It's about who has the right to do what. It's about who has the right to own what.'

A chill moved down Lyra's body and raised the hair on her arms. It always came back to ownership.

'Let's say you have an idea, a good idea, and you want

to share it. To make sure other people can use it. But it was your idea, so you should get rewarded.' Anju was talking very slowly, like the nurses at Haven always had when they were forced to address the replicas directly. Maybe because they had known all along of the holes that would eventually make shrapnel of their brains; maybe they had already zoomed forward in time and seen the replicas idiotic, unable to control their bodies, paralyzed and silenced and then dead.

But didn't Anju know that Dr O'Donnell had given Lyra special medicine? Didn't she understand that Lyra's brain would be saved?

'You mean paid,' Caelum said, and Anju nodded.

'Exactly. So *licensing* takes care of that. We license a thing so that we can then replicate it all over –' she caught her use of the word, and smiled at them as if they were all sharing a joke – 'and make sure that no one uses it illegally, for free.'

In the outside that was the most important rule: that nothing was free, and everything would be paid for, one way or another.

Then something occurred to her. 'Were the replicas licensed?'

Anju barely moved, but nonetheless Lyra was aware that everything, even her skin, had suddenly tightened. 'What do you mean?'

She *was* stupid. She must be. 'Were the replicas licensed?' she repeated. 'Is that why the Gods –' an old habit, to think of them that way – 'I mean, why Dr Haven and Dr Saperstein were allowed to make so many of them?'

Anju seemed to relax, and Lyra wondered why the first question had bothered her. 'No, no,' Anju said. 'You can't license human beings. Licensing is for . . . well, for ideas. Techniques. Methods. Let's say I invented a new way to manufacture a chair, for example. I might patent that, and then sell it through a licensing agreement, so other people could use my method when they made their own chairs. Do you understand?'

Lyra did understand, at least in general terms. Licensing was a way to make money off replicating ideas, as far as she could tell. But she *couldn't* understand why CASECS needed a person like Anju Patel. Haven had never had a licensing department. She would have heard about it.

'Can you license a medicine?' Lyra asked, trying to puzzle out why CASECS, with its nest of cluttered offices and the smell not of antiseptic but of old carpet, made her uneasy.

'Oh, sure,' Anju said, and Lyra felt instantly better. That was all right, then. CASECS made cures and licensed them because in the outside world money was everything. 'You can patent a medical technique, too. About a hundred medical patents are issued per *month—*'

Anju broke off suddenly, and glancing up, Lyra saw that Dr O'Donnell had returned. In the split second before she knew Lyra's eyes had landed on her, she appeared baldly angry: it was like a raw, hard flush had ruined her complexion, even though Lyra didn't think her color had actually changed. The stain was invisible, and as soon as she saw Lyra she smiled and her face smoothed over.

'You must be so tired,' she said. 'All the way from Tennessee, all by yourselves.'

'I can have Sonja round up some blankets,' Anju said.

'Already did.' Dr O'Donnell didn't look at Anju, and her tone swept a thin band of cold through the room. She was obviously angry at Anju for speaking with the replicas, but Lyra didn't know why.

Anju left without another word. A moment later another woman appeared, this one even younger than Anju and with the stoop-shouldered look of someone who got tall very young, carrying an armful of blankets.

She also seemed as if she wanted to speak to Lyra and Caelum, but Dr O'Donnell intercepted her before she could even step foot in the room.

'Thank you, Sonja,' she said, in the same tone she'd used before on Anju. Lyra didn't remember this tone of voice. It reminded her of someone she knew, someone not from Haven but from outside, but she couldn't think who.

More holes, maybe, or she was simply tired. Her whole body ached. Her mind felt like a bruise, throbbing with a single message of pain and tenderness.

Dr O'Donnell had small white pills for Caelum that Lyra recognized as Sleepers. She felt a rush of sudden affection: the Sleepers were everyone's favorites, those small soldiers that herded you off into a mist of dreaming. But when Lyra reached out for her dosage, Dr O'Donnell shook her head.

'It isn't safe,' she said. 'Not when you cracked your head. I'll have to wake you every few hours. Sorry,' she said, but any regret Lyra felt was outweighed by the sudden pleasure of Dr O'Donnell's expression, which softened into the one she remembered so well. Instead Lyra got reddish Advil pills, slick and sugared on her tongue.

Caelum settled on the couch next to Lyra's. He hadn't said much since Anju had first appeared, except to say he wouldn't leave Lyra, and when Dr O'Donnell tried to place a blanket over him he caught her wrist, and for a moment they were frozen there, staring at each other.

'I'll do it,' he said. But already Lyra saw him relaxing, as the Sleepers did their work.

'I'll be here all night,' Dr O'Donnell said. 'Just shout if you need something.' She smiled at Lyra, and momentarily the changes to her face, the new wrinkles and the slightly thinner skin, were erased. 'And I'll see you in a few hours.'

She turned off the lights. It was surprisingly dark. The window was covered by thin slat-blinds but must have been facing away from the parking lot, toward the fence and beyond it, the woods. The only light at all came from a tissue-thin crevice around the door, which appeared as a result like a faint, glowing silhouette. But Lyra could still hear the muffled rhythm of music, although after only a minute, it cut off abruptly. Then: footsteps ran like water, and whispered voices outside their door soon flowed away.

'Caelum?' Lyra whispered. Then, a little louder: 'Are you awake?'

He didn't answer for so long she thought he wouldn't. When he did speak, the edges of his words were round and soft, as if they were melting on his tongue. 'I don't trust her,' was all he said.

Lyra wanted to be angry with him. CASECS and its unfamiliar sounds, its dizzying arrangement of cubicles and ceiling tiles and cluttered desks and new names, had exhausted her. 'You don't know her like I do,' she said. 'That's all.'

Caelum didn't respond. After a minute, she heard his breathing slow and realized he was asleep. She closed her eyes, expecting to drop quickly into a dream, but instead she found her mind cycling, insect-like, landing quickly on old memories, on visions of Haven, on quick-splice images she'd thought she had forgotten.

She was still awake when the door opened again. She thought at first it was because Dr O'Donnell was coming to check on her. A band of light fell sharply across her eyes. She squeezed her eyes shut, and was about to ask for water when she heard an unfamiliar voice and froze.

'Are you sure they're sleeping?' It was a boy's voice, totally unknown to her.

'Positive. O'Donnell was hunting around for Ambien.'

Because of the lightening of the colors behind her eyelids, Lyra knew they were standing there in the doorway, staring.

'It's weirder in person,' the boy said, after a minute. 'They look so . . . normal. Don't they?'

'What did you think? They'd have three heads or something?'

'Shut up. You know what I mean.' Then: 'Do you think . . . do you think they dream and everything?'

'I don't see why not. Dr O'Donnell says they . . . like we do,' the girl whispered, so softly that even the rustle of Caelum's blankets when he turned blew some of her words away. 'She never had proof before. So many of the others were morons. She told me some of them couldn't even use the toilet. But these . . .'

Caelum rolled over again, and so the boy's response was

lost. When he finally settled down, the girl was already speaking.

'. . . depending on what you use them for.' There was a long stretch of quiet, and Lyra feared, though she knew it was impossible, the girl would hear the knocking of her heart and know she was awake and listening. 'Everyone always thought AI would come from computers. But we did it first. Biology did it.'

For a long time, they didn't speak again.

'It's kind of sad, in a way,' the boy said at last.

'You can't think of it like that,' the girl responded. 'You have to remember there's a purpose.'

'Cha-ching,' the boy responded. Lyra didn't know what it meant.

'Sure,' the girl said. She sounded annoyed. 'But that isn't the only reason. We can save hundreds of thousands of lives. Maybe we'll even cure death.'

'Who knew,' the boy said, 'eternal life would spring from a cooler in Allentown, Pennsylvania?'

He closed the door, sealing out the light. Lyra's heart was beating fast. She rolled over to face Caelum, trying to slow the frantic drumming of her pulse, listening to the sound of their intermingled breathing. She thought about what she had overheard: the talk of AI, which she didn't understand; licensing, the key to eternal life. She had mis-understood many things, but she had understood that the key was here, somewhere in CASECS, locked in a cooler.

Perhaps the key was in the medicine that Dr O'Donnell had given her. Or perhaps it was a real key, or a kind of medical equipment.

Though it should have been an electrifying idea, instead it made her uncomfortable. At Haven, they had tried to be gods by making life: and so the replicas had suffered for their miracle.

She wondered what it would look like to cure death, and who would have to suffer for it.

As her mind wandered through strange corridors that bordered on dream, she thought for some reason of a bird they'd found on one of the courtyard pathways when she was a child: a scrawny brown thing, smaller than her palm, it must have mistaken the reflection in one of the windows for an aerial pathway and flown straight into the glass.

She remembered the way it had tried to hop to safety as the replicas had crowded around it, and her sudden lurching awareness of death all around them, not just in the clean white folds of the Box, not contained or containable. And then Calliope, who was then only called number 7, had stepped forward and driven her foot down on top of it, so hard they all heard the *crunch*.

It was broken, Calliope had said. *It's better to kill it. It's the right thing.*

But Lyra had suspected, had known, that she had just

wanted to know what would happen. She was curious to know what it would feel like, that small fragile second when a life snapped beneath her shoe with the sharp crack of a flame leaping to life from the head of a match but in reverse: the sound of darkness, not light.

EIGHTEEN

WHEN SHE FINALLY SLEPT, SHE had a dream of standing in the middle of a large metal chamber that vibrated like the interior chamber of Mr I, while Anju spoke over the roar, explaining how to license chairs.

Leaning forward over the railing, Lyra saw hundreds and hundreds of chairs lined up along the tongue of a conveyor belt, and for some reason she was repulsed by them, by their jointed design and the crooked look of their spindly legs – until, looking closer, she saw they weren't made out of wood or plastic, but out of human arms and legs, human feet, thousands of bodies hacked up and rearranged and made available, Anju was saying, for sale on a large scale.

She woke up sweating. The morning, which should have been filled with a buzz of activity and voices, was instead profoundly quiet. Caelum had opened the blinds, and his face was cut into horizontal stripes of light.

'How are you feeling?' he asked her, without turning away from the window.

She sat up, shaking off the sticky remnants of her dream. Her whole body was sore and her legs were purpling with enormous, flower-shaped bruises. But her head was clearer. Maybe the medicine was working already.

'Better,' she said. 'What are you doing?'

He turned to face her. 'The windows are barred. It doesn't make any sense. There's nothing but telephones and office rooms and computers. So why bar the windows and put up the fence? Why security?'

'They want to keep people from getting in,' Lyra said.

'Why? If they're making medicines, if they're curing diseases, why all the secrecy?' He shook his head. 'They're hiding something.'

Lyra was annoyed. Caelum saw danger in everything and everybody. But it was easy for him to doubt. He wasn't the one who needed a cure.

And what bothered her most, deep down, was that she knew he was right.

'Maybe they don't want anyone stealing from them,' she said. She was about to tell him what she had overheard in the night – about the key to eternal life, about the magic cooler – when the door opened and a blond girl came in with a paper bag that said *Dunkin' Donuts*. Her face was shaped exactly like a circle, her eyes like two exclamation points of surprise.

'Dr O'Donnell said you might want breakfast.' She looked nervous, Lyra thought – as if she were the one who felt out of place.

'Where is Dr O'Donnell?' Lyra asked.

The girl looked startled, as if she hadn't expected questions. 'Putting out fires,' she said, and Lyra frowned. 'I don't mean real fires,' the girl added, seeing that Lyra didn't understand, and she giggled a little. 'It's just an expression.'

'It means there's been an emergency,' Caelum said. Lyra looked at him, surprised. 'I heard Rick say it.'

Thinking of Rick and the people who had taken him made Lyra feel nauseous again. She wondered whether they were still out there, searching for her and Caelum. She wondered whether she really had seen the man at UPenn or only imagined it; she wondered if they could track her to CASECS. But Dr O'Donnell would protect her.

She'd promised.

'What emergency?'

Now the girl definitely looked nervous. 'Dr O'Donnell says you have to eat something,' she said, avoiding the question entirely. 'I have some water for you, too.'

She deposited the bag on top of the mini fridge and, as

she went to root around inside it, toppled the small vial of special medicine that Dr O'Donnell had left, stoppered, for Lyra's morning dosage. Lyra shouted and Caelum made a dive for it.

But it was too late. It hit the ground and opened, liquid seeping out into the carpet. For a second, Caelum stayed there, his hand outstretched. Then he drew back, and Lyra felt a sharp pain: as if something hot had gone straight through her lungs. Unexpectedly, tears came to her eyes.

The blond girl stared from Lyra to Caelum and back. 'What?' she said. 'What is it?' She followed the direction of Lyra's gaze then, and gave a quick laugh. 'Oh,' she said. Carelessly, she snatched up the now-empty vial and tossed it once, catching it in her palm. 'Don't worry. It won't stain.' Lyra could only stare at her.

'I *mean* –' the girl sighed and slipped the vial into her pocket – 'it's just saline, anyway. Salt and water never hurt anybody.'

'She lied to me.'

They were alone again. The girl had left them, promising to get Dr O'Donnell, frightened perhaps by Lyra's stillness. This hole was worse than any yet, because she was conscious, she was aware, she was remembering. But she felt that enormous walls of darkness had grown to enclose her. She was shivering at the very bottom of a pit. Caelum was speaking to her from somewhere very far away.

'We have to go. Lyra, listen to me. We have to find a way out of here, now.'

'Why did she lie to me?' She was so cold. Her hands and lips were frozen. Corpses grew cold, she knew; she had touched one before, the day that she had found number 236 dead, her wrists cabled to her bedposts. 'It doesn't make any sense.'

'Of course it does.' Caelum grabbed her shoulders. 'They're all liars, Lyra. Didn't I tell you? Each and every one of them is the same.'

She didn't want to believe it. But when she closed her eyes, she saw memories revolving, taking on new dimensions. She had overheard Dr O'Donnell fight with Dr Saperstein, and had always believed it meant that Dr O'Donnell loved them. But if she'd really loved them, why hadn't she tried to end the experiment? She had once tried to convince Emily Huang to stand up to God. But she hadn't stood up herself. She hadn't exposed Haven.

She had just left.

She had left to do her own experiments, to do whatever it was they really did at CASECS. To *license*. All the times that Dr O'Donnell had read to Lyra and the others, had taught them about the stars – was that simply its own experiment?

Maybe all people were the same – they all wanted

different things. But they all demanded the *right* to want whatever it was they wanted. They all thought of it as their birthright.

Caelum let Lyra go. He turned back to the door and tried the handle: locked, from the outside. He aimed a kick for the door and Lyra didn't even startle at the noise. Dr O'Donnell had lied to her.

All people were the same.

There was nowhere to go, nowhere for them to run, no time left for her. What did it matter whether she died here or somewhere else?

'We shouldn't have come here.' Caelum's voice cracked, and Lyra wanted to tell him it was okay, that it didn't matter anymore.

'What choice did we have?' Everywhere Lyra turned she hit walls and more walls. 'I'm running out of options, Caelum. I'm dying.' It was the first time she'd ever admitted it to Caelum.

When had she become so afraid of dying? For most of her life, she'd seen death as deeply ordinary, almost mechanical, like the difference between having a light on or off. She was afraid that death would be like falling into one of the holes, except that this one would never end, that she would never reach the bottom of it.

She couldn't stand to look at him, at the angular planes of his cheekbones, at his beautiful eyelashes and lips, all of it undamaged, pristine, *beautiful*. She was unreasonably angry at him – for being so healthy, for being so beautiful.

Because she knew, of course, that Caelum was the reason she was afraid. She'd never had a reason to care about whether she lived or not. Caelum had given her the reason. Now he would continue, while she would end.

'Don't,' she said, when he tried to touch her. But he got her wrist before she could turn away from him.

'Hey,' he said, and put a hand on her face, resting his thumb on her cheekbone, forcing her to look at him. 'Hey.'

They were chest to chest, breathing together. His eyes, so dark from a distance, were up close layered with filaments of color. She felt, looking at them now, the way she did when looking up at the dark sky, at the stars wheeling in all that blackness.

'I would trade places with you if I could,' he said. He moved his hand to her chest, and her heartbeat jumped to meet his fingers. 'I would trade in a second.'

'I know,' she said. She was calmer now. He had that effect – he softened her fears, blunted them, the way that when night fell it softened corners and edges.

'I'll stay with you, always,' he said. 'I want you to know that. I'll never leave you again. I'll go with you anywhere. Anywhere,' he repeated, and then smiled. 'You tamed me, remember? Like the little prince tamed the fox in the desert. And you named me and made me real.'

She wanted to tell him she loved him. She wanted to tell him she was afraid. But she couldn't get the words out. Her throat was too tight.

Luckily, he said it first. 'I love you, Lyra,' he said.

'Me too,' she managed to say.

He kissed her. 'I love your lips,' he said. 'And your nose.' He kissed her nose, then her eyebrows, then her eyelids and cheeks. 'I love your eyebrows. Your cheeks.' He took her hand and gently brought her pinkie finger into his mouth, kissing, sucking gently, and now the distinction between her body and his began to erode. She was his mouth and her finger, his breath and her heartbeat, his tongue and her skin, all at once. 'I love your hands,' he whispered, moving finger to finger.

'Me too,' she said, and closed her eyes as he knelt to kiss her stomach, explored her hipbones with his tongue, naming all the places he loved, all the inches of skin, the seashell parts spiraled deep inside of her, filled with tides of wanting.

But her wanting wasn't a right. It was a gift. It was a blessing. She came to it on her knees, holding out her arms.

'Me too,' she said, and every place he kissed her, her skin came alive, and told her she had to live.

NINETEEN

THE LOCKS AT CASECS HADN'T been made to keep people prisoner – especially people like Lyra and Caelum, who were only half-people, raised in a place where a thousand different locks controlled the motion of their daily lives. Lyra and Caelum knew locks that beeped and locks that spun, locks that clicked and locks that jammed. Each of them had its own language, its own clucking tongue.

They rooted in Dr O'Donnell's desk. Lyra turned up a business card like the kind the Suits had carried into Haven, dropping occasionally like scattered jewels for the replicas to collect: this one carried the name Allen Fortner. She knew this must mean that Dr O'Donnell had business with the Suits, or wanted to, even before she turned up a to-do list that included the item: *Call Geoffrey Ives.*

Rifling through a notepad, she found many to-do lists, and many calls to Gemma's father.

She wondered whether he was already on his way.

More likely, he had simply sent someone to take care of Lyra and Caelum; he was the kind of person who spoke through his money.

She stuffed her pockets with paper, with Post-it notes, with business cards and scrawled reminders. Evidence, although she still wasn't sure what it proved. But every piece of paper, every scrap, hardened a sense of rage and injustice.

If she had any time left, any time at all, she would take the words and light them on fire so they would explode everywhere; they would drift like a cloud and blacken Dr O'Donnell's name, and CASECS's name, and Geoffrey Ives's name too. Even if she died, she would find a way to make the words live.

In the bottom drawer, behind a rubble of loose pens, they found a handful of bobby pins. Caelum straightened out one of the bobby pins and inserted it into the keyhole, wiggling until he heard it click. In less than five seconds, they were free.

The hallway was empty, and branched in both directions. Lyra saw no exit signs and couldn't remember which way to go. The night before, she'd been too overwhelmed to pay attention. Caelum had been brought in by security and was distracted by a small cluster of people who had gathered to watch, but he thought they should turn left, and so they did.

Caelum was right about the rest of CASECS: it was

all carpeted hallways and offices marked with unfamiliar names, conference rooms and cubicles. Lyra saw signs of the previous night's celebration: a bottle of wine, uncorked, and plastic cups that had pooled liquid onto a conference table. There were coffee mugs still exhaling steam at empty desks, and abandoned jackets, purses, and cell phones everywhere, suggesting their owners had, indeed, come to work only to be spirited away.

Fear moved like a film of sweat across Lyra's body. The hallway seemed to keep unrolling extra feet, stretching endlessly past the same bleak workstations, as if it were expanding. She kept spinning around, thinking she heard footsteps on the carpet, expecting to see Dr O'Donnell bearing down on them. But they saw no one but a guy wedged into a cubicle, fiddling with a grid of numbers on his computer, ears obscured beneath palm-sized headphones. He didn't see them.

Finally, the hallway dead-ended and they turned right, startling a girl holding a bakery box. She nearly dropped it, yelped, and turned to hurry away – as if *she* had reason to be afraid of them.

'We have to hurry,' Caelum said, as if Lyra didn't know. But she spotted a set of double doors where the girl had whipped out of sight around another turn, and she and Caelum grabbed hands and ran.

Lyra's heart was gasping. As they got close she thought

it might burst; she saw a keypad like the kind they had used at Haven, which required an ID to swipe. But the doors had been propped open with an old paperback book, and beyond them was a stairwell and a sign pointing the way to further levels.

The stairs went down, and twisted them around several landings, past a level called Sub-One, which was unlit. Through a set of swinging doors, Lyra saw a vast room filled with nothing but old machines, abandoned workstations, and freight containers. The double doors opened at her touch.

'In here?' she whispered to Caelum. But just then, a patter of footsteps passed overhead, and he shook his head and pulled her on.

As they descended, the air got noticeably cooler. Lyra remembered what the boy had said about a refrigerator. She pictured an enormous, chilled space, like a dead heart, filled with endless chambers.

The stairs bottomed out at a heavy metal gate; this one was closed and required a digitized code to open. Beyond it was a plain white windowless door, fitted with yet another keypad and marked with a small sign that simply said: *Secure Area – Live Samples*. Lyra's blood rushed a frantic rhythm to her head, and in its rhythm she heard the certainty of dark secrets. Whatever CASECS made, whatever Dr O'Donnell built with all her wanting, it was here.

They had no choice but to backtrack. The climb left Lyra winded and she had to rest on the landing, leaning heavily against Caelum, before they slipped once again through the propped-open doors at the top of the stairs. Maybe, Lyra thought, there was no exit. Maybe Dr O'Donnell had trapped them, the way in the early days Haven had placed rats in mazes that didn't lead anywhere, to test how long it took for the sick ones to learn all the dead ends.

They turned again, and this time Lyra's heart leapt: an exit sign pointed through a set of doors only twenty feet away. She was so happy she failed to register the sudden swell of voices. She slipped easily away from Caelum even as he tried to grab her.

'Lyra, wait.'

But she had started toward the sign already, hooked on the glowing comfort of its syllables. *Exit.* A funny word, and one she had only lately come to love. At Haven, she had always thought the exit signs were taunting her.

She was halfway there when the wave of voices finally broke across her consciousness; as if the sound was a physical substance and she had mindlessly stepped into its current. Forty or fifty people were gathered in a conference room to crowd around a wall-mounted TV. Had they been turned to face the hallway instead, Lyra would have been visible. She was rooted directly in the middle of the doorway, frozen with sudden terror.

Dr Saperstein was staring directly at her.

For a confused and terrified second, she mistook the image for the real thing and thought he was really there, staring bleakly over all the CASECS employees, pinning her with his eyes. But of course he wasn't. It was just an old picture, an image made huge by the television. Almost immediately, Dr Saperstein vanished, and a female newscaster with stiff black hair and an even stiffer smile took over the screen.

The rush of blood in Lyra's ears quieted. But just for a minute.

'. . . confirmed that Dr Mark Saperstein was indeed found dead this morning at an undisclosed location . . .'

A microwave beeped. No one bothered with it. They were all still. Lyra felt as if the air was being pressed out of her lungs.

'Though Dr Saperstein had just undergone a spectacularly public fall from grace, culminating in this week's protests at his alma mater, the University of Pennsylvania, the police have denied reports that his death was a suicide. . . .'

Dead. Dead. Dead. The word kept drilling in Lyra's mind. Dr Saperstein was dead. God was dead. She should have been happy, but strangely, she was just frightened. It had never occurred to her that God would die, or that it was even possible.

She was less than fifteen feet from the exit. No one had seen her. And yet she couldn't move, and even Caelum hesitated, teetering on the edge of the doorway as if it were a river he was worried about crossing.

Eight seconds, maybe ten. Twelve at a stretch.

God had died, and with him, the replicas' only reason for being.

Was a terrible reason better than no reason at all?

'There they are. Get them. *Get* them.'

Lyra turned and saw Dr O'Donnell charging them and trailing a small crowd of people behind her; among them were three guards and the girl who'd dropped the bakery box.

And at the same time, in response to her shout, everyone in the conference room turned and spotted Lyra.

She ran. Caelum was shouting over the sudden chaos, and though she couldn't hear him, she could feel him a step behind her. They had a small advantage, but it was enough. They were steps from the door, inches, they could get outside, they would be free—

But even as Lyra reached for the door, it opened forcefully from the other side. Caelum managed to pull up, but Lyra was thrown backward by the blunt collision, as with a hard and hollow smack the door caught her in the side of her jaw. She landed on her back, breathless and dizzy. Through a fuzz of dark shapes she saw a whip-thin man, soaked with toppled coffee, gaping at her.

Caelum tried to get her to her feet but by then Dr O'Donnell had caught up, and the guards drove him to his knees, and Lyra saw a thicket grow above her: a nest of mouths and unfamiliar faces, long arms that looked like weapons. Cold fingers locked her wrists in place. Some-one sat on her ankles.

They look so real, somebody said.

You'd never know.

Be careful how you handle them, please. That was Dr O'Donnell. *It looks like they may be the last ones.*

TWENTY

THIS TIME THEY WERE PLACED in an unused office whose only furniture was a set of metal filing cabinets and two chairs brought in for Caelum and Lyra to sit on, although Caelum remained standing. The door required a key. Dr O'Donnell had locked them in herself.

'Give me a minute,' she'd told them, almost apologetically. She couldn't stop pretending that she was on their side. She probably didn't know the difference.

Standing with her ear to the door, Lyra could hear Dr O'Donnell speaking to someone in the hall.

'She says they came here on their own, with no help. I doubt she knows a thing.'

There was only silence in response, and Lyra realized that Dr O'Donnell was talking on the phone. Her skin tightened into a shiver. Dr O'Donnell knew the Suits. How long would it be before they arrived?

'She hasn't mentioned Gemma at all, but I can ask.' Another silence. 'You think she ended up there by mistake?'

Lyra leaned so hard against the door, sweat gathered in the space behind her ear. For a long time, Dr O'Donnell said nothing, and Lyra worried she might have hung up.

But then she spoke again. 'I'm sure she's okay, Geoff. I'm sure she made it out.' Then: 'No, I understand that. But she's a smart girl. You've said so yourself.'

Lyra put a hand on the door and pressed, imagining she could squeeze her rage out through her fingertips, harden it into blades that would slice them free. Geoff meant Geoffrey Ives. Though she didn't understand much of the conversation, she understood that something bad had happened to Gemma.

Something had happened to her by mistake. She was in trouble. And Lyra knew, without question or doubt and without knowing how she knew, that it was because Gemma had come to warn her.

Had Gemma, like Rick, been taken away?

She thought of Jake Witz hanging by his belt, and the purple mottle of his face.

The memory brought back a roar of sound, a memory of Haven exploding into flame, and the char of burning skin carrying over the marshes. She nearly missed the next thing Dr O'Donnell said.

'I see. So how many of them escaped?' Then: 'We can still use them, you know. If we could spin it—' She broke off. After another minute, she spoke again, this time so close to the door that Lyra startled backward and could still hear her clearly. 'Well, maybe it's for the best. Public support will be the trickiest. If word gets out that they can be violent . . .'

The last thing she said was, 'I'm praying for Gemma.'

Lyra couldn't help but wonder whether anyone in the whole world was praying for her and for Caelum. She doubted it.

Then Lyra had to stumble out of the way, because Dr O'Donnell turned the key in the lock and opened the door. For a half second, Lyra didn't recognize her: the lines of her face had converged into a baffling question mark.

'Sit,' Dr O'Donnell said. Neither Caelum nor Lyra moved. 'Go on. Sit. Please. I won't hurt you.'

'You're a liar,' Caelum said. 'Everything you say is a lie.'

Dr O'Donnell sighed. She must have gone home at some point to change; she was wearing different clothing than she had been last night. Lyra hated her for this – that she would think to go home, that she would think to shower, that Lyra and Caelum were so small in the orbit of her life they hadn't even caused a ripple in her routine.

'I wasn't lying when I said I could help you,' Dr O'Donnell said. 'I'm sure I don't need to tell you this, but you're in a difficult position. You're not supposed to exist.'

Although she said the words gently, Lyra knew them for what they were: sharp, weaponized things, knives designed to make her bleed. She wouldn't argue, or cry, or show that they had landed.

'What happened to Gemma?' she said.

Dr O'Donnell looked momentarily startled, and Lyra was glad: she had an advantage, however brief.

Dr O'Donnell recovered quickly. 'You're very observant,' she said. 'I'd forgotten that.'

'There wasn't much to do but observe at Haven,' Lyra said. A wave of dizziness clouded her vision, and she wanted to sit down but didn't want to give Dr O'Donnell the satisfaction. 'What happened to Gemma?'

'I don't know,' Dr O'Donnell said, after a short pause. 'No one knows. It seems she disappeared on Sunday morning.'

So. It *was* Lyra's fault.

Dr O'Donnell moved away from the door – slowly, as if Caelum and Lyra might startle, as if there was anywhere for them to go. 'Can I ask you a question?' She held up both hands when Caelum started to protest. 'Then you can ask me anything you want, and I'll be honest. I promise to tell you everything you want to know.'

Caelum's eyes locked briefly on Lyra's. She shrugged.

'Go on,' Lyra said. Finally, she took a seat, hoping that Dr O'Donnell hadn't noticed her relief. Caelum, however, stayed where he was. 'But then it's our turn.'

Dr O'Donnell called up a smile with obvious difficulty. 'I promise,' she repeated. Since Caelum wasn't sitting, she took the empty chair instead, and drew it across from Lyra, so they were almost knee to knee. She leaned forward, and Lyra was sure she would ask about Gemma.

But instead she said, 'Do you know how many replicas escaped Haven after the explosion?'

Now Lyra was the one who was surprised.

'Why does it matter?' Caelum asked.

Dr O'Donnell barely turned her head to give him a tight smile. 'You said you'd answer first.'

Lyra shook her head. 'I don't know,' she answered honestly. 'Caelum and I were hiding. We got under the fence. . . .' When she closed her eyes, she could still see the zigzag of flashlights, and hear the rhythm of helicopters threshing the smoke beneath their propellers. Dozens of them, passing back and forth, back and forth. She remembered screaming. 'There were rescue helicopters, though. So there must have been some. Dr Saperstein survived, didn't he?' Dr O'Donnell nodded. 'The explosion happened in A-Wing. But there wouldn't have been replicas there.'

Dr O'Donnell was quiet for a bit. She clutched her hands, making her knuckles very white. Were they really the same hands, Lyra wondered, that had smuggled books onto Spruce Island, had touched Lyra's forehead when she was feverish?

'Why?' Caelum asked again. When she looked down at her hands, he said, 'You promised to answer.'

Dr O'Donnell shook herself, as if she were passing out of a rain. 'I never liked what Dr Saperstein was doing at Haven,' she said. 'Research of that magnitude . . .' She cleared her throat. 'Secrets breed violence. The bigger the secret, the bigger the violence.' Suddenly, she stood up, moving not toward the door but to a barred window with a view of nothing but a blight of straggly trees. 'Dr Saperstein is dead. His secrets killed him. And it's possible – it's likely – that the replicas he brought up from Florida managed to escape.'

'Where?' Lyra asked.

'I don't know.' Dr O'Donnell turned to them when Caelum made a noise in his throat. 'That's the truth. I don't know. Somewhere in Lancaster County, only an hour or so south of here. That's all I know. We weren't exactly on the best of terms.'

'He was suing you,' Lyra said, parroting back what Sebastian had told her. Again, Dr O'Donnell looked surprised.

'You were always very smart,' Dr O'Donnell said. Lyra wanted to hit her.

She gripped the sides of her chair, as another wave of dizziness nearly took her sideways. 'What do you make here, if you aren't making cures?'

Dr O'Donnell turned back to the window. She waited so long to answer, Lyra began to think that her promise had also been a lie.

But finally she did. 'Dr Haven and Dr Saperstein were convinced that their work could only be done in secret,' she said. 'That was wrong.'

'You said that already,' Caelum said.

'Just *listen*.' A sigh moved from Dr O'Donnell's shoulders down her spine. 'I've spent years doing nothing but speaking to people – scientists, engineers, politicians, even – about how important this research is. How important it should be.'

Lyra decided she hated that word – *important*. The way Dr O'Donnell said it made her want to spit. As if it were a beautiful piece of glass, as if Dr O'Donnell was beautiful just because she carried its syllables around on her tongue. How many people, Lyra wondered, were dead because of someone else's importance?

'That's what we do at CASECS. We promote research. We give hospitals, facilities, even governments the chance to do their *own* research. That's where you come in.' Dr

O'Donnell turned away from the window again. She wasn't smiling. 'There's nowhere else for you to go. I know you understand that. If you leave, you'll eventually be caught by the same people who wanted to erase you in the first place.'

'I'm dying anyway,' Lyra said. 'Aren't I?'

Dr O'Donnell winced, as if Lyra had fired something sharp at her forehead.

'You lied about a cure,' Lyra said, although the words curdled in her mouth and left her with a bad taste in her throat. 'Admit it.'

Dr O'Donnell looked down. 'There's no cure,' she said softly. But Lyra thought, unbelievably, that she really sounded sorry about it. Still, the words fell like a thin knife, Lyra felt, slicing the world in two. She remembered the moment that Caelum had grabbed her wrist and she'd seen his mud-coated nails and felt the strange warmth and newness of his touch, and then a rocketing blast had driven her off her feet. She had thought, then, the world might be ending.

Instead it was ending here, in this room.

'We hardly understand prions,' Dr O'Donnell said. 'Dr Saperstein understood them better than anyone in the world, probably, and he wasn't looking for a cure. The whole point was to study a class of disease that we knew hardly anything about. To see how it could be manipulated, to understand it by making different variations and observing their effects.' She shook her head. 'He was collecting data. It *had* to be incurable.'

Lyra thought of all the replicas she'd ever known – Lilac Springs and Rose and Cassiopeia and the hundreds of numbered ones they'd never named – standing in a vast row against a blinding sunshine, looking like pen strokes on a page. Looking like data.

'So why does it matter?' Lyra said. 'Why does it matter, if I'm just going to die?'

Dr O'Donnell looked up. 'I'm offering you more time,' she said.

Years collapsed in a second. Just for a second, Lyra fell back into the fantasy of Dr O'Donnell as her savior, as her mother, as her friend.

'We don't want anything from you,' Caelum said.

At the same time Lyra asked, 'How?'

Dr O'Donnell spoke in a quiet rhythm Lyra knew from their Sunday readings. 'Most people in the world – the vast majority of people – don't even know it's possible to clone human beings. They've heard about cloning sheep, and cloning human organs, even. Dogs, apes, cows, on rare occasions. But Haven's work was kept so confidential – secret, I mean – that most people, if you told them a single human clone was alive in the world, eating, breathing, thinking – *they wouldn't believe it.*'

When Dr O'Donnell spoke, it was like the soft touch of a Sleeper. Lyra's mind turned dull and soft and malleable. 'You're our proof.'

She could have laughed. She wanted to cry. 'I'm not proof.'

'I didn't mean it that way,' Dr O'Donnell said. 'I only meant—'

Lyra cut her off. 'No. You don't understand. I'm not proof. I'm not even a replica. I wasn't made at Haven. I wasn't made at all.' She felt both satisfied and sickened at the fault line of disappointment that shook Dr O'Donnell's face. 'You didn't know? I have a father. His name is Rick Harliss. I had a mother too, but she didn't want me, so she gave me over to Haven and then she died.' Saying it out loud gave her the good kind of pain, like digging in the gums with a fingernail. 'I wasn't made by anything except accident. No one wanted me at all.'

That was really what had made Caelum so special to her: he wanted her. And not just because of her body and what he could do with it, but for her, something inside neither of them had a name for, the stitching and the thread that held her whole life as a spiderweb holds even the sunlight that passes through it. 'There were more of us at Haven. Not just me. Replicas are expensive.' She remembered that day on the marshes, the soldier saying,

You know how expensive these things are to make? 'I guess that means I was cheap.'

Dr O'Donnell shook her head. 'I'm sorry,' she said. Lyra wanted to ask whether she was sorry for Lyra or for herself. 'I . . . heard rumors. But that was all before my time.'

It was the most dangerous kind of lie: the one the liar believed. 'That's convenient for you,' she said. She felt a hard, ugly pull of hatred. Was this all the world was? They'd escaped Haven only to find that Haven existed everywhere.

Dr O'Donnell stood up. She stared down at Lyra as if from an enormous height. But when she spoke, she sounded calm. 'If you understand anything, I want you to try and understand this,' she said. 'We're all doing our best. We always have been.' But her mouth twisted around the words, and Lyra wondered if on some level even her body knew that was a lie – or at least, that it wasn't an excuse. 'Haven was a crazy place – such a crazy time for everyone. . . . I was posted there for three years and I remember I would leave for the holidays, step off that launch, and hardly remember how to be human. . . .' Bad choice of words, and she seemed to realize it. Lyra and Caelum had no idea what any of it meant: the holidays, family, Haven as a fluid world that allowed passage in and out. 'Some people might think what we did was wrong. Maybe it was. But it was also a miracle. It was, maybe, the first scientific miracle.' She almost looked like she might cry. 'You make choices. You make sacrifices. Sometimes you make the wrong choices. Then you work to correct them. That's what science is about.'

Lyra wanted to argue, because she knew there was some problem of logic there: there had to be. Anyone could give names to anything – Dr O'Donnell had taught her that, when she'd given Lyra her name. If you could do anything you wanted and then call it *doing your best*, you could invent anything, excuse anything. There had to be a center somewhere. There had to be a truth.

But suddenly, Lyra found she couldn't bring up the words she wanted to say. The word *center,* for example. She could picture it, see it as a hard little seed at the back of her tongue, but she couldn't find the word. This was a hole of a different kind. She wasn't dropping into it. It was reaching up to swallow her. Lyra thought of the pages she'd eaten in Sebastian's bathroom, and the words all dissolving into her blood. She wished she hadn't: now she was nauseous and thought that they were the things poisoning her, saw the letters reconfigure themselves into deformities, like little mangled prions, and float carelessly toward her heart. Words could make anything: that was their great power, and their great danger. Lyra saw that now.

Dr O'Donnell had already started moving for the door when Caelum spoke up again.

'I have another question.'

She turned around, keeping her hand on the door.

'Someone blew up Haven because of their idea of God,' Caelum said. 'You know that?'

Dr O'Donnell frowned. 'I'd heard.'

'And Haven was for science, and it killed people, too.'

Dr O'Donnell said nothing.

Caelum took a step toward her, and then another. Dr O'Donnell's whole body tensed.

'My question is this.' He stopped when he was no more than four inches away from her, and Lyra could see how badly Dr O'Donnell wanted to flee, how hard she was trying not to throw the door open and run. 'If it's okay to kill people for science, or for God, is it okay to kill people if you think you need to?'

'Of course not,' she said sharply.

'Why not?' He spoke the words softly, but she flinched.

'I – I don't expect you to understand.' She couldn't control herself anymore. She wrenched the door open, forcing him to step back. 'The world isn't black and white. There are no easy answers.'

Still, Caelum wasn't done.

'You said the world isn't black and white. But the world isn't like you think it is either,' he said quietly. Dr O'Donnell froze. 'I watched and I watched. There were days I watched so much I thought I wasn't even a person, just an eye. And even I know that when you push, and you keep pushing, someday, sometime, someone is going to push you back.'

Dr O'Donnell turned to face him, very slowly. 'Are you threatening me, Caelum?'

'I don't need to,' he said. 'That's just the way the world works.' He smiled, too. 'We all do our best, like you said.'

Dr O'Donnell opened her mouth, but Lyra couldn't hear her response. A sound filled her ears like the sifting of wind across a desert, a sound of huge emptiness, and her body disappeared, and Dr O'Donnell and Caelum and the room disappeared, and darkness lifted up and swallowed her like a wave.

TWENTY-ONE

SHE DIDN'T EXIST AND THEN she did again: she was drinking water, and as the cold touched her lips and tongue and throat, it poured her back into herself. She was so startled she nearly choked.

Dr O'Donnell was gone.

So was Caelum.

She couldn't remember where the water had come from – it was in a mug, and there was writing on the mug, but she couldn't seem to bring it into focus; the letters were meaningless geometry. She couldn't understand where Caelum had gone, or Dr O'Donnell, and in fact she couldn't remember their names or what they looked like but only that there had been other people with her, a sense that she'd been left behind.

The room smelled bad, and in a lined plastic trash can there was vomit mixed with a little blood. She knew it must be hers, but for a long time she stared at it, revolted and uncomprehending: she didn't remember throwing up. She tried to move to the window but found that she was instead pushing on the door, pushing and trying to open it. The door was locked.

She turned around and the room also turned, swung and changed direction, and just as the letters had disintegrated, the whole place had ceased to have any meaning. She saw lines and angles skating in space like the cleaved wings of birds in the sky, and she couldn't tack any of it down or make sense of it. *Help,* she wanted to say, but she couldn't find the word for help. There was a sound in her ears, a hard knocking. And after a bit she recognized that she was hearing her own heart, and the idea of a heart came back to her, four interlocked chambers webbed with arteries.

At the same time, words loosed themselves from the dark hole and soared up to her consciousness: *room, chairs, rug.* Every time she found the word, the shape of the thing stopped struggling and settled down and became familiar.

She was still in the unused office. Caelum had been with her but he had argued with Dr O'Donnell and now he was gone. Outside, the light had been reduced to a bare trickle that bled through the tree branches: it was evening. But Caelum had argued with Dr O'Donnell in the morning.

She had lost a whole day.

Think. Someone had brought her the mug of water. She was sure it hadn't been there earlier. That meant someone must be close, and in fact when she went to the door again and leaned up against it, she could hear the murmur of voices.

Dr O'Donnell wouldn't hurt Caelum, not when she wanted to use him to show off. So Caelum must have been removed either to another room in the building, or somewhere else entirely – which meant first that Lyra had to find him.

Second that they had to escape.

Another wave of nausea tipped her off her feet and she sat down and bent over, waiting for it to pass. At least she didn't throw up again.

When she felt better, she moved to the file cabinets and opened all the drawers one by one, hoping to find something she could use to get out. But they were all empty – she didn't find so much as a pen cap. Even if she could slip out into the hallway, she would need an ID to swipe in and out of doors. But Dr O'Donnell, wherever she was, had of course taken hers along.

Think, think. Along with the water, someone had left her a pack of gum, probably because she had been throwing up. Lyra got a small, electric thrill.

An idea, a very small one, a very desperate one,

condensed through the fog of her brain.

She fed a wad of gum into her mouth and gnawed, then went to the door again; the murmur of voices, probably from an adjacent office, continued uninterrupted. Someone was watching TV. She lifted a fist and banged several times, and after a brief and muffled discussion, footsteps came toward the door. She quickly spat her gum into one hand, and thumbed it into two portions.

The door handle jumped around while someone took a key to it. When it opened, Lyra saw a girl with chunky black stripes in her hair and very thick glasses.

'Oh,' she said, and took a step backward, as if she hadn't expected Lyra to be there. 'Oh,' she said again. 'I *thought* I heard you knocking.'

'I need to pee,' Lyra said. The girl tried to step in front of her, but she shoved into the hall, wedging the gum right into the locking mechanism, forcing it in deep: a trick Raina had taught her.

The girl took a few quick steps away from her – Lyra realized she was frightened, and didn't want even accidental contact. The halls were dim, and Lyra knew most of the employees must have gone home for the night, although she could hear the ghost *clack-clack* of invisible fingers on keyboards, and a few offices still spilled their light onto the carpets.

In a narrow office across the hall, a boy was hunched

over a laptop, watching something. He quickly thumbed off the volume. Lyra's heart swelled: his ID was lying next to his computer, coiled inside its lanyard at the edge of his desk. Her fingers itched to take it.

'What does *she* want?' the boy asked, jerking his head toward Lyra, and even though he sounded tough, Lyra knew he was afraid also, and just trying not to show it.

'She has to use the bathroom,' the girl said, in a desperate whisper, as if it was a secret. 'Where's O'Donnell?'

'Still on the phone,' he replied. 'She said she might be half an hour.'

So: Dr O'Donnell was still here. That was good. It likely meant she hadn't taken Caelum somewhere else, somewhere that would require a car. But Dr O'Donnell had said she'd be back in half an hour; that didn't give her much time to look.

'Should I . . . take her?' the girl asked, still shying away from Lyra as though she were diseased.

The boy blinked. 'Well, *I'm* not going with her.'

'Dr O'Donnell said not to go anywhere. . . .' The girl trailed off uncertainly.

Fear could be used. The nurses at Haven had been afraid; they had acted as though the replicas had something sticky on their skin, something that might spread through contact and turn them into monsters. But back then, Lyra had not known how to use this to her advantage.

Things were different now.

'I threw up in the trash can,' she said. 'There's some on the floor, too.'

'We heard,' the girl said. She avoided Lyra's eyes. Lyra knew the girl was afraid she wouldn't be able to find the difference between them, the reason she had the key to the room where Lyra was getting sick and not vice versa.

'Did Caelum get his medicine?' she asked. This made the girl and boy turn to stare at her. 'The other one,' she clarified. 'The male.'

The girl looked worried. 'What medicine?' she asked loudly, as if Lyra might otherwise fail to understand.

'He has medicines,' Lyra said. 'He always takes them. Otherwise he'll get sick worse than I did.' She held her breath as the girl chewed on her thumbnail. If she went to get Dr O'Donnell, Lyra would have to admit Caelum didn't take medication.

She counted heartbeats, one, two, three.

'Can you go and get Sonja?' the girl said finally, turning to the boy. Lyra let out the breath she'd been holding. 'Can you ask whether the other one said anything about medicine?'

'*Now?*'

'Just ask,' the girl said. 'I don't want to get in trouble.'

The boy leaned to hoist himself to his feet. He grabbed his ID, winding the lanyard between his fingers, and

Lyra's heart skipped down into her fingers. 'In one of the cold rooms?'

The girl nodded. 'Sub-Two,' she said, and Lyra had to bite her lip to keep from smiling. Now she knew where Caelum was.

But she was careful to keep her face blank, to look as dumb as they thought she was. To watch without seeming to pay any attention at all.

She saw: the way the boy slipped his ID in his back pocket when he stood.

'I really need to pee,' Lyra repeated.

She saw: the girl relenting. 'Come on. Make it quick.'

Lyra followed her into the hall, head down, obedient as a cow. Dumb, docile, harmless. The boy glanced at her with barely concealed pity before turning to lock his office door.

She saw: the loop of lanyard visible above the stitching.

All she had to do was hook it with two fingers as she was passing.

Harmless.

In the bathroom, she used the toilet and washed her mouth out in the sink. There was no time to waste. Once Dr O'Donnell returned, Lyra would lose her chance.

The girl had waited in the hall. When Lyra emerged, she saw the boy retracing his steps, making a search of the hallway.

'I had it right here,' he was saying. Another sleepy-looking employee had come to her office door, blinking and yawning, as if she'd just been napping. 'Right here, in my pocket . . .'

When he looked up and spotted Lyra, he blinked, and Lyra was seized by sudden panic. But his eyes traveled through her down the length of carpet.

Of course. He wouldn't think to check her or look in her pockets. They thought she wasn't capable of it. Too dumb to lie. Too dumb to plan.

Lyra followed the girl back to the empty office, taking a seat quietly as the girl tried, and failed, to make the key work. She made a face when she saw the gum jamming the lock. 'I don't *believe* it,' she said. Suspicion tightened her face. 'Did you do this?'

'Do what?' Lyra asked stupidly.

The girl rolled her eyes. 'Worst night ever. Just stay here.'

Lyra nodded, dozy as an animal.

She counted the girl's footsteps until the carpet had absorbed them completely.

She stood up, steadying herself against the wall. She had to be careful, to stay clear of any holes that might grab her.

For the moment, the hall was clear. She went quickly,

scanning for hiding spots, checking door handles lightly with her fingers, looking for open offices. She ducked into the bathroom again when she heard voices, but the sound of a closing door quieted them. They had gone into an office, whoever they were.

She found her way to the stairwell without seeing anyone else. The doors were still propped open by the same book, its pages furred with moisture and age.

The first basement level was still dark, still full of the lumpy silhouettes of old equipment. She kept going, listening carefully for footsteps, since the turns concealed the landings beneath her. The girl with the striped hair had probably already discovered she was missing: Lyra had a minute, maybe two, before the girl panicked and launched an all-out search.

She reached Sub-Two, and the gate locked with a keypad. She nearly cried when she saw that it required a numbered code: she'd forgotten all about it. Her palms were sweating and dizziness rose like a sudden swarm of insects. She leaned against the gate, sucking air into lungs that felt like paper.

She imagined her whole body strapped with fear and anger. She imagined burning up with it, like the woman who, arriving at Spruce Island, had detonated the dozen homemade explosives lashed to her body. She imagined screaming so that all the windows shattered, so the roof blew off, so that everyone above her was consumed in flame.

She imagined fire.

She wheeled away from the gate and backtracked up the stairs, leaning heavily on the railing, until she spotted what she wanted: on the landing of Sub-One, directly across from the swinging doors, a small red-handled fire alarm. At Haven the alarms had been enclosed by plastic, surfaces warm and smudgy from the fingers of all the replicas who'd touched them for good luck and connection.

Pull down, the alarm said.

She pulled.

The noise made her teeth ring. It vibrated her eyeballs. Immediately, the stairs filled with the echoes of distant shouting. She rocketed across the landing and hurtled past the swinging doors, into the dark recesses of the empty basement level.

From where she stood, she could see a steady flow of people up the stairs from Sub-Two. But not Caelum. She kept waiting for him to pass, but all she saw were strangers made identical by their confusion, by the quick-flash way they passed behind the glass.

She counted them all, the way she'd counted beads of IV fluid from the drip bag: *two, seven, nine, fourteen, fifteen, sixteen.* Still Caelum didn't come.

The blur of people slowed. She counted three heartbeats

when no footsteps rattled the landing, when the window stayed empty of passing faces.

Hardly thinking, she pushed once again from her hiding place through the swinging doors and hurtled out into the open stairwell. She sprinted down the stairs, no longer thinking of being caught, thinking only of Caelum, of reaching him, of losing her chance.

As Lyra crashed around the corkscrew of stairs, she saw the gate at the bottom of the stairs was only just swinging closed. She saw the inch of space between lock and gate as a narrow tether. She leapt, shouting, reaching for it the way she might have reached for a rope, and got a hand through the gate just before it clicked shut. Her mouth tasted like iron relief, like blood. Beyond the gate was the door marked *Secure Area – Live Samples*, which she opened with the stolen keycard.

It was very cold.

For a moment she stood with goose bumps lifting the hair on her arms, suddenly confused by a vision of Haven unrolling in front of her, by the collapse of past and present. But it was just an illusion: this hall looked almost identical to so many hallways at Haven.

There were no offices here. There was no carpeting. Just a long linoleum hallway and windows overlooking darkened laboratories, doors barred and marked with *Do Not Enter* signs, cameras winking in the ceiling. Her stomach turned. She'd forgotten all about the Glass Eyes, and she felt a pull of both homesickness and revulsion.

Almost as soon as she started down the hall, a man with an Afro and a goatee turned out of one of the laboratories, shouting something. She froze, thinking he was angry, or that she'd been caught. Then she realized he was just asking her a question.

'Is it a drill or what?' he said, and she realized, too, that he had no idea who she was. Dr O'Donnell had told her there were one hundred and fifty people who worked at CASECS: he must simply have mistaken her for one of them.

'Not a drill,' she said, and had to repeat herself twice over the noise. 'Everybody out. I'm making the rounds,' she added, when he started to respond, and she continued past him down the hall. Maybe that was the secret, and why at Haven the doctors and nurses had been able to lie for so long. People were trained to believe.

Lyra counted two laboratories, each of them a fraction of the size of Haven's. Some of the pieces of equipment were familiar. She recognized them from the vast, brightly sterile rooms where the doctors had done all the making, had with a shock of electricity made an egg swallow the nucleus, the tight-coiled place where DNA nested, of another person's cells.

But CASECS didn't make replicas. Dr O'Donnell had

said so herself, and Lyra didn't think it could be a lie. If there were other replicas, Dr O'Donnell wouldn't be so desperate to use Caelum as evidence.

Dr O'Donnell had said CASECS helped other places do research. But Lyra hadn't thought to ask what kind of research she meant.

Or maybe she *had* thought to ask. Maybe she had known, deep down, and she didn't want to hear the answer.

Understanding was like its own kind of alarm – so loud, so overwhelming, that the only choice was to ignore it altogether.

There were just three other doors in the hall, and one of them wouldn't open. But the second one did and inside she found Caelum, sitting on the floor, knees up, head down on his arms. She called his name at the precise moment the alarm was silenced, so her voice echoed in the sudden quiet.

'Are you hurt?' she asked. A stupid question. When he stood up and came toward her, his face was pale, and she noticed new cuts and bruises on his cheek.

'The guard,' was all he said.

He didn't hug her, but from a distance of several feet he lifted his hands and touched her face and smiled.

'We have to go,' he said, and she nodded.

But she hesitated when she registered all the industrial

freezers, the careful labels and printed signs. The whole room was full of them. Storage freezers, of the kind that kept embryos cold, on ice, until they were ready for use.

And suddenly she knew.

Who knew eternal life would spring from a cooler in Allentown, Pennsylvania?

We give hospitals, facilities, even governments the chance to do their own research.

'They're not making replicas,' she said. 'They're selling them.'

'They're selling *how* to make them,' Caelum said. Lyra remembered what the woman Anju had said to explain how licensing worked: *Let's say I invented a new way to manufacture a chair . . .*

'They're making new Havens all over the place.' He even smiled, but it was a terrible smile, like a new wound. 'They're replicating Haven all around the world.'

PART III

TWENTY-TWO

AS A COP, REINHARDT KNEW lies, but he also knew coincidence. Coincidences happened all the time, everywhere. Plenty of rookie cops wasted time giving too much weight to the kind of background coincidence that blew through every life, every death, every case.

Coincidences happened everywhere, all the time: but they didn't happen in the *same* place, at the *same* time.

That was called a pattern.

The girl who'd called herself Gemma Ives, that skinny little thing with eyes eating up her face, wasn't any of his business. He had plenty of other cases to worry about, *actual* cases: three other missing-persons cases had landed on his desk in the past six months alone, two of them teenagers from the same low-income district where he'd grown up, one of them a forty-five-year-old stay-at-home mom on the board of her children's PTA who'd disappeared in February on her way to the gym. No signs of violence, but no activity on any of her credit cards, either, nothing to indicate whether she was alive or dead. Only yesterday he'd found her in Florida, living with an ex-con who'd retiled her roof last summer. Reinhardt still hadn't figured out a way to tell her husband.

As far as he knew, the girl wasn't in any trouble at all. Just because she'd lied about her name didn't mean she'd lied about heading for Pennsylvania to see her doctor.

Of course, she couldn't have been headed to see Dr Saperstein, since Dr Saperstein was dead. It had been all over the morning news. That was coincidence number one.

Maybe she'd lied about his name, too. But it was funny she'd chosen his name in particular, and funny she'd chosen Gemma Ives's name, too. Because after Detective Reinhardt had seen the real Gemma Ives's picture, and after he'd Googled around a bit, he found that Geoffrey Ives and Dr Saperstein, now deceased, knew each other, from a place called Haven, a research institute off the coast of Florida.

The girl, the skinny big-eyed girl, had said she came from Florida.

And if you were counting – which Detective Reinhardt wasn't, because it wasn't his business, because what did some skinny, desperate stranger matter to him? – but if you were, you would count coincidences two and three.

And you would know that three coincidences were two coincidences too many.

Of course, anyone could imagine meaningful connections where none existed. It was all a question of wanting. If you wanted to find a thread between JFK's assassination and a UFO sighting in New Mexico, you could be sure you would hit on one eventually.

But Detective Reinhardt didn't want to find a thread. He didn't want to see a pattern. He wanted to forget the girl, and forget Gemma Ives, and the smell of moneyed lies that leaked off her father, and the skittish look of his wife, like someone awakening in an unfamiliar room from a terrible nightmare.

He certainly didn't want to find significance in the presence of federal investigators on a missing-persons case. He didn't want to find it strange that they'd grilled him about the girl and her cousin – or whoever he was – he'd picked up Sunday night, though Mr Ives had said previously that Gemma knew no one of her description.

He didn't want to find it suspicious that his captain, usually so forthcoming, shut down Reinhardt as soon as he'd thought to question their participation.

He didn't want to see, and he didn't want to care, and he sure as shit didn't want to spend Wednesday, his only day off, making the twelve-hour drive to Philadelphia.

He would have to stop for gas on the way out of Nashville.

TWENTY-THREE

THERE WOULD BE NO THIRD chance to escape. Maybe Dr O'Donnell would lock them in cages, or cuff them to a bed, as some of the replicas at Haven had been cuffed. Or maybe she would simply grow tired of protecting them, and hand them over to one of the Suits who wanted Lyra and Caelum dead.

You aren't supposed to exist, she had said.

Whose fault is that? Lyra should have asked.

Every second they delayed brought them closer to disaster – and yet they went through the laboratories, smashing everything they could, knocking equipment from the countertops, shattering microscopes, dumping out chemical samples. Lyra knew Dr O'Donnell and her staff would recover soon enough – they could buy new equipment, order new chemical samples – but it made her feel better. Every test tube that shattered, every hundred-thousand-dollar piece of lab equipment that crashed and splintered into pieces, seemed as it broke to simultaneously split open a kind of joy inside of her.

Finally, there was nothing left to destroy.

The hallway carried distant echoes, footsteps overhead, voices shouting words she couldn't make out. People looking for them.

They were halfway up the stairs when the rhythm of footsteps narrowed above them: in her head, Lyra saw sound like a cloud that had collapsed into a single dark stream of water. She recognized Dr O'Donnell's voice, and the panicked response of the girl who'd escorted her to the bathroom earlier.

'In here,' she whispered to Caelum, and she pulled him past the swinging doors into the vacant offices on the basement level. Through the cutaway window, she saw Dr O'Donnell pass, followed by the girl and the boy whose ID she had stolen. There were other employees with them, brown and white and tall and short, but all with the same identical expression of tight-cinched panic.

They didn't dare turn on a light and so they went slowly through the dark space, feeling their way, toward an emergency exit sign that floated up through the murk of shadows.

More shouts, increasingly urgent, vibrated through the ceiling and floated up through the floor, like a dust they disturbed with their feet. It seemed they weren't getting any closer to escape, as if the darkness kept unrolling.

'Wait,' she said. She couldn't breathe. When they reached the emergency exit, a barred door, she was so dizzy she had to stop, leaning heavily against it. 'Wait.'

Suddenly she wasn't sure. Dr O'Donnell was right: there was nowhere for them to go. She wondered how much time she even had left. One week? One month? Two? Would they spend the rest of her time simply running, like this, in the dark, trying to stay ahead of the people who wanted to erase them? And what would happen to Caelum once she died?

It was terrible to think that he would go on, and terrible to think that he wouldn't.

'We have to go,' Caelum whispered to her. 'They'll find us here.'

Lyra still couldn't breathe. The room was spinning, and ideas began losing their shape: Rick was warming soup in the microwave; there were men passing through rows of beds, touching the replicas with their fingers. She recalled the strange, sweet stink that had sometimes carried back to Haven from the ocean, when the winds were right and the disposal crews hadn't gone far enough to burn the bodies of the dead. Time, the present, was like a hook; she struggled to hang on.

'Where will we go?' she said. Caelum's breath was hot

on her cheek. The dim light of the exit sign gave shape to his shoulders and neck. 'Dr O'Donnell was right. No one can help us.'

'It doesn't matter if she's right or not,' Caelum said. His hand found hers in the dark. She was shocked by the sense that her heart had traveled down her arm into her palm, and that he was holding that instead, fragile and alive. 'She doesn't have the right to say,' he said. 'She doesn't have the right to choose.'

Lyra swallowed. She felt like crying. 'I'm going to die,' she whispered. 'Aren't I?'

He leaned forward. His lips bumped her nose and then her jaw and finally her lips. 'Sure,' he said. 'But not yet. Not today.'

Elbowing open the door, they found instead of stairs a cavernous loading bay. They ran together, even though the effort made her gasp, and she kept fearing they would hit some obstacle, a sudden wall that would surprise them, although there were dirty bulbs set in the ceiling that switched on with their movement and she could see there was nothing to stop them.

Caelum found the switch to control the rolling doors and the noise rattled her whole body: it seemed to take forever before they'd inched high enough for Caelum and Lyra to duck beneath the gap.

Either her sickness or her fear began to cut things into clips: a short stretch of pavement and a fence they couldn't climb. Dumpsters to their right. To their left, a sweep of red light: a fire truck had come, although as Lyra watched, the lights went dark and the truck began to shimmy itself into a turn. She couldn't see the parking lot or the front gates they'd snuck through; they'd come out the back.

They skirted the building, looking for other gates, or places the fence wasn't reinforced. But the only way out to the street was through the manned gates. And the fire alarm had driven the staff out into the parking lot; there were still a half-dozen people milling around in front of the double glass doors.

They could wait for the crowd to break up, but that just meant it was even more likely that Dr O'Donnell would catch up. The only other option was simply run for it. Charge straight through the lot and count on surprise. The fire truck was just nosing toward the driveway. They might even be able to hitch a ride out through the gate when they opened it.

'Think you can make it?' Caelum asked her, and she knew he was thinking what she was: why stop now?

She nodded, although her legs felt wobbly and she knew that there was always a hole waiting for her, waiting like a long throat to swallow her up.

He took her hand again, and she was glad. A sudden,

strangling fear made her want to cling to him, to tell him that she loved him. But she couldn't make the words come up. They were stuck behind the fear, which glued her lungs and made it hard to breathe.

'When I say go,' he said. 'Go.'

It was a good thing they were holding hands. She wasn't sure her legs would have started moving if he hadn't yanked her forward. They came around the side of the building, charging straight toward the group of people still milling outside, texting, one of them smoking a cigarette; but by the time anyone thought to look up, they were already blowing by the crowd, weaving through the few cars in the lot and sprinting to follow the fire truck as it approached the gate.

Everyone was shouting, and touching off explosions in her head. The gate was opening to let the fire truck through. They were too slow. They wouldn't make it. But Caelum wouldn't let go of her hand.

Almost there. The truck had slowed to maneuver through the gates. They were ten feet away, then closer. They were going to make it.

'Stop, stop, *stop.*'

Dr O'Donnell's voice was high and clear: it rang out like a bell. The fire truck braked abruptly, and Caelum threw out a hand to keep from cracking into the bumper. One of the firefighters leaned out the driver's-side door and cranked around to see what all the noise was. Lyra saw his mouth moving, saw the way his eyes darkened when they landed on her.

Stop. Lyra was screaming, too, or she thought she was. Then she realized she had only been screaming in her head. She threw her voice as hard as she could, hurled it like a stone. 'Stop! Please! Help!'

He retreated, yanking the door shut; she didn't know if he'd heard. The fire truck jerked forward another few feet, and that did it – Lyra gave up, she dropped, her knees gave out and she stumbled. Caelum caught her and tried to draw her in another direction, toward the parking lot. But she could barely stay on her feet. She was too tired – of running, of hiding, of hitting walls, of finding that every face concealed a sharp set of hungry teeth.

Then Dr O'Donnell threw herself between them and the truck.

'Wait,' she said. Her hair was slicked by sweat to her forehead. 'Just wait a second, okay?'

Caelum had to put an arm around Lyra's waist just to haul her backward. Her feet had stopped obeying her. Her whole body felt as if it were as flimsy, as weightless and useless, as an empty sheath of skin.

But Caelum wouldn't give up. 'Come on, Lyra. Come on. Move.' He was still shouting, although it was suddenly very quiet.

And then, with a start, she realized why: the fire truck's engine had stopped growling. No more exhaust plumed from its tailpipe. And almost as soon as she noticed, the door opened again, and the firefighter dropped to the pavement from the cab. Another one followed, a woman, this time from the passenger side. Both of them wore heavy rubber suits that made funny squirting noises when they walked – that was how quiet it was.

'Is there a problem?' The firefighter who'd been driving had sharp eyes, placed very close together, as if they'd been made that way just to notice every detail.

'Please,' was all Lyra could say. She was still winded, still gasping for breath – partly from the run, partly from a dizzying sense of relief.

Dr O'Donnell pivoted neatly to face him. 'There's no problem.' In an instant she transformed. She had been begging them to listen, begging them to stop. But in a split second, she shimmied into a new skin, and Lyra was seized by a sense of dread. 'I'm sorry you had to come all the way out here. Honestly, we didn't expect them to react like this.'

He looked from Dr O'Donnell, to Lyra and Caelum, and back again. 'What do you mean, "react"?'

'They're patient volunteers,' Dr O'Donnell said smoothly.

'She's lying,' Caelum burst out.

But Dr O'Donnell didn't miss a beat. 'Sometimes our volunteers get anxious. Sometimes they get paranoid. It's the first time anyone's ever tried to stage an escape, though.'

She slid over the words as if she'd been waiting for years to use them. And Lyra hated her so violently, the hatred blew her apart into a thousand pieces.

Because the worst part, the absolute worst part, was that Dr O'Donnell truly believed she was good. She was surprised that Lyra and Caelum weren't grateful; that they didn't see the way she wanted to use them as a kind of gift.

Because deep down she thought, of course, they didn't deserve it. Because she thought that it was *obvious* they didn't.

And that made her worse, even, than Dr Saperstein. Saperstein had treated the replicas like objects, but at least he never pretended.

Dr O'Donnell thought the replicas should love her for helping them pretend that they were worth something, when it was so obvious they weren't.

The woman's coat was folded down at the waist. She thumbed her suspenders. 'So it's some kind of medical research?'

Dr O'Donnell smiled. Lyra couldn't believe she'd ever loved that smile. 'That's exactly right,' she said. 'Medical research, pharmaceutical testing. All voluntary, obviously.'

'She's lying.' Lyra could finally breathe, but the effort of speaking, of trying to be believed, made her words come in hard little bursts. 'She's been keeping us locked up. She won't – she won't let us go.' Then: 'You can't believe her.'

Dr O'Donnell didn't even glance at Lyra. 'Paranoia, like I said.'

The firefighters exchanged a look. 'They seem pretty upset,' the man said doubtfully. But Lyra could tell he was wavering.

'Of course they're upset. They're having a bad reaction to a new SSRI.' Dr O'Donnell grew taller, swelled by her lies, or maybe the world shrank around her. She sounded calm. She looked calm. Lyra couldn't imagine what she and Caelum looked like. 'And I can't help them unless we get them inside. They should be monitored. We should be watching their heart rates.'

Lyra saw at once that Dr O'Donnell had won. She watched the firefighters tip over into belief; she saw them shake off their doubts, like a kind of irritant.

'Please—' Caelum tried again. But his voice broke, and Lyra knew that he, too, had seen.

'Thank you for coming out here,' Dr O'Donnell said. 'We really appreciate it.'

The firefighters had already turned back to their truck. Though they were only a few feet away, Lyra saw them as though from the bottom of a pit, as if they had already vanished into a memory.

'Wait.' She cried out from the bottom of a long tunnel of anger and fear. 'Wait,' she said again, as both of them turned back to face her.

Dr O'Donnell showed her irritation, but only briefly. She was busy playing a role. 'Really, we should get them inside—'

'She said she would let me call my mom,' Lyra blurted out. Caelum tensed.

But Dr O'Donnell looked at her with blunted astonishment: it was as if her polish was only a mask, and someone had elbowed it off.

'She promised,' Lyra said, feeling her way into the lie. If Dr O'Donnell was going to make up a story, Lyra could get in there, could hook her hands around it and make it hers. 'She said I'd be able to call if I got scared.'

Dr O'Donnell licked her lips. 'I never—'

But this time, the firefighters were on Lyra's side. 'For God's sake, let the kid call her mom,' the man said.

For a half second, Dr O'Donnell and Lyra locked eyes. Dr O'Donnell squinted as if they were separated by a hard fog, and Lyra wondered what she saw. That Lyra was small and young. That she was stupid. That she was *dying.* Just like Calliope, all those years ago, and the bird. *It was broken,* she'd said. *It's better to kill it.* For weeks afterward Lyra had dreamed of the bird coming back to life, but enormous, and swooping down through the dorms to peck their eyes out, one by one.

Dr O'Donnell even looked vaguely amused. Of course she knew that Lyra had no mother.

Of course she knew, or thought she knew, that Lyra had no one to call.

Maybe that was why she didn't put up more of a fight.

She shrugged. 'Okay,' she said. She took her phone out of her pocket, and, after punching in her code, passed it wordlessly to Lyra.

She'd been trained to memorize number series, of course, so that the doctors at Haven would be able to collect data points, would be able to track how quickly her mind was breaking up. And she'd been trained to observe, too: not intentionally, but she had been trained.

And in the real world, she'd been trained to lie.

Lyra pressed the numbers very slowly, making sure she got them right.

Now Dr O'Donnell was frowning. 'Honestly, this isn't standard. . . .'

But the firefighters said nothing, and stood there, watching.

Lyra brought the phone to her ear. She pressed it hard,

the way she had with those seashells Cassiopeia had collected long ago, and her breath hitched. It was ringing.

Once. Twice.

Answer, she thought. *Answer.*

Dr O'Donnell lost patience. A muscle near her lips twitched. 'Okay. That's enough.'

'Wait,' Lyra said. Her heart was beating so loudly she lost track of the number of rings.

Answer.

And then a fumbling sound, and a cough, announced him.

'Reinhardt.' His voice sounded rough, but also comforting, like sand.

She closed her eyes and watched his name float up from the darkness, resolving slowly, like a distant star captured by a telescope.

'Detective Kevin Reinhardt. Hello,' she said. Her throat was tight. It was painful to speak. When she opened her eyes again, Dr O'Donnell was staring at her. Shocked. Hands hanging at her sides, limp, like old balloons. 'You picked me up in Nashville. You gave me your number and told me to call if I ever needed help.'

It seemed that everyone was frozen: Caelum, watching her, and the firefighters, watching her, and Dr O'Donnell, slack-faced and dumb. Only the insects sang, a noise that sounded to her like a motor.

She took a deep breath. She had never been taught how to pray, but she did pray, then, without ever having learned it.

'I need your help,' she said.

TWENTY-FOUR

FOR A SHORT TIME, THE firefighters waited with them on the road, pacing in the quiet and talking into their radios, casting cautious glances at Lyra and Caelum from a distance, as if they were fish and too much attention would cause them to startle away.

Then a cop arrived to replace them, a woman with a high forehead and a long nose that reminded Lyra of a hanging fruit. She wanted to talk, to understand, to hear Lyra's side of the story.

But though the woman was kind to her, and though Lyra liked the look of her face and the slope of her nose, she didn't want to talk to anyone but Detective Kevin Reinhardt. She didn't even want to get into the police car: she was tired of strangers and their doors.

So instead, she and Caelum sat on the curb, with the police car parked a dozen feet away, watching the last trickle of car traffic out of CASECS. Dr O'Donnell and the other CASECS employees weren't in trouble, exactly, because the trouble couldn't be reported or understood when neither Caelum nor Lyra would talk, as the policewoman explained to them more than once.

But they weren't exactly not in trouble, either. CASECS wasn't invisible anymore. She kept her hands in her pockets, touching the drift of words, notes, telephone numbers. Proof.

And so the employees who had lingered to work late, or to catch a glimpse of Lyra and Caelum, spilled into their cars and flooded the exit gates, and tried to vanish. Lyra thought of cockroaches flooding from a clogged drain.

She tried to pick out Dr O'Donnell's car in the sixty or so that passed. But the cars looked the same, and the drivers, inside of them, looked the same too: hunched shadows, leaning over the steering wheels as if that would make them go faster. As if they could escape whatever was coming, just by leaning forward.

He arrived an hour or so before sunrise, when the darkness was like a scowl that had folded deep into itself.

They waited for him in the car while he spoke to the policewoman who had by then sat with them for hours.

It was hot. An empty cup of coffee in the cup holder had scented the whole car with hazelnut.

Finally, he returned, and put the car in drive without saying anything except, 'I brought you snacks.' At Lyra's feet was a bag of gas station food and water. Caelum ate three bags of beef jerky, and Lyra drank two bottles of water.

Then Detective Reinhardt said, 'Do you want to tell me your real name, at least?'

Inexplicably, the question – how kind it was, how gentle, and how difficult it was to answer – made tears come to Lyra's eyes.

'Which one?' She turned to the window, swiping her tears away with a palm. 'I've had three so far.'

And then, after hours of silence – after years of it – she talked. Detective Reinhardt was listening quietly, not saying anything, not interrupting to ask questions, just listening. She told him everything: Haven, all the replicas, Jake Witz, Nurse Emily Huang, Gemma Ives and how she'd saved them. Dr O'Donnell and CASECS; a world full of places where people could be manufactured, like furniture, for different uses. About Rick Harliss, her real father, and the people who'd taken him away.

Afterward, he was quiet for a long time. Lyra couldn't tell whether he believed her, and was too tired to ask.

When he finally asked a question, it wasn't the one

she expected. 'Do you have any idea where Gemma might be?'

Lyra shook her head. 'I heard that she was missing.'

'Missing,' he said. He appeared to be choosing his words carefully. 'And in quite a bit of trouble.'

Caelum spoke up for the first time. 'What kind of trouble?'

Detective Reinhardt appeared to be chewing the words. Lyra liked that about him. Too many people used words without thinking. 'I'm out of my element here,' he said finally. 'I'm flying blind.'

'What kind of trouble?' Caelum repeated.

'The Lancaster County Sheriff's Office is looking for Gemma,' he said, with some difficulty. 'I got a call about an hour before we talked. Because you'd given me her name,' he added, and sighed. 'Funny coincidence.'

Lyra looked down at her hands. 'It was the only name I could think of.' Then: 'Gemma's my friend.'

'That's what the sheriff's department figured, too. They thought you might be a clue.'

'A clue to what?'

Detective Reinhardt hesitated. 'Several people were hurt – badly.' He cleared his throat. 'They were killed. There was a witness. He described a girl Gemma's age, matching her description.'

'It wasn't her,' Caelum said, and leaned back.

'The witness got a good look at her,' Detective

Reinhardt said. 'He was very specific. And—' He broke off. Now his whole face corked around his mouth, like there was a wrestling match between them.

'And what?'

He shook his head. She noticed then how tightly he was holding the wheel.

'Dr Saperstein and the Ives family have history. A long history.'

'Because of Haven,' Lyra said.

'Okay.' He exhaled. 'Okay. Because of Haven.' He didn't believe her, not totally, not all the way. But he didn't disbelieve her, either. 'Dr Saperstein was found not far away from where the victims were discovered. And the Iveses are there, now, in Lancaster. They drove straight from Nashville. Look, like I said, I'm flying blind.' He held up a hand as if Lyra had argued with him. 'But where there's smoke, there's fire.'

'But Gemma wouldn't hurt anybody,' Lyra said. 'She couldn't.'

He shook his head. 'Sometimes people can do a good job of hiding who they really are,' he said, as if Lyra didn't know that. 'Some people put on their faces the way you and I put on clothes.'

'Exactly.' She was growing impatient. 'The faces don't mean anything.' But when he glanced at her, puzzled, she could tell she'd misread him. He *didn't* understand. He had listened to her without really absorbing it. Maybe he thought she was making it up. 'It's like you said – people can wear different faces. And different people can wear the same face, too. It's not Gemma,' she repeated, a little louder. 'So it must be one of the others.'

'One of the others?' Detective Reinhardt's voice cracked.

'Yeah. I already told you.' She pivoted in her seat to look at Caelum. 'At CASECS, Dr O'Donnell said some of the other replicas might have escaped. Wherever Dr Saperstein was, they couldn't have been far off.'

Detective Reinhardt was quiet for a bit. 'So you're saying that Gemma Ives has – has replicas? That she was . . . cloned?'

'Of course.' Lyra was too tired to be polite. 'Were you even listening?'

'I was, I just—' He broke off. 'Bear with me, okay? It's a lot.' He took a hand off the wheel to rub his temples. 'So you think – you think one of Gemma's replicas is responsible?'

'I know it,' she said. She leaned back against the head-rest. She thought of Calliope, number 7, squatting to nudge the broken bird with a knuckle before straightening up to smash it beneath her shoe. Lyra had thought at first she intended to help it fly again. 'I bet I know which one, too.'

TWENTY-FIVE

THE DAWN CAME, WEAK AND watery, bringing a patter of light rain. Lancaster was long spools of dark green, fields and forests: at any other time, Lyra thought, it would be peaceful.

But now, helicopters motored down over the nature preserve and hovered there like giant mosquitoes. Unmarked, but obviously military grade. There were snipers wearing camouflage visible inside.

'You're sure you want to be here?' Detective Reinhardt asked, and Lyra realized she'd been clenching her fists so hard she'd left marks.

She nodded. 'I want to help Gemma,' she said. 'Gemma helped me.' But she was afraid. She was afraid she would not be able to help. She was afraid of the Suits, afraid Detective Reinhardt wouldn't be able to protect her, afraid that he would try.

But she could no longer be invisible.

Detective Reinhardt drove slowly, showing his badge whenever they were stopped, which was often. The interstate was completely blocked off between the exits to Loag and Middletown, as were all the local roads bordering the Sequoia Falls Nature Preserve. Police had come from all over the state, some of them on their days off.

Detective Reinhardt had said little since they'd reached Lancaster, and had ordered Lyra and Caelum to stay in the car with the doors locked when he climbed out briefly to speak with a cluster of police officers. But she had picked up rumors, whispers, words carried back to the car like a kind of contamination.

There were *kids*, dozens of them, maybe even more than that, running loose.

Not normal kids, either. Twins, triplets, even quadruplets. Skinny. Feral. Covered with blood.

'Creepy as shit,' she heard one cop say, when Reinhardt swung open the door. 'Everyone's saying that guy Saperstein must have had them in juvenile lockup, but I never seen a juvenile lockup makes kids like these. It's like something from a horror movie. You can't make this shit up.'

You can make up anything you want, Lyra felt like calling out to him. *Even horror.*

But of course, she stayed quiet. She imagined the

whispers blowing like tiny seeds from one person to the next. Words were little things, of no substance at all. But they were curiously stubborn. They rooted.

They grew.

It was easy enough for Reinhardt to get through the various cordons. All he had to do was show his badge. Only one trooper seemed interested in Lyra and Caelum, and leaned down to stare at them in the backseat.

'Picked 'em up ten minutes ago trying to hitch a ride,' Reinhardt said easily, before the trooper could ask. 'Must have come from Saperstein's JDC – they won't say where they've been, got no ID on them.'

Wordlessly, the trooper backed up and waved them through the line, shouting for another trooper to move the sawhorses out of the way.

After that it was easy enough; they pulled over and Reinhardt nosed his car into a thick entanglement of growth, so it was partly concealed. As they climbed out of the car, Lyra could hear the distant whirring of the helicopters, and felt the hairs rise on her neck.

Reinhardt had gotten a copy of the map the search teams were using to organize their efforts. He had marked the approximate location of each of Gemma's sandals, which had been located several miles apart with a piece of fabric that might have come off her clothing.

Caelum immediately pointed to several shaded-in

squares a fingernail's distance away from where a search crew had turned up her second sandal.

'What's that?' he asked Reinhardt.

'Those are farmhouses, turn-of-the-century settlement. I'm talking turn of the *last* century. Three cabins, totally run-down. But the police checked the cabins early this morning,' he added. 'I heard it over the radio. Apparently some kid from one of the Amish farms rang up to tip them off about the cabins – he'd walked seven miles just to find a pay phone.' Reinhardt smiled. 'He was scared his parents would find out. I guess the place is popular with teenagers around here when they want to be alone. Some things are the same from Lancaster to Miami, huh?'

'She couldn't have gone far without any shoes,' Lyra said.

Reinhardt looked at her. 'She made it more than two miles with only *one* shoe,' he pointed out. 'Besides, the police were already there. They cleared the cabins.'

'Maybe she hid,' Lyra said. 'She wouldn't know she could trust them. She might think they were coming to get her for what happened on the farm.'

'I thought you said she didn't do it,' Reinhardt said. 'That it was one of the other – the others.' He still couldn't say *replica*.

'She didn't,' Lyra said. 'But she wouldn't know that

they knew that.' That was what people did when they escaped: they found a place to hide. Caelum had hidden successfully on the island for several days when he was 72, even though there was an armed military guard on the perimeter, even though there must have been fifty people looking for him. It was because he'd stayed on the island, exactly in the middle of where he was supposed to have escaped, that no one had found him.

Besides, places had feelings to them, just like objects did: they whispered things, absorbed secrets and quietly pulsed them back. But most people didn't hear. They didn't know how to listen.

Lyra listened, and she heard a whisper even in the lines on the page. A lost and abandoned place, for lost and abandoned people.

'She could have planted the shoes,' Detective Reinhardt said. 'She might have wanted to throw people off her trail.'

'Why would she plant them so far apart?' Lyra shook her head. 'She might be underground. She might be in a basement or – or hiding under a bed.'

She could tell that Reinhardt didn't think so. But he folded up the map. 'Someone's going to find her. They'll stay at it until they do. The dogs will get a scent.'

'The dogs look for dead bodies,' Lyra said. She remembered how the soldiers had brought dogs onto the marshes after the explosion to scent the trails of blood. She didn't hate dogs, though: she knew it was just their training. 'Besides, it rained.' She and Caelum had slid into the water to avoid being caught, and Cassiopeia had been located instead – located, and then permitted to die, flagged for collection later.

Reinhardt said nothing.

'There,' she said, and pointed again to the ghost-silhouettes of the long-abandoned settlements. The paper dimpled beneath her finger, and hissed the smallest of words. *Yes.*

It was still raining when they set off into the woods, using a compass Reinhardt had on his phone. If they kept straight north from where they had parked, they would eventually hit the old settlement.

It was harder going than Lyra had expected, and she had to stop frequently to rest, overwhelmed by sudden tides of vertigo.

She was falling more. It was like there was a wall up between her brain and her body, and only some of the messages made it through. This was, like the holes, a symptom of the disease as it progressed: she'd seen it at Haven, even, though at the time she hadn't known what it was, and had believed it was just a problem in the pro-cess going wrong. Replicas got sick. They forgot their numbers and then how to use the bathroom and then how to walk and swallow.

She was glad neither Reinhardt nor Caelum asked her if she wanted to go back, though. Caelum just helped her up, every time, without saying a word. And Detective Reinhardt went ahead, scouting the easiest routes, and trying to break apart the growth where it was thickest to make it easier for her to pass through.

It took several hours, but at last they saw, through the tangle of natural growth, the hard sloping angle of a roof and a little stone cottage. The settlement had been made in a literal natural clearing, although growth had reclaimed the area, and one house was little more than rubble, punctured by the hardy fists of oak trees that had grown straight up through a collapsed portion of the roof.

As soon as Lyra saw the place, her stomach sank. It was obvious that Gemma wasn't here. It took only a few minutes to check the two standing houses: they were each a single room. Inside was a litter of cigarette butts and empty soda cans. But no Gemma. She was glad, too, that Reinhardt didn't gloat about it, or say he'd told them so.

Instead, he said, 'I'm sorry.'

'I thought she'd be here,' Lyra said. Her stomach felt like it had coiled itself around her throat. 'I really did.'

'She'll turn up,' Reinhardt said. 'I promise.'

Lyra just shook her head. She knew he was trying to

make her feel better, but she knew, too, that it was a promise he had no ability to keep. In the distance, she heard
a faint hollow clacking – the noise of a woodpecker, or
maybe a squirrel, cracking two stones together. An empty
sound.

Lyra was reluctant to leave. Though Gemma was
obviously not here, she kept feeling that she'd missed
something, kept turning around to stare even as they
began to retrace their steps. The houses, dismal, lurching
on their feet. Piles of rot and leaves. The trees puncturing
the beams. An old circle of stones. Maybe a fire pit, or a
garden.

And not a single sign of movement, nothing but the
hollow drumming that made her heart ache with lone-
liness.

They started back the way they'd come, and Detective Reinhardt took the lead again. They'd barely left the
cabins behind when they heard him shout. Caelum put
a hand on Lyra's elbow, to help her go faster, and they
pushed forward through a leaf-slicked trail marked by the
detective's footsteps in the mud. The rain was coming
harder, beating its percussion through the trees.

She saw Reinhardt, moving through the mist toward
a girl in a filthy dress, and from a distance, for a second,
even Lyra was confused: Gemma, it was Gemma, they'd
found her.

But immediately the vision passed. The girl's body was wrong, and her hair was wrong, the way she stood with her arms very still and tight at her sides was wrong, all of it just a small but critical distance off, like a door hanging an inch off its hinges.

Not Gemma. Calliope.

Caelum realized it too. He dropped Lyra's arm and started to run, an instinct, as if he could physically get between Calliope and Reinhardt. Lyra started to call out but it was too late, Detective Reinhardt had crossed the distance. He reached out to put a hand on her shoulder even as Caelum shouted, 'No!'

Calliope moved quickly. It was like a sudden pulse of electricity had brought a statue to life. From an angle Lyra saw only the quick motion of her hand and then Reinhardt, leaning heavily on her shoulder, so it looked as if he would pull her into an embrace.

Then he released her and stumbled backward, and Lyra saw the knife handle stuck in his abdomen, and blood already darkening his shirt. He reached for the gun holstered to his belt, but only grazed the grip before pulling away again quickly, as if it had scalded him.

For a split second, just before Caelum reached her, Calliope met Lyra's eyes. Lyra was shocked by the feeling; she stopped moving; it was like running into a wall, a huge hand of immovable stone. She thought then of the statue of Richard Haven, which had been built from the wrong stone, so that quickly its face had begun to dissolve in the rain; by the time Lyra was named, its eyes were gone, and its nose, and even its lips, so it looked like the blank face of a clock without numbers or hands: like a warning of some terrible future to come where no one could see or speak or hear.

Then Calliope turned and ran, wrenching away from Caelum when he tried to grab her. Caelum hesitated. Lyra knew he was torn between the urge to go after Calliope and the desire to stay with Detective Reinhardt. But they couldn't let Calliope get away.

'Go,' Lyra said to Caelum. And then, when he still didn't move, 'Go.'

Finally, he took off after Calliope. She had a head start, but she was weak; he would catch her easily.

Lyra dropped next to Detective Reinhardt when he sat down heavily.

'I'm okay,' he said. But he was chalky-looking, sweating. The good news was that Calliope had stuck him in the stomach, not the chest; she'd missed his heart by a mile. 'I'm okay.'

'You have to keep pressure on it,' she told him.

'I know. I'm a cop, remember?' He tried to smile, but pain froze his expression into something horrible. 'God. When I saw her standing there . . . She looked so lost. . . .'

'That was number seven,' Lyra said. Calliope didn't deserve her name; Lyra couldn't stand to say it out loud.

'Poor kid.' Detective Reinhardt coughed and then cursed, his face screwed up with pain. Lyra couldn't believe it: Calliope had stuck him with a knife, had caused him all this pain, and still he felt sorry for her. 'Do me a favor. Get my belt off, okay?'

She unclipped his duty belt, which was heavy. The gun he carried in his holster was the same as the one Rick Harliss had taught her to fire, only a little heavier. A Glock. Lyra thought the word fit. It was a loud, angry word, and it sounded like an explosion.

Lyra was suddenly furious. 'You should have killed her,' she said, thinking of the way Detective Reinhardt had fumbled for his gun. 'She would have killed you.'

Detective Reinhardt shook his head. 'She's just a kid,' he said.

'She's a replica,' Lyra said, but Detective Reinhardt shook his head again.

Lyra saw then that he really, truly didn't understand the difference. That to him, there *was* no difference.

She had been told she was supposed to love Rick Harliss because he was her father, and because he loved her. But she had never felt as if she loved him, and she had worried simply that she didn't know *how*. Even the way she felt about Caelum, she thought, might not be love at all, but something different, something she had no name for. Hadn't she heard again and again at Haven that the replicas weren't all-the-way human, they weren't real people, they were simulations of people, precisely because they *couldn't* love? Damaged, monstrous, soulless – these were all different words for the same thing.

But in that moment, and though she hardly knew him at all, she knew absolutely that she loved Detective Reinhardt. It was complete and undeniable, and it changed the whole world around her, like being submerged in a warm bath for the first time. If she could have chosen a father, she would have chosen him.

The gun was cold in her hand. But its grip felt familiar.

'Stay here,' she told him. 'I'll be right back.' He didn't say anything, and she wasn't sure he'd heard. His whole face was screwed tight around his pain now, as if it too had been winched around the knife.

She'd been right: it hadn't taken Caelum long to catch up to Calliope, and Lyra found them quickly. He had gotten her facedown in the wet leaves and pinned her arms behind her back. But she'd obviously fought him. There were deep scratch marks from his cheekbone to his jaw, and a bite mark on the back of his hand.

When Lyra approached, Calliope tried to lift her head. But she couldn't manage it. She thudded down into the dirt again, one cheek flat to the leaves, the other catching the drive of the rain. But her eye, swollen with rage, rolled toward Lyra, like the eye of a spooked animal.

Except that Lyra didn't feel sorry for Calliope, not one bit.

'I thought you were dead,' Calliope said. Because of the way her head was angled, her voice was distorted. It was a terrible version of Gemma's voice: it was the same 15 percent wrong as the rest of Calliope.

Lyra ignored that. She knew Calliope likely meant that she thought Lyra had died on the marshes, but she couldn't help but feel, too, that Calliope had seen immediately how little time she had left, that the disease was starting to show on her skin. 'Where's Gemma?' she said.

'I don't know any Gemma,' Calliope said, and Caelum gave her a nudge with his knee. Her tongue appeared quickly to wet her lower lip. She was nervous, and Lyra was glad. 'I don't know where she is.'

Lyra didn't know whether to believe her, but it didn't matter, anyway. Calliope would never tell her the truth.

'Why'd you do it?' she asked. 'You killed that family. You left Gemma to take the blame.'

'I didn't know what would happen,' Calliope said. Then: 'Why do you care, anyway?'

'Gemma's my friend,' Lyra said.

Calliope's pupil was so large it seemed to swallow all the color in her eye. 'Friend,' she said, and the rain suddenly changed its pattern through the leaves, creating a ripple sound like laughter. 'You were always one of the dumb ones. They'll kill you. You know that, right? They're all the same. They'll pretend to help you and then they'll hurt you, again and again, just like they did at Haven.'

Lyra had always felt anger as a kind of heat burning through her. But now she was freezing cold. As if from the grip of the gun her whole body was turning to metal very slowly. Calliope had known the truth about Haven, just like Caelum had. But not Lyra.

Was it true, then? Was she really just stupid?

Was she being stupid now?

'Let me go,' Calliope said. 'You're not going to kill me. So let me go.'

'Not until you tell me why,' Lyra said. The trees chittered under the pressure of the rain. They threw the question back at her, and made it sound ridiculous.

'Cassiopeia was dead,' she said. 'Number six was dead. Numbers nine and ten, too. They never made it out of the airport. And number eight doesn't count. Even if she did escape, she couldn't last long.' Calliope pulled her mouth into a smile, exposing an incisor tooth, graying and sharp. 'I wanted to be the only one.'

Lyra closed her eyes. She stood and listened and thought of her whole life like a single point of rain, falling down into nothingness. Calliope was still talking, wheedling now, sounding young and afraid. But Lyra could barely hear her. *Let me go, Lyra. I'm sorry. I'm so sorry. I didn't mean to. I was so scared.* It was the strangest thing, as if Calliope wasn't talking at all, as if Lyra was just remembering something she'd said years earlier.

She thought of Detective Reinhardt and Gemma lost forever, and those people on the farm, lying in one another's blood. Detective Reinhardt had said that some people could wear faces, could slip them on like masks.

Lyra opened her eyes. 'Do you remember the baby bird that flew into the glass?' she asked. Funnily enough, she felt calm. 'It flew into the glass and broke a wing. I thought I could nurse it.'

Calliope frowned. 'No,' she said. But Lyra could tell she was lying.

She could see it so clearly in her mind: the way its tufted feathers fluttered with every breath, the shuttering of its tiny beak, how scared it was.

'You stepped on its head to kill it,' Lyra said. The barrel of Detective Reinhardt's gun was slick and wet but she felt it, slowly, warming in her hand. 'You said it was the right thing to do, because of how it was broken. Because there was no hope of fixing it.'

Calliope went very still. The whole world went still. Even the rain let up momentarily and seemed to gasp mid-air, deprived even of the will or energy to fall. Calliope's fear smelled like something chemical. Lyra saw her calculating: right answer, wrong answer.

'I don't remember,' Calliope said finally, and all the rain unfroze, all of it at once hurtled down fast and thick to break apart, as if trying to blow itself back into elements purer than what it had become. The feeling came back to Lyra's hand, warmed her fingers and wrist and arm as she raised the gun. It spread down through her heart, opening and closing like the wings of a bird in her chest.

'Funny,' she said. 'I never forgot.'

She didn't need more than one shot, but she fired three anyway, just to be sure.

TWENTY-SIX

THE WARMTH FLOWED AWAY FROM her as quickly as it had come. She didn't feel sorry, or sad. She didn't feel anything at all. The bullets had ruined Calliope's face, and forever destroyed her resemblance to Gemma. There *would* be only one now: the right one. Still, she wasn't sure whether she had done the right thing, or why she felt so little. Maybe there really was something wrong with her – with all of them.

'What's going to happen?' she asked suddenly. She was too afraid to meet Caelum's eyes, so she stared instead at the leaves turning to pulp in the rain.

'I don't know,' he answered. Caelum was always honest. It was one of the things she loved about him.

Suddenly she felt like crying. 'I'm a replica, really, aren't I? I'm more replica than anything else.'

He touched her face. His fingers were cool and damp.

She blinked at him through the rain webbed in her lashes.

'You're Lyra,' he said. He smiled, and she fell down into his love for her, touching every layer, and this kind of falling was like its opposite, like flying instead. 'That's all. That's enough.'

Lyra was relieved to find that Detective Reinhardt was on his feet, leaning heavily against a tree. When Caelum reached for him, he said, 'I'm okay, I'm okay,' and even managed to smile.

They had no choice but to give up their search for Gemma. Detective Reinhardt needed help, and it would take longer for someone to find them out here than it would for them to make it back to the car on their own.

Slow. One foot in front of the other. Stop to rest. Lyra turned her face to the sky and whispered an apology to Gemma, for leaving her behind. For failing.

The rain had dropped off, faded to a bare mist, and the leaves shook off their moisture, so it sounded as if high above them, in the cage of the branches, tiny feet jumped from branch to branch. Lyra smelled mulch, rot, growth, and the pure wet sweetness of new blood, of life.

Lyra smelled her old life burning. Every day, the past was burned and you became something new from the ashes.

Lyra smelled burning.

No. She smelled *fire*.

Detective Reinhardt must have smelled it at the same time, because he winced and grunted, ordered Caelum to stop. But Lyra had already turned. She'd already spotted a thread of smoke unwinding above the trees, back in the direction of the cabins, and she'd already started to run.

TWENTY-SEVEN

DIMLY, LYRA WAS AWARE OF shouting: the gunshots must have drawn the attention of the searchers. She had been worried about coming across police officers in the woods; she was worried they would ask questions that Detective Reinhardt didn't know how to answer.

But now, she thought of nothing but Gemma, her *friend*.

She saw through a break in the trees the architecture of the old cabins, and the smoke coming from somewhere beyond them. She had approached from the back and had a view of collapsed stone timbers and a ruined hearth.

She circled around to the front, completely mindless of the way her heart was jumping arrhythmically in her chest, mindless of the little moments of dark that shuttered her vision for seconds at a time. *Gemma, Gemma, Gemma* was the only rhythm she could hear. The long finger of smoke was all she could see.

The ground was smoking. Or at least, that's what it looked like to her from a distance. But as she drew closer, she saw a blackened door laid flat over a lip of stone, and the smoke flowing out from an opening beneath it.

She dropped to her knees, soaking her jeans. She got her fingers around the old door and pushed, recoiling as the column of smoke thickened, carried up by a surge of air. Blinking to clear tears from her vision, she spotted a mass of uniforms coming toward her through the trees – troopers, police officers, firefighters.

'Here,' she screamed. At the bottom of a long well, Gemma was curled up next to a smoldering fire, which blew its thick smoke into the air. Lyra felt as if she were falling, and leaving her body behind. 'Here. Here.'

It seemed to take forever for her to lift her hand. She saw it waving there, tethered to the narrow cable of her wrist, and it looked like a distant balloon, like something that didn't belong to her at all.

'Here, here, here,' she shouted, again and again, as all the uniformed men and women came toward her through a scrim of smoke. Maybe it was a trick of the smoke, or maybe not: but funnily enough, all those strangers fractured in her vision into a kaleidoscope of different angles, and she saw them coming toward her not as a wave, not as a group, but as individual points of color, as individual hands reaching to hold her, as individual arms that caught her just before she dropped.

TWENTY-EIGHT

LANCASTER GENERAL LOOKED LIKE THE Haven from her dreams: full of windows that let in long afternoon sunlight, when the clouds eventually broke up; full of the reassuring squeak of footsteps, and the smell of floor polish and fresh flowers. Lyra was placed in her own room and hooked up to an IV to deliver fluids and Zofran to get rid of her nausea. Her window looked out onto an interior garden, just like the one at Haven, except there was no faceless statue here. Just flowers, and benches where visitors sat in the sun.

The IV fluids made her feel better right away, and she began to drift, rising and falling through different dreams: in one, she and Caelum lived in a white house that looked just like the one at April's grandparents', and Detective Reinhardt brought them mail, but every single one of the letters he delivered turned into a white bird and flew away.

She woke up because she thought a bird wing swept across her face; it was dark already, and she was startled to see Kristina Ives, Gemma's mother, draw away.

'Sorry,' she said. She looked embarrassed. 'You were so still – I wanted to make sure you were all right.'

Lyra sat up in bed. For the first time in days, she wasn't nauseous, and movement didn't give her vertigo. A reading light was on in the corner, and Kristina Ives had obviously been sitting there: her purse was on the floor next to the chair, a magazine rolled up inside of it. 'Where's Caelum?' she asked.

'He went to check in on Detective Reinhardt. Both of them are fine,' Kristina said, before Lyra could ask. 'Detective Reinhardt was very lucky. The knife missed all his major organs.' She smiled. She looked very tired, but she was still extremely pretty. Lyra thought she was a little bit like the rose in *The Little Prince*. She'd been sheltered behind glass for a long time. But she was loyal. She knew what love was. 'I want to thank you,' Kristina went on. 'You found Gemma. I can never repay you.'

'You don't have to,' Lyra said. 'Gemma found me once. We're even.'

To Lyra's surprise, Gemma's mother reached out and took her hand. Her skin was incredibly soft, and Lyra was shocked to recognize the scent. Lemon balm. Her expression changed, too. When she smiled, it was like light passing into a room through an open door.

'I want you to know I'm your friend,' she said. 'You can trust me to help you however I can. Do you believe me?'

Lyra nodded. She was overwhelmed by the tightness in her throat, and by the feeling, at the same time, that paper birds were winging up through her chest.

The door opened, and Lyra turned to see Caelum and Detective Reinhardt. The detective moved slowly, and a bulk of bandages was visible beneath his shirt, wrapping his abdomen. But he was smiling.

'You shouldn't be up,' Kristina said, releasing Lyra's hand with a final squeeze.

Detective Reinhardt waved her off. 'I'm good as new. The surgeon said so himself.'

Caelum came right to the bed. 'Hey,' he said. He put a hand on Lyra's face, and she turned so she could kiss his palm. 'How are you feeling?'

'Better,' she said. For once, it wasn't a lie. 'Much better.'

'I'm going to go check on Gemma,' Kristina said. She picked up her purse and hugged it.

'I want to see her,' Lyra said, sitting up a little straighter. 'Can I come and see her?'

'Of course.' Kristina smiled. 'She's just down the hall. You were the first person she asked about – you and Caelum, both.'

After she had left, Detective Reinhardt moved to the

window, parting the blinds with a finger. Lyra thought he was giving Caelum time to lean forward, quickly, and kiss her.

'You get some sleep?' Reinhardt asked, and Lyra nodded. 'Incredible how different the world looks on the other side of a nice sleep, isn't it?'

She wanted to tell him about her dream, but she was too embarrassed. He eased into the chair in the corner, wincing a little.

He waved off Caelum's help.

'I'm okay,' he said. But he sat for a long time with his chin down, eyes closed, breathing hard. Lyra even began to think he'd fallen asleep. Then, at last, he looked up. 'I'm afraid I have some news about your father.'

Lyra knew just by looking at him what he was about to say.

'He's dead, isn't he?'

'Yes.' He looked her directly in the eyes. She liked that about him. That he wouldn't look away, even though she was sure he wanted to. 'Found at home, at the trailer park, only yesterday. Looks like an overdose.'

'That's impossible.' Caelum's voice leapt almost to a shout. 'It's a trick.'

'Caelum, please.' Reinhardt sighed. 'I'm on your side, remember?' Caelum wheeled away and went to stand by the window. Lyra wondered whether he was thinking about how he and Rick had fought. She knew he would be sorry he had never had the chance to apologize.

She was surprised that she was the one who couldn't make eye contact with Detective Reinhardt. She looked down, blinking back her tears.

'I promise you, Lyra, I'll make sure your father gets his justice. I'll make sure you do. Do you believe me?'

She nodded. For a long time, he said nothing. She liked that about him too: he wasn't afraid of silence. He had learned to find comfort in it.

'They've still got those vultures by the main entrance, waiting to pounce,' he said. There had been a crowd at the hospital when they arrived: police officers but also men and women holding phones, video equipment, cameras that went flash-flash. 'I don't imagine any of us are getting off easy.'

The nurses had sworn that no one would be able to get to Lyra so long as she was in the hospital – she'd been worried, initially, that Geoffrey Ives or one of the other Suits would simply creep in and murder her while she was sleeping. There were even police officers monitoring every visitor to and from this portion of the hospital. But what would happen once they left?

Detective Reinhardt seemed to know what she was thinking. 'They're going to want to ask you questions,' he said. 'There's going to be a lot of nosing around. I expect a department inquiry. Well. I *asked* for a department inquiry.'

Lyra had worried that Detective Reinhardt might be disappointed when he found out she had stolen from Dr O'Donnell's desk drawer. But instead, he had hugged her. He had lied for her, too, and told the state troopers who found Calliope's body that he'd been the one to shoot her, after she rushed him with a knife.

There's no hiding this anymore, he told Lyra on their way to the hospital, as she drifted in and out of consciousness. *There's no covering up.*

'I don't blame you,' Detective Reinhardt went on now, 'if you had other things on your mind. Things you wanted to do, for example.'

Detective Reinhardt was looking intently at his cuticles. That was how Lyra understood: he was giving them a way out. He understood she didn't have much time left.

'I like buses,' she said. Caelum took her hand. 'I wouldn't mind riding some buses again.'

Detective Reinhardt heaved out of his chair, using both arms for leverage. 'Amazing things,' he said. 'You can go coast to coast on the Greyhound bus line, from Maine to Santa Monica. Did you know that?' He started limping toward the door. "Course, they won't discharge you yet. Not without wanting to know your story. And the front entrance is crawling with press.' He paused by the door, turning back to smile at Lyra, and she saw in his expression love, actual love, the kind she'd felt for him in the woods. She barely knew him at all, but he was family. 'Of course that's the problem with hospitals. Always have to be a million exits, because of fire regulations. You can't cover them all. I saw a stairwell right by the ladies' room, led right down into the parking lot and not a single person standing guard.'

'Thank you,' Caelum said.

Detective Reinhardt nodded. Then he turned around and fished something from his pocket. 'Oh,' he said. 'I had one of the nurses run out and pick this up. Thought it might come in handy. Pay-as-you-go. No code.' He tossed a cell phone in the air and it landed at the foot of Lyra's bed. 'Don't worry. My number's already in there.'

It was brand-new, made of plastic, and had little numbered buttons. It had a fake-leather case, which snapped closed and could hook to a belt.

Lyra's throat closed up entirely.

Thank you, she tried to say. But she couldn't get the words out.

Detective Reinhardt seemed to understand. He touched his fingers to his forehead, once – a kind of salute – and was gone.

Lyra didn't need to ask where Gemma's room was; all she and Caelum had to do was listen for the babble of April's voice. Though Lyra didn't know April well, she knew her voice right away.

April was sitting at Gemma's bedside. With her were two women Lyra assumed must be related to April. One of them had April's warm brown eyes, and the same nest of curly hair. The other one kept a hand on April's shoulder.

'Looks like you have some more visitors,' Kristina said, when Lyra and Caelum entered. She, too, had drawn a chair up to Gemma's bedside.

'You're awake,' Gemma said, sitting up. She was pale but smiling.

'You're *heroes*,' April said through a mouthful of candy, pivoting around to face her. 'Twizzler?'

Lyra shook her head. But Caelum took one.

'Come on.' The woman with the curly hair gave April a nudge. 'Let's leave them alone for a bit, okay?'

Kristina took the hint and stood up. 'I could use a cup of coffee, actually.'

April frowned. 'Yeah, sure. But we'll come back, right?' She pointed a Twizzler at Gemma. 'You can't get rid of me that easily.'

'I wouldn't dream of it,' Gemma said, and rolled her eyes.

Kristina bent down to kiss her daughter's forehead. 'I'll be right back,' she said.

Lyra almost laughed. And she nearly cried, too. The

sun through the blinds looked almost solid. It was beautiful, she thought. It was all so beautiful.

She would miss Gemma.

Maybe Caelum knew what she was thinking, because he reached for Lyra's hand and squeezed.

'How are you?' Gemma asked, after the others had left. 'How are you feeling?' That was so like Gemma: she was the one who had nearly died, and still she was worried about Lyra.

'We're fine,' she said. Caelum's hand was warm in hers. It was both true and not true, of course. She was still dying, of a disease for which there was no cure.

But it was like Caelum had said: she wasn't dead yet. Not today.

Already, the words she'd taken from Dr O'Donnell were beginning to turn, to flow, to do their work.

'April was right,' Gemma said. 'You're both heroes. I can't believe you found me.'

Lyra wondered whether anyone had told her about Calliope. She knew that Gemma would be sorry, even though Calliope was broken, even though Calliope had killed people. That was the kind of person Gemma was.

'That's what friends do,' Lyra said. 'They find each other.'

Gemma beamed. It was like her smile split her face open, and sunshine poured out of it. 'Exactly.'

The look on Gemma's face, the way she smiled, the understanding that Gemma would mourn Calliope even though Calliope had never mourned anyone – all of it warmed Lyra's whole body and moved her forward, to Gemma's bedside, compelled by an instinct that for years had remained buried. But now it broke free of its casing. She made her body into a seashell and gathered Gemma in the curve of her chest and spine. She didn't think about doing it. Her body just knew it, remembered the impulse, the idea of warmth and closeness, as if all along the knowledge had been there, working through her blood.

And for the first time ever, Lyra and Gemma hugged.

'Thank you,' Lyra whispered into Gemma's hair, which still smelled, faintly, like smoke. Words were funny things, she thought. The best ones carried dozens of other words nestled inside of them. 'Thank you,' she repeated.

I love you, she thought. *Goodbye.*

TWENTY-NINE

THEY COULD HAVE BEEN ANYONE, going any-
where. There was a joy in that, in the absorption: they
were caught up in the great big heartbeat of the world.
They were infinitely large and infinitely small. They
were a single vein of feeling, an infinitely narrow possibility that had somehow come to be.

They could have vanished, right there, from the
bus stop, and who's to say whether anyone would have
noticed, what would have changed, and whether somewhere in the rippling universe a wave would turn or fall
or change directions.

But they didn't vanish.

They sat in the sun, sweating, holding hands, and
avoiding the gum on the underside of the bench when
they moved their legs. They breathed the smell of exhaust.
They saw people pass, a wash of sneakers and colors and

cell phones. They sat for hours without speaking, without moving, without impatience or desire. Their hands were so tightly intertwined that looking at them you could not immediately say which was whose. The sun wheeled through the sky; it turned its infinite cartwheel and blinded them when they stared directly.

And Lyra, sitting there, knew at last that she had found her story. It was not, after all, a story of escape and fear and fences. It was not a story about power, and so, after all, she did not have to play the role of sacrifice.

The story, *her* story, was about a girl and a boy on a bench, holding hands, watching bus after bus arrive and leave again. And because it was her story, that was all right: there was no hurry, no rush to get anywhere. The universe slowed, and both the past and future fell like a shadow flattened beneath the sun. The girl and boy sat, and watched, and time dropped a hand over them. It held them there, together, safe, and in love.

And in her story, they stayed that way.